WHITE
BADGE

WHITE
BADGE

A Novel of Korea

Ahn
Junghyo

First published in Seoul in 1983.
Translated from the Korean by the author.

Copyright © 1989 by Ahn Junghyo.
All rights reserved under International and Pan-American
Copyright Conventions. Published in the United States by

Soho Press, Inc.
1 Union Square
New York, NY 10003

Library of Congress Cataloguing-in-Publication Data
Ahn, Junghyo, 1941–
White badge
p.   cm.
ISBN 0-939149-16-8
I.   Title.
PS3551.H48W4   1989
813′.54—dc19   88-38506
CIP

PART ONE

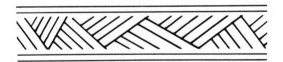

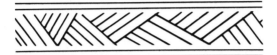

The woman peddler, who sold cabbages and radishes from the basket she carried on her head, was making her early morning round of the neighborhood, hawking.

"Caaaaaabbage! Raaaaaaaaadish!"

I walked out of my house to the road leading to Five Mounds Park. The paved road, still wet from the rain last night, was already bustling with people on their way to the park for morning exercise. In my tidy suit, shiny shoes and straight neck-tie—attire that looked so out-of-place among these healthy, casually-dressed people—I joined this flowing procession of the cheerful. A man and wife in loose gym suits bicycled up the slanted road, their

3

hips wiggling right-left-right-left in perfect concert; a whole family out for a walk, everybody in clean tennis shorts; a little girl with a big red comical ribbon on her head, sitting astride her father's neck; a trio of grandfathers with white plastic jugs going to the fountain to draw the fresh unprocessed water; a group of fat grandmothers with small feet in smaller sneakers waddling up the road, carrying towels and badminton rackets and shuttlecocks; five girls with the same blue headbands, who probably roomed together and worked at the same factory, jogging hop-two-hop-two; people jogging up, people jogging down; a lean middle-aged man walking backwards: all the happy people coming to Five Mounds Park every morning from the Pulgwang, Ungam, Yokchon, Kusan, Kalhyon and Sinsa districts to breathe the fresh moist air before beginning another routine day. Someone gave the Johnny Weissmuller yell, playing the urban Tarzan, as he did at this hour every morning on the hill behind Suguk Temple. I joined their procession because I wanted to float in the stream of ordinary happy life shared by all these ordinary happy people. How simple and easy it looked, for them. Perhaps something happy would happen to me today, I thought.

A dozen young men in bright scarlet uniforms, probably members of a neighborhood cycling club, pedaled down the road, stooping low, making slow, interchanging, waltz loops, and wheeled around the curve lined with newly pruned young plane trees. These people did not seem to have too much difficulty in finding their happiness. They found their simple joys easily because they did not waste themselves and their lives in a futile quest. They were happy because they kept their dreams as they were—dreams. Perhaps I had been wrong to think that a life hounded by unrealized dreams was better.

The world-record speed of a snail, established on glass in 1970, was 2 feet in three minutes, 0.00758 miles per hour. We used to drive our jeeps at 110 kilometers per hour on Highway 1 in Vietnam to avoid VC snipers. Now I crawled my life away like a mollusc. Like a slug. Slugs are hermaphroditic, I thought. Must be very convenient in procreating. But I was a sterile slug.

The guard at the gate of the Combat Police Unit watched the stream of morning people come and go, jogging and bicycling and rambling. The guard was armed with an M-16, although the main duty of Seoul's combat police was to crack down on anti-government demonstrators with tear gas shells. How badly we had wanted such M-16s in Vietnam. In the first six months we were not supplied with these newly-developed rifles and had to fight with heavy, inconvenient, single-loading M-1s against an enemy fully armed with automatic weapons.

Over the slanted road, past the Green Belt and then past the border of the metropolitan city and the neighboring Kyonggi Province, I walked among the joggers and bicyclists and strollers until I arrived at a lone cottage by the watch tower. In the open-air front yard of the wooden shingled cottage they sold snacks and hot soup for those on the way back home after exercise; families or groups of people, their hair wet with sweat, sat around the log tables to eat green bean pancakes, roast potato slices, cow blood soup, steamed pig hooves or makkolli rice wine. I took a seat at a roadside table and ordered a bowl of hot rice soup.

By the archery range, cordoned off for the night by a straw rope, two middle-school girls were playing badminton, giggling every time they missed the bird. And they missed every time. Yellow jackets and red tee-shirts and tight white pants. Springy youth. Wondrous, pure, innocent. Yes, those girls soon would pass the first gates of maturity, and then begin to feel and distinguish the different shades of despair, rebellion, fear, delusion. The conflict would commence. I had begun to look back at the road not taken, I thought.

Why had I been always obsessed by a sense of alienation, of feeling that I was somewhere else, somewhere I did not belong, while my life was progressing by itself out of my reach? Why was I always tailgated by the anxiety that I should be at some other place doing something else? My life was running away from me. What was the important thing I was destined to do here, now, today, on this spot, in this phase of my life? There must be something else I had to do in the given hours of my life other than checking the wrong fonts, redundant expressions, broken type or awkward phrases on the printed page, squatting before my desk day after day after day after day. I was sure I was wasting the only life I was given to live.

After soothing my empty stomach with the hot soup, I continued on down the paved road and arrived at the open ground among the pine trees at the entrance of the park. For some time I loitered about, watching the groups of people cheerfully sweating through their aerobic workouts, posing rigidly in a yoga contortion on a mat, stiffly flexing their limbs like slow-motion break dancers, jogging or walking around the marked trees counting three-hundred-and-thirty-six, three-hundred-and-thirty-seven, wiping their sweating faces with the towels hanging on their necks or hips, pedaling, or having an early breakfast and leisurely watching others. Near the park gate, I queued with the old ones carrying white plastic water jugs, took a bus and came straight downtown.

At 8:04 a.m. I entered the office, plugged in the coffee pot, and sat down before my desk to read the morning newspapers. U.S. Develops Soundless Sub Equipped With 8 Torpedo Launchers. Chinese Pilots to Be Trained in U.S. U.S. Willing to Purchase Chinese-Made MIG-21s for Training Purposes. Efforts to Maintain Military Superiority of South Korea Over North. U.S. Assistant Defense Secretary Warns About Possibilities of North Korea's Invasion of South . . .

The front page was, as usual, bursting with warlike phrases and all sorts of intimidating military-related stories. I turned a page, but they were the same old pieces all over again. Saudis Order Immediate Shoot Down of Planes Violating Territorial Air. Airborne Early-Warning Platforms Useless—Information Transmission Too Slow. USSR Plans Deployment of Blackjack Bombers to Far East. Iran Violates Limited Ceasefire, Shells Civilian Districts in Al Basrah. Japan Alerts Fleet on Spotting Russ Planes. Killing Robots Operated by Artificial Brain— Effective for Defense of Pipelines, Airports . . .

Page 3 was also screaming madly about armed conflicts. The ailing earth. The Russians suddenly stepping up their mopping-up operations along the Afghanistan border, the intensifying confrontation between Prime Minister Gandhi and the Sikhs, the Moslems and Communist guerrillas rampaging on Mindanao in the Philippines, General William Westmoreland suing Mike Wallace and CBS in another grueling battle of the doomed and rejected Vietnam War, Iran and Iraq wasting themselves in lethal attrition that did not seem to get anybody anywhere much, the Strait of Hormuz turning into a powder keg, Chinese and Vietnamese troops clashing, the American CIA sinking more and more deeply into the mire of Latin America, the eternal religious conflicts in Belfast . . .

The fog, that had thickly filled the gray space of the urban sky, slowly cleared off, and another day of noise and smog set in. At nine o'clock all the employees gathered for civil defense force training in the auditorium on the third floor. The instructors showed us some old scratched and hazy slides of the Korean War; the anniversary of its outbreak was only days away. Robert Capa's *Life* photograph of the refugees crossing the bombed, skeletal Taedong River Bridge, of course, was included in the show. Another slide showed heaps of dead bodies scattered in the snowy field like abandoned bundles of rag. A familiar snowscape of my child-hood. There was also the much-used slide showing Hungnam Port in a snow storm where an estimated 100,000 refugees had gathered to escape on the retreating U.S. naval ships from the North Korean and Chinese Communists. The countless heads jammed on the pier re-minded me of the newsreels dramatizing the desperate Vietnamese trying to enter the American Embassy compound in Saigon in the final week of the regime.

The narrator of the slide show suddenly got emotional explaining in her propaganda falsetto, "And remember our young boys in the 1950s who volunteered to fight as student soldiers against the Communist aggressors." I remembered. The sorrowful refugee life in Pusan. The shanties built with broken planks and C-ration boxes. The massacred civilians, their hands tied with barbed wire. Dead bodies piling over dead bodies. Mass killings casually done by human beings of other human beings.

My maternal uncle was mobilized as a student soldier and spent painful days of hunger and cold, herded from one place to another on drafty freight trains; he was sent home one year later, emaciated and terrified, because the army had no weapons with which to arm him and his comrades. There was also a black-and-white slide of a young boy standing alone in the rubble of a bombed ruin. The boy looked just like me at that time—dirty, ragged, starved, frightened, full of lice. There were so many "war orphans" and orphanages when I was a child. And so many pickpockets and bootblacks. The GIs called the pickpockets "slicky boys" and called us "gooks," the degenerate form of *Hanguk*, meaning "Korea," and we called the American soldiers Yankees or *bengko*, meaning "big nose." The relief goods sent by American Red Cross and other organizations were the most luxurious riches for the destitute Koreans—clothes, watches, pencils, thread, papers, toys, and so many beautiful marbles.

When the war broke out I was a second grader in grammar school, and I had to support my family by selling American cigarettes and polishing shoes on the streets. In wartime soldiers and men and women, and even children, had to do things they would not do in a normal society. One night my father sneaked into a stranger's rice paddy, cut the rice ears with his scissors and stuffed them into a paper bag, then stole back home through the moonless dark. My mother wept to see the handful of rice he had stolen for us.

We twined straw rope and sold it to barely sustain ourselves. The whole family used to file the jags off rough aluminum chopsticks all day long to make enough money for one meal of pressed barley and "trash soup." We did everything and anything that could feed us.

My father was imprisoned for several months on charges of cooperating with the Communist enemy because he had been forced by the People's Army to work for the district police station, but we were not too sad, for he had not made much money anyway, while consuming most of the food. A few days after his release my mother asked him to look after "the shop" while she did some laundry. The shop consisted of a small pan and a rusty iron tray which she spread on the ground in the back alley by the prison to fry slices of cuttlefish and display them to tempt the hungry children in the neighborhood. When my mother finished washing the clothes and went back to the shop, she found my father guiltily sitting before the empty tray. It was a sunny day: I still vividly remember the spinning dazzle of the summer sun that afternoon. He had starved too long in prison to keep his hands off those delicious cuttlefish fries. My mother wept again because my father had eaten "the whole shop."

My life had been a succession of wars. When I was born in December of 1941, the Japanese were bombing Pearl Harbor and attacking the Phillippines. Born during the Great War, I spent my childhood in the Korean War, and then a part of my youth fighting in Vietnam. If somebody asked me to tell about my childhood, I would have endless stories about the days when I sang military songs, like "Over the Bodies of Fallen Comrades-in-Arms" or "Brave Fighters Flying to the North," instead of nursery rhymes. And more endless stories about the snow-covered ridges and hills I had to walk over during days and nights with the serpentine procession of refugees, the bombings, dark smoke rising from bombarded Yongsan depot, the bread the retreating American soldiers left behind at the school playground, the C-ration cans the GIs threw at us from the passing trucks, the relief supplies shipped by the United States Red Cross, the naval bombardment from Inchon night after night, the soldiers' hardtack that was the only delicacy we war children had, the wheezing roar of the military trucks retreating at night, the prostitutes for the U.N. Forces called "the U.N. Princesses," my father dragged away by the Communists for labor mobilization, the miserable meals of "piggie soup" (the garbage from the U.S. mess halls boiled again after removing coffee-grounds, cellophane paper, broken razor blades and other inedibles) or the gruel of liquor lees and sticky rice, the clothes infested with lice, the arrowroot that you kept chewing forever for its sweet juice, the Lucky Strike cigarette packs with big red circles, and the famous euphemism of "the tactical retreat" that actually meant the U.N. Forces' defeat by the Communist Chinese troops. And of my sister Kija whom we had to abandon in the snowy field because we could not take her with us . . .

Alarmed by the rumor that the Chinese troops, who were overpowering the U.N. Forces everywhere with their "Human Sea Tactics," would soon sweep down to Seoul, my family fled to Sosa. My father remained in Seoul to watch the situation till the last minute, but he could not join us again until the war was almost over because we were forced to leave Sosa before he finally came to find us. We had been at grandmother's for a week or so when American and Korean soldiers swarmed into Simgok village and told everyone to evacuate because the Communists would arrive soon. So we had to leave without father. Mother and grandmother packed some of the things that they thought were absolutely necessary for our survival on the road for an indefinite period and a neighbor kindly allowed us to load some of the "refugee bundles" and my siblings on his ox-cart. A second grader at that time, I plodded interminably to the south, trailing after my mother along the road that seemed to stretch out to infinity. The refugees trudged over the white mountains. Carrying bundles of clothes or bedding or cooking tools or rice or other necessities, carrying them on their heads or backs or hugging them in their arms or holding them in their hands, they meandered to the south like a long white thread. Near Anyang, we saw soldiers blocking the road. They said we must leave all carts and wagons there because they would impede the flow of the military retreat. Men and cattle could go on, but not vehicles. In a snowy field littered with countless carcasses of discarded carts and wagons, the refugees packed their bundles smaller so that they could carry them. Mother and grandmother could carry almost nothing, for my siblings could not walk. My sister Kisuk, who was two years younger than me, had died of tuberculosis immediately after the war broke out and my youngest sister Kihyon was not born yet, but there were still three of them—Kija, Kijong and Kiwan—whom somebody had to carry. Mother and grandmother could carry one child each but one still remained. And they had no idea how far we still had to walk. So they had to give up one child. They decided to abandon Kija. She was squint-eyed because, mother used to say, she had not had sufficient nourishment. She had to share mother's milk with my brother Kijong who was born nine months after her. Besides this physical defect, she had the disadvantage of being a girl. My mother and grandmother reasoned that a girl should rightfully be sacrificed to save two sons. They spread several layers of thick bedding that they or other refuge families had discarded on the snow-covered field, set Kija upright on them like an image of Buddha, placed two more layers of warm clothes on her head and shoulders, wrapped her tiny hands with woolen mufflers and put a rice ball on her right palm, and placed several more rice balls in a row on the bedding spread before her knees so that she could eat them later when hungry. We continued on our way south, my mother crying her heart out the whole time. Kija, who was four years old then, did not cry because she did not know what was happening to her; holding a rice ball in her wrapped hand, she just stared blankly after us, as we deserted her in the middle of nowhere.

Mother kept weeping and wailing for over an hour, looking back over her shoulder again and again although we could no longer see Kija, until grandmother finally suggested we give up the flight. They could not abandon my sister, even if we were all to be killed by the Communists. When we breathlessly returned to the open morgue of the carts and wagons, Kija was still there, like a miracle, alone among the bundles of bedding and clothes and furniture discarded by the refugees, still holding the frozen rice ball in her tiny hand wrapped with a green woolen muffler. What would have happened if she had not stayed there for two hours, if she had gone astray? She did not even cry when we went back to fetch her. And my mother smiled and grinned, sometimes sobbing hysterically, all the way back to Sosa, pulling the cart carrying my three siblings. She even smiled at the North Korean soldiers when we met them on Soreh Hill near grandmother's house.

My co-workers were on their feet, filing out of the auditorium. I realized the civil defense force lecture had mercifully ended.

2

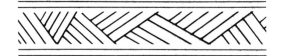

"We're in big trouble," Pak Namjun, the director, began to squeal even before we took our designated seats around the new oval table. Summoned to the "emergency" meeting were the managing editor, the three editorial chiefs, the production manager and the general affairs manager. "It's already July, and the vacation season will start in a few weeks. Soon we begin handing out vacation bonuses, but business looks very bad on the delivery and collection chart. Sales are dropping fast; the usual summer slump in the publishing business is here again. And this year the returns of books from local stores have increased sharply. We need some emergency measures to tide us over this serious crisis. We must have one or two quick bestsellers to keep our cash flow in the black."

At every meeting, Director Pak wanted someone to come up with a project that would sell at least 100,000 copies in a month. Nam Hosik, chief of the Second Editorial Department, suggested we might have an easier summer if we could buy the right to publish *Destiny in the Winds*, an epic novel appearing in a local daily newspaper, as soon as its serialization was concluded in mid-August. But everybody at the meeting knew that suggestion should have been made at least two years earlier; four other publishers had been competing to buy these rights for over a year, each offering from 5 to 10 million won in advance payments against royalties, with no obligation to refund it under any circumstances. Lee Wonse, chief of the First Editorial Department, tried to persuade the director, again in vain, that this publishing house might as well try some surefire project, such as a heavily commercial novel about the affluent and materialistic business world, with sufficient pornographic doses to vault it onto the bestseller list immediately.

"How about the translation side?" This was a recommendation invariably made by Choe Inhwan, the managing editor, at almost every meeting called by the managing director to squeeze an impossible bestseller out of us. "Have you read any good books lately, Mr. Han?" he asked me, and I thought his question sounded like a book advertisement. "Maybe we can find a good book for translation that would sell."

I told them about the books I had read lately: *The Truth That Killed* by Georgi Markov, who was dubbed the Solzhenitsyn of Bulgaria, Saul Bellow's *Him with His Foot in His Mouth*, William Kennedy's *Ironweed* that had won the Pulitzer Prize in the United States but was completely unknown in Korea, and Arthur Miller's *Salesman in Beijing*.

"*Salesman in Beijing?*" asked Director Pak. "What's 'Beijing'?"

"It's the same as Pukkyong. They used to romanize it 'Peking' in English, but it is now spelled 'Beijing'."

"Oh. Is that a new Arthur Miller play? I saw the other play about the salesman."

"This is not a play," I explained. "Arthur Miller visited Pukkyong when *Death of a Salesman* was produced there, and this book is about his experiences in China. . . ."

I was aware that I was making a mistake and I should shut up or talk about something else, but somehow I kept discussing what was totally irrelevant to this gathering. I was supposed to explain to them what recent books would be bestsellers if translated and published in Korea. Instead I lectured them on transitions in Chinese culture since Mao Zedong's death. The horde of Honda and Suzuki motorcycles that had been polluting the air of the Saigon streets now fell upon Red China on its way to continental conquest; Pacmen were gobbling up the computerized symbols of modern Western civilization in the video game rooms of Shanghai; the mandarin community observed developments in the Persian Gulf and the dangerous confrontation between President Marcos and Senator Aquino through news broadcasts on television sets imported from Japan; *Tess of the D'Urbervilles,* the movie, was shown in the Chinese cinemas; *Star Wars* and *The Winds of War* were translated into Chinese; the younger generation ate beefsteak with forks and knives and drank martinis at Westernized restaurants as China, the Middle Kingdom of the Universe, slowly, lazily, opened its eyes and took in the breathless changes going on in the global community . . .

"They couldn't even dream about it when Mao Zedong was alive, but these days Chinese musicians perform such Western composers as Beethoven. When they held a concert of Brahms' Second Symphony—"

"What's the Chinese listening to Brahms' symphony got to do with our selling books this summer?" Director Pak said, annoyed.

He was right. All the trashy knowledge packed into my cerebrum had nothing to do with the main flow of my work life—producing books for Sejin Publishing House—or the world in general. Why did I talk about all those useless things at the meeting? I knew from repeated experience that my jargonic spree would, without fail, evoke Pak's ire. He could not understand why I had to keep talking about irrelevant things at the wrong times and places. I could not understand it either. I blankly gazed at the rain streaming down outside the window. Daylight would last 14 hours and 32 minutes today.

It was a long afternoon. The meeting seemed to go on and on forever. Since we did not have any substantial prospective publication plan for the next spring season, Pak Namjun, the managing director, had given vague instructions for us to work on a five-volume collection of some sort that could be sold as a set at the beginning of the new academic year, and Choe Inhwan, the managing editor, had assigned me to draw up a project that would delight the director. I had to prepare proposals to provide the editorial panel with several choices because presentation of one single project was liable to give a bad impression, one of negligence and lack of commitment on my part. By afternoon I was suffering too much from tedium and fatigue to pitch those projects, one after another, as if each of them was worthy. I felt I was conducting a disoriented orchestra before a deaf audience. Why should I go on prattling empty words into that hollow room, without response, or even an echo?

"You mean Sir Winston Churchill wrote a novel?" the managing director asked, glancing over Item #3 in my 12-page memo.

"Yes," I said. "He wrote one when he was young."

"*The Unknown Novels of the Famous.* That's interesting. Will you tell me a little more specifically about these novels, Mr. Han?"

I did. Sarah Bernhardt's short novel about four people traveling on a balloon, Winston Churchill's novel about a liberal fighter in Africa written when he was serving in the army in India, oil magnate H. L. Hunt's novel about a totalitarian government, Benito Mussolini's serialized novel about a cardinal's mistress, and movie star Jean Harlow's about high society in the 1920s. And Harry Reasoner also wrote a novel, a love story."

"Harry Re- . . . who is he?" Pak asked.

"He's an anchorman of '60 Minutes,'" I tried to explain.

"Sixty minutes? What sixty minutes?"

I explained, and segued into the commercial feasibility of the *Mysteries of the World* series and *The 50 Greatest Short Novels of the World.*

"Where did you find all this data, anyway?" Pak asked, more curious about my working methods than the content of my presentation.

"From books," I said, but did not elaborate, because I decided it would be better for the managing director not to know the truth, that I had discovered those facts in a book of trivia.

For almost three hours I continued my monologue, as dull as a recitation of public library catalogues. None of the seven proposals I had prepared was accepted.

When office hours were over, Nam Hosik, the chief of the Second Editorial Department, invited me for a shot of soju with roasted pork before going home, but I did not feel like getting drunk. I declined, yet I did not want to go home early either. So I went roaming downtown aimlessly. I passed an underpass and then an overpass, and then the Joongang *Daily News* building, a tea house, a florist's shop, a spacious open parking lot, a slouching American Negro soldier in plain clothes, and then the shady back alley leading to the courthouse, where I came out onto the bustling street again. Noisy. Dizzy. I felt a nauseous hunger.

Bulky buses swollen with commuters rolled away. People were lined up by the roadside taxi stop. I trudged, alone, among the numerous faceless people hurrying toward their destinations. Home. Or friends. Or lovers. They hurried away but I had no reason to. Shuffling amid the melee of the urbanites, I was not sure where I should go. A fat woman with sausage lips yawned in the aluminum kiosk displaying foreign slick magazines covered with the flesh of Occidental females. *Penthouse, Playboy, Oui, Stag, Swank*—the naked girls in full color, their long legs converging at the dark triangle of the spotlit pubic hair. An accentuated microscopic reality.

After an hour-long wandering, I went down to the subway station in front of Toksu Palace, but I did not have any intention of getting on the train taking other people home. Somebody tugged me by the elbow and said, "I think you're Han Kiju, aren't you? Remember me?" It was Chang Sunho who had been a classmate of mine in our graduating year at the high school. Snake Fish, that was his nickname. "Where're you going?" he asked me.

"There." Pointing nowhere with my chin.

"You busy tonight? Got an appointment to keep or something?"

"Not particularly. Why?"

"I'm on my way to the alumni meeting at the Scandinavian Club in the Medical Center compound. It begins at eight." He glanced at his watch. "We get together every other month. Did you get an invitation by some miracle?"

"No."

"Why don't you come with me, if you're not busy tonight? You don't need an invitation, anyway. You used to be the monitor in our class, didn't you? Everybody will be glad to see you. You so rarely—hell, you never show up at the alumni gatherings. Coming?"

I decided to go with him. I had nowhere else to go. Perhaps old classmates would not be such bad company on an evening like this. As we went down to the City Hall subway station under the ancient palace, we exchanged superficial questions and answers like two diplomats beating around the bush. "Where do you live?" We exchanged addresses and phone numbers. "Where do you work now? Do you often meet the old gang?" I shook my head, waiting for the train. What does one have to talk about, anyway, when he meets someone for the first time in ten or

fifteen years? Their respective jobs, wives, kids, cars? The deplorable
political unrest in the country? I suddenly had a strange dizziness, some
filmy delusion passing by me. Something was terribly wrong with me. I
had a throbbing urge to hate something definite.

The fourteen old classmates wedged in uncomfortably around the
table, seemed to have met quite often at the bimonthly gatherings. They
exchanged lively talk, calling one another by the nicknames of our high-
school days, about the party to be held at a Chinese restaurant next
week for the sixtieth birthday of Horse Head, the geometry teacher, the
fund-raising project to build a new library building, the belated marriage of a classmate whose name I could not remember, the increasing
American pressure over trade inequities and a golf course that was
opening at Anyang in September. They had gathered there to enjoy
small talk by themselves. Their clean hair trimmed impeccably, their
proper uniform neckties tight and straight, they were talking to one
another in a private, exclusive language all their own. Implicitly boasting about their success, their wealth, the proud report cards of their
sons, the lavish life style of their wives and their future prospects in
their professions. I was not sure what I was supposed to do or say in
order to begin to fit in with them. I realized I did not belong. Why had I
allowed Snake Fish to take me to this reunion of strangers?

"By the way, what do you do these days?" Im Chigyu, a wholesaler of
screws at Chonggyechon Market, finally recognized my mute invisible
existence and attempted to lead me into the vivacious conversation.

"I work for a publishing house," I mumbled.

A very disappointed and pathetic expression flashed over Im's unc-
tuous face—I believed he was laughing at me inwardly, though—and he
said in a disbelieving, sympathizing voice, "I thought your I.Q. was 180
or 190 or something." He could not understand why I, with that
marvelous brain, had failed to make a lot of money or become a politician
or something.

Sure, with that remarkable brain I had jiggled the malfunctioning
batteries of my mind for three hours this afternoon to secure my
biological survival. As I remained silent, not knowing what might be an
appropriate defense against Im's inquisitive accusation, all fourteen
boys around the table fell silent too, like actors who had forgotten their
lines. Then, like dormitory children immediately after a silent prayer at
meal time, they began to pleasantly chat about a club at Socho-dong

where lesbians presented excellent shows in the private booths. In their excitement they quickly forgot my existence again.

While their conversation hectically darted back and forth over the table, I withdrew more and more deeply. I felt I was snared by billions of fine invisible glass fibers, a dragonfly caught in a choking web.

The knowledge that I had a mental quotient superior to that of most people around me had been a cause of frustration all my life. Even at a young age people expected perfection and peerless excellence from me: I simply had to score the highest marks. My report cards were straight A's throughout my elementary, middle and high school years. Everybody took it for granted. If I solved something nobody else could, they took that for granted, too. I was a matter-of-fact person, whose achievements surprised no one.

My mother wanted me to be a world-famous violinist; she believed a highly developed brain could do anything in the world. My father wanted to live a rich and respected life as the father of a prominent judge or an influential prosecuting attorney. I think my parents did not have the slightest doubt that I would become a prosecuting attorney with staggering wealth and almighty power, who would travel all over the world on weekends as a renowned violinist. They expected too much from me, as did everyone else, just because my intelligence quotient was a few notches higher than ordinary. The boys had often relished watching me corner the physics teacher, that mean and vicious man enamored of corporal punishment, with a complicated and knotty question that the bespectacled neurotic could never answer despite his own weeks of homework. Those same males were now sitting before me, successful and middle-aged, wondering why my celebrated brain had failed to get me anywhere in this world of easy money and quick fame. So did I.

I had fallen victim to these expectations too, and eventually came to cherish unreasonable ambitions for myself. I was foolish enough to believe that I was entitled to live any kind of life I chose to. Some time before entering college, I realized I was not the weaver of my own life: I was merely tracing lines between the dots punctured in the cardboard world for me by other people. I did not exist except as someone's expectation. So I decided not to fulfill Father's dream of my becoming a prosecuting attorney or an influential politician. And I decided not to become the doctor or celebrated musician my mother envisioned in her future. I decided not to become an Einstein, or a Mozart, as if I had the choice.

I majored in literature, a decision that lacked any sense of purpose or direction. At school I avoided the girls who liked me because I was "intelligent" or "bright." I also avoided acquiring any systematized body of knowledge in an established field lest I should some day alight on a tangible "achievement" that might attract anybody's scrutiny. I did not want to be categorized. I wanted to run away to where no one knew me and start a totally new life from the very beginning. After I graduated, I refused to go to the United States for further study, and enlisted in the army as a private.

My great grandmother once said she had been astonished, sixty years ago in her youth, when she heard a passing Japanese in a modern Western suit pipe a fart on the street. The image of a gentleman belonging to the colonial ruling class simply was not associable with any base animal functions of the physical being. Indeed, it is hard to imagine Cleopatra sitting on a flush toilet. But all men are biologically equal. And I hoped to be a common person swimming along with the flow, not an object of curiosity. This strong wish for a rebirth as an anonymous person had much to do with my late marriage.

When I was stranded by a typhoon for nine days on Huksando Island along with a photographer from the newspaper I was then working for, I met a girl—an ordinary girl—staying at an islander's home with her friend, also stranded in the middle of their travels along the South Coast. She and I spent several innocent days together like two children, exploring the island, fishing by the lighthouse and collecting flat pebbles, while the photographer and her friend were cleaving non-stop at the harbor inn. I married her seven months later because this anonymous woman liked me even though she knew virtually nothing about me except that I was a reporter who had been to Vietnam as a private soldier.

After discussing various ingenious ways of making money, the middle-aged boys concluded our small reunion and went out to Ulchiro Street. They split into several groups of four or five so naturally that I suspected they did this every time. I hesitated for a moment, not knowing where to turn, and, following a half-hearted tug by Snake Fish, joined the group of Chang Sunho, Im Chigyu and Ko "King Miser" Taechi who ran an inn at Pildong. They hailed a taxi in front of Kyerim Cinema to go to a private bar with partitioned rooms at Yaksu District, without asking me if I was interested. Since I stayed with them, they took it for granted that I was.

The private bar had the suggestive name of The Ride — "You can have a hot ride in there, if you want it on the spot," Snake Fish told me with a chuckle and a wink. Outside, it was decorated in traditional Korean style with tiled roof and wooden gates, but the drinking rooms inside were completely sealed shelters, like carpeted hotel rooms, for undisturbed pleasure, fully furnished with separate toilets. Snake Fish and the other boys seemed to be steady customers, for each of them had a favorite who was sent in immediately. The girl assigned to me had a beguiling chaste look, her hair trimmed unpretentiously like a high-school student. While the routine prelude of obscene jokes was verbally shared among the customers and the girls, a bottle of Blackstone whiskey was emptied promptly. I watched the giggling face of the girl sitting next to me, a girl barely seventeen who seemed to have an inexhaustible repertoire of lewd riddles in the vein of "What is the stick with bristling hair at one end that keeps pumping in and out of a dark small hole and makes the hole ooze with white juice in ten minutes? It's a toothbrush."

"You're a strange man indeed." Hong Sonja, the girl assigned to me, snuggled up to my neck like a purring cat. "Aren't you going to give me some fun? A man is supposed to touch a girl. Or should I touch you? I hope you know at least that much of etiquette when a girl is sitting next to you."

"But he's got the brain of a genius. He has an I.Q. of 190 or 195 or somewhere around that," Snake Fish said, chuckling. "He knows everything about everything and I guess he should know a lot about women, too. Maybe your service hasn't been good enough to make him notice you."

"Is something bothering you?" asked Hong Sonja, ignoring Snake Fish's commentary. "If something is on your mind, just tell me. I will make you happy."

A little after one o'clock we left The Ride. Snake Fish, King Miser, and Im Chigyu, the wholesaler of screws, exchanged some whispered words with the girls as if plotting something. It looked as if they had practiced this ritual. When we came out of the house, they walked some 20 meters up the alley, turning at a barbershop at the corner, and stopped by a post box. They waited, chuckling and chattering. They did not explain to me why we had to wait there, but I waited with them without asking why. They were very drunk, having emptied three bottles of whiskey, but showed no indication of going home.

"You can stay out tonight, can't you?" Snake Fish said. It was not a question, but a confirmation.

I still did not want to go home. "Why?" I asked. "You guys going to go to a nightclub and drink all night?"

He answered me with another question. "What do you think of the girl who sat next to you tonight? She was Miss Hong, wasn't she?"

"She was all right."

The four girls who had been with us came out of The Ride and hurried to the post box where we were waiting. It was apparent that there had been some sort of arrangement. Im Chigyu, King Miser, and their girls walked away towards Changchung Park, and Snake Fish hailed a passing taxi for me and Hong Sonja. He pushed me into the taxi after the girl, slammed the door shut, and whispered to me through the rolled-down window, "I have already settled things with this girl, so you don't have to pay for anything except the room," and then stepped back, grinning triumphantly.

We drove to Itaewon. She knew the way well enough to give the driver directions for a shortcut. I could see she had often stayed at the inn. I did not care.

Led by the inn-maid to a corner room on the third floor, I felt I was going astray, as if the man now heading for a secluded cell with this girl was not me but a stranger I had never known before. All of a sudden I was a detached spectator floating in the air above and watching a wretched man in my body and a young girl infested by venereal disease follow the guiding middle-aged woman carrying a water jug and towels, shampoo and roll of tissue paper on a tray along the dark corridor to the shady den of unclean pleasures.

I took off my socks in the room when the maid was gone and sat timidly on the edge of the much-used bed with its chipped headboard. The girl, without any hesitation, took her few clothes off and piled them quickly on the worn out grey sofa. I was intimidated. She was not a bit self-conscious about her nakedness, not even trying to cover her hairy part from my nervous stare. When I was finally naked too, we sat on the bed to face each other. The broken windowpane had been glued together with blue paper cut in a flower pattern. Outside late-hour taxis scampered like mad bulls along the deserted street looking for stragglers.

It suddenly occurred to me that I would not have an erection now. The law of inertia. The centrifugal drive of instinct. When did I have sex with my wife the last time? Three months ago? Four? I could not remember. I needed some time and reassuring darkness. I rose, a solitary body standing naked, meek and unprotected, in the desolate and obvious surroundings.

I said hesitantly, "How about a bath? It's so hot and humid."

"Bath can wait," the girl said and laughed. "Don't you think we got something to do first?"

She apparently wanted to finish her work quickly and get some sleep. When I touched her, the girl was more than ready. She responded spontaneously, clasping like a boa constrictor with her slithering arms and pulling me down into herself. I abruptly turned lethargic, feeling emasculated. I was at a loss because the girl seemed to be hastening, pressing me to push on and on, when I was not even ready to begin yet. The girl kept moving busily, her legs twining about mine, leading and prompting me this way and that. I tried, but a while later, helplessly gave up. The woman also stopped, frankly disappointed, and let me go. She stared at me, puzzled, went over to the sofa, sighed a low and restrained sigh, and then smoked one whole cigarette very slowly, the sweaty skin on her breasts reflecting the yellow electric light. I crouched at one corner of the bed like a pile of discarded rags, humiliated. After the final long drag, the naked woman slipped into the bathroom. I heard the long *shoo* of the shower. The girl chuckled. Twice. I blushed.

I wanted to restore my lost confidence and pride by any possible means but I was still not ready when she finished her shower and came out of the bathroom with her flushed body so fresh and seductive. The girl waited for a while, still hoping, and looked down at the naked drooping male. She was disappointed again. I shrank further, my diffident libido hopelessly dampened.

She began to dress slowly. I wanted to stop her but was not sure enough of myself to do so. Lying uncomfortably in bed, I smoked, feeling stupid. She pulled up her panties, hooked her bra by twisting her arms back like an Indian demigod with many arms, threw on her short black slip that barely covered her navel and lay down beside me gently. I watched her, smoking. She kept quiet, waiting, until I finished the cigarette and crushed it in the ash tray on the head board, and then said, "I think this is the first time for you. You seem to be embarrassed. It *is* the first time, isn't it? Whoring, I mean."

I said nothing, because I was too ashamed to defend myself. I felt an odd frustration mixed with shame, guilt, enervation and discomfiture. I could vividly imagine what this girl would say to my old classmates when they went back to The Ride after the next get together two months hence. "Your friend who was here last time with you," she would say, "that genius friend of yours, Mr. I.Q., you know. Isn't he a eunuch or a psycho case? I tried every trick I know to get him aroused, but he simply doesn't know how to fuck. He may know everything about everything, but he certainly does not know one thing." Everybody laughing. Laughing and laughing again.

I gave up, and the girl did not demand any more. We talked. Intermittent meaningless words, barely sustaining the conversation. And then we talked some more. Until we really began to talk. Although our working and living conditions were worlds apart, I noticed that she was also drifting in turbulent waters, an outcast. Somewhat like myself. As we sobered up, she and I talked on and on, not listening much to the other as if we were competing about who was a more dramatic failure.

She said, "I had many fathers. Because my mother kept changing her husband all the time. I think she collected husbands. When I was young, I used to have a new father every year. And every time my mother introduced me to a strange new father, my family name changed too. If I had a father with the family name of Kim, my family name was Kim, and I became a Pak if my father was a Pak. Then I became a Choe and a Yun, too. My last father, when my mother died of too much opium smoking, was a Hong. That's why I am a Hong now."

I had read this story in a novel twenty years ago somewhere. But I did not mind if she had stolen an episode from an old novel. Life itself was full of plagiarism, anyway. The girl said she was living a lamentably miserable life at a cheap boarding house at Chonggyechon with her younger sister who worked at a laundry house. She hated her seedy boarding house so dreadfully that she would go to The Ride as soon as she got up, around eleven o'clock in the morning, and spend the whole afternoon playing flower cards with other girls.

Around 3 a.m. she murmured herself to sleep. I could not fall asleep, blankly gazing at the ceiling stained with rain leaks. As my mind cleared more and more to a crystal sobriety, I saw the whole day, with so many confusing and incoherent happenings, rapidly pass before my eyes. Was this the odyssey of my life? This particular day ending with the funeral of my libido? Was this the proper time for a trumpet elegy to wail over the grave of my defunct animal identity?

I floated in the air and watched my abandoned self, alive and dead, beside the unused female body. I blinked slowly like a big, foolish and impotent yellow toad. The reptile deprived of breeding ability. Mental castration. The man unable to reproduce himself. That pathetic image reminded me of the skeleton lying alone in a dark cell in Yun Tongju's poem.

I made another try a little after four o'clock, the final attempt to confirm my dormant potency. I peeled up her short black slip. The girl remained motionless, asleep, but when I had removed the other two pieces of scanty clothing, she began to help, still asleep but moving slowly, effectively. It was a very brief motion, though, that did not last longer than ten seconds. I was too uneasy. I just squirmed for a while on top of the woman and then slid down, feeling stupid again.

The girl woke up during the short intermission. Wiping herself with tissue paper, she chuckled. She had chuckled like that earlier while taking the shower. "What was that?" she said.

"What was what?" I said.

"What's the matter with you?" she said. "So quick. Like a bird."

She fell asleep again. I waited for the morning so that I could get out of this shameful room and go to the office. I was sorry for myself, for everything that had happened to me that night. I am physically and spiritually exhausted, I thought, my instincts shredded and abraded. Even the ecstasy of lust could not help overcome the choking pressure. Joy was a rustic concept. Pleasure might exist in cities, but not happiness.

She woke up around six, had another quick shower and dressed. She glanced down at my listless body and smiled. "I don't have any sex disease now," she said, "but I want you to go to a drugstore in the morning and get some terramycin. I like you. I don't know why but I've come to like you somewhere between last night and this morning. So I don't want you to get into trouble with your wife because of some dumb disease. You'd better take precautions. But I am clean. You have to believe me that I don't sleep with too many men."

She smiled again. An angel of a whore. Still smiling, she quietly stepped back out of the room and closed the door, click, leaving me behind, alone, in the crumpled bed of something unconcluded. Her smile distracted me.

I went to a urologist near Piccadilly Cinema in the morning, and during the urethra suction, due to extreme fatigue and lack of sleep, I fainted because I could no longer stand on my shaky legs.

It was a perfect defeat.

3

It had rained steadily for several days and Inwang Hill loomed faintly through the dark grey mist. Gloomy weather. I had startled myself awake. It was 5:18 a.m. I had fallen asleep on the wooden floor of the upstairs living room with the verandah doors open, as I often did on summer nights. I sat up on the flower-patterned rush mat and folded the blanket slowly.

I cannot just wait passively for something to happen to me, I thought, and hurriedly washed and dressed, hastening like a host who wanted to be out by the gate to welcome the guest before he arrived. I could not hear my wife anywhere; she might still be asleep in her room downstairs. Brushing my teeth, I thought I should be prepared to encounter her before leaving for work.

I finished dressing. I waited for a while, pacing in my study, then went downstairs. My wife was asleep on the sofa in the downstairs living room. She might have fallen asleep while watching television until all hours last night. There was no sign of my parents-in-law in the house; they might have gone to the fountain by Suguk Temple, I thought, as I slipped out silently.

All morning in the office, I was stalked by a sense of urgency and absence. But I was not sure what I was supposed to do. I decided to take some time, be alone, think. After lunch, I lied to the managing editor that I had an appointment with the novelist Choe Tokchin at the Doll's House. Instead I went to Namsan Hill to saunter up the promenade and take the cable car to the top, right in the middle of the work day. It was indeed a childish whim to go there like a tourist visiting Seoul for the first time.

In the Octagonal Pavilion atop the hill, several leisurely old men were quietly looking down at the city, musing or dozing. Apartment buildings and official residences for foreign diplomats and military personnel were snugly set among the trees on the ridge below. The daytime fog of gaseous waste turned the distant mountains surrounding the city to faint violet shades.

Escape. I tried to imagine a possible way of escape from the city that kept dragging me into its maze. A desert. I visualized myself living in a desert. I imagined myself lying on sand and looking up at the night sky where the stars were pouring down like shattered-crystal fragments. Down there ten million souls wait for their salvation in those piled up buildings of this monstrous great city. A horde of drifting people whose souls had failed to take root in the lifeless organism called The City. They were slaves of agony but did not know why they were agonized; they were slaves of fury but did not know why; they were slaves of despair. And I was one of them, an unnoticed citizen bored by the monotony and tedium of the mass life. I was not even trying to hold myself erect.

While the human race was stupendously reproducing to cover the surface of the earth, I had not made any contribution. Perhaps I was one incapable. But was I really? I would find out today. I decided to go to the

Catholic Medical Center, the general hospital located at the foot of Namsan Hill.

I took the cable car down. The start of the rainy season had threatened for days, but the sky had cleared and it was scorching inside the box of glass and iron dangling high in the air. "Are you sure you're the responsible party?" Choe Inhwan, the managing editor said one evening while we were out drinking. "Maybe it's the soil that's bad, not the seed. You'd better go to see a doctor yourself."

But what if it *was* the seed that had been responsible? What if I were medically proven to be defective? If the doctor found . . .

I hesitated again as I crossed the underpass by the Prince Hotel, wriggling through against the milling crowd like a minnow swimming upstream. My legs were leading me to the hospital but my mind was fleeing.

The sultry back alley was teeming with the urbanites, souls imprisoned by overlapping organizations and partitioned offices. The procession of non-existences. What dignity and nobility could a man assume and maintain in this collective of statistics?

I trudged on. Plod, plod. It was boring—ennui. I was trudging towards a distant goal, vaguely conscious of my destination, heading for a trial that would deliver a medical verdict upon my human qualifications. At least I was heading in that direction. I felt mid-summer despair; summer was always merciless to me. I was depressed by my abstracted life and my nagging sense of extinction. I felt my heart would burst from the weight of an unbearable incubus pressing on my chest.

Why should I be so hypersensitive about simple reproduction? In the near future life would be created by a scientific process at a canning factory. The human race had already entered the era of deciphering and revising the structure of deoxyribonucleic acid, the era of mass producing geniuses by amplifying brain waves, of dividing the spermatozoon inseminated outside the body. Last night Peter Jennings reported a quaint legal dispute concerning rights of inheritance as between a woman's child from her first marriage and her unborn fetus, inseminated by the sperm of a man, not her new husband, who had died in a plane crash.

After pacing back and forth several times before the florist's shop, I entered the hospital with a detached feeling, as if I were visiting a friend there. This was the first time that I had ever been to a hospital for such an embarrassing purpose: a man going to see an obstetrician. Other patients shuffled around in the corridor with painful expressions of sickness and anguish. I waited my turn sitting on a bench in the dark corner. Squeezed among other waiting patients, surrounded by the pungent sterilized smell, I looked around at nurses carrying medicine bottles, a young intern with his hands thrust in the sagging pockets of his white gown, and the patients in loose crumpled clothes passing by with pathetic expressions. Again I felt I did not belong here. I was a misfit everywhere I went. I did not belong anywhere and that awareness made me feel small. Very small.

Sitting on the wooden bench I thought about the beginning moment of life. When does an individual human being start to exist? At the moment of ovulation? When it is still a spermatozoon swimming around the testes? But sperm is a mere potentiality of a human being. Hemingway once wrote about a girl in Kansas City who had chosen to become a prostitute so she could freely swallow high protein sperm because she thought it would cure her tuberculosis. Is the moment when inorganic matter is compounded into an organism the beginning of human life? A woman produces only 400 ova in her lifetime while a man is responsible for producing as much as 500 million spermatoza in one single emission. One man's lifetime sperm production can total $3 \times 10^{10} \times 35$. But I doubted I would ever catch up with that magnificent male performance in my life.

It was finally my turn and I explained my predicament to the doctor. The gynecologist, a man in his early 40s, who looked sickly pallid, sent me to the adjacent laboratory with a scribbled note. The sallow lab technician in his late 30s, who had been reading an English medical journal, glanced at the doctor's instruction slip and told me to produce a sample of my sperm. "The nurse will help you," he said. I thought he meant that a nurse would help me collect the sample and wondered if she would use her hands or what. A young nurse with a long face, who was so tall that I had to look up at her like the Statue of Liberty, brought me a gray packet of condoms and gave it to me with an extremely efficient attitude, saying matter-of-factly, "Please go to the bathroom and get a sample." She looked tired.

I always found it difficult to produce a urine sample at a random moment, but it was literally impossible for me to enter a dark suspicious toilet booth, pull down my pants halfway to my knees and then, standing up, produce an artificial ejaculation. I tried, rustling and stroking, for ten minutes I guess, until I decided it would never work. I gave up and

timidly went back to the lab technician; I did not have the courage to
discuss this impossible matter with the nurse. I asked him politely if it
would be all right to collect the sample somewhere outside the hospital,
probably with someone's help, and bring it to him later in the afternoon.
He chuckled knowingly and said, "No problem. But you have to hurry
here as soon as you get the sample."

Awkwardly conscious of the soft rubber roll in my pocket, I came out
of the hospital into the bustling street. I felt helpless, cornered. I did not
know what to do. I could not go to my wife, explain to her about my
humiliating situation and beg her to help me; somehow she had become
an invincible enemy in my eyes lately. Nor could I go to find a prostitute
in broad daylight like a horny widower, and ask for a weird favor. Maybe
Hong Sonja of The Ride might help me, but I was afraid to see her again.
I still blushed whenever I recalled what she had said to me that night:
"What's the matter with you? So quick. Like a bird." I thought about
using a milking device, a sucking thing that was shaped like an old
model of a honking automobile horn. It was miserably comic to imagine
that round squeeze-rubber hanging down there like a clown's red nose. I
chuckled. There was no other way, it seemed, but to find a whore. But
where could I locate a prostitute at this time of day? They did not run
their telephone numbers in the classified ads. If I rented a room at a
downtown inn and asked the maid, offering a fat tip, to call one of the
girls under contract with the inn, she might get me one. But that did not
seem to be so easy either. It was too obvious and embarrassing to enter
an inn at this hour, and it made me feel sad and miserable when I
visualized myself waiting all alone in an empty seedy room for a prostitute to show up.

After roaming around downtown, I decided to get on the first bus at
the first bus stop I came across to rest my tired legs for a while. The bus I
got on was going to Pogwang-dong.

The daytime bus, collecting one customer here and one there, looked
leisurely and forlorn. They were not going anywhere in particular, and
if they were, nobody was in a hurry. I got off the bus at Itaewon and
shuffled along a street lined with bars and discos and clubs of dubious
nationality. The whole street looked dead; this district for the American
soldiers stationed at Yongsan would come alive at dark. I finally made up
my mind. I was defying the voice of my fate if I did not solve this matter
before the day was over, so I called the technician at the hospital and

said, "I haven't collected yet, you know, and I want to find out when you close the laboratory."

He laughed, and said, "I will wait here for you until five o'clock. If you can't make it by then, you may come in tomorrow."

I hailed a taxi and went directly to The Ride at Yaksu-dong. Without any hesitation I entered the dark hall of the wine house and called out like a policeman on a raid, "Anybody home?"

Several girls, who had been giggling and joking and cheering while playing flower cards in a corner room, abruptly quieted. The red velvet-covered door opened and a young girl peeked out suspiciously. It was the girl who had entertained Snake Fish that night. She did not recognize me, so I had to explain to her who I was and who I was looking for. Her head disappeared into the room and momentarily Hong Sonja craned her head out, to see who had come at this odd hour.

Hong recognized me at one glance, but was as surprised as if she had encountered a yeti on a tropical island. "Oh, Mr. I.Q.," she said, merrily.

She hurriedly stumbled out of the room in her crimson slippers, tidying her hair with one hand and putting on a cheap red blouse that revealed her shoulders and bare chest down to the cleavage. I asked her if she could go out with me for a while.

"Sure," she said promptly, probably thinking I wanted to have sex with her now, and handed her cards over to Snake Fish's girl. She changed her shoes and followed me out to the alley. When I told her we needed some place to discuss a private matter, she led me to a teahouse on the second floor of a noodle shop across an overpass. The name of the teahouse was White Violet.

"How come you deigned to visit this worthless creature?" she asked teasingly, her eyes glinting blue with curiosity, sitting next to the glass globe in which several tropical fish idly floated around. She seemed pleased that I came to see her again even though our last encounter had not provided me with much satisfaction.

I explained to her the perplexing situation I was in. My wife must have had herself checked at the hospital, I told her, and I wanted to check myself, too. Hong attentively listened to my distressing story. In fact she listened so sincerely, not interrupting me even once with a question, like a virgin girl listening to a timid love confession from a pimpled boy, that I gradually shed my shame and embarrassment.

Detecting some faint response in her solemn expression, I felt like the dark clouds of agony were passing off.

"I will help you," she said. That was all.

Hong and I went to the inn where we had stayed the other night. Although it was still daylight, both the inn maid and Hong behaved so casually that I suspected she came here often with afternoon guests. Hong asked the maid to give us the very room where we had slept last time.

"I think a familiar room would be more relaxing for you," she explained. "You must be very tense now, aren't you?"

Until I finished my shower to calm down, she quietly waited in bed, naked under the sheet. And then she began to help me enthusiastically, using both her hands and mouth. Watching her black hair covering my abdomen, I recalled Trau's mother, Hai—and Sergeant Chon Hisik who wept so loudly, prostrate atop the Vietnamese whore, thrusting violently and sobbing as violently. He was already dying that night.

Surprisingly, it did not take much time for me to get what I wanted. While she carefully held up the condom like a fluttering butterfly, I hastily dressed, without even washing myself. Her thumb and index finger held it like a dreadful poisonous insect, the other three fingers spreading outward. I took the slippery rubber, its upper end knotted tight, from her outstretched hand, wrapped it several times with tissue paper, put it in my pocket and hastened out of the room. I rushed down the hall, and then stopped at the top of the stairs, detained by an afterthought. I realized I had not even said goodbye to Hong, and looked back at our, yes, *our* room over my shoulder. She was standing by the threshold, carelessly covering her breasts with the sheet, only her torso leaning out of the room, and smiling at me like an innocent child.

When I reached Taehan Cinema, it occurred to me that I had not paid anything to Hong. I did not ask the taxi to turn back because I was running short of time. Hong did not seem to matter so much now, anyway. Holding the small mushy rubber pouch tight in my palm, I was afraid I might squeeze it too hard and the thin skin would burst and lose the little oozy clot of life liquid. What if the spermatozoa died anyway? Worrying that the precious spermatozoa might die, if there were any of them in the balloon, I ran up the hospital stairs like a breathless fireman.

Still feeling a little self-conscious in her presence, I submitted the condom wrapped in several layers of tissue paper to the Statue of Liberty nurse, who promptly delivered it to the technician. I waited anxiously, trying to forget what I was doing, trying not to worry about the examiner's verdict, to think about something else, anything else than what was going on in the laboratory, thinking about the Big Bang, the beautiful rings of Saturn, Carl Sagan's voice, Ptolemy's epicycles, Jules Verne's journey to the center of the earth, Magellanic Clouds, the beauty of the gas cloud of the Crab Nebula, and the rotating radio beam of a pulsar blip, blip, blip, blip, blip, blip. I tried to calm my heart, thinking about the sea, the whitecaps of the waves, the squeaking of whales, the ugly look of the red sea raven, the camouflage of the peacock flounder, the fishing boats of the East Sea, the summer typhoons on the South Coast, an owl, the Kingston Trio. About 15 minutes later the examiner buzzed and told the nurse to send me in. When I went in, he was sitting before his microscope with the sample of my semen smeared on the slide under the illuminated lens.

"Looks fine to me," he said, grinning. "They swim around mighty lively."

The lab technician pushed his microscope toward me, saying I could take a look if I wanted to. I pulled my chair next to him and, crouching uncomfortably, looked into the eyepiece. On the slide, magnified by the lenses, I saw the tadpoles with thin elongated tails wriggle around in the pool of whitish grey protein that the Kansas City prostitute used to swallow to cure her tuberculosis. The tiny little worms swimming around seeking the moment to create a human being, they were the agents of life itself in this glass world. These little wigglers testified with their humorous dance that I was capable of creating a new life. But I did not have a child.

I did not feel the ecstasy I had expected. There was no bliss, nor even a shade of joy in my heart. I had vaguely, or perhaps ardently, hoped and somehow anticipated this, but the primordial life forms on the glass slide brought disappointment and nihilistic despair. I *was* one of those wriggling things. These things, these primitive worms would develop into human beings who might heatedly discuss Jaspers and Mayakovsky, torture themselves through sleepless nights lamenting their unrequited love, start wars to sate their sanguinary urges and feast on mass killing, hate one another or shed sentimental tears gazing at the yellow moon on autumn nights. And because of these worms I had worried so much. How I had agonized because of them all these years. And why were they jerking about so fitfully, their futile wandering already begun in the protein pool?

I awkwardly bowed thank you to the gloating examiner and the towering nurse, and shuffled out to the street where humans were still broiling under the ferocious summer sun. In ancient days Roman generals returning home from a victorious battle crashed through the walls instead of entering the city by the gate. But the urge to demolish a wall, I felt now, had nothing to do with my hypothetical triumph in confirming the potential for continuing my physical existence.

It was almost closing time. There were two messages for me waiting on my desk. One was the invitation to the annual gathering of the Han family presently residing in the Unpyong District. The other message said Pyon Chinsu had called again—twice—that afternoon.

We had been in Vietnam together. I had not seen him since. Thirteen years.

While most of the city population was asleep in the hours between yesterday and tomorrow, a new day began. Five o'clock that morning in front of South Seoul Gas Station across the Han River we were to rendezvous. Of the nine members in the fishing party I was the first to arrive at the appointed place, carrying the ice chest slung over my shoulder. I was alone and had nothing else to do but wait for others to show up, so I squeezed into a roadside canopied cart, to soothe my empty stomach with a bowl of peppery noodles.

By the phone booth outside a bar hostess was intently counting the tips she had earned entertaining drunks all night long.

Three night-club waiters in white uniform shirts squatted on the imitation marble steps of a tall black building and passionately inhaled arid cigarette smoke until their cheeks were sucked in. A street-sweeper, stooping like a life-sentenced prisoner, pulled the garbage cart to the curb where a shapeless old woman was selling snacks to the wanderers of the dark.

Blankly staring at the counter, I wondered what was the secret about me that everybody knew but I did not? I felt I had missed a step somewhere. Why did they keep watching me with such sorry eyes?

The physics teacher was in charge of my high school class in the graduating year. He was very surprised and disappointed when I brought him my college application form to get his recommendation. "Why don't you study something in the field of science?" he said. "You have such a superb brain, you know." He did not know it was the superb brain that was bothering me at the time. If I had become a physicist or a mathematician or a master in a field my old high-school teacher had determined my aptitude indicated, I might have fared far more easily in the world.

My father was so angry. He would not give me the matriculation fee or the tuition fees, or any money I might need for my college education, when I told him about my decision to major in literature. He thought it was something "only sissy boys with no brains" studied, instead of going where I was really supposed to go: "a good respected school with good prospects for a bright future." He gave me a choice of getting money myself to go to college or giving up further education and running his hardware shop after high school, if I really intended to waste "four years reading story books."

I knew he meant it. My father, who ran a shabby store at Kongdok market, was too poor to invest in me for any abstract possibility of future success. But he would support me all the way, he said, if I changed my major to law or engineering or medical science that guaranteed more security and faster cash return. "You just get your mind straight," he said, "and I'll see that you get graduated from any damned expensive school, even if my back breaks."

So I had to find some way to make the money for college. I was sure I could get scholarships until graduation, but no school offered free entrance at that time. I rushed to the American Air Base at Kimpo

Airport when I found a help-wanted advertisement in a newspaper. They were looking for interpreters to work on the base for the American military. I waited for two sweltering hours in the quonset hut at the air base, but the Korean clerk did not even allow me an interview with the American hiring officer when they found out how young I was and that I wanted to work only during the summer vacation.

After trying two other places for a part-time job, I finally decided to go to the east coast where they said one could get a summer job easily as a fisherman during the busy cuttle-fish season. I left Chongnyang-ni Station at night and went cross country to arrive at Kangnung after a sweaty, exhausting 12-hour journey in a stinking local train that seemed to stop every five minutes. In Kangnung I took a local bus full of fishy smells, chickens and poverty, and traveled along the coast all the way up north to Kojin, the military city just below the Demilitarized Zone. Carrying two bushels of rice on my shoulders, I went to see the biggest shipowner in town, a stalwart man with a rugged sun-tanned face and six cuttle-fish boats. I was supposed to give him the rice in advance for the meals I would eat on the boat during the fishing trip. The shipowner was apparently short of hands and immediately allowed me to work on one of his boats. "I am really impressed," he said. "A young boy like you doing this kind of hard work to go to college. That's the way, I say. If you want this job back next year, you will be welcome."

Under our contract, the ship's owner was to take 60 percent from the gross sale of all the cuttle-fish I would catch, and my share was the remaining 40 percent. I agreed to all the terms concerning profit share, labor requirements and repair expenses, because I could make enough money for my college entrance with this fishing contract. There were two other part-time fishermen like me aboard our boat. We were scheduled to leave Kojin and sail all the way down to Pohang, chasing the cuttle-fish schools, anchoring at eight major harbors on the coast.

We fished only at night, lighting up the whole boat brightly with electric bulbs as big as zucchinis hanging on the wire fixed between the two poles at each end of the boat. To catch the cuttle-fish gathering around the boat attracted by the bright lights, we would drop anchor and lower the holder to prevent the boat from tangling all the lines. We used spinning wheels to roll up the line with some thirty hooks, and when the line was too heavy with the fish on every hook, we had to shake off some of them by releasing the line so that the spinning wheel would not break. We had to wear long rubber raincoats to keep the cuttle-fish ink from soaking our clothes. The fishermen on the boat, working at night, looked like ghouls dredging up dead bodies from the sea bottom.

At dawn we sailed to a port to auction off the catch to a wholesaler at the cooperative market. Leaving the shipowner's share with the purser, who attended the auction as a witness, I went to an inn for an uncomfortable two-hour nap in a close, shabby, back room. Then I dropped by a bait shop, dragging my worn-out, half-asleep body, to buy fishing line and a handful of hooks to repair the damaged rigs. Back aboard, I had several painful days when a hook impaled my sole while I was running the line between my big and second toes to straighten the looping knots.

Whenever the boat made a stop at a large port, one or two fishermen were replaced by new men but I had to stay till the end of the trip because I needed all the money I could get that summer. And one night, while shaking off some cuttle-fish from the overloaded line, I suddenly burst into silent tears, grieving that I had to start my adult life like this. Nobody on the boat could see the tears because my face was flooded with the ink spewed by the angry cuttle-fish.

After entering college with the fishing money, I continued wasting my life. Going to war, marriage, a resentful and short career as a reporter, and then this work at the publishing company—they were all aborted, bungled misadventures that drowned me in a swamp of shame and disillusionment. I chose this life but it certainly was not a gratifying choice.

The streets were deserted but for stray humans, occasional taxis and bulky trucks scampering past like frantic rats and enraged bulls.

The canopied noodle cart was noisily alive inside. Three youthful men babbled about their good old marine corps days and three young ladies of dubious reputation, somewhere between beauty parlor girls and whores, apparently picked up on the street by the ex-marines, guzzled down boiled ark shells. Beside them a girl of about twenty, with billowing ebony hair, was fast asleep among the dishes of live octopus, cucumber slices and liquor bottles strewn over the serving board, her face down on the oozy plank. To this passed-out girl a man of sleek appearance, eight years her senior, was giving a philosophy lecture as outlandish as his immaculate attire, so totally out of place in this cheap joint. "You see," he said, "that was the logic so often quoted by the sophists. . . ." He was busy expounding when the girl suddenly sprang up and rushed out from under the draped canopy of the cart. The young philosopher hastened after her, puzzled, and a while later I heard the young girl vomit loudly by a telegraph pole. The philosopher went away, disillusioned, muttering, "What a fucking night." The girl staggered into the morning.

Shortly my companions arrived. We were going to drive to the sea. Seagulls would fly overhead, dropping white stains on the grey-green water, and the hills and islands would float in the distant mist. The sea was one of the few things I really liked in this world. That was why I chose to go with Yo Hyonsu's fishing party that Sunday, instead of joining the anglers who preferred the easier catch of crucian carp now busy spawning at the reedy edges of fresh water reservoirs. Our van passed Suwon and Palan, and then stopped at Choam to buy ice. I dozed to make up for lost sleep and then we arrived.

We left Maehyang Village on the hired motored boat, had a hasty breakfast on deck and reached the waters off Pang Island in half an hour. We fed line into the sea but there wasn't a bite. We knew it was too early in the season for rock fish, yet knowing this fact did not blunt our disappointment. Summer had come early this year, but the fish under the sea did not seem to have noticed.

Our skins began to tan by early morning, but there was still no bite. We searched around several rocky islets looming darkly above the water, but there was no pulling twang of the line yet. We decided to go far out to Ippa Island beyond Kukhwa Islet. As we endlessly plowed through the calm water of the bay, two dark seals rollicked on the surface, their wet backs shining black in the sun.

Whether on a lake or on the sea, your mind keeps wandering when the fish stay away from your bait. Mundane thoughts. Not spiritual meditations. Vaguely conscious of the tingle on the inside skin of the knuckle where the line is hooked to detect the vibration of a nibble, I was remembering. *I wouldn't care if you have a baby by another woman.* These words haunted me so often the past two months. I could vividly visualize the resigned but firm expression of my wife staring at my eyes as if to penetrate into my fortified core when she said them. What it meant was bluntly simple: I might produce a child by another woman, any woman, and that child my wife would raise as if it were ours—her own—because she might have been responsible for our failure to continue the bloodline.

From ancient days childlessness was one of the seven justified reasons for expulsion of a wife even if it was the husband who was sterile. Defunct traditions sometimes survive in one's psychology and my wife was probably acting out the feminine virtue of a traditional Korean woman by granting the institution of a concubine. A surrogate. Could I have allowed my wife to have a child by another man if I had turned out to be responsible?

She had made this extravagant suggestion because I was so strongly against adoption. I was not sure of myself in undertaking the obligation of raising, and loving all its life, a child abandoned by a total stranger when I was apparently unable to love my own wife. "Having a child is the easiest thing on earth for all other women," my mother said spitefully only a few days before she passed away. But why did my wife suddenly come up with that idea almost half a year after my mother's death? Did she sense I had been considering, though remotely, the possibility of divorce? But was I not convinced that divorce would offer me no new turning point for my life? I rubbed my eyes. Not having a child was hardly the whole reason why I was unable to love my wife.

It was around one o'clock. The heavy round sinker was sucked into the muddy bottom of the sea several times and finally it found a promising rocky bed so that I had to concentrate on the repetitive motion of jerking the line so as not to let the sinker get stuck in the cracks of the rocks. Something attacked the lugworm.

A rock trout as big as my forearm floundered in the air, dangling at the end of the line, its grey scales shining. Everybody on the boat got busy as the rock fish started swallowing the bait of loach with their savagely big mouths, and my mental activity turned extremely simple and perfectly coordinated as I continued feeding out the line, shaking, snatching and winding the spool.

The boatman expertly sliced the fish we caught to prepare *sashimi,* and we relished the juicy raw fish with *soju* drink and we joked and talked and laughed, our faces tanned red by the blazing afternoon sun.

The fishing boat headed for shore a little after four. The wind had grown somewhat stronger when the tides shifted, and the boat pitched slowly over the swaying waves. While we were chatting about plans to have a fishing party next week to officially open this year's season and to design a cap for the members of this fishing group, the boatman suddenly changed direction. Near Pang Island another fishing boat with a jammed engine was bobbing in the middle of the bay and the stranded anglers, standing along the gunwale, waved their jackets like flags to hail for rescue. Malfunctioning engine. Stranded. Drifting. They were workers from a Seoul company exporting stuffed toys who had gone out aboard two leased boats as a springtime company picnic.

The crestfallen group on the becalmed boat squatted down on the deck as meekly as grammar-school children when our boatman shouted it was dangerous for them to stand up. "The owner of that boat used to boast so much that his boat is as fast as an arrow because it is mounted with an automobile engine." Our skipper, towing the troubled craft to shore, seemed to relish the whole situation. "Look what happened to the fastest fishing boat in the bay."

It was almost ten in the evening when I returned home. Quickly I finished my shower and had supper. My wife went to bed right after the meal and I watched *Bestseller Theater* on a commercial channel and then David Letterman's *Late Night* show on AFKN, the American military channel. When there was nothing more to watch after the national anthems of Korea and the United States of America, and then the dancing snow of molecules, I turned off the TV and started reading the paper. As I read the desperate persuasion of the text for an electric fan advertisement, the telephone rang.

Pyon Chinsu. He said, "Is this Sergeant Han Kiju?" Reaching out for me through the telephone in the middle of the night, out of nowhere, like a wraith that had suddenly been resurrected. His unreal voice hovered in my dim living room. He said he would have hung up if I had not answered the phone in the first three rings. He would have hung up because it was such a late hour. It got on my nerves a little, however, that he spoke to me in a falsetto as if he was trying to convince me of his calm. He kept talking about incoherent and trivial things that could hardly justify his untimely call. He said, "It's been so long since we've seen each other, Sergeant Han. We've not met since Vietnam, have we? I hope to see you some time." Then he hung up. Without even saying good-bye.

I hung up, feeling not so pleasant, went to the kitchen, took out a bottle of beer and pressed dry cuttle fish, went up to the upstairs living room and then out to the front verandah. Since my house is located on an elevated part of the neighborhood, I could watch the dark humps of Inwang Hill and the street lights of the Ungam District area from the wisteria chair of the verandah. In the distance, the red light blinked atop the broadcasting transmission tower on Namsan Hill. Down there in the alley, the neighborhood fraternity chief was enjoying a late summer night drink with three elders under the grimy Coca Cola parasol in front of the mom-and-pop store. The smell of burning pine needles wafted to me from somewhere near the fountain in the gulch next to Suguk Temple behind my house.

I sipped my beer, alone, looking around the acacias of Songjong Girls' High School, the golden lights sprayed over the streets and buildings of the district, the crimson neon cross atop the steeple of a church, and the bright lights undulating like the contour of bony plates protruding from the backs of stegosaurs along the ridges of the mountain behind the Presidential House. The numerous lights guarding the Chief Executive. Once a president who lived there sent us to Vietnam for whatever reasons he deemed right and profitable for his nation. International prestige, perhaps, or an expression of gratitude to the U.S. for their helping us during the Korean War. Or national welfare. Whatever the reasons. The blood money we had to earn at the price of our lives fueled the modernization and development of the country. And owing to our contribution, the Republic of Korea, or at least a higher echelon of it, made a gigantic stride into the world market. Lives for sale. National mercenaries.

PART
TWO

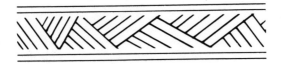

5

The military train that
carried us south to Pusan Port looked like a
long giant hearse hastily made of planks
torn from apple crates, the black locomotive covered with a Korean flag as large as a
sail, the tarred boxlike cars decorated with
flower wreaths at both doors, festooned
with cheap paper in motley colors,
bleached by repeated use, draped thickly
over the whole train.

I felt everything around me was death.
Darkness, the sea, the stars, the wind, the
sky, everything of the night, even the situation that made us sail down the South
China Sea aboard an American naval ves-
sel carrying us to the war in the land of
probable no return. The 2,200 Korean sol-

diers aboard the USS *Patch* headed south, ploughing through the waves
and foam of the dark blue sea. They had to fight for one year. The ship,
the whale-like mass of iron, plunged through the wrathful waters.

In the cabin the soldiers were loaded layer upon layer in triple tiered
bunks, like pollacks stored in a refrigeration room. Sergeant Chon
Hisik, pillowing his head on his arms, was blankly staring at his naked
feet that kept rising and falling with the slowly pitching motion of the
ship. I thought his toes were very ugly; his heels and toes were still
blistered and calloused from the tough commando training we had gone
through. He looked around the cabin, lying on his back and moving his
eyes only. The drooping lone electric bulb looked melancholy. The 3rd
Platoon of the 9th Company was accommodated in a dreary cabin with
naked pipes and steel beams. Only Sergeant Shin "Sissy" Pokchin and
the radioman, Sergeant Chi "Tap-Tap-Tap" Taesik, were asleep in the
corner bunk. Several soldiers, exhausted by days of seasickness, exchanged casual chatter intermittently, sprawling among the duffle
bags, tightly packed knapsacks and shovels, M-1 rifles and helmets piled
here and there among the pipe posts. The crumpled white sheets of the
empty bunks looked like shrouds.

The farther south we came the warmer the weather grew, and it was
now as sultry and stifling in the cabin as inside a hemp sack.

Corporal Yun Chusik, who carried the three nicknames of "Toffee
Vendor" (who accepted all sorts of junk for toffee), "Ancient Car" and
"Junk Dealer" because of his inexhaustible, passionate love for the
second-hand; Sergeant Kim Mungi, who every so often boasted, smirking, that he was the master of pen pal management; Corporal Kim
"Yeller" Chaeo; Corporal Song Pyongjo, the AR gunner who never
missed a drinking bout; Sergeant Chong Sangchol, the leader of the 1st
Squad; Private Yun "Boar" Chilbok and Private Chon "Catfish" Chilbok
who were called together "Private 14 blessings" because their common
name Chilbok meant "Seven Blessings"—they looked like the prisoners
on death row abandoned even by their own families, sitting together to
find consolation in one another.

"Something's fishy about Ninh Hoa, the place where we're going to be
stationed," Yeller said.

"There he goes again," said Sergeant Chang "Piggie" Taejun, the
leader of the 3rd Squad.

"The boys who've been with the Tiger Division said if you have heat
prostration, you lose your appetite and easily fall sick all the time. What

if Ninh Hoa is a miserable little hole in the middle of nowhere? If you're struck with malaria, they say, you're as good as dead. That's what I heard. Honest truth."

"Did you think we were going to Vietnam to play a soccer game or something? You really got an early start on getting scared—even before taking your first step on Vietnamese soil. What kind of a soldier are you, anyway?"

Yeller Kim's discouraging ravings about all sorts of weird rumors were frequent: about centipedes, stringy snakes, mines, booby traps, bamboo spears, poisons. Where he had collected all this nobody knew. But Yeller never ran out.

"You don't need to worry about those things." Piggie Chang flopped down on the bottom bunk. "Vietnam isn't as dangerous as the DMZ in Korea. You used to have hard times when you served at the division stationed near the UN Hill, right? North Koreans infiltrating through the DMZ mine field to cut your throats. Safe, uh? The life for enlisted men is easier in Vietnam, I think. And you must remember how hungry you used to be at the Korean frontline camps. But you'll never go hungry in Vietnam, and you'll have fancy Western meals, beef and all, every day. You certainly tasted the American C-rations they sell at the Seoul black markets. Nice, eh? That's what you're going to eat in Vietnam— C-rations—meal after meal, day after day. Besides, when you get to the battle zone, there won't be that much sadistic discipline and abuse by those boys who just love to pull rank all the time. You will get much more pay because you'll be paid by both the U.S. and ROK governments, and you can see a foreign country. How else could you even dream of touring a foreign country in your miserable lifetime as a poor country boy? Do I have to list any more reasons why you have to love this war?"

"But what's the use of it all if you get killed?"

"Are you crazy? How can you get killed by the Cong who look like they've starved for a month? You must have seen the pictures of the Vietcong—just bags of bones dogs would like to lick all day long."

"But I heard the Blue Dragon guys were really beaten up by the Cong several weeks ago," said Private Chong Sangchol, crushing his cigarette butt on the pipe post of his bunk. "There's a rumor that our division may be sent to the Cambodian border or the Mekong Delta to relieve some U.S. force, so you might as well start to worry a bit. It's logical, anyway, that we would be deployed to a hot battle zone as soon as we get used to the Vietnamese climate and terrain. Blue Dragon marines and Tiger

Division have been doing so much fighting up to now. It's time for us to replace them because White Horse Division is such a new and fresh force. That's the prevailing logic, I guess."

Sergeant Chon Hisik, who had been mutely listening to them, sat up on his bunk, scratching his side. "Why did you cowards come all the way here if you're so scared of fighting? You could've petitioned for DMZ duty instead of a Vietnam combat mission when you were given the choice. Or you could've just deserted, if you think running is better than dying. The Corps Commander surely knew what she was saying when she said, 'Poor thing, such a pitiful young boy going to the war'." Corps Commander was the nickname of the woman who owned the tavern at Yangpyong, where we had bivouacked.

"There's still a way out for anybody who doesn't want to fight this war," said Piggie, climbing back to his bunk. "Shoot your foot. You'll be crippled, maybe, but you can get home in no time and be kicked out of uniform as sure as hell."

"Let's talk about some pleasant things like Vietnamese whores, bananas, mango or coconuts." Corporal Chon Chilbok, half of the 14 Blessings, tried hard to hide the frightened expression on his hollow face which was pallid from seasickness.

Yeller ignored Chon's plea. "The Vietcong are cunning and sly," he said. "They are hideous creatures."

"Well, we are finally here. So weary and depressing it has been for such a long time, but we are here after all." Corporal Min Chonggi leaned against the starboard wall and stretched his legs. "I wonder why they made us wait so much. We're going to soon see a Vietcong, or King Kong, or whatever, and find out if all that heavy training will really pay off."

"I thought we'd never see the Vietnamese land or even begin this voyage until we were discharged from the army as we kept packing and unpacking our knapsacks and weapons because the departure was delayed time and again," said Corporal Song Pyongjo. "Six times. Postponed six goddam times!" Then he imitated firing his automatic rifle with his crooked index finger, *tit-tit-titt*ing through his clenched teeth. "I'm going to get at least thirty of those slimy bastards."

Min and Song were both from the military town of Wontong, Kangwon Province. They enlisted on the same day, underwent basic training at the same boot camp, were assigned to the 3rd Reserve Unit for the frontline forces, and wound up as riflemen of an infantry company under the 2nd ROK Army Division far up north. They were like close twins, always together, a perfect duo who virtually demolished two taverns at Yanggu before volunteering for Vietnam duty. If there was any dirty job to be taken care of, these two were always there, ready to take over when everybody else threw their arms up helplessly, and it naturally was their job to steal a piglet from the pigsty of the village cigarette shop when the buddies agreed during the drinking party at Yangpyong Tavern that they wanted to have roasted pig, Viking style, as a side dish for their soju. The reason why they volunteered to go to Vietnam was simple: they preferred to go to the war and show the world what they really were good at rather than wasting their precious youth washing clothes and dirty underwear for the soldiers of slightly higher rank, cutting firewood in the snowy mountains to warm the barracks in winter, plucking arrowroot vines to weave camouflage nets for the vehicles, or twining straw ropes for whatever use the master sergeant wanted them.

"No more showing off for us. Too bad." Corporal Song yawned loudly. "Everybody on the street would look up to us like great heroes when they recognized the shoulder patch of the infantry division soon to leave for Vietnam. But, alas, those glorious days are over."

"Yeah, it was really nice—to be a hero and respected."

Corporal Min was the kind of soldier who got excited with a primitive vigor whenever he sang a military march or heard a pompous motto like "dauntless warriors of Democracy," or "vanguard of peace" in the indoctrination broadcasts from division headquarters. Believing that he would experience in Vietnam an adventure that would be the proudest and most thrilling in his life, he took to the guerrilla training with zeal and dedication, and even encouraged Corporal Song and other soldiers to learn combat skills well. Intimidated by their attitude, even the drill instructors, famous for their sadistic cruelty, shunned these two soldiers, whose glaring, murderous eyes made them seem impatient to kill somebody, anybody.

"We had good times at Yangpyong, yeah," said Corporal Min, grinning. "The tavern girls were crazy about the soldiers going to Vietnam, you know. Office girls, beauty parlor girls, factory girls, bus girls, even college girls and other nice girls, they all were dying to get a fuck from a Vietnam-bound soldier. They used to take their clothes off in twenty minutes on the first date."

"It was a really good time."

"I heard girls are an easy lay just before they leave to study abroad or when a boy enlists in the army, but when you say you're going to Vietnam to fight— Well, they opened their legs right away as wide as castle gates. You don't even have to ask because *they* ask you to let them serve."

"It's really nice to be a hero."

"Did you have many send-off consolation fucks?"

"Sure. I used to have a rented room at Yangpyong Inn for that particular use. I had six girls there, all virgins. You know something? That inn was really noisy, night and day, with brave warriors attacking the girls. 'Oh! Ugh! Ugh! Oh! Ugh! Ugh!'"

I met Private Pyon Chinsu when I went out on deck after midnight for some fresh air. The humid air below decks was compressed by the heat to the suffocation point. Pyon Chinsu's eternally mournful expression and unsure posture often aroused in others the instinctive urge to protect him at first. Typically, he was sitting on the coiled pile of hawser at the most secluded corner of the quarterdeck, watching the gurgling foam chasing and then falling away behind the ship. The USS *Patch* had been trailing this white foam for a week.

Pyon took pride in that, in his civilian life working for Taehan Cinema, he could paint Charlton Heston, Burt Lancaster, or any American, British, French or German male actors, "including Curt Jurgens and Jean-Paul Belmondo," better than most other billboard painters in Seoul. Yet he had made a big mistake when he got drunk one day while serving at the Korean frontline town of Chorwon. Drunk on makkolli rice wine at the company PX, he drew a picture of his vicious sergeant copulating with a mule. Somebody took the drawing and posted it on the company bulletin board so that everybody could have a good laugh. They were too drunk and forgot to remove it before daybreak, and the sergeant saw it. The sergeant did not laugh. Private Pyon got every possible disciplinary punishment and was beaten to a pulp almost every day for two months until he could not stand it any longer and volunteered for Vietnam duty. That was the only way out for him. Private Pyon never wanted any part of the actual war. When he dreamed, he always saw something about Vietnam in his troubled sleep. He eventually came to be afraid of sleeping. During the commando training he trembled constantly and he frequently suffered diarrhea from his nerve-wracking terror. The anxiety crawled around in his stomach.

We had endured three months of special training, dangling on the ropes hanging high in the scorching summer sun on the perpendicular cliff of Yongmun Valley. One day the noontime heat suddenly started to cool and it was early autumn. We were loaded on trucks and transported to Yangpyong Station through yellow clouds of dust rising behind the MP convoy jeeps. The weather was sunny and cosmos blossomed cheerfully along the rice paddy dikes and the dirt road we used to march or shuttle back and forth along every day. At the railroad station the military band played the song of the White Horse Division and other stupid military songs that we kept hearing night and day during training, and high-school girls in short-sleeved white blouses and blue-black skirts sang Christian church hymns for us.

There was a brief send-off ceremony. The train loaded with soldiers gave a long reluctant hoot and slowly started. The late afternoon sun was paling towards evening. In the rice paddies along the tracks, farmers waved as if to students on the way to an autumn excursion, and a lone country woman waddled along the dike, wriggling her hips like a big fat duck. Going home, she was.

It was after dark when the train puffed into Yongsan Station in Seoul for a brief stop before changing tracks. Another military band played the same military songs over and over again on the platform illuminated by electric lights festooned along a wall of barbed wire. Several generals with golden stars shining on their collars gave us another mechanical send-off around midnight, but nobody was interested in the fixed protocol rituals. The soldiers swarmed to the train windows, as large as prison cell peepholes, to find the faces of their families and sweethearts in the howling crowd trying to break through the military police cordon. Trying to see the soldiers once more, just once more, before they would leave for the war, the crowd was milling, a pandemonium, pushing and pulling the military police who, with cudgels and rifle butts, tried to keep the people away from the black ugly train. Amid the shrieking, the soldiers confined in the train waved their hands to the crowd, to everyone, hoping their loved ones would see them, although they could not find them. Young girls stamped their feet or hopped like kangaroos because they did not know how else they could express their frustration. Many wept. The military band played noisy military songs. Many waved handkerchiefs or small Korean flags. The whole Yongsan Station raged in the dim yellow light.

Private Pyon said he could not forget their faces, their screams. Even though there had been no face in the crowd that he had to look for.

The train, studded with colorful festoons and flower wreaths and national flags, slid out of the metropolitan city and dashed again through the dark. The train stopped at almost all large cities, perhaps to wait for the rails to be cleared of commercial trains. Families of soldiers or mobilized students were waiting at each station in the early dawn hours to welcome and then send us off with cheers and sobs. The local housewives rushed to the small windows of the train, searched inside the cars with flashlights, standing on their tiptoes, to offer cookies or apples to the boys. Middle-aged women from the Red Cross filled our canteens with ice water, weeping like mourners. The whole world was asleep but the railroad stretching out in the dark towards Pusan was wide awake. Wailing, stamping our feet, we were glaringly awake throughout the night.

Around three o'clock in the morning when the train passed Taegu and plunged into darkness once more, someone began to sing, hesitantly, a ballad that we knew by heart because we had sung it so often on the way to the training grounds.

Then, all at once, the soldiers joined the song. When the first song was over, someone started another military ballad, and the rest of us promptly joined him. Beating the helmets on their laps with their palms, they chorused the song of the White Horse Division and then all the songs they knew, one after another. They screamed at the top of their voices, screamed not to hear the desperate outcry of others if they screamed hard enough themselves. The singing quickly spread to the other cars, in both directions, the soldiers sweating in the stuffy sealed compartments and howling until their throats turned hoarse and sore. The military train sped through the dark, singing, screaming, wailing.

Pyon Chinsu said he could never forget that night. And he could not forget either the morning of the dazzling sun when our ship secretly slipped out of Pusan to the open sea, like a doomed exile.

One more sunrise, and we would be in Vietnam.

Private Pyon, who had been stooping over the railing like a hunchback, suddenly raised himself erect and pointed to the west. "What is that?" he said. "What is that over there?"

I looked. Above the southwestern horizon, four incandescent flames popped out like cotton blossoms in the dark space and blazed on for a while. They were too bright, too big and too close to the horizon to be stars.

"They must be fireworks," Private Pyon cried. "There're some more of them over there. It must be Vietnam out there. The Viet folks are shooting up fireworks to welcome us because they heard we're coming. They must be really nice people, waiting up for us at this hour."

"Are you crazy?" I said. "Can't you even recognize flares?"

I went down to ask the kitchen police about the flares, and the American seamen preparing breakfast for the Korean infantrymen aboard their ship confirmed that the U.S. marines operating around Da Nang must have engaged the enemy near shore.

"*Now* we're going to have some action," said Corporal Song Pyongjo, his teeth and the whites of his eyes gleaming.

The sun was blazing hot in the sky, strangely mild. A welcoming ceremony was held on the golden sand of the beach for us, the officers and soldiers of the advance contingent of the White Horse 9th ROK Army Infantry Division. Vietnamese military officers, an ARVN major who was also the Khanh Hoa Province governor, American officers, Korean officers, and Vietnamese high-school girls in gauzy pink or white *ao dai* greeted us with flower wreaths. Afterward we loaded onto trucks waiting in single file on the paved roadbed and set out to Ninh Hoa.

Sputtering cyclos and Lambretta minibuses dashed around the streets that spread out radially in all directions from the enormous white Buddha seated in the center of the city, and four AFRVN bombers in formation droned inland. Signs of bright and colorful alphabets, with French diacritical symbols, hung outside the mud houses that looked like the huts at an oasis one might see in a Hollywood movie about the nomads in an Arabian desert. As our convoy vehicles crossed Xe Chai Bridge, a boy, perhaps ten, suddenly sat up on a passing wagon pulled by a decrepit old horse and made an exaggerated motion of sex with his hands, shouting, *"Con gai boocoo boocoo daksan. Vum vum, vum vum!"* When we were young boys like him during our war, we also flashed a similar motion to the passing American soldiers at Sosa, shouting, *"Ssibi, ssibi!"*

Moving out of Nha Trang, we passed a cemetery for Vietnamese civilians, flat graves with beautiful tombstones, and beyond the cemetery on a hill appeared a tall odd chimney, spewing white smoke. The chimney was made of old oil drums, welded one on top of another. An MP from the 100th Logistics Command assigned to our truck said, "That's the field crematorium for the Korean soldiers. All the KIA's in this tactical zone will go there."

I stared. It meant *I* would turn to smoke there if I should get killed. At the Hongje Municipal Crematorium back home the stokers would not pound the bones of the creamated remains fine enough unless you gave them a fat extra tip. The smoke—who could that be?

At the foot of the hill behind the cemetery, the whole area looked like Dresden after the air-raid, garbage from American and Korean units piling over the whole place and a swarm of flies attacking us like a sticky downpour. The soldiers tried to drive away the flies, standing on the open trucks to wave their arms like dancing shamans exorcising pestilence, but the fully armed soldiers were totally helpless in the swirl of the fierce insects collecting on them as if to suck the blood of living bodies. I felt goose flesh all over my body, thinking, this is a swarm of vampire flies that has been sucking the streaming ooze of decaying corpses just a minute ago. When we finally escaped, our faces felt bloated like drowned bodies, the skin puffed from countless suctions by the buzzing short-winged monsters. I felt sick to my stomach.

When I looked back at the garbage dump as our truck was grunting up the steep ridge, I saw Vietnamese villagers gathered where a truck had just unloaded refuse. The Vietnamese picking through the crumpled cans and stained leavings were grotesque. In these people I saw Korea twenty years ago. During the War, when my family was drifting around after our house at Kongdok Market in Seoul was gutted by the retreating People's Army, we spent a summer near a school at Inchon, where my father worked as a carpenter at the American base close to the school and Mother ran a small shop at a nearby intersection of a three-forked road. Every day I used to go to the garbage dump a little distance off from my house. Often my foot was cut by a used razor blade, on the sharp teeth of a broken saw or a jagged lid of a can, but the cuts were worth it because the whole family could feast on pig soup at dinner if I happened to find a piece of meat among the garbage. So the mud puddle in the middle of the rice paddies where the Americans dumped their trash was a cornucopia for us village children. Sometimes you would have good fortune and unearth oranges, Hershey chocolate wrapped in sleek brown paper or Brach's jelly candies of five different colors shining like jewels in their cellophane wrappers. One day the American soldiers dumped a heap of chicken legs that had quite a lot of meat still hanging on the bones. I filled my large sooty milk can with the chicken legs and proudly brought them home. Mother boiled a delicious soup with those bones and meat and barley, even adding some precious rice. Where had I found all those chicken legs, Father asked. I told him. That night, he took a rusty tin bucket from the kitchen and asked me to show him the way to the dump.

The Vietnamese in *calico noire,* the black pajama-like clothes, and the Lambrettas loaded with chickens and bicycles on the roof, moved aside to give way to the procession of trucks. The old women, whose gums had turned black from constant chewing of betel nuts, waved in welcome, grinning wizened smiles under their conical *non* hats. A local soldier, an M-1 rifle slung upside down over his shoulder, trudged along Highway 1. A locomotive and several cars of a derailed train, obviously lying abandoned on their sides for years, rusted dark and twisted in the middle, lolled alongside the road. On the hilltop outposts, around which even the shrubs had turned to loess color in the scorching heat, armed American soldiers were standing guard for the new incoming Asian troops.

The convoy crossed a bridge. Unclean boats floated in the filthy water below. At both ends of the span fishmongers sold sliced raw fish wrapped in oily leaves. Shanties lined up along the riverside; Vietnamese militiamen, wearing caps like baseball players, loitered in the dirty street. Entering the plain beyond the bridge, I vaguely sensed the creeping fear that hovered about the road ahead. There were no people in sight. I could see through the swaying mist of the shady, sagging leaves of banana plants along the road, the isolated seaside hamlets ahead.

The fear subsided. I began to enjoy the peaceful pastoral scenery. This was a different country. The trucks sped along the narrow road in the quiet sun, bumping up violently at the spots where the asphalt was torn out.

The railroad parallel to the highway ran around the foot of an ominously lush hill; the rails, probably never used since Dien Bien Phu, were rusted as if coated with red dust. A young boy with a long whip herded his black buffalos to one side of the road and vacantly watched the speeding trucks.

After we passed the fishing village of Ngoc Diem, the trucks began to speed up to discourage snipers. Boats were afloat in the South China Sea. The warm sunrays glimmered on the waves, and I saw some old fishermen mending their nets under the palm trees in the yards of the solitary huts near the road. On the left, dark brown buffalo stood stupidly. The rice paddies were yellowish green with new shoots or fully ripe dark-green or golden, or already harvested. The sun and the hills and the plain and the sea and the fishermen and the rice paddies were too beautiful to associate with war, yet we were filled with a slight giddiness, a faint sense of nothingness.

We supposedly had come to this remote foreign land to participate in an international armed conflict, but the only thing we did on a nameless hill was to stand guard most of the night hours and, from sunrise till dusk, burn the thorny bushes to clear the land, dig foxholes and trenches, dig garbage dumping holes, dig drainage ditches, dig pits to build bunkers around—forever digging, like mole crickets.

More and more soldiers began to complain out of disappointed relief. They spent sultry boring days waking up at daybreak, undergoing the roll call with a lot of shouting, singing military songs, eating bland C-ration meals, listening to the old Korean popular ballads or folk songs on tape-players, digging holes everywhere, piling up sandbags, clearing the ground for a helipad, digging ditches to be ready for the approaching monsoon season, digging some more to bury the C-ration cans that kept piling up. It was so hot while the sun was up that sweat streamed down backs and arms and chests but the soldiers were short of water even for drinking, not to say washing, so if anyone wanted to clean his body he had to stand naked outside the bunker, with his helmet like a basin, and wait to catch the natural shower water, then wash quickly, busily rubbing the soap during the short daily squalls. If he was not fast enough, the breathlessly short rain would leave the sticky lather smeared all over him like mucus.

At dusk the soldiers clad in thick flak jackets went out to the listening posts. Squatting in the foxholes and looking over at the dismal Hon Heo Mountain crouching in the dark, we would argue about what kimchi soup of a certain eatery in downtown Seoul tasted like, reminiscing about all the nice Korean delicacies at the famous restaurants in different provinces. In endless nights out in the field the soldiers would exchange idle talk about generals of different nationalities, Saigon, political assassinations, Ho Chi Minh, the American riches and the Vietcong.

Corporal Kim Chaeo, the Yeller, claimed, "If you become a prisoner of an urban Vietcong at a whorehouse or at a bar, the Regiment guys said you will be freed if you pay your captor. Yankees are released for two hundred dollars a head and a Vietnamese militiaman for fifty. That's the going price."

"How much is a Daihan worth? We should be worth at least a hundred dollars apiece."

"If you get bitten by a Vietnamese centipede, I heard, you die instantly. Your flesh starts decaying blue and black as soon as the centipede bites. Watch out if any creature climbs up your cot when you go to bed."

The soldiers smelled stale because their fatigues, washed with rain water, had not been dried properly. Gradually they were forgetting the war as they spent tedious hours talking about mosquitoes, snakes, the wonder of aerosol spray, scarce water, socks, spiders, DDT and the insipid rice imported from Vietnam that we had had to eat in the 50s post-war period when Korea could not produce enough. "And we are eating that same rice in another war," Sergeant Chon Hisik said, chuckling.

Sergeant Oh, the orderly for the company commander, did not have to dig so much. Instead, he washed and ironed the captain's clothes, polished his boots and devoted himself to becoming a perfect house boy. "Imagine coming all the way to Vietnam to shine boots," he often scoffed. When there was some leisure time in the afternoon or early evening, he would come down to the bunkers to join us and strum his guitar, singing, sometimes imitating a medicine peddler: "Ladies and gentlemen, even a porcupine looks handsome and beautiful in the eye of another porcupine of different sex." He would crack jokes in the stifling heat, and whenever he saw the captain return to his quarters, he threw his guitar to Piggie Chang and rushed to prepare a helmetful of water for the captain's swollen feet, usually throwing in a punch line to close his clowning monologue: "Now the main event of the Indochina War is about to begin!"

One evening Sergeant Oh spat on the tip of the captain's boot to polish it and said, "I got a letter from home asking me if I'm sick or wounded because I don't write home often enough. Me sick? Ha, they'd die laughing if they knew I'm healthily licking all the boots in Vietnam."

War was truly dull.

It was less boring when we went to Nha Trang to escort the mail truck once in a while. As a precaution against Vietcong snipers, vehicles were allowed to travel between Ninh Hoa and Nha Trang only when there were at least ten.

The soldiers of the 966th Field Artillery Battalion kept shelling for hours even though no enemy was visible. With cigarette filters stuck in their ears to prevent the tympanic membranes from bursting, they were another unreal group. War was annoying, wearying.

In the days when I used to be governed by conceptual thinking, I believed a war was a sacred struggle between two or more causes or ideologies contradicting each other but respectively lofty and noble. War was a profound and sublime expression of human desire, I thought, and that struggle was an essential evolutionary process for realization of ideals, of glorious triumphs for mankind, although it would exact the toll of some tragedy and unhappiness among the petty, insignificant individual beings. War was a sanctuary of masculine strength, while the merciless conflict to death was an ascension of ordinary man towards divinity. So much for theory. We just kept digging, every day.

"While other boys of the Blue Dragon Brigade and the Tiger Division enjoy all the action out in their hot tactical zones, we just keep guarding the cool empty house in the rear like a stupid dog," Corporal Min Chonggi muttered.

I was depressed by the weary expectation that we would forever do chores in the rear area, contrary to the hopes I had secretly entertained. The sultry days passed. The war was just like the monotonous lecture of a summer afternoon at college; I could not find anywhere the war I had read about in Remarque, or the Homeric war of heroes who spoke with poetic eloquence and performed courageous acts.

And then one night, the soldiers asleep in the bunkers were awakened by sputtering gun fire. Somebody shouted, "Red alert! Red alert!" We dashed out, grasping rifles and cartridges and hand grenades. We jumped into the trenches and scattered to our assigned fighting positions. The combat was progressing at the listening post five hundred meters in the direction of Xuan My to the east. Tracer bullets zipped out trailing red tracks across the darkness, and the noise of indiscriminate firing added urgency to the whole situation. The report from the listening post said forty plus Vietcong were believed to have infiltrated the company perimeter. Since there was only a platoon of the friendly force at the listening post, the 2nd and 3rd Platoons were ordered to move out to assist. The reinforcement was commanded by the executive officer, second in command.

But the fighting was already over by the time we arrived at the post by the drain ditch. The smell of burnt gunpowder was still sickening but the shooting had stopped. The soldiers lying dumbfounded on their stomachs and speechlessly staring at the rice paddies ahead of them, would not even speak to us when we arrived to help them. They were still dazed.

The executive officer scurried around, stooping low, to check for losses. Not a single casualty. Silence hung over the field, and we spent the night lying among the thorny brush, ready for action at any moment, for we suspected the enemy might attempt a second wave of attack.

Long hours elapsed and the day broke. At 0400 hours, the executive officer ordered the 2nd Platoon Leader to go out and check for enemy casualties. Leading the listening post team, the platoon leader crawled out along the rice paddy dike to the spot where the enemy had been first spotted.

The team returned in twenty minutes, trudging carelessly, following the platoon leader with a troubled expression. When the executive officer asked if they had found any enemy dead, the platoon leader simpered, embarrassed. "There're twenty-six dead buffalo out there, sir. In the rice paddies."

Vietnamese farmers usually left their buffalo out in the field at night and sometimes the Vietcong would come down from the hills to take the animals away for food. In the active combat areas buffalo herds would roam around like wild beasts after their owners had fled to take refuge. Someone at the listening post must have spotted some of these drifting buffalos and mistaken them for Vietcong infiltrators. The soldier had opened fire and everybody followed suit, mobilizing all the firepower they had. Our first combat.

In the morning when the sun rose over the horizon of Dong Hai, the East Sea, about thirty inhabitants of Lac An paid a group visit to the Division Headquarters, confirmed the fact that it was the 9th Company of the 29th Regiment which had had an "engagement" with the buffalos, and then swarmed to our company base to ask for an interview with the captain who was having a hasty breakfast of C-ration soup and rice before hurrying to the battalion commander to report about the humiliating mistake. The villagers demanded compensation. The captain was disconcerted; he had never heard of anybody paying for cattle killed in acts of war. At a loss, he called Regimental Headquarters, which was in charge of civic actions concerning the Vietnamese locals, and eventually the G-5 of the Division Headquarters started negotiation with the village elders. The agreement was made that the Daihans would pay a total of 520,000 piaster—20,000 piaster per head—to Lac An inhabitants to compensate for the untimely slaughter.

The trouble did not end there. Two days later, ten representatives of the village came to ask the captain for a second interview. They came dragging a buffalo with a broken left hind leg and demanded some sort of compensation for this miserable animal also, because Division Headquarters had paid for the dead ones only. A perky young Vietnamese policeman, with a heavy pistol drooping in its holster like a hammer, did all the talking. He was fuming with unnatural anger. The villagers stood by and watched the show absentmindedly. While the argument was going on, the gawky owner of the buffalo remained in the background constantly grinning and stroking his goatee with gnarly fingers. Driven into a corner, our captain promised to do his best to see to it that the old man with the constant grin was properly compensated for his buffalo. The villagers departed, without the broken beast. The crestfallen captain sighed, and sighed again, not knowing what to do about the wounded buffalo left standing in front of his quarters. The creature blinked its big mournful eyes, stretching its neck out as if waiting for the guillotine blade to swish down.

Corporal Lee Kwanil, a good friend of Sergeant Chin Sochol at the clinic of Division Headquarters, said, "Leave it to me, sir, I can handle it all right," and asked for the captain's permission for him to use the commanding officer's jeep for a couple of hours.

We heaved the buffalo into the trailer of the jeep, drove down to the division clinic, had the broken hind leg of the buffalo cast in plaster, then drove to Lac An and delivered the animal to eternally grinning Huong. In broken English we explained that the medical personnel had given the beast good medical care so it would be fine. The old man probably had not understood one single word but he continued to smile broadly, repeatedly thanking us, *"Cam on, cam on ong."*

The next day the villagers were back with the limping buffalo, led by the saucy young policeman. The police officer demanded we buy the buffalo because the old man could not use it for farming any more, even if the broken leg would some day heal. Corporal Lee, speaking for the commanding officer, said we would not buy it because we could not eat its meat. The policeman scornfully argued back, why don't you *Daihans* go get the Vietcong instead of butchering and crippling the helpless cattle of poor peasants?

Lieutenant Choe Sangjun, the 3rd Platoon Leader, was disgusted by the whole nonsensical situation and wanted to express his exasperation dramatically, but the only curse he knew in Vietnamese was *"Xau lam."* So he said it, very loudly and with a lot of fury, but to very little effect. However, that single phrase was apparently not sufficient to exhaust his anger; he picked up his carbine, loaded it, stuck its muzzle in the policeman's forehead, and shouted, *"Chung toi di Daihan!"* What Lieutenant Choe said simply meant "We go Korea," but I think what he had meant to say was that we would rather go back home than risk our lives to fight for worthless bastards like you and your stupid buffalos.

The policeman flinched and a while later, he and the villagers went back home with the sad limping buffalo.

Six villagers demonstrated at downtown Ninh Hoa the next day, waving two placards and chanting, "Daihan go home! Daihan go home!" It was an infinitesmal and insignificant incident in the big picture of the war, but the concept that Vietnamese inhabitants, regardless of their number, demanded at a public rally that Koreans leave, looked gravely distressing in the written reports. Naturally the captain had to explain the same things over and over again to various officers of higher and higher rank. This international incident petered out finally after we collected money among ourselves and paid the villagers for the buffalo.

It was a lousy war indeed, as Sergeant Chon Hisik said.

Chon Hisik had enlisted in the army two months earlier than I did. He was not exactly a close friend during our advanced commando training at Yongmun Valley, but we spent a lot of time together in Vietnam since he was the squad leader and I the second sergeant of 2nd Squad, 3rd Platoon of the 9th Company. It took quite some time for us to build a friendship because we were so different from each other.

Sergeant Chon had an aggressive, extroverted personality while I was a reticent type, very selective in choosing friends. Not many dared to approach him during our training in Yangpyong because disconcerting rumors concerning him were circulating among the barracks. Some believed he could smash a stone to dust with his taekwondo-trained fist. And he always looked stern.

When he was in a better mood, which was actually almost all the time, he enjoyed playing practical jokes on his buddies, most of whom feared and laughed at his blunt sense of humor. He was quick to lose his temper, but once he fell for someone, he was an unbelievably loyal friend. He was a man of probity and integrity, a gallant man in a somewhat melodramatic sense, one who seemed to belong to another century. Sergeant Cho Ichol, who had been in the same unit with Chon before their transfer to our Vietnam-bound division, told us several times that Sergeant Chon had owned a small wrestling gym on the second floor of an iron foundry at Yongdu-dong in Seoul. Chon himself never mentioned anything about his legendary wrestling and fighting skills. The only thing he had ever told us in that connection was a terse remark that he was not afraid of any dark alleys. From his log-like arms and twitching biceps, when he clenched his fists to imitate the Mister Korea contestants, we could make a wild guess how strong he was, but nobody dared to test his strength in action. And he considered all sporting apparatus as some sort of sacred implements for his religious worship of physical fitness. If he caught anybody sitting on weight lifting disks or dumbbells, that act of profanation would never go unpunished, as Sergeant Cho had warned us repeatedly.

On the other hand, part of him was capable of blindly stupid dedication. If anyone in the company kicked up trouble and was thrown into "the monkey house," it was always Sergeant Chon who made the first visit to the military lockup with cigarettes, candies, our army newspaper *The Comrade*, or anything that would make the life of the detained soldier more bearable. Some argued that his persistent lockup visits were an aftermath of his own experience at the monkey house, but we did not find out, even after his death, if it was true that one night when the moon was irresistibly bright he had climbed over the barbed wire fence behind his barracks and walked six kilometers in a daze like a sleepwalker down to the railroad station to take a train home to see his sweetheart. But it was his girl Sujin who later, more or less, led him to his death on Hon Heo Mountain.

He did some quaint or weird things at times. One day when the bunkers were deserted and quiet because most of the soldiers had been sent to Cam Ranh Bay to escort the sixty-five jeeps issued by the U.S. Army to the White Horse Division, I found him sitting on his cot, naked except for the dark green military shorts, carefully studying his navel, holding a match stick. I asked him why he was so absorbed in umbilical contemplation.

"You look like the naked Buddha entering the world of enlightenment," I said.

He said he wanted to remove the filth that had collected in the folds inside his navel, showing me the black dirt that looked like mouse droppings imbedded in the pattern of apple seeds, but he was afraid to scrape them out with the match stick because Piggie Chang had told him it was dangerous to clean them out.

"If cold air gets into the guts through your belly button, Piggie said, your inside will get all fouled up and you will die eventually. Those dirt pieces are protecting the frail skin inside the folds."

He never took the chance of risking his life by removing the filth. Instead, he wrote Dr. Han Kugnam, a radio show medical consultant, to ask if it was all right to clean out one's navel. The doctor never replied to this inquiry.

Two soldiers from Division Troop Information and Education detachment brought us one American and one Korean movie two months after we reached Viet Nam. From them Sergeant Chon rented a Bell & Howell projector and the two reels of films for five dollars in American military payment certificates, which was the currency also used by the Korean soldiers in Vietnam. Chon paid one dollar to Private Pyon Chinsu who prepared several posters to the best of his professional ability and pasted them on the company bulletin board and at the entrances of all the bunkers. The posters read:

DON'T BE ON A KIA LIST
BEFORE SEEING THIS FANTASTIC MOVIE!

Title: *EGLUB EHT FO ELTTAB* and *FLAC EHT.*
Time: Starts at 10:00 a.m.
New Show Every 30 Minutes.
Place: 2d Squad Bunker, 3d Platoon
Admission: One A.P.C. Dollar.
NO CREDIT! Where would we collect
the money if the VC got you???????
!!!Children No Admittance!!!

The soldiers swarmed to the 2nd Squad bunker because a rumor, spread by Sergeant Chon himself, got around that the show was a fantastic sex film borrowed from the American soldiers for two cases of Korean canned beer obtained through the 30th Regiment stationed at Cam Ranh Bay. The movies Sergeant Chon showed the gullible soldiers on the screen of two white sheets of typing paper fixed on the sandbag wall were one reel each of the American war movie *The Battle of the Bulge* and the Korean melodrama *The Calf.* When the soldiers belatedly found out that the movie titles on the poster had been spelled backward to cheat them, they screamed to get their money back.

Sergeant Chon said, grinning, "Watch the movie just for five minutes and then decide if you really want your money back or not. You'll never again see a movie like this in your whole life."

The soldiers packing the bunker were grumbling and puffing at their cigarettes, as the TI&E soldier in charge of the projector rolled the film, backwards. The movie was hilarious. Spitting out unintelligible dialogue that sounded like Vietnamese, full of implosive sounds like *hieoc, thuoc, ciak,* a young boy fell from his father's arms to the ground, ran backwards as fast as a pony stung by a bee on its haunch, and disappeared over a hill, waving his hand; while the father, also running backwards, jumped into the house, hips first.

In *The Battle of the Bulge,* a dead soldier leapt up backward, coming alive, as if pushed off by the earth, and a rifle flew up from the ground like the strange flying objects in a kungfu movie and stuck to his hand like a nail drawn by a magnet, and the soldier ran backward until he slid into the trench like a lizard slipping back into its hole. In the next scene, the white smoke filling the whole screen shrank to the size of a cotton candy and then was sucked into the cannon of a tank rolling backward. The soldiers went crazy over these images on the paper screen. They enjoyed themselves so much—applauding, cheering, whistling, yelling, laughing—that nobody asked for their money back any more, and every show after this uproarious premiere drew a full house.

Later, counting the MPCs he had earned for a day's work, he said, "A sergeant's monthly pay we Korean soldiers receive here, for risking our lives in this miserable war, is a mere 46 dollars, but look what I've made from this ass backwards movie show. Sixty-seven heavenly dollars! This sure is a safer way to make money around here, right? When I go home, I may start a business out of this thing. You just pitch a big picnic tent somewhere at Ui-dong or Tobong-dong, and show backward movies to the hikers coming down from the mountain in the evening, and between the shows you can sell them rice wine, too. Just buy an old military movie projector and several reels of outdated films from the Chonggyechon back alleys, and you have a drinking cinema of your own. And a really prosperous business it will be."

7

Private Pyon used to
paint the billboards for Taehan Cinema
in Seoul before he was drafted and then
shipped to Vietnam in 1966. He was such a
shy and timid boy that he had never dated
any girl. But given the exotic landscape and
imminent danger of the war zone, suddenly he was worried that he might die
without ever experiencing sex. So he went
to the brook at the foot of Hill 24 one
afternoon and surrendered to a mobile *con
gai,* a sort of traveling whore who haunted
the brookside with a mattress rolled under
her arm for conducting her quickie
daytime business with the Korean soldiers.

He was still suffering from the clap
when we went out to our post that night.

The poor boy used to go to the regimental clinic every day with a box of canned beer or anything he could afford for a penicillin shot incognito. But his penicillin trips were soon widely publicized among the soldiers of the 9th Company through anonymous notes posted on the company bulletin board. In the bunkers they would stay away from Pyon, who kept wiping the greenish pus from his thighs with tissue paper. Some of his buddies teased that Private Pyon might be the last to get a VC but the first to get VD. At any rate, nobody was happy to share a foxhole with him. I was not.

The division headquarters and the main force of the 29th Regiment had finished deployment, and the troops of the 9th Company had ringed the company's base with barbed wire entanglements and claymores. Every night they were sent out to ambush—to intercept and make contact with any Vietcong elements that might try to infiltrate the hamlets of Lac An, Tu Bong or Xuan My on the Lac Ninh plain. The uncharacteristically flat field of Lac Ninh stretched out towards the sea and the hovels of Lac Binh and Lac An loomed faintly in the moonlit darkness. Of all the nightly missions of our company, the most important was to guard the brook located at the end of the new bumpy dirt road bulldozed by an American military engineering detachment, a 500-yard gash through brush in the middle of a zone supposedly hostile. The brook provided potable water for the division and regimental headquarters, which were not yet furnished with any water service. The military band attached to the 9th Division Headquarters had built bunkers by the spring, but we, the soldiers of the 9th Company, had to actually guard this resource. The protocol toy soldiers whole use in this war began and ended with bugling twice a day in front of the flagpole.

The eight of us were divided into four teams, dispersed along the brook. Each pair dug a small hole to squat in, then spread a poncho at the bottom of the foxhole to prevent humidity from the wet soil seeping in through our pants, scattered tobacco all around to keep away the snakes, and installed telephone wire connecting the positions so that we could signal one another by tugging the line in case of emergency. We crouched down to confront the darkness. We waited in vain late into the night. Private Pyon kept rustling tissue paper beside me in the dark. Our task was to protect the stream from possible poisoning. The guard duty was no longer the cinch it used to be. The VC were close. Seven Vietnamese militia men and twenty-seven villagers had been abducted in Khanh Hoa province alone since the election. The chilly silence made my hair bristle up on my nape as I imagined Vietcong infiltrators noiselessly crawling to us across the rice paddies. The fishing village of Tu Bong was barely visible among the blurred contours of the terrain. We had never been to any of the nearby villages although more than a month had elapsed since our arrival. In truth, we feared the villages. There, we believed, the innocent lived together with the Vietcong fighters for we were told so many times that Vietnam was a country where you could never distinguish the friendly villagers from the enemy. You never knew whom you might smile at and whom you should shoot. In this eternal guerrilla warfare, they said, you never knew when the enemy would strike, or where. So we avoided anyone with a Vietnamese face and listened to bizarre stories, like the one about an American soldier whose penis had been severed with a razor blade by a whore who actually was a female Vietcong fighter, or about restaurants where they served poisoned food.

Squatting uncomfortably in the tight foxhole and placing my chin on the cold butt of my M-1 rifle, I blankly gazed at Route 1 that stretched out, cutting straight through the rice paddies beyond the brook. In the silvery silence, bleached white by the moonlight like a black-and-white photograph, the road appeared, at one end, from a patch of darkness, ran a long stretch, and then disappeared into another dark patch at the other. Up Route 1 to the north the Korean troops of the 28th Regiment, or the Goblin Unit of our 9th "White Horse" Division, were stationed at Tuy Hoa; the Tiger Division at Qui Nhon, the Blue Dragon Marine Brigade at Chu Lai, and then the American marines at Da Nang. Farther north was Hue, and then the 17th Parallel, the non-existent border dividing the North and the South. The Demilitarized Zone was extremely militarized, like the DMZ in Korea. To the west, Route 19 stretched out to Ban Me Thuot, An Khe, and then to the Cambodian border that was webbed with the criss-crossed Ho Chi Minh trails. South lay the seaside city of Nha Trang. A great white sedentary Buddha in the middle of that palmed city gazed down on the dwarfish human beings surging around in the turmoil of war. Farther down was Cam Ranh Bay, leased to the American military for a period of one hundred years. Then Phan Rang, where you could find the Montagnard mountain soldiers. And then the beaches of Vung Tau, where our non-combat Dove medical unit was enjoying a comparatively pleasant war. Finally, Saigon and the muddy Mekong Delta infested by the fierce warfare.

East, west, north, south—the enemy elements were active everywhere. For twenty years and more this war had been going on, going
nowhere. What should we do—and what *could* we do—in this country,
in this complicated war that we did not know anything about? We just
dug all day like grave-diggers, and then squatted in our holes by the
brook at night. To guard water.

Hon Heo Mountain crouched like a huge turtle in the dark by the sea
of Dong Hai beyond the fields. They said there was a Vietcong regimental headquarters on that mountain, but we did not know when we would
actually go there and engage them in a real war. The past month had
been a bore.

The military band's bunkers were quiet, the buglers peaceful. Not
everybody worried about the war, I thought. The buglers enjoyed a
comfortable sleep, the way the Vietnamese did, believing the Americans
would do all the fighting and dying for them. We were to fight in
Vietnam in American uniforms, wearing American helmets, using
American weapons, eating American C-rations, smoking American
cigarettes and being paid by the American government. But we had all
hoped when we left Korea that the Americans would do all the dirty jobs
for everybody else so that we could just enjoy the exotic countryside,
like tourists. The sticky insect repellent and sweat seemed to saturate
the pores all over my body. I dozed, exhausted by the heat.

Reduced to a pulp by fatigue, I had difficulty breathing, as if my
stomach was stuffed with carbon monoxide and I had succumbed for a
brief moment. Unsure if it was sleep or a slip into temporary unconsciousness, I woke up when I heard Private Pyon Chinsu rustle the
tissue paper to clean himself. Almost instinctively, I fished from the
pocket of my flak jacket Vietnamese red peppers, no bigger than bees,
that stung so as to make your eyes burn with tears. Slowly I chewed,
with my molars, to drive away my drowsiness, vaguely thinking it must
be two o'clock in the morning or perhaps three, when the mortar shell
exploded.

An appalling terror streaked through my spine. I shrank myself and
pulled the telephone wires in both directions to sound the alert, not
realizing somehow that it was hardly necessary. The explosions
sounded like tin sheets tearing. White flashes popped and vanished in
the rice paddies ahead of us.

"VC! They're coming! The Vietcong are coming!" screamed Pyon,
voice choked, hugging his helmet and crouching in the foxhole, trem-

bling. In the next foxhole, Sergeant Chang Taejun was breathlessly calling the company commander on the EE-8 field telephone.

"Mortar, sir. We can't see the enemy yet but I think they're coming in from eleven o'clock, sir."

We could not open fire, the target was not yet exposed. I craned my neck and looked around the field. Between the yellow explosions and white flashes popping in the rice paddies near Lac An village, I heard hissing sounds like that of a flying whistle. The enemy was there, somewhere near Lac An. But it was the villagers shelling us. Or were they?

"What should we do, sir?" Piggie Chang, the squad leader, screamed to somebody back at the company.

What should we do? Eight soldiers in foxholes by a brook, facing an abandoned open field, with mortar rounds advancing towards them—towards us—coming to kill me and kill Piggie and kill whoever we had out there.

"The shells keep moving towards us, sir. The shells are marching in a straight line towards us. We'll be hit unless we take cover somewhere else, sir."

Private Pyon started to hiccup.

"Retreat to the military band bunkers!" Piggie Chang hollered. "Pass the word! We're ordered to retreat to the trenches of the buglers!"

There was nothing to think or hesitate about. In a war, soldiers are unicellular animals, following orders. I was not responsible for my own death if I died.

Gripping the sling of my carbine, I scrambled out of the foxhole, shouting, "Run! Run to the trenches!"

Private Pyon, curled up like a porcupine and continued hiccupping, frightened, as he had been since the shelling started.

"Let's go! We'll get killed if we stay here!"

"I . . . can't"—hic—"go"—hic—"Sergeant Han. My legs are"—hic—"stiff. Like . . . like . . ."

"Run, you bastard. Run!"

He climbed out of the hole, hiccuping violently. The other six were scampering madly towards the trenches of the military band bunkers. I ran, my hand pressing down the U.S.-made helmet. It was too big. My rifle was also too big for my small Oriental physique.

I glanced back. Private Pyon stumbled after me, hugging his rifle, as yellowish flames exploded in the dark behind him. The rounds were chasing us. What if I am hit in the leg? Crippled.

Dashing toward the bunkers, I saw the buglers in their shorts and shirts gathered outside to watch the fireworks of the mortar shells.

"Hey, there goes another!" *Wham!* "Did you see that one? Over there, over there. It was really great."

"And there, too. Look!" *Wham!*

I jumped into the trench, panting, desperate.

Friendly artillery began to pound the rice paddies across the brook as the eight of us leveled our rifles at the invisible enemy. We crouched in the half-dug trenches; the buglers had not even dug their holes right. The crops of the peasants were being shredded by mortar and howitzer. Private Pyon vomited profusely in between his hiccupping fits. The sour smell upset my stomach, too.

The shelling stopped—both sides—almost simultaneously.

We waited. Ten minutes crept by. It was very quiet under the wan moon. I couldn't believe the barrage of shells that had poured down furiously all over the place. There was no smell of gunpowder. Frogs began to croak loudly again.

"Boy, it scared the shit out of me," said Piggie Chang, stretching his legs and removing his tipped helmet.

"Look here, Private Pyon," Sergeant Kim Mungi grumbled in a sickened voice. "What have you eaten so much of to produce that enormous heap? Clean it up. Right now."

Even in that confusion and flurry, Private Pyon complied without a single word of protest. He scooped it up with his bare hands and threw it away, hiccuping.

As this was our first encounter with the enemy in any form since we had arrived in Vietnam, we were somewhat mystified by the Vietcong shelling and were curiously relieved at the evidence that a war was indeed going on in this country. We would not go home not having seen combat.

When the stunning shock of the unexpected enemy fire subsided, the soldiers started to talk, and soon were chuckling and bantering with one another:

"Where do you think the shells came from?"

"From that village over there, I guess. Is that Lac An?"

"It was a belated gun salute from the Cong to welcome the arrival of the Daihan."

"They probably wanted to find out how strong our fire power is." The chatter stopped with this serious observation. "Some sort of a test, you know."

"They wanted to give us a good scare," someone else said.

Like young boys gone to a whorehouse for the first time, the soldiers resumed their jabber, asking one another, What did you feel, what did you think during the shelling? And boastfully they confessed they were not scared at all, that the shelling was actually exciting. Pyon Chinsu, still hiccuping crazily, was the only soldier in the trench who did not join that bombast.

Piggie Chang asked me what I had felt when we were chased by the mortar shells.

I told him the truth—that I feared the possibility of being crippled by shrapnel, more than dying.

"You certainly did the worrying the right way," Piggie Chang said. "A perfect death is far better than to get wounded and spend life as a cripple. You're as logical as ever, my boy."

"If you get killed in action, you will become a laudable model of a filial son," said Corporal Kim Chaeo, who used to be a driver before he was reclassified as a combat soldier for Vietnam duty. "The U.S. government offers a fat compensation for all the Koreans killed in this war, so your death will make your parents rich."

Piggie nodded. "They give rewards to the wounded too, I heard."

"But you've got to trade in your life if you need some real money."

Corporal Hwang Chanhi, who had been recently transferred to our company, joined the lively conversation. "But you can't use the money if you're gone."

"We're talking about filial virtues, not benefits for ourselves, remember?" Piggie Chang said, blowing the dirt off the muzzle of his rifle.

"But what could we do for a living if we had to return home crippled?" Corporal Kim said. "The reward for the wounded won't be enough to support you for your lifetime."

Hwang Chanhi said, rising, "I got it. You know what the beggars do on the downtown bus in Seoul, don't you? Remember the melodramatic speech the beggars give to win the passengers' sympathy and pennies? Listen." He hemmed twice to clear his throat. "Ladies and gentlemen in the bus, this wretched soul here lost both legs in Vietnam and now begs of you generous alms."

Piggie Chang tapped his helmet with his bayonet to imitate the elimination chime of a radio show contest. "You failed to make the finals because you lacked emotional conviction," he jeered. "If you're so pompous, nobody's gonna give you a single penny. You don't want displays of ego in the begging business."

"All right, I'll show how you're supposed to do it," said Kim Chaeo, as he put down his rifle on the dirt mound of the trench and stood primly like a docile grammar school child preparing to sing before his class. "Ladieeees and gentlemen in the bus, this poor man now standing before you joined the expeditionary forces of the Korean crusade to Vietnam for preserving peace and freedom in Indochina." With all the pomp and glory he could muster, he mimicked the endlessly repeated cliches of the Defense Ministry pamphlets supplied all combat soldiers, and then suddenly changed to a pathetic tone. "But I lost my legs while fighting for the buglers."

"Did you attend oratory lessons in high school or something?" said Corporal Hwang, chuckling. "I've never seen any driver as well versed as you are."

Listening to their jokes between Private Pyon's fitful hiccups, I wondered at how concepts of spiritual death, with all their philosophical undertones, would sound amongst the profanity. Was the tragedy essentially a big joke? I was not at all sure whether romantic concepts of heroism weren't actually comic farces.

Private Pyon drank a whole canteenful of cold water, holding his nose. He stopped hiccupping. The exhausted sun rose, pouring down rusted light over the battered rice paddies.

8

Of the total division, nineteen soldiers died during the first month. None lost his life in direct combat. Their Killed In Action classifications were hardly heroic ones: a 105-mm howitzer gunner of the 51st FA lost his life when the gun barrel blew off while shelling to scare away VC elements that might be concentrating on Hon Heo Mountain; a private of RCN Company, 29th Regiment was killed during a regular patrol by a primitive booby trap rigged on a tree branch; a 30th Regiment master sergeant, fearing snipers, died when his jeep was overturned while speeding through a gum plantation. We found it hard to believe that nineteen soldiers had already died in a war that did not seem to be any more dangerous than night guard duty in the Korean DMZ.

And then, there were the real KIAs. The first casualty among us was Lee Kwanil, who had been transferred to our company after our deployment in Vietnam. He was an oddly funny guy. Corporal Lee wore an Omega wristwatch. Maybe he wore the best watch among the 50,000 Korean soldiers stationed in Vietnam.

I heard a distant Chinook helicopter flying towards Hon Heo Mountain, sputtering drowsily over the yellow landscape of Lac Ninh plain. The nine of us, forming a line as short as the cut-off tail of a lizard, were out on our regular daily patrol to Hill 24.

The soldiers were cheerful. They had reason to be. More than 80,000 letters had arrived at the Division APO last night, an average of five letters for each soldier, probably more than thirty for Kim Mungi, the pen pal specialist. Letters certainly made them happy. And the canned kimchi, sent by a big construction company in Seoul through its branch office in Cam Ranh Bay as a gift to the combat soldiers, had been distributed to them this morning. For the soldiers who had to put up every day with three meals of tasteless Vietnamese rice accompanied by C-ration stew that reminded us of the piggie soup of the Korean War days, even a single clove of garlic was such a precious treasure that they used to bite it off little bit by bit and chew it with a mouthful of rice mixed with some hot pepper paste to whet their appetite. A whole can of deliciously sour and spicy kimchi was a blissful feast for the soldiers, who eventually had a big lunch of Korean rice with the pickled cabbage that refreshed their stomachs with a delightfully hot tang. On top of all this, there would be a show this evening at the U.S. chopper detachment barracks a little distance down the hill. In a few hours, they would watch the big white women strip-teasing, going stark naked to reveal the last secrets of the blond pubic hair. That was real entertainment. The soldiers had been bored to death by the dull shows staged by the amenity troupes organized with over-the-hill comedians like Yang Hun and Yang Sokchon, the Korean copy of Abbott and Costello, or obscure singers and dancers nobody had ever heard of.

Now Sergeant Chon Hisik hummed Sergeant Saddler's "The Green Berets" in a jolly spirit while Corporal Kim Chaeo and Private Song Chunsik and Piggie Chang and Lee Kwanil prattled on:

"This is really a deplorable country. They say two thousand ARVN soldiers desert and 400 more get killed by the Cong every week."

"If you go down to Saigon, there are French *con gais* too. For forty
dollars they give you the best treatment you can dream of. The six-nine
sucking and . . ."

"I wonder when I can ever mount a white mare. You get nowhere by
digging your whole life away in this miserable place."

"But we've finally got somewhere in our lives, haven't we? Getting
paid in American dollars, smoking American cigarettes all the time and
drinking American beer."

"And you wear American shorts, too."

"Did you hear the story about the young widows of Ninh Pung
Village? Every night you can hear a mile away the wailing chorus of the
young women hungry for something to fill their empty groins—"

A shot. A single shot.

I just stood there, vaguely thinking the shot, the single shot, must
have been some sort of illusion, because the sun was so dazzling and
everything was so quiet around me. But the soldiers who had been
walking ahead of me dispersed right or left and vanished out of sight in a
flash, all of them, like the countless little crabs on the silt at an estuary,
disappearing underground at a whiff of wind, and I could see nobody, all
of them hidden behind trees or rocks, and Corporal Lee Kwanil, who
had been slashing away the thorny branches and tendrils with his
machete some twenty meters ahead of me, tried to pull himself up, his
knees buckling Elvis Presley-like, trying not to fall back, not to collapse,
and then his legs bent and folded weakly, collapsing like a jellyfish, and
he flopped down.

All this happened in one single moment. When I saw the blood
stream down from his torn side as he silently fell, I thought that was
wrong and I hit the dirt quickly. I felt the raspy blades of grass scrape my
cheek as I leveled my rifle at something, at nothing, ahead of me. It was
so quiet. The Vietcong had fired just one round so as not to expose his
location; we could not tell where the bullet had come from.

Hiding among the thorny undergrowths, I clicked the trigger catch of
my carbine from semi-automatic to full-automatic, fed a bullet into the
chamber, and slid back to conceal myself behind a rock heated hot by the
afternoon sun. In the stifling smell of the roasting soil, I looked around.
Lying flat on the rough grass, Sergeant Chon Hisik, Corporal Kim
Chaeo and Private Song Chunsik were curling like porcupines behind
the fat spiky cactus, ducking their heads, but Piggie Chang stretched
his neck from a sunken pit to take a look at Corporal Lee Kwanil.

I looked over at Lee, too, sprawled like a knocked-out boxer on the grass. From his side spilled red blood that looked too clean and transparent to be associated with death. Strange it was. Ghastly, illusive it was that the person called Lee Kwanil, who just two or three minutes ago had cheerfully yammered about the naked blond dancers of the fantastic shows at the U.S. chopper squadron, had ceased to be a living person in a few seconds. He was, all of a sudden, an inanimate object.

The sticky blood flowed like molten red toffee and curdled around a patch of grass, as the dead man stared at the sun with his glassy eyes, his surprised mouth agape.

The sound of the shot had vanished from the air. Not caring whatever had happened on Hill 24, farmers herded their buffalos in the distant rice paddies and the Dong Hai Sea glittered, reflecting the sparkles of sun rays beyond the peaceful green fields.

Piggie Chang shouted for the sniper to come out with his hands up, — "*Di ra! Gio tay len! Lai lai! Lai lai!*" — and then opened fire at the bamboo grove. We also opened fire. We had to do something. Spent cartridges burst out from my rifle and scattered on the ground. Beautifully shiny cartridges. But the VC sniper was not in the grove. The enemy was nowhere. We ceased firing, Piggie first and the rest of us after him this time too, embarrassed and ashamed because there was no response from the enemy.

I looked over again at the body of Lee Kwanil, only twenty or thirty meters from me, and I thought, It can't be, people can't die like this. There must be something, something more serious, something else like rain or dark or a wailing woman . . .

When Piggie Chang tried to wriggle out of the pit like a giant tadpole to approach the dead body, another shot rang out. Piggie Chang slid back down.

Watching the abandoned body that was exposed to the enemy but out of anybody's reach from our side, I suddenly had a frightening sense of identification: the body out there was me. And I did not want to be discarded like that. I wanted to drag the body away and hide it somewhere nobody could see. In death, man was not much different from a dog, and it was a profanity to display a death in the open like that. It simply was not right. Yet I was utterly incapable of saving Lee Kwanil from that lonely abandonment.

A long, long while later reinforcements arrived from the company and we searched the area around Hill 24. We could not find any trace of the sniper. Not even the two cartridge shells.

When a chopper flew in to take away Corporal Lee's corpse, I loaded the heavy body with Piggie Chang. The Omega watch on Lee's wrist ticked vigorously. Along with the samples of hair, fingernails and toenails he had submitted to the HQ Company of Division Headquarters just for this occasion, as all of us had done upon our arrival in Vietnam, the crate containing the white powder of his cremated remains, his belongings, and the Omega watch, would be sent home.

That night of the first official KIA, the nocturnal shelling of random targets intensified. The nightly shelling that we used to consider ridiculous and pointless suddenly began to mean something to us. The soldiers going out for ambush in the evening looked glum with silent anger. The war was not silly or ridiculous any more. One single death it was, but it changed everything.

The shells of 155-mm howitzers whistled away through the dark air, orange flashes popped like noctilucent flowers on the western ridge of Hon Heo Mountain and disappeared shortly after, and then the sound of explosions rumbled through the ground. The nightly intimidation shelling of the ominous mountain had continued for three days, and at daybreak Operation Bulldozer was to begin to clean up the VC elements from the villages of Lac Ninh plain.

Flares kept whizzing up above the dark rice paddies, belching white tails of smoke, falling through the drizzle like tiny white parachutes, burning and vanishing in mid-air into darkness. The pale light of the flares brightened the dark wet soil piled up around the bunker. The heavy roof covered with dirt and palm leaves, soggy with rain water, sagged down to depress the waiting soldiers. Contrary to the weather forecast by the U.S. Air Force, it began to rain a little after midnight. The rainy season was about to begin.

The narrow bunker was in a deep pit lined by vertical rows of C-ration cases stuffed with dirt. On the crowded cots the soldiers were writing last-minute letters home. A few oiled their rifles, squatting before the flickering light of the lamp improvised from C-ration cans. Butcher shined his bayonet, swearing he would avenge Corporal Omega Watch's death. Corporal Kim Chaeo was packing the green combat rations into his knapsack, piling the cans all over his cot and shaking them one by one alongside his ear so as to find out what was inside because he could not read the English words on them.

We were as dirty as beggars. Since everyone faithfully believed in the superstition that a bath, haircut, shave, the trimming of nails or having sex before or during an operation would bring bad luck, most of the soldiers were filthy, their eyes glinting like those of Negro soldiers in the dark, for they had not even washed their faces for three days. I had not washed my face for three days either; I did not believe in any superstition, or even in religion, but who wanted to take any unnecessary chances.

I heard a field telephone bleat in the next bunker like a big mechanical cricket. My knapsack was packed so tight that not even a strap hung loose. Using it for a pillow, I thought about the villages we were to attack in a few hours.

By now the villagers must have heard that we would launch an operation against them. The Vietnamese non-coms and civilians working for Division G-5 had fled early in the evening, without any notice or explanation. They had fled, leaving the war to us. Most of the inhabitants in the objective areas of this mopping-up operation were innocent peasants, but we had to ferret out the Vietcong, who might have infiltrated them, to eliminate the secret enemy contact points within our area of operation, so that friendly outposts could intercept the night attacks of the enemy, secure the bases and chase the VC into the mountainous terrain in the central highlands later on. At least that was what the CO explained to us. The villagers already knew somehow about our forthcoming maneuver. We would march into their villages, declaring that we had come to rescue and protect them from the enemy threats, but what would they think and feel about the foreign soldiers barging into their houses to drive them away at gunpoint? What did we, or our parents, think when the U.N. Forces, the Americans and the Turks swarmed into our villages during the Korean War to liberate us from the Communists and then raped the village women at night? I visualized the villagers who might be hiding in the underground shelters dug beneath every house, or perhaps they had left their homes with their belongings, and I remembered the endless procession of the Korean refugees trudging to the south over the snow-covered mountains. But where would the Vietnamese take refuge in this war that had no frontline or rear?

I thought of Trau, the boy I had met at Dong Hai beach at Xuan My. There was an R&R center for the Korean soldiers on Xuan My beach. The sign "R&R Center" in red paint on the broad plank looked like a joke because this place was just a piece of deserted sandy beach segregated by barbed wire entanglements to keep off the Vietnamese, as if it was a pocket of Korean territory. It was almost empty most of the time because the Korean private soldiers were rarely granted R&R of any sort, while officers had better places to go, and all the rest and recuperation activities those few coming here enjoyed were swimming, volleyball or just sitting idly around. We occasionally went there for a dip because the 9th Company was responsible for safety and protection of the facilities there. One day I saw little Vietnamese children swarm outside the barbed wire fence, calling, "Hey, Daihan, give me chop chop!" I conversed in English with one of the boys across the barbs. This boy opened the can I had thrown to him and ate the beans with the white plastic C-ration spoon he carried with him. Then, simpering, he asked me for cigarettes in Vietnamese Korean: "*Dambai, dambai.*" I gave him a pack of Winston and asked how old he was, and his name, and where he lived. I was attracted to him perhaps because he reminded me of myself twenty years ago when I had done the same thing to American soldiers and given them a dirty gesture if I got no can.

Trau was twelve years old, a fifth grader at Xuan My Elementary School and lived at Tuc My. He lived alone with his mother, ate two meals a day at home, and skipped lunch if he could not get any cans from Yankee or Daihan soldiers. He was a precocious child, who had learned very early in his life that childish innocence and honesty did not help survival in war at all. He could smile any time he wanted to if needed, and I got the impression that he would never cry in any tragic or painful situation. He could easily throw a bomb at a Korean military base if a Vietcong offered him something to eat for a week. There was no need for him to feel any guilt in doing so if it was necessary for survival, for he was simply performing a duty to life.

I met Trau again several days later at Ninh Hoa. He played harmonica with another boy his age at the intersection of the three-forked road by Ban Cong High School, and a barefooted five-year-old girl in a pale pink dress was dancing to the harmonica tune like a French automaton. Many Korean soldiers who happened to be in town for a public demonstration of taekwondo martial arts gave coins and cans to these three pathetically beautiful child beggars.

I brought the three children to a nearby eatery and bought them fried rice. Trau, expertly handling the tall ivory chopsticks, swaggered a lot to show off that he had a *Daihan linh,* a Korean soldier friend. When I asked him who that little dancing girl was, Trau said he did not know. He explained that he had met the little girl in the pretty dress on the street, "and I think, I make money." He had promised to give her 50 piasters if she danced for his begging. "I make *muoi ba* (13) cans *hai tram Dong* (200 piaster)," he said, grinning. He was pitifully bright for his age. That was all.

I worried about Trau, for his village, Tuc My, was included in the objectives of Operation Bulldozer. I could not fall asleep. And the day broke.

Turnout at 0300 hours, rendezvous at 0400. I finished the breakfast of pound cake and ham in the early dawn, and went down the dusky hill with two hundred men of the company marching in a column to the command post of the 3rd Battalion, the first rendezvous point. The vehicles that would carry the troops to the battle were waiting in a long line in the dark.

It still drizzled. Orange electric light beamed out of the big command post tent pitched in the middle of several camouflaged bunkers. Soldiers plodded along the grassy rice paddy dike and converged from different directions in the misty light trickling out of the tent openings.

Radios cautiously screeched somewhere. It was a little chilly because of the steady rain. I rolled down my sleeves. Ten minutes later, the soldiers fastened their knapsacks onto the sides of the trucks as they boarded. Scattered here and there some distance off the road, the soldiers who would remain to defend the base were guarding the trucks, their ponchos and sagging fatigues soaked dark by the rain. Their helmets were pulled down low over their faces. By the jeep beside a large puddle, Captain Kim Sanghyop, the company commander, was giving last-minute instructions to the platoon leaders, his flashlight shimmering on the military map wrapped in waterproof acetate. His lieutenants marked something on their maps.

Officers drove their jeeps back and forth among the soldiers. There were occasional shouts of orders. Radios suddenly hissed with traffic. Truck engines began to idle. The sloppy road grew noisier and noisier.

In the hazy dawn light I saw the palm trees and other shapes and contours standing or stirring around the command post. At 0500 hours the trucks, with their cautious low beams on, started moving out along

Highway 9. The drizzling rain swayed like a fantastic veil over the South China Sea. Raindrops hung along the edge of my helmet, stared at me transparently for a while and then fell away. Jeeps, trucks and armored personnel carriers rolled out carefully in the fading darkness.

Pfc. Song Chunsik, sitting opposite me in the truck, sucked his wet cigarette, concealing the glowing light with his cupped hand. The muzzle of the M-1 rifle leaning against his shoulder, like all other weapons in the truck, was covered with a vinyl wrapper to prevent the rain water from trickling into the barrel. There were thin dark rings under his eyes, I thought.

The asphalt was wet, as were the trees and the deserted houses of Thon Xuan Hoa Village. The one-story houses looked like bungalows at a seaside resort. The thatched huts among the rice paddies were empty; the villagers had left this hamlet after years of harassment from the Vietcong. Where could they have gone to find a refuge in this war that did not bother to discriminate between the front and the rear? The rusty burnt-down skeleton of a Lambretta overturned by a Vietcong mine, shrubs, the sky, grass, hills—the whole world was wet in the rain. Through the palm trees, the vehicles advanced.

I glanced again at Private Song, and I secretly studied the expressions of other soldiers in the covered truck. I was afraid to look into their eyes. Why did these soldiers on their way to battle look so innocent and meek? Guarding all directions with their leveled rifles, the quiet soldiers were carried to the battlefield.

Jeeps drove back and forth among the trucks like cowboys herding cattle, the officers spitting terse orders to the heavy trucks crawling along the rain-swept highway. The trucks carrying the 9th Company veered off from Highway 9 near Lac An and we were ordered to get down. The other companies continued their advance north. We promptly spread out, each platoon deployed by its leader. Our fatigues sagging, we were sent out along the rice paddy dikes.

The assignment given to the 9th was not a search-and-destroy mission as we had expected; instead we were to guard the perimeter of the Command Post. We were ordered to dig in around the big floppy tents pitched on the prominently exposed twin hills. These were immediately christened by the soldiers as "the Boobs of To Kumbong" after the celebrated breasts of a glamorous Korean movie actress. We were to guard the Tactical Command Post from the enemy who would never come near. The soldiers, who had anticipated action, were disappointed.

"I guess we'll keep digging for a year—all the way home—without firing one single bullet," Sergeant Chon Hisik grumbled, whacking a twisted bough with his machete to remove the visual obstacles around his foxhole. "That would certainly be a great contribution of ours to the war effort—not wasting any ammo. Imagine. All that fuss to prepare for combat and then coming out here to dig in and stand guard . . . Stand guard! What the heck do they think we are? Stupid MPs?"

Having cut down all the thorny branches around me with the side blade of my entrenching shovel, I sat down on the red slippery ground and looked down at the plain, faintly aware of the cold rain water wetting my hips. The rain had stopped, and the plain, where the operation would be conducted for twenty days, was completely block-aded by ten o'clock in the morning. The CP was so conveniently located on the hill overlooking the whole operational zone that I could visualize the commanding officers at the CP tents atop the hill pointing at different spots on the chessboard of the rice paddies with long swagger sticks and telling the troops to move from here to here, as if they were playing a giant chess game on the field with live soldiers.

Clusters of farmhouses were dispersed in the field of green and gold, patterned by rice plants. The dikes crisscrossing among the paddies re-minded me of the irrigation canals in the Korean countryside at Sosa where I used to go fishing with nets in my childhood. A lone cart road stretched through this landscape and the drearily majestic Hon Heo Mountain rose menacingly high to the left of that country road. The palm trees around Hill 24 must look like furry green crosses from up there.

White sand glittered through the palm trees along the shining blue water of the Dong Hai Sea. A swarm of little birds, probably sparrows, swept around, startled by the noisy engine sputter of choppers flying towards Tuc My. How could human beings kill one another in this crystal sunshine?

The fierce sun poured through the canvas camouflage cloth as soon as the rain had stopped. The heat from the burning metal of my helmet scorched the crown of my head and the grass stifled me with its radiating hot breath. The propaganda warfare van at the Tac CP was repeating the warning to the inhabitants in the operational area that they should move out to safety because a military maneuver would soon begin in their villages; the warning, given in the Vietnamese language, with so many implosive syllables, sounded like a long taped speech played backward.

Absent-mindedly I gazed at the soldiers digging foxholes. They had a look as bored as that of grave-diggers at a municipal cemetery. Picking up my shovel to continue digging my foxhole, I saw Vietnamese in black clothes and conical hats appear around the bamboo grove beyond the bridge on the cart road. They trudged towards us along the path from Lac An Village.

"Aren't they VC?" asked Private Pyon Chinsu in a frightened voice, putting down his shovel and quickly putting on his helmet.

The soldiers stopped digging and watched the Vietnamese, some fifty of them, worming up the hill to the CP. They picked up their rifles for an unlikely but prospective combat.

"I don't think they're Cong," Piggie Chang said, narrowing his eyes. "No VC would come out like that and get killed when the fight has not even started."

"The man in the lead carries a white flag," Corporal Kim Chaeo said. "You don't have to worry if they're real VC, because they're coming to surrender."

"Be careful," said Master Sergeant Han Myongsun, chambering a bullet. "Vietcong are wicked and cunning bastards. They might approach us pretending to surrender and suddenly hurl hand grenades at us when they come close enough."

They were not Vietcong. They passed by our position about twenty minutes later and headed for the Tactical Command Post. The one carrying the white flag in the lead was an old man with short pointed goatee, and the other old men following him were either barefoot or wore crude Ho Chi Minh sandals, made of car tire treads. Like a funeral procession, they went mutely with the white flag and bowed, gathering their hands before their chests, the Buddhist way to formally greet the armed soldiers waiting for them with loaded rifles. The soldiers let them proceed to the battalion commander's tent.

"They must be the villagers seeking safe refuge as instructed by the warning announcement," said Sergeant Chon Hisik.

"But isn't it strange that only fifty villagers responded to the warning?" said Piggie. "At least one thousand inhabitants must be living in this area."

"Maybe most of them have decided to stay and defy the Daihan warnings," said Sergeant Kim Taegi. "Who cares, anyway? These Viets are none of our business as long as we have no chance of actual combat in this operation. Let's dig."

We dug.

When I got the message from Sergeant Chi Taesik, the radioman, that the executive officer had summoned me, I went to the temporary company CP housed in a deserted farmhouse. It was never happy news if First Lieutenant Lee Taehun was looking for me. Probably he needed my French to communicate with the Vietnamese. Most Vietnamese, especially older ones, spoke French fluently the way older Koreans spoke Japanese. When I reached the half demolished farmhouse surrounded by piles of bombing debris, he was sitting astride an empty ammunition case by the broken window.

"Really glad you're here," said the lieutenant, already rising to leave. I followed him out to Highway 1 where APCs were lining up and waiting for the order to move into the villages. "They need your French real bad. The chief of Lac An Village is at the Tac CP with some villagers demanding an interview with the battalion commander. This Vietnamese goat keeps babbling something to the commander and all the officers around but there's no interpreter available because all the Vietnamese non-coms working for G-5 fled last night. No wonder this country is in this mess. Everybody runs away for his own life. They totally lack the will to fight for their own survival. And our Division G-5 doesn't have any officer who can speak Vietnamese well enough to communicate with this old man who keeps talking and talking. The village chief can speak French well, though. And that's why the Battalion HQ is looking for someone who can speak French and talk to that prattling goat."

Lieutenant Lee took me to the Battalion CP and we reported ourselves to Lieutenant Colonel Min Hijun, the G-5.

"Fucking Vietnamese," Colonel Min said, taking us to the Tac CP. "They never know how to appreciate us even when we risk ourselves to fight for them. You know how they pestered us, Lieutenant, asking for compensation for the dumb buffalos and then demonstrating in the streets because we neglected to pay them for one single miserable beast with a broken leg. Have you heard the latest? The Khanh Hoa county chief, who's a mere ARVN major, filed an official complaint to the division commander demanding an apology because that bastard and the prestige of his nation—he actually used that expression—were besmirched when that son of a bitch had been seated in a lower row than a Daihan colonel at the dedication ceremony of a reconstructed classroom at a Phan Rang high school."

When we arrived at the Tac CP, the battalion commander and two other officers were sweating to comprehend what the Vietnamese village chief with the white flag was trying to explain to them or to pass their own ideas, if possible, into the old man's closed brain, using all sorts of exaggerated gestures and speaking a queer pidgin language somewhere between English, Vietnamese and Korean. The other old villagers stared suspiciously at the Korean soldiers and clung together like a human ball. Outside the big tent, about 50 meters above them on the hill, the staff officers who had come out from the division headquarters to observe how the operation was going, sat around on the cots and idly chatted about the old days because there was not much action down at the plain to watch through the spotting scope.

"It's true the Vietnam War is dull," Major Kim Hyonguk, the judge advocate, who had served with the special forces unit of 8240 KLO during the Korean War, indulged in reminiscence, his black eyes twinkling. "The Vietcong is a really weak enemy. Think of the war we had to fight fifteen years ago. The Vietcong are so weak they cannot direct this guerrilla warfare to their utmost advantage although they can choose time, place and fighting method. During an operation at Siniju, we organized two five-man squads to strike the enemy simultaneously from both ends . . ."

Lieutenant Lee Taehun waited on the grass next to me for Colonel Min to explain to the battalion commander why we had been brought there. He frowned and muttered in a low voice so that the colonels could not hear him, "What kind of a war is this? Officers coming out to watch the battle, complaining that this war is boring, yawning—what is this? A baseball game or something? The older officers say they've never seen a war as boring as this and then talk about the old war when they got all the excitement in the world. They think the old war was a Glenn Ford movie or something. And they regard these soldiers as kindergarten children on a picnic. But in this war, there exists tragic death and you can witness heroic . . . heroic . . . heroic something, don't you think so? Just as love seems to be the most precious and sublime thing in the world to each individual experiencing that particular love, the particular war that one personally goes through is the most painful and bloody experience to that person. And a man matures through this personal experience of war."

While the lieutenant was thus philosophizing, I looked down at Highway 1 in the direction of Ninh Hoa. Down there on the road, the

Vietnamese farmers who had come from the villages outside Lac Ninh area gathered here and there to watch the Daihan soldiers swarm around in the field. Some of them even brought chairs to enjoy the spectacle of the live war game more comfortably, and there was a family having a meal of noodles on the highway, too. The passing Lambretta mini buses would stop to see what was going on and then drive off when they noticed nothing much was happening. For these people the foreign armed soldiers sloshing across the green rice paddies and the helicopters sputtering around overhead were a rare entertainment in their tedious lives. While the colonels were chattering and watching the show from the hilltop and the Viet farmers were enjoying themselves down at the highway, Operation Bulldozer was forging ahead as the foot soldiers faithfully carried out their part.

With the battalion commander, Lieutenant Lee Taehun, the staff officers and a bunch of the Korean war correspondents who had flown in from Saigon to observe and report on this first major military operation by the 9th ROK Infantry Division, I went down the hill to the waiting farmers.

They were led by Nhat Tien, who was about seventy years old and spoke French a lot more fluently than I did. The old man said the villagers had heard the warning announcement but did not want to be evacuated. He emphatically added then that the peace-loving inhabitants of all the non-hostile communities in the plain sincerely hoped the Koreans would cancel this operation.

"We, the inhabitants of Lac Ninh plain, cannot consent to this military action. In other words, sir, we don't want to permit you to use our land as a battlefield. Nobody wants a combat action to take place at our villages. If you kill pigs or chicken, intentionally or not, during this operation, we're the ones who will have to suffer those losses, and what about the rice paddies that the Daihans would trample all over? We don't want our crops to be damaged. If our houses are destroyed, who will be responsible for building them again for us? We are poor peasants. We don't have the money to build our houses again every year. And I want to tell you honestly that we're no longer interested in the military situation. We don't care much which side wins the war. If you go through a war, the same war, whatever kind of a war it may be, for twenty years, sooner or later you fall into the rut of indifference when all the fancy talk about ideologies or causes seems to be vain and futile. What is important for us now is the basic matter of survival. We simply don't want any more of this war.

"It doesn't matter much who wins it, because it will keep on sacrificing countless lives on both sides. This war is going on forever. Whenever new forces occupy our land, we have to pay the overdue taxes to the new liberators, and this is a great burden to us because they try to collect all the arrears once they can reach us. If ARVN liberates us, the Viet government immediately dispatches its tax-collectors, and when the VC liberates us, they demand their own overdue tax in turn. How can we go on living when we're harassed by both sides?

"I have yet to see if it's true or not, but I read in the leaflets and propaganda books distributed by the Korean troops that the Daihans are humanitarian soldiers who consider the safety and welfare of the Vietnamese populace a matter of first and foremost importance. If you're really faithful to your propaganda commitments, please do not bother us, sir. And why do you have to care if we live under VC pressure? We don't care. One steady pressure is better than two alternating pressures that tend to accelerate each other. We want to farm and live peacefully. That's really all we want. If this battle can end the war, we wouldn't mind losing our homes, or even some lives. But this is not going to be the final battle. You've come from a foreign country and you're not going to live here forever. It's perfectly all right for you if you burn down the whole village to search out one or two VC infiltrators and then move to a new tactical zone, but what about us who have to remain here and go on living?

"When the Vietcong come back, they'll torment us because we've cooperated with the Daihan forces. Maybe they'll behead me and several other village elders. Then who will be there to protect us? The Vietcong sneaked into Tu Bong one night about three months ago and eliminated two families who were suspected of having cooperated with an ARVN intelligence detachment. They buried everyone of those two families, even a two-year-old child, leaving only their heads above the ground, and then hacked their skulls with an ax until the mushy brains and blood spattered all over the yard. The villagers were forced to watch the whole process of execution so that they could learn a lesson. Have you ever seen such a gory scene, sir? Such a gruesome punishment inflicted on your own next-door neighbor?

"I did learn a lesson. The lesson that a useless death is indeed a meaningless loss. So, please do not reprimand us for asking you to cancel this operation and allow us go on living as we have been."

The operation was delayed because of this unexpected incident. If the inhabitants would continue to refuse to leave their villages, it would be a beastly job to screen all the local people in the target area and pick out the VC suspects or sympathizers.

The battalion commander tried to persuade the old man for two hours, but Nhat Tien kept repeatedly asserting his views in a calm, undisturbed voice. The staff officer of Operations at Division Head-quarters soon arrived by jeep to join the persuasion, but to no avail. The infuriated G-3 staff officer blew his top, swearing profusely in Korean, but nobody could exercise any influence over the old man who stub-bornly refused. Lieutenant Lee Taehun busily noted down something in one corner of the tent; tonight, I thought, there would be a special entry in his personal diary about this situation. The Korean war correspon-dents asked the Information Officer for an interview with the village chief, because this quaint behind-the-battle confrontation could make a nice story, but the old man did not answer any of their questions.

Eventually the regimental commander had to report to division head-quarters about this hitch in the first phase of the operation, and a staff meeting was summoned in the evening. Most of the villagers returned home at dusk but Nhat Tien and six other village elders decided to stay until they were notified of the decisions made by the emergency staff meeting. The seven Vietnamese were accommodated at the tent next to the 9th's CP, and after a C-ration supper with us, they waited quietly.

I spent the night in the same tent with the Vietnamese elders, for I had been told to stay with them until "this nonsense could be settled" and "keep a close eye on those gooks."

Holding my breath once in a while when I could no longer stand the strange, unique, millipede smell of the Vietnamese people—some sol-

diers said that was the scent of the soap they used—I lay down on the cot
to relax and gazed at Nhat Tien. The old man, with bony fingers and
emaciated face, smoked a thin cigarette by the entrance of the tent,
squatting like a frog to see if anybody was coming from the Tac CP to tell
him the outcome of the staff meeting. From his solemn expression
somehow I could detect an air of aloof detachment. And in his person,
somehow, I could feel the agony of Vietnam.

After midnight when everybody else was asleep, I tried to lead him
into a casual but personal conversation. The old man was not willing to
talk to me at first, but began to answer my questions intermittently a
while later; perhaps he felt obliged to me for at least that much courtesy
because of my help that afternoon in conveying his wishes to the Korean
commanders. About an hour later, however, he was freely talking about
himself and what he had gone through in the past.

He had left his home in Khanh Hoa Province at the young age of
eighteen in 1911 when France seized power in Vietnam with the
establishment of *Conseil de Gouvernement de l'Indochine* after China's
abrogation of the 1885 Tiensin Treaty. He went to Saigon and was
educated by the French. Then he worked for the Indochina Trading
Company, managed by the French, until 1930 when he launched a
political career by organizing a political party with some of his young
friends, who advocated pacifist causes, to compete with the Communist
Party headed by Nguyen Tat Thanh and the radical nationalist party
Viet Nam Quoc Dan Dang.

As Nguyen Tat Thanh changed his name to Ho Chi Minh and
expanded his Communist influence in the north, he, ambitious Nhat
Tien, joined the Hoa Hao Buddhist sect that emerged in 1939 from the
poverty-stricken Mekong Delta. He actively participated in the political
struggles against the Trotskyites and the Communists who tried to
infiltrate the higher administrative echelons of Saigon. When the
Vichy-sponsored Vietnamese regime was attacked in 1941, both by the
Japanese and the Thais, the French governor-general had to hand over a
part of Cambodia and Laos to Thailand through the 1941 Tokyo Treaty.
At the end of that year, Nhat Tien went to the northern Tonkin area to
join against the resistance of the nationalists, who were supported by
the Japanese Allied Forces. But he left Hanoi later and returned to
Saigon after he grew skeptical about the political ideologies to be
advocated by the future independent government because he realized
how fast the League for the Independence of Vietnam, or Vietminh, was

absorbing the nationalists in the South through active organization of the Communists. They were called Viet Nam Cong San Communists or Vietcong. Southern Vietnam was thrown into turmoil after Ho Chi Minh's proclamation of the Democratic Republic of Vietnam on September 2, 1945 and the outbreak of guerrilla warfare. Just before the arrival of the Allied Forces, and return of the French forces early in 1946, he gave up his political ambitions and returned home, "lost in the mire of international politics and disillusioned by the greedy struggle of the dwarfs for power."

"I noticed the Daihan officers and correspondents stare at me queerly this afternoon as if I were a mad man." The old man's face was deeply lined. "Maybe they thought I behaved that way because I was ignorant of the meaning, the flow and the future of this war. But it is you, the Daihans, who plunged into this war without fully understanding what is actually going on. I guess very few of the Koreans understand why this war has been going on so long and what kind of a future this nation can expect. But we know. You Koreans say the Vietcong is a weak enemy, but you're misinformed. I don't know who is responsible for your misinformation, but you don't know your enemy as well as you should. You will realize how wrong you are about the enemy if you go to the northwestern region, the central highlands, the Mekong River Delta or the Cambodian border. A real war is going on there."

The old man stretched his withered legs, exhausted, and leaned against the pole supporting the front flap of the tent. "We don't feel a sense of affinity with you, or with any foreigners, because we have shed too much blood in this land, our land, because of foreigners. France, China and Britain trampled this country because they coveted our fertile soil. So did Japan. Later, however, we cherished a vague hope for peace, although the nation was divided at the 17th Parallel in 1945. Another civil conflict raged when the opposing political ideologies of communism and democracy confronted each other in North and South. Ho Chi Minh crossed the Chinese border in 1951 and swept southward with support from China, and the United States began its intervention in 1952. The Americans did not want the war in Korea linked with the Indochina conflict and the whole Asian continent turned into an uncontrollably vast war zone. That was how this country was divided into two half nations."

Nhat Tien believed that the Vietnamese populace was rapidly absorbed by the National Liberation Front, because more and more people resented the Catholic-dominated policies of Ngo Dinh Diem and Ngo Dinh Nhu and their secret political organization opposing the national election to unify the nation. The NLF organized in 1960. The People's Revolutionary Party that emerged in 1962 strengthened the Vietcong power, taking advantage of the political unrest and popular resentment. The Communist guerrilla forces of 25,000 in 1963 increased more than tenfold in three years, while Hanoi regularly dispatched 50,000 troops to the south every year. They had occupied virtually one third of the South Vietnamese territory, fighting against 720,000 Vietnamese, 510,000 American and 50,000 Korean troops.

"Statistically, your side is superior, of course," the old man said. "But it's the psychological attitude that really matters in this war. I know what I'm talking about, Sergeant. Vietminh advocates the nationalistic cause of saving the country from foreign powers, and the Viet people do hate the foreign influence that prolongs this war. Because they have suffered enough—suffered so long from foreign colonialists. And the South Vietnamese administration does not have sufficient organized strength to counter this mass sentiment of the populace.

"We cannot trust the Americans either, because the strong public opinion opposing this war at home will ultimately defeat the United States itself. Nor is our own government dependable enough to build our hope upon."

Following the death of Ngo Dinh Diem in the military coup of 1963, General Duong Van Minh's regime was also overthrown in 1964 by Nguyen Khanh, and Phan Khac Suu seized power through yet another military coup in the same year. Nguyen Khanh made a comeback the next year but again had to surrender the power to Nguyen Van Thieu in 1965. The people were not even sure if their government existed and was actually functioning somewhere in Saigon. "Who on earth would cherish any loyalty or patriotism for a government like that?" Nhat Tien said with a sigh.

The village chief, in a low subdued voice, said, "I lost four sons in this endless war. My eldest son joined the Vietnamese Army when it was inaugurated in 1949 to fight the partisans. He served as a liaison officer and eventually fought on the side of the French forces who wanted to colonize this country. He died at Dien Bien Phu—while fighting for the wrong side. My second son was a public servant faithful only to the Diem regime, and he probably committed every possible bureaucratic abuse of power and graft known in this world in order to accumulate his personal wealth, and one day in a dark back alley of the Cholon district in Saigon, his severed head along with his ID card was found wrapped in a white cloth on which the words 'Traitor to the Nation' were written in his own blood. We never found the rest of his body. My third son, an ARVN paratrooper, is known to have been killed in action near Hue, but there's a rumor that he might have deserted after shooting an officer of higher rank. My fourth child just disappeared when he was fourteen. Probably kidnapped by VC. Now you may understand a little the reason why I had to say those things in the afternoon. I've met Vietcong, and cooperated with them when they asked for food. A village chief is the primary target for Vietcong terrorism if he does not cooperate with them. Your head is chopped off or your guts blown out if you refuse to collect rice from the villagers and give it to them. It's that simple. You may think I am a coward, but bravery or cowardice has no tangible meaning whatsoever in this kind of a war. You just go on living, observing the minimal duty necessary for a human being to survive."

I heard raindrops spatter again on the canvas flaps of the tent. From the heavily sagging roof of the tent a drop of rain fell to the old man's forehead and trickled down his cheek. He hardly noticed. Later Nhat Tien and the village elders returned home when they were promised that the inhabitants would be amply compensated for any unnecessary damages they might suffer during the operation.

Evacuation of the villages in the plain began early. The villagers left their homes carrying their belongings and chickens and fatherless babies on their carts, and herding pigs or buffalos. They passed through the Korean check points to go to the refugee camps at Xuan My and Ba Hai. It took one full day for the AID and the Reconnaissance Company to verify the "political inclinations" of the individual farmers and accommodate them at the two camps.

In the evening of the second day we heard the first combat sounds of burping machine guns and flying mortar shells. Like the bloody urine of an invisible giant, tracer bullets streaked down to the dark plain from a chopper hovering in the dark sky. A flare popped above Duc My and slowly fell to a Tu Bong hill, spraying white light over the rice paddies, and weakly flickered off into the black space.

Another day broke.

The Tac CP was very quiet as the number of the staff officers coming to watch the game of war decreased and the correspondents from Saigon rushed away to the refugee camps with the TI&E staff officer; the colonel in charge of public relations had been restless because his division would not get much publicity coverage out of this operation. This morning he had barely managed to persuade the reporters to cover the refugee processing system at the camps with one of his beloved propaganda cliches: "You can write a nice human interest story, I guess, about the humane Korean troops who wouldn't start combat until all the innocent villagers were evacuated to safety."

No enemy resistance of any importance was reported to the CP, but the orioles, the radiomen, kept chirping ceaselessly in the battalion radio communications truck. "Report on the mole hunt. Over." Screech. "Mole hunt completed at peony cherry plum orchid (6325) area. No rats but August smoking pipes captured." The snub-nosed radioman wrote down the report with a felt pen on his sleeve and bare arm because he could not find any paper at hand: no VC, 8 rifles captured. All day long the 9th Company soldiers just watched. Spectators. Another day elapsed.

Flares brightened the field all night. Automatic weapons burped somewhere once in a while. Mosquitoes kept biting through our clothes. Sticky insect repellent oozed all over my body. Another dawn broke.

Some exchange of fire with the enemy had been expected because the encircling troops were closing in tighter, but it was as tedious and weary as any other day. The commanding officers were impatient and irritable because there was no visible response from the enemy. There would be no remarkable entries in their reports. Maybe we were surrounding an empty field and shelling and tearing apart paddies that were miles from the actual VC positions. We would have to pay for these rice paddies that were now apparently destroyed "unnecessarily." It was really annoying to fight an enemy who would not respond. The war correspondents flew to the Tiger Division at Qui Nhon, telling the information officer to notify them of the results of this operation, if there were any, through the Saigon press office at the Combined Headquarters of the Korean Armed Forces in Vietnam. They knew from experience that there would not be any news for their weekly dispatches from this wasteful operation.

Another day elapsed, and another and another.

On the seventh day the first VC suspect was captured. The encirclement had tightened so closely that I could hear the 10th Company radioman shout over his machine at the other company closing in from the opposite direction: "Hey, you fucking bastards, you're shooting at us! Hold your fire! Hold your fire!" A VC courier took a shot at the 6th Company spotters and was wounded while trying to infiltrate this tight ring probably to contact unidentified VC sympathizers and deliver instructions from a major Vietcong element in Song Da Ban. He was captured by 3rd Company soldiers while running from the 6th. As when somebody scored the first goal in a tedious soccer game, the soldiers were suddenly animated and fussed around the field like snake hunters, stabbing the ground with their bayonets to seek out underground shelters. I found it hard to call this comical farce a combat operation.

The 9th Company, which had not fired a single shot—while the rest of the regiment killed six and captured one VC suspect, and seized 27 rifles—was finally relieved from the duty of guarding the Tac CP, which apparently had no need to be protected in the first place. We moved to the Ba Hai refugee camp to replace the reconnaissance company, who were to join "the second phase of Operation Bulldozer." The duty of looking after the Vietnamese farmers accommodated at the seaside school building was not a bit more exciting or interesting than the nine days of guarding the hilltop tents. "Washing the assholes of the Viet peasants, this is what we really needed, sure," Sergeant Chon Hisik grumbled, kicking at his tightly-packed knapsack.

It began to drizzle again when we finished rigging up our tents in the school playground. Since I had nothing else to do in the afternoon, I snooped around the classrooms, trudging the damp musty corridors, vaguely hoping to find young Trau or Nhat Tien.

The refugees looked miserable and weary, like flood victims. An old woman was cutting her grandchild's hair with her big scissors. An old man, perhaps eighty years old, sidled up to me, gave me a clumsy military salute, demonstrated a smoking gesture and thrust his hand out, baring his decayed black teeth to simper pleadingly. Another old woman showed me her ragged clothes, probably hoping I would bring her new ones from somewhere. From where? The buttocks of the child standing timidly beside her were streaked red from his mother's whipping. A young woman sobbed silently, gazing at an old man who busily yammered on and on some unintelligible words, crawling on the floor with his behind high to explain something. Several children played under a tall tree with a helmet dented by a bullet. A pregnant woman was shivering helplessly, squatting on the ground in her soaked raincoat under the dripping eaves of a classroom.

I could not find any young males among the refugees anxiously waiting for the operation to be over so that they could go home. Young men were busy killing one another on either side of the Vietcong or the South Vietnamese Army. There were so many old people and women and children, and the absence of young men so conspicuous, that I no longer doubted the authenticity of the rumor that even the most insignificant petty officers in Vietnam had three or four wives because they were so short of men.

Although I failed to find Nhat Tien—perhaps the old man had been sent to Xuan My camp—I met the boy, Trau, late in the afternoon. I opened a C-ration can with my bayonet and was eating beans with a tiny white plastic spoon sitting on my upturned helmet when a beggar boy slouched towards me, looking into the tents and asking the soldiers, "Hey, White Horse uncle, you boocoo ration have yes? Give me? Give me chop chop?"

I did not know who that boy was at first because half of his head was wrapped with a grimy blood-soaked bandage.

I recognized the beggar boy when he came to the very next tent and I rushed to him, surprised to see his messy appearance.

"What happened?" I asked, pointing at his bandage. "This blood, I mean."

Trau looked around furtively, eyes flashing like a burglar's. He took me behind an old tree, looked around once more, and then removed the bandage from his head.

"This pig blood," he said, grinning. "I tie blood bandage Daihan give me boocoo ration." He proudly showed me the C-ration cans he had collected in the sagging bag hanging from his belt.

I was at a loss, not knowing what expression I should assume before this boy. I could not scold Trau. I could never scold the young boy who, at his age, should be reading fairy tales about the adventures of Flower Lady and Star Maiden on the cotton clouds, or dressing up to go to the zoo with his parents.

We sat down under a tree dripping with big raindrops and talked about casual things.

"All villager scared Daihan attack our villages," said Trau, scraping out with the plastic spoon the remaining beans from the can to finish my supper. "Daihan kill everybody, they say. But I know Daihan no kill."

After emptying the can Trau tied the bandage again on his head and asked me if I would go with him and meet his mother. I said yes and went back to the tent to fetch my helmet and rifle. I followed the boy to a classroom crowded with refugees crouching like frightened quail on the straw matting.

Trau's mother, squatting by the door, was eating a ball of rice distributed by the soldiers, resting her chin on her folded knees. She was at least three years older than I was but still looked like a virgin girl, her dark long hair billowing down her back; she looked so young probably because she wore no makeup and her bare skin was glossy with the faint lustre of bursting life. Her big black eyes somehow reminded me of wild geese. When Trau said something quickly to her in Vietnamese, she tried to smile, her face slowly brightening up. Trau must have told her about me, I thought. I took off my helmet and said hello to her in English. Her name was Hai and she could not speak English very well.

The next day the G-5 staff from division headquarters brought a truckload of clothes, mostly underwear, to the refuge camp and asked the 9th Company to distribute it to the refugee farmers. We tried to maintain order so that the villagers could equally share the clothes, but so nimble were the hooklike hands slithering in and snatching out the clothes from all directions, that I just wanted to get away from the truck, leaving the clamorous crowd to other soldiers.

I put down my rifle across the exposed roots of an old tree and sat on its stock. I blankly watched the young Vietnamese children playing with shiny used cartridge shells by the school latrine, remembering me and my wartime childhood friends playing with live cartridges and gunpowder on the ridge of Soreh Hill at Sosa. We used to be the house boys for the American soldiers during the Korean War, and now the starved Vietnamese children were the house boys for us. Watching the young barefoot boys, the duplicates of myself, playing with the spent cartridges, I could not predict the future of these children, born in the war and fated to grow up in that same war, these children mired in the monstrous sinking republic infested with police officers and petty public servants and revenue officials who were engrossed in the pursuit of personal profits, fighting viciously to steal the last hoard of the ruined family, the corrupt politicians and administrators indulging in their perpetual hegemony for ephemeral power, the intellectuals poisoned by skepticism and defeatism, and the apathetic ordinary citizens like these daily cocooned in their hammocks hanging amidst the bombed rubble.

Somebody tugged at the sleeve of my trousers. I looked down. A young girl in a very clean white cotton dress, four or five years old, was squatting before me with a pinkish smile, thrusting out her tiny hand with tiny pinkish fingers.

"Chop chop?" the little girl said.

I searched my pockets but could not find anything to give her, not even a stick of chewing gum. I pantomimed for her that I had nothing with me and fell to the ground, hugging my stomach with an exaggerated frown, to tell her that I was also starving to death. When I raised myself, dusting my knees, the little girl smiled an understanding smile and hopped away.

I watched the refugees fighting in the dust around the truck to grab the clothes from the soldiers. I saw Trau who was standing a little distance off from the desperately waving crowd. The bandage of hog blood now gone from his head, the boy calmly watched the commotion. I noticed a pile of clothes at his feet. Momentarily a girl about eight years old came over to Trau and added another pair of trousers to the pile and Trau gave her a C-ration can. Then the girl went back to the commotion in the rising dust, wriggled through the howling crowd, and stood before a soldier handing out the clothes. She just stood there, innocently, not even thrusting her hand out. The soldier soon noticed the pitiful girl helplessly standing among the struggling grownups and promptly gave her a shirt. The girl quickly went back to Trau and collected another can. The boy pointed at another soldier handing out the clothes at the other side of the truck and the girl again wriggled into the crowd to reach the unsuspecting soldier. Remembering Trau and the little girl begging on the Ninh Hoa street, I chuckled, thinking, this boy would make a great master of a whorehouse some day, owing to his extraordinary flair for doing business with girls. But on second thought, I realized there was nothing funny about that. I was sorry to have entertained such a cruel thought about the boy. The other day Corporal Kim Chaeo threw stones at the town urchins running away with the C-ration cans they had stolen from our jeep parked before a grocery store in Ninh Hoa. I cursed and swore at him angrily that day; I thought the soldier had done wrong, throwing stones at the boys who had to turn into thieves because of the war. Corporal Kim could have been right, I thought, watching Trau. I was confused. I was not yet adept at judging anything about this country at war. Still, it was wrong for Corporal Kim to have thrown stones at the children that day.

The little girl, who had thrust her hand out at me a few minutes ago but had to go away empty-handed, hopped back to me. She smiled her pinkish smile again, offering me a paper bag containing a handful of cookies, and gestured that I could eat them.

"*Ong an gi khong?*" she said. "Chop chop. Okay."

On the thirteenth day of the operation, the 9th was finally relieved from guarding and maintaining order at Ba Hai refugee camp, but our new job was not so satisfying either. We were ordered to search again the two villages of Lac Binh and Lac An, where the Special Forces and the recon company had already searched during the first phase of the operation, and destroy any enemy elements hiding in underground shelters that the first wave might have missed. It was a humiliating job for any combat unit, but we had our orders. Glory was for the generals. The task was, however, better than guarding the hilltop tents or the Vietnamese peasants.

The piles of fresh red soil looked like scabby scars in the field of green grass at the spots where the Special Forces had buried and then excavated claymores and flare mines for retrieval when moving to a new position. Yellow shiny howitzer shells were scattered in the watery bed of rice paddies. There were empty C-ration cans everywhere. The foxholes clustered on a dike like crab holes. Grey buffalos, lost, loitered around leisurely and then scampered away, startled, when a gunship fired a rocket somewhere nearby. A hen peacefully pecked at a worm by the sewer ditch in the empty village. The signal corpsmen hurried to lay out the emergency telephone lines across the hamlets. A swarm of flies were sucking at the sticky death on the red entrails squeezing out of the torn belly of a buffalo butchered by shelling. The barbed wire entanglements installed by the narrow pathway as a defensive obstacle, and then abandoned by the ARVN troops years ago, were rusted dark brown. Mud-spattered A-tents were pitched along the path and two recon company soldiers were taking a catnap under the crumbling red barbs. Ankle-deep mud and stagnant rain water in the bomb craters. The soldier musing absent-mindedly on his crumpled poncho before the naked door post of a bombed house. The earthen wall crumbling. Somebody had spread palm leaves in his foxhole to cushion the clammy bottom.

The flat earthen huts in the village had no doors and the dark rooms were permeated with the stuffy scent of incense. In a shady corner room a wooden Buddha statuette was ensconced on an upright altar decorated with gaudy paper and cloth strips. Every house had a secret escape tunnel in the kitchen leading to the back yard or the open field—to run away from the Vietcong as well as from other intruders—and a bomb shelter inside or near each hut. My family used to have a bomb shelter like that at Kotchori in Puchon County where we had taken refuge. Years ago.

We searched for two days but failed to find any evidence even remotely related to possible Vietcong presence in the vicinity. The soldiers were tired and annoyed.

"I think what we heard about Vietnam at home was all lies," muttered Sergeant Chon Hisik, crushing an empty can with his hands. "We could have seen much more action at a rabbit hunt. Too damned boring. We haven't even seen a Vietcong, have we? It's really crazy to fight against a foe you can't see anywhere. Why the hell don't they come out and fight us?"

Everything was a repeat of everything else in our version of the war, the same situations eternally duplicating themselves, and the drama we had expected, or imagined, did not exist anywhere. We were exhausted and despondent, futilely tiring ourselves.

If the Allied Forces really wanted to terminate this war, or get anywhere at all, they had no other choice but to cross the 17th Parallel and overrun Hanoi. But that drastic final action would certainly spur the expansion of the war with inevitable Chinese intervention, as well as provoking fierce opposition worldwide. Armistice, on the other hand, would require that South Vietnam hand over a big chunk of territory below the 17th Parallel to Ho Chi Minh, and there was little chance that the National Liberation Front would respect the ceasefire agreements afterwards.

We kept digging in the watery rice paddies and the back yards of the peaceful seaside village. The enemy was not there. I felt my whole life would be wasted in that one single year I was supposed to spend here.

We found some consolation, though, in the last few days of the operation because the 9th Company was given the initiative in attacking the small patch of ground surrounding Hill 24, where we had witnessed Corporal Lee Kwanil's death. Some Vietcong might have been trapped there in the last nook which had not yet been searched by any of the friendly forces. We waited for the day to break, listening to the mortar shells blasting all over the hill throughout the night, hoping we would have a face-to-face encounter at long last.

The yellowish day broke over the field overcast with the nauseating smell of gunpowder, and the darkness began to peel off to reveal the clear blue sky over the Dong Hai sea. After spending the night on the pricking bed of sticky leaves on the slope, I scratched the mucus out of the corners of my eyes with the nail of my little finger, gargled with salty water to freshen my stuffy mouth, had a simple breakfast of crackers and cabbage pickles, and packed my knapsack.

When we finished organizing search parties after the regular roll call, the CO received a radio message from Battalion Headquarters not to leave the present position and to wait for further instructions. The company force of 140 men, who had been excited by the anticipation of assaulting the hill by themselves while other companies maintained the encirclement, were exasperated again.

"How much waiting do we have to do for one damned operation?" grumbled 2nd Lieutenant Choe Sangjun, the 3rd Platoon leader.

"Captain Oh of the Army Intelligence Detachment is on his way here," said Captain Kim Sanghyop, the company commander, tapping a cigarette out of the pack. "A Vietnamese woman surrendered herself as a VC sympathizer at the Xuan My refugee camp about an hour ago and confessed that her Vietcong husband is now hiding somewhere near Hill 24. That woman is worried sick about her husband because she heard we're going to launch a concentrated attack over the area, and she asked the intelligence people if his life would be spared if she brings him in. AID gave her a deal, of course. She volunteered to go out to find and persuade him to surrender without resistance."

As the blood-colored rays started to spread over the grassy slope, a muddy jeep arrived at the foot of the hill and a Vietnamese woman stepped down, escorted by a stocky captain with narrow squinting eyes.

"*De theo toi,*" Captain Oh told the woman and came over to us. The woman glanced at us, and then at the hill, with her swollen eyes. The intelligence officer explained something to the company commander. Then he explained something to the woman and gave her two sheets of printed paper. The paper slips were safe conduct leaflets in Vietnamese, Korean and English, the written guarantee of safety for Vietcong defectors.

The woman read the safe conduct slips and nodded approvingly. Her tense face was stained with dust and tears. Gripping the ticket firmly in her trembling hand, she began to climb the slope. With long black hair billowing down her back, the woman in black pajama clothes disappeared into the thorny brush. We waited.

The woman returned in less than a half hour. She came down the hill alone. She still held the safe conduct leaflet in her clenched fist. She did not cry. Captain Oh asked several questions of the listless woman and then told the company commander that she had found her husband in a puddle of muddy water, dead. With a dazed expression, the woman went down the hill and drove away in the jolting jeep, around the deserted Buddhist shrine and along the bumpy road. The sky was clear and the green landscape of the field glistened as if sprayed over with crystal particles. The jeep disappeared into the glimmering sunlight.

"Move out!" the company commander shouted.

Like passengers who had been waiting all night for a local train at a countryside station, the soldiers slouched up slowly, picking up their rifles and knapsacks, and started to climb the path.

We found the dead Vietcong soon. There were two of them. They were sprawled in a watery bomb crater, so covered with slime and blood that we could not tell where they had been hit. The torso of one body was half buried in the dirt, his bony heels sticking out, and all the ten fingers of his hands were cupped as if trying to grab the empty air. I saw the traces of where the woman must have been digging in the earthen debris by their faces.

The dead husband of the woman who had volunteered to go into the combat zone—maybe he was the sniper who had killed Corporal Lee, I thought, trudging down the slope several hours later.

The Korean newspapers, delivered to our company the next week, carried big stories under headlines like: ROK TROOPS OPEN VIET HIGHWAY 1, even though we had only waddled around the rice paddies of a peaceful plain for weeks and then returned to base, but the newspapers insisted that we had somehow opened the highway that stretched all the way from Saigon to Hanoi which had been untraffickable for twenty years. But in truth the road remained impassable, and not much had happened on Hill 24.

I cannot remember if the boy Trau suggested it first or I asked, but we agreed it was time for me to make a visit to his house. I was curious. Somehow I believed his life might be the same as my own during the Korean war, and his house identical to our shabby hovel by the three-forked road at Inchon where we stayed temporarily when my father worked as a carpenter at the American base nearby. Carrying a bag stuffed with chocolates, chewing gum, and some leftover C-ration cans containing pound cake and turkey, I went with the boy.

Trau lived at Tuc My, around the Xuan My cliff, with a commanding view of the Dong Hai sea. The clear green expanse of

the South China Sea stretched out to the horizon from one end of the
small seaside village situated just beyond the local cemetery filled with
dwarf cactus and white stone crosses. Inland, grey buffalo, as massive
and menacing as rhinoceroses, loitered amidst the green and golden
patterns of the rice paddies that spread far out to the grey rubber trees
planted along a dirt road with geometric regularity by the French.
Trau's house had not had its grass roof replaced for at least three years;
there was nobody at home who could do man's work. The bleached
thatch reminded me of a Japanese farmhouse, but the walls and the
outside structure had a definite Western look, showing the French
influence over popular Vietnamese architecture. In another Asian
country it might be mistaken for a villa built by a misanthrope at a
seaside resort, as the house was elaborately fenced with flowering
tropical plants. But it was surprisingly barren and gloomy inside. The
dusky space, that did not even have any partitioning between the
bedroom and the kitchen, was sparsely occupied by one double bed, a
hammock, and refrigerator. Everything looked too conspicuous and
enormous in the dank rectangular cavern. There was an old wooden
chest chipped in over a dozen places, spoons and bowls piled neatly on
e earthen sink, some clothes and two new conical *non* hats hanging on
unpapered plaster wall, a pair of spare sandals, old magazines, and a
ful of odds and ends. The floor was plain dirt, and I noticed some
on cans, coffee jars, a bayonet, and other army supplies heaped in
rner. Trau must have collected this loot. And by the southern
v I saw gauzy pink woman's underwear hanging like a quaint half-
hat feminine color did not seem to belong in this dismal house.
did not seem to have been notified of my coming. I was Trau's
t, anyway, not Hai's. Her nonchalant attitude showed that she also
ght my visit had nothing to do with her. Hai and I did not exchange
formal greetings nor did we need an introduction, for we had
dy met at the refugee collection camp. She just gave me a simple
owledging smile without any modifying words and offered me a cup
ang on a lacquered wooden tray. Her black straight hair billowed
own to her waist like a sweeping river when she stooped down to put
the tray on the bed; I was sitting on her bed because there was no other
place to sit. She was in a thin beige *ao dai* dress that clearly revealed the
seductive shoulder straps of her black brassiere underneath. A subdued
peace emanated from her calm face; she spoke very little. Sitting astride
his hammock, Trau tried to prompt an intimate—or at least a friendly—

conv᎐ ᎐tion between Hai and me, busily studying our expressions alt᎐᎐nately, posing as an interpreter with his broken English and scanty Korean vocabulary.

I suggested that all three of us to go together to the beach, because it was depressing and irksome to sit around and continue a tedious limping conversation in the damp and dreary house. Trau said something very fast in Vietnamese, tugging at his mother, who blankly gazed at me for a moment. Then she said, "Okay," in English, packed some fruit from the refrigerator in a shopping bag, and followed us out into the blinding sun.

White foam rolled up to the shore with the lapping waves. Swaying palm trees dozed in the languid afternoon. There were no seagulls. Shells half-buried in the sand glittered like quartz. Trau dog-paddled around in the shallow water while Hai and I enjoyed the pleasant drowsiness on the hot sand.

Half an hour later, Trau hurriedly put on his clothes, saying he had forgotten to bring a floating tube from home, grinned at me, and then hopped away toward the thatched house. When Trau disappeared around the fence, Hai and I felt lost, like two uninvited guests at a family wedding party. We waited for a while but Trau did not come back. I realized Trau had gone somewhere not to return. That little boy made himself scarce so that his mother and I could have the privacy he thought we needed. A precocious boy, Trau was. Had he schemed to get his mother a lover?

Since it was apparent that Trau had disappeared to let us get to know each other, I thought it senseless to sit mutely and just look at each other like two idiots at their first encounter. I tried to chat with Hai about someti᎐g, anything, but that was not a matter as simple as I had assum᎐.

"Do you speak English?" I asked in English.

She kept quiet for a while and then said, in English, "I don't know. I speak little." She showed how little with her fingers.

I tried to ask if she had any other relatives, but she knew too little English to explain anything. She kept silent, thinking. A short pause ensued. Then she said something in Vietnamese that I could not understand. I had not been in Vietnam long enough to speak fluent Vietnamese.

I told her that I could not understand: *"Khong biet."*

Another pause.

I asked could she speak French? *"Parlez français?"*

She hesitated for a moment, thinking again, and then said she could, *"Un peu,"* a little.

Somewhat relieved, I told her in French about my family back in Korea. Hai looked at me in consternation. She could understand the basic words, like *pere* and *mere,* but not my explanations about them. She was at a loss, blushing, as I tried to elaborate a point, and apologized self-consciously, *"Je ne comprendre pas."*

So I started to speak slowly and distinctly. Hai listened attentively, and quickly smiled when she understood something, but then as quickly turned uneasy, perplexed, lost in a maze. I had to give up. This conversation was too much of a torture for Hai.

After another long pause, it occurred to me that the Southeast Asian countries belonged to the same Chinese cultural domain as Korea. With new hope twinkling in my mind, I picked up a shell and wrote in the sand:

知漢字 Meaning: know Chinese letters?

Hai's face brightened. She emphatically pointed at the letter 'know', nodding her head with a confident smile.

We began to communicate through the most primitive method of writing and erasing Chinese letters in the sand, I with the shell and Hai with her slender index finger. It was like a pantomime. We even added drawings when the ideographs could not amply deliver what we wanted to tell the other person. We were as mischievous and jubilant as young children secretly scribbling on a neighbor's fence. Hai even laughed.

Once we decided to behave like children, there was nothing to be ashamed of, and we did not hesitate to perform charades and antic gestures, sometimes using onomatopoeic sounds. The dazzling sunshine poured down over the exultant beach.

I went to see her again about seven weeks later.

After the operation over the Van Gia area, the 9th Company and Ngoc Diem, a fishing village near Xuan My, established a relationship under the G-5 guidelines to promote "Dai-Viet friendship" as a part of the Division's psychological warfare programs. We followed up with routine good works indicated in the manual—building and donating a community clinic to the village, distributing rice and clothes to the villagers, sponsoring the elders' party and other ceremonious local events.

The elders' party, one of the first things the Korean soldiers did when their unit moved to a new area to win over the hearts of the populace, was held at Ngoc Diem's village square. All the old men and women in the vicinity were invited to this public and rather ostentatious celebration so that the Vietnamese peasants might witness and tell the neighboring hamlets that the Daihans respected their elders as much as the Vietnamese did theirs, because both nations considered filial piety a traditional institution and a major virtue in their similar community life.

Festoons of colorful paper strips and Korean and Vietnamese flags hung from one palm tree to another all around the square as at an autumn sports competition for the countryside grammar school children. The old farmers, everyone with the identical emaciated Ho Chi Minh look, in identical pajama-like black garb, and towels tied in an identical way around their heads like Indian turbans, sat in two files facing each other along the lengthy plank table loaded with coconuts, Korean ginseng wine, canned beer, bananas, and cold food, wearily waiting for the feeding time to begin after the speeches by the Khanh Hoa Province officials and the Korean army officers. The indifferent wizened faces of the elderly guests showed absolutely no excitement, or any other emotion, while the army photographers were busy taking propaganda pictures of the grateful beneficiaries for tomorrow's news release dispatch to Saigon. These pictures would be sent to Korea via diplomatic pouch by the press corps in Saigon, and in a week the Seoul newspapers would simultaneously carry the identical stories and pictures provided by the military, pompously emphasizing the Daihan humanitarian approach to this difficult war. The farmers did not care. They would have a free drink. They had been tortured and cheated and used by every group of people that had crossed their path.

The eating started, while a martial art squad in white uniforms gave a taekwondo martial-arts demonstration, the favorite entertainment presented at various ceremonies and public events. The village children, barefoot and tanned dark like Negroes, gathered in the square to watch the Daihan *linh* giving terrific yells and breaking planks and bricks and roof tiles with their naked knuckles. At another corner, the village women of all ages were kicking up a row, grabbing the clothes and C-rations distributed by the G-5 soldiers. At the newly dedicated clinic, that had been constructed next to the square for the convenience of the photographers, Sergeant Chin Sochol and two other medics from the Division Headquarters Clinic were handing out some household medicines or applying ointments to the infected cuts and boils and blisters of the frightened children and the decrepit aged patients, who looked like they were suffering from starvation rather than sickness.

In the afternoon, I managed to slip out of Ngoc Diem, asking Sergeant Chon to cover for me. "Hey, where're you going?" he asked. "AWOL on the battlefield is punishable by a firing squad, you know that? You so homesick you decided to walk all the way home or what?"

I just told him it was important for me to go to Tuc My, and I might as well go there this afternoon since Tuc My was so close to Ngoc Diem. "Getting an official leave from the CO is so difficult, you know," I said. Sergeant Chon Hisik did not ask me anything else, for he knew where I was going. And he believed it was an important matter if I said it was. I sneaked out of the village, carrying a bag in which I had packed several C-ration cans and walked for twenty minutes to Hai's village. I knew it was dangerous to walk around the Vietnamese countryside alone, but somehow I was not so much concerned about my personal danger that afternoon. In my pocket, there was Tabu, a gift of perfume for Hai. I had made a special trip weeks earlier to the Division PX with Sergeant Chon to buy that perfume.

"Imagine Sergeant Han Kiju buying perfume!" he had teased me, grinning. "What's the historic occasion? You found a *con gai* lover or what?"

I told him about the exchange Hai and I had had through the Chinese letters scribbled in the sand.

"Hey, what do you know! Gentle cats steal the fish first, they say." He laughed. "Who could have ever guessed that you'd find a lover here? And a married woman, too. A secret love affair with a married woman? You? Jesus!"

"She doesn't have a husband," I said, defensively. "She's a widow."

Around four o'clock I arrived at Hai's house. I stopped before the gate, decorated with moist red flowers, and called for Trau. There was no answer. I called again, but still there was no answer. Nobody was home, and I was at a loss, not knowing what to do. I decided I had better wait inside until Trau or Hai returned home; the curious sidelong glances of the villagers would make me uncomfortable if I just stood there by the gate, waiting, like a jilted serenader. I was about to enter the gate when a sallow-faced Vietnamese man in a police uniform, about thirty and very short, hurried out of the house like a fleeing burglar, glanced at me with a frown and then went around to the back yard. Momentarily I heard him start the engine of his motorcycle and blast away along the dirt road to Highway 1.

Something was not right. I felt I should not be there at this moment. Perhaps I should have gone back to Ngoc Diem, but I had a bag stuffed with C-rations for Trau. And the Tabu. I stepped inside, somehow driven by a psychological need not to believe what I had just seen. No policeman had come out of the house, no one. I wanted to believe that Hai had not been with any man that afternoon. She could not be doing such a thing in her own home. In broad daylight. I must have seen an illusion.

Hai, in that conspicuous gauzy pink slip that had been hanging by the window like a symbolic banner, stood helplessly at one corner in the shade, where she could not hide much of herself. Clumsily trying to conceal her breasts and thighs with her hands, she blushed scarlet as if she had been caught red-handed in sin. She apparently had seen me waiting outside and then coming in, but was too flurried by my sudden appearance to tidy away the tracks of her shame before I entered. Her disheveled hair and the crumpled sheet on the bed, and a used tissue discarded on the dirt floor, plainly showed me what had been going on there a minute ago. I did not know what to do. I just stood there, vaguely hoping for someone to appear and give me directions.

The shock and despair slowly ebbed from Hai's expression to be replaced by overwhelming sadness, and then she turned to face the wall. Covering her face with her hands, she began to sob silently, her shoulders throbbing almost invisibly. I put down the C-ration bag on the floor and went over to the corner to turn Hai toward me. She would not look at me, now weeping uncontrollably like an innocent child. I knew the best thing I could do was to leave her alone. After a perplexed pause, I took out the cold tiny glass bottle from my pocket and placed it in her trembling hand. She gazed down at the perfume bottle in her palm, wet with tears.

I walked around the rice paddies near the village to spend some time before returning to Ngoc Diem so that Sergeant Chon would not get curious why I came back so soon. But one hour was still too early.

"Boy, it was quick," he said, chuckling.

Several months later Hai told me that she had been a "part-time concubine" to the police officer. Until she "become frien'" with me, the policeman used to drop by to sleep with her about twice a month, but he did not give her any money nor provide means for her livelihood at all. In a country where men were so rare, a young widow could not expect anything more from any man than an occasional visit to her bed. Hai also confessed to me on another occasion that she had to go out to Nha Trang to solicit American soldiers one or two nights a month when she and Trau had virtually nothing to eat. The policeman had probably mistaken me for a day customer when we came across each other that unfortunate afternoon. After our accidental encounter, the officer stopped coming to see her, because he believed Hai had become a full-time prostitute inviting her customers to her home. The policeman would not have much trouble getting other willing women elsewhere.

"This may sound corny, but it's all because of this damn war," Sergeant Chon said, when I told him about the policeman. "But you have to thank this miserable war for meeting Hai. She is not wholly responsible for her wretched life, you know, and you could show some sympathy for her, okay?"

It was not exactly out of sympathy alone that I went to see Hai again. As I went through combat and one operation after another, I realized she was a shelter for me, an escape from the ordeals of the war. When an operation or a patrol mission lasted a long time and my whole body began to smell like a rotting rag in summertime, I often escaped in my imagination to the sunny shore where Hai and I had scribbled in the sand. At times I even felt grateful for that precocious Trau, who had brought his mother and me together by his little scheme. Returning to the base from the jungle after a long mission, I used to feel a reassuring consolation stir quietly in my heart with the expectation of seeing Hai again.

After the policeman incident she grew conspicuously self-conscious, speaking very little and keeping constantly alert to my moods. Whenever I went to her house, she behaved in my presence like a repenting wife—a taciturn spouse forever grieving over a sin that her husband had forgiven a long time ago but which she could never absolve herself of. It did take a long while, but she gradually overcame her guilty feeling. In the meantime, my Vietnamese improved fast and I taught Hai French and English. Our communication was getting better day by day, and I felt we were collaborating on a cautious exploration. I also came to know a lot more about Hai herself.

Her name meant "two" in Vietnamese, and when I asked her why she had a numerical name, she gave a very simple explanation. "My family many children," she said. "Seven daughters. One son plus. Parents give us number names, *Mot, Hai, Ba, Bon, Nam, Sau, Bay, Tam.* One, Two, Tree, Paw, Pie, Sic, Sec, Ate."

Her husband, Thanh, died as an ARVN *thieu-uy,* a second lieutenant, four years earlier during a night engagement with the local Vietcong on a bridge at Ban Me Thuot. I could not understand exactly what had happened on the bridge that night because she gave up the detailed explanation when she found it too difficult to describe the circumstances surrounding his demise, but I could understand that Thanh had been hit in the leg, fell into the river, and his body was never found. Her parents and siblings had scattered in all directions during a Vietcong night raid against their village so as to escape public execution by the VC. An army officer's family was a prime target for terrorism. Hai had never gone back home since. Nobody in her family had. Her older sister, Mot, used to run a vegetable store at Da Lat, and Bon had been a dancer at an American Air Force club in Tan Son Nhut Airport. Hai was not sure where they were now. She had heard from a relative in Phu Cat that her old father, a retired ARVN master sergeant, had been hanged by the Vietcong at Ben Ghe last fall. She knew nothing about the rest of her family.

We met once every two or three weeks and strolled along the beach, exchanging broken dialogue, smiling, laughing, throwing sand at each other. We, the two abandoned souls seeking shelter in each other, became affectionate and attached, like a brother and sister. When I was with her, I did not want to recognize or accept any other reality except for our own small world by the sea. She seemed to feel the same way about us, about me, about the Tuc My shore that exclusively belonged to us. The two of us existed all alone on that isolated golden shore. Not even Trau was allowed to intrude upon our sunny beach, and the boy knew it. Trau always stayed away when Hai and I were out on the sand.

II

We were growing tough, tempered by the real training—in the jungle—learning the quick and sure skills to find and eliminate the enemy. Our daily life was an endless succession of airlift deployments, search-and-destroy operations and night missions. We were supple and tenacious, like a whip. The war was slowly revealing its true aspects to us as the months accumulated.

In the ten days after the conclusion of the fifth Operation Bulldozer, sixteen Vietnamese civilians were killed when a Lambretta hit a mine installed by the Vietcong at Xe Chai Bridge. In another incident, three American soldiers lost their lives at Van Gia and all weapons were taken in the VC raid on an ammunition truck heading for the 28th Regiment Headquarters at Tuy Hoa.

More and more discomforting rumors circulated. The scattered forces of the regular 2nd NVA Division had infiltrated south through the mountainous terrain and were now closing in from north of the 9th ROK Infantry Division's operational area to secure their new stronghold in Khanh Hoa Province. These infiltrators were expected to join with the local VC elements and launch a massive offensive against the Koreans in the Ninh Hoa area. According to the analysis of the intelligence gathered by the Vietnamese agents planted in various villages and the reconnaissance missions by our troops, a major battle was imminent.

One day the whole family of Hoang Van Thai, the farmer at Tu Bong who had been supplying information on Vietcong movements in the Lac Ninh area, were executed by the enemy. The villagers said a platoon of Vietcong fighters had come down from Hon Heo Mountain and raided the village in the middle of the night. They forced the villagers out of their homes to the village square, tied the Hoangs, including the four-year-old daughter, together, ordered them to sit on a bundle of dynamite sticks and blew them up.

Since then information conspicuously decreased but the recon reports on enemy movements suddenly increased. The enemy was ceaselessly moving, gathering somewhere near us.

The soldiers pretended to be calm but I could see the anxiety shrouding their faces. If we went out to the listening posts at night, the palm trees and the rice paddies and the hills and the field, and everything around us, seemed to slowly swell with a grotesque terror in the suffocating dark. As days passed more and more soldiers were infected by a nagging, contagious fear that the unseen, unknown enemy was approaching.

The AIU report predicted the primary target was the 51st Field Artillery Battalion located only 700 yards northwest of Division Headquarters. The attack would help boost the morale of the local Vietcong, who were being pressured by the newly deployed Daihan forces, and win sympathizers locally. It was a basic strategy of General Vo Nguyen Giap, the operational brain of Ho Chi Minh since the Dien Bien Phu days. But there was no doubt that their ultimate target was Division Headquarters itself.

Amid this uneasy atmosphere, the 9th Company moved out to a hill

near Tu Bong and built a new tactical base to intercept the advancing
enemy from the Hon Ba Mountain region. We built bunkers, piled up
sandbags and C-ration boxes filled with dirt, installed a three-fold
barrier of barbed wire entanglements and buried claymore mines all
around the base. The nervous soldiers hastened their work, worrying
that the enemy might attack before the defenses were completed. The
company commander was irritable all the time, flaring up at his men
every minute. And night after night, the 9th Company, the northern
protector of Division Headquarters, waited in the dark surrounded by
foreboding silence.

The night the 3rd Platoon was out in the trench 300 meters outside
the barbed wire barrier surrounding the company base, we were responsible for the defense of the outer perimeter until daybreak, when all the
listening posts and ambush squads would come back in.

It was almost the lunar fifteenth night of the month, and so bright
was the moon that we could read letters from home by its light. The
soldiers were relieved because the sky was cloudless; the enemy would
not foolishly attack us on a clear night like this, risking exposure in the
moonlight.

Corporal Kwon Yongjun urged Piggie Chang to tell about the fancy
hip work of Pak Kwija, the girl who had given Piggie a farewell fuck in
broad daylight at Yangpyong Inn, so we had to hear the same old story
yet again. Corporal Chae Mugyom was mumbling about the wondrous
chewing tobacco he had found in the U.S. Army-issued Sundry Pack.
Sergeant Chi Taesik, the radioman, reported to the company CP that it
was all quiet and put down his PRC-6 on the floor of the trench to smear
sticky insect repellent on the nape of his neck. Yun "Boar" Chilbok
shook the ration cans one by one to listen and decide what he would have
for a snack. Sergeant Chon Hisik was writing a very long letter to his
sweetheart, Sujin, using the stock of his M-1 rifle as a writing pad, and
his tri-color ball-point pen for emphatic visual effects, clicking it again
and again, and every once in a while going back to read what he had
written so far on the thin decorated stationery he had bought yesterday
at the Regimental PX especially for her. Pyon Chinsu was not doing
anything at all.

It was 0100. Corporal Chae had been mumbling and sucking at the
chewing tobacco like a cow rolling the cud in her mouth, his chin
resting on his folded arms. Suddenly he stiffened beside me. He craned
his neck quickly, tapping my forearm, braced on the dirt mound of the

trench, and croaked in a choking voice, "Look, Sergeant. Over there. At twelve o'clock. Something moving."

The soldiers around us looked out at the moonlit field, grabbing their rifles, suddenly freezing as if electrocuted.

From the thorn brush, two hundred meters in front of us, something flat, like a huge lizard, crawled out slowly. The alert signal was passed from one soldier to the next in the trench by whispers and nudging elbows. We silently fastened the chin straps of our helmets, cautiously fed cartridges into the chambers of our rifles, checked flak jackets and quietly prepared for the combat. The radioman reported the situation to the CP. Some soldiers whispered in the eerie brightness of the moon:

"Cong? Right? Vietcong?"

"Isn't it strange they try to get us at the full moon?"

"Wonder if it's a buffalo."

"No chance. Buffalos don't crawl on their bellys."

"Maybe wild dogs looking for leftovers."

"There's another. At three o'clock."

We could not know when and how they had sneaked up so close, but two more of the flat lizard-like forms were slithering over the rice paddy dike about 50 meters away, the width of a boulevard. They were not buffalos nor roaming curs. Two Vietcong, their naked bodies smeared all over with dark slimy mud for camouflage, were sliding across the watery rice paddies towards us, the slings of their heavy AK 47A assault rifles tied round their wrists. They were VC all right. Daring to launch an attack on a night of a bright moon like this, defying logic, flouting the conventions of war. Foolishness is merely another face of genius. Rebels. Revolutionaries. Breaking old rules.

"They probably wanted to see us more clearly," someone whispered.

I heard Piggie Chang squawk breathlessly. "VC! They're coming! Report to the CP! Tell the CO we have a visual contact with the enemy!"

"Real VC? Are they real VC?"

I could not hold my rifle firmly enough; somehow I felt my wrist bones had been disjointed. There must be more of them, a lot more, than these three. Somewhere, in the dark out there . . . Those three must be the scouts, and soon, hundreds of them would swarm over us, hundreds and hundreds.

"What should we do, Sergeant Han? Open fire?" somebody asked me, but I could not tell whose voice it was. I was too shaky and confused.

"Calling Seagull, calling Seagull," the radioman whispered some-
where, but I could not tell where he was either. "This is Weasel Three.
Seagull, Seagull, the rats are doing Hong the Magic Boy towards us.
Respond, Seagull; respond, Seagull."

The enemy was moving. I felt my whole view was crowded with their
dark heavy shadows. This was the first time that I had ever seen the live
moving enemy before my naked eyes; the enemy crawling straight
toward us, toward me.

Staring at the three Vietcong gliding across the rice paddies, I
dreaded the moment when we would have to shoot at each other, face to
face; I dreaded the inevitable moment inching towards me along with
the dark crawling shapes. Could I shoot straight at those Vietcong?
Could I shoot and kill them, aiming at their skulls as we had learned to
do at boot camp, in commando training, as we had learned from the drill
instructors and the manuals, placing the target lightly on the level line
of the front and rear sights, holding your breath calmly and then
squeezing the trigger the way you squeeze the toothpaste out of the
tube, the way you squeeze a girl's soft nipples.

"We have to wait," Sergeant Chi Taesik said to Sergeant Chon Hisik
when he finished his radio report to the CP. "The CO will give us
further instructions soon enough."

Captain Kim Sanghyop ordered us to wait for a while and observe
enemy movements while he reported the situation to the 3rd Battalion
Headquarters and alerted the 51st Forward Artillery Battalion. We had
to remain still until we could confirm the size of the enemy main force
and its direction of advance.

My breath skipped every once in a while as I waited, barely standing
on my shaky legs. Why was I so afraid? Why did I now fear the war that I
had often considered a ridiculous and contemptible farce? Had I a
sudden premonition of my own death? Was this it? The military crematorium at Nha Trang, a handful of ash, the samples of hair and nails
the HQ Company clerk had collected from us, home, the National
Cemetery at Tongjak-dong, a white cement cross at my grave . . .

Pyon Chinsu said, in a terrified voice, somewhere in the dark trench,
"There's more coming, corporal, over there. From the banana grove."

About fifteen Vietcong emerged from the banana grove, sank into the
knee-deep rice plants that began to stir and ripple as the black slimy
creatures wriggled towards our position, and then more enemy—more
than a hundred of them—rose slowly here and there like enormous

shoots of human plants growing out of the ground. They began to walk towards us, not crawling on their bellies this time, but walking erect toward us like professional hunters approaching the bush where their game was hiding.

"Hundreds of Cong, Seagull, hundreds of them! I can't even count them, sir!"

The company commander urgently ordered us to immediately open fire but the soldiers had already started shooting everywhere; they did not need to wait for the official recognition of the emergency. Flare mines popped off here and there to brighten the perimeter and my vision blurred in the madness of noise, nauseating gunpowder smell and insane cacophony of indiscriminate firing.

"There're more than five hundred of them!"

"We're going to die. We will die. All of us!"

"Shoot! Shoot, bastard!"

Hundreds of half-naked Vietcong swarmed across the rice paddies, shooting. They looked so enormous, every one of them, the dark shapeless forms splashing across the water, dashing towards us. Scattered rifle shots, a scream, someone yelling, spasmodic burps of automatic weapons, the flash of an exploding hand grenade, tracer bullets flying away like a glowing red arrow leaving a clear track in the dark air, rockets and mortar shells whizzing over our heads from the company base to the enemy positions, bursting incandescence of exploding claymores, recoilless rifles and machine guns blasting off, 105-millimeter howitzer shells tearing up the rice paddies. And in this stormy orchestra of killing noises, I suddenly heard a gruesomely distinct sound. The Vietcong beating their gongs. They made the dark air vibrate. The enemy was coming to us, dancing to the incantatory sound as primitive as Scotch bagpipes. And then, through some mysterious malfunction in my nervous system, I suddenly could not hear anything. I was deaf to all sound around me. The silent pantomime of killing flashed and swayed in the dark film of air like a billowing gigantic negative of a black and white photograph montaged with bullets and shells shattering and spattering into a million fragments, and empty cartridge shells bursting out of a machine gun, the white moonlight bleached whiter by the flares, the dark cannibals dancing and surging toward us like a huge wave across the etched rectangular patterns of the open rice paddies. I could not even hear my own rifle firing.

I was startled back to chilly consciousness a while later when a hand grenade exploded just before the trench, throwing a shovelful of dirt in my face. The haze cleared off, and the cracking rifle shots and thundering booms and various resonant notes of explosions poured in to envelop and swallow the savage *clang-clang-clang* of the gongs. The enemy seemed to have been nailed behind the rice paddy dikes by the friendly fire; they stuck to the ground like turtles and continued firing back at us, the muzzles spitting flickers of white splotches among the dark lumpy shapes on the dike.

I glanced at my watch. The battle had been going on for forty minutes, but I could not tell what the overall situation was like. I had no time for such a leisurely analysis. I just continued firing at the field of disturbed dark. As if swept by a mass motion without any motive or purpose, mechanically driven by subconsciousness, by instinct, we shot up the flare bombs, pulled the pins and threw hand grenades, replaced the magazines of our rifles, fired and fired again into the long night. We had to defend our lives by ourselves, because reinforcements could not reach us until daybreak. We did not need any logical strategy for that— to survive, that was the only thing that mattered to us.

The muzzle of a machine gun glowed faintly in the dark with the red heat of too much firing; Sergeant Chon Hisik gasped and sucked at his canteen. The chaos before the Creation surrounded my whole being. Suddenly the sound of gongs rose to a clanging roar, sweeping over the earth, and with a battle cry, the Vietcong fighters arose from the ground like numerous squirming larvae crawling on the long wavy tentacles of a giant octopus, and started to swarm toward us again.

It was at this moment that Pyon Chinsu caught my eyes. When I looked around to see how others were facing the enemy I saw their pale faces perspire in the moonlight, and three soldiers away from me, I also saw Pyon Chinsu crouching in the bottom of the trench, his rifle abandoned on the dirt abutment, whimpering. I could not actually hear him weep, but the contorted mouth and the crumpled muddy face showed every sign of his crying. Hugging his knees with his hands, his shoulders twitching, he sobbed.

Nobody paid any attention to what Pyon Chinsu was doing. They did not have any time to look aside. I looked away from him, feeling repulsed. I clicked my carbine to semi-automatic with stiffened fingers and fired one shot after another into the emptiness. That was the only thing I could do for the moment against the frenzy of the Vietcong attack.

I had an illusion that the eyes of the Vietcong rushing to us were suddenly enlarged to enormous dimensions like a bizarre face whose one particular part was blown up by a warped lens. Their enormous eyes, spouting icy phosphorescent glints, seemed to be staring at me, at me alone. And I thought the flame shooting out of my rifle was a destructive power spurting from my desperate urge to eliminate the other life for the sake of preserving my own. The gigantic eyes of the enemy and the flashes spurting out of the muzzle kept growing, enlarging, swelling until they filled the whole flare-littered sky. That spitting flame was an agonized scream of life.

Again I could not hear the sounds of the killing tools; I could hear only the thud and splash of the bodies falling, dead, into the rice paddies. They were dying! They were dead! And then instantly chaos poured down again from the sky. Waving their hands, hurling grenades, shrieking, roaring, the enemy threw themselves into our trench, surging over the helpless soldiers trying to fight off the sea with feeble sticks. They did not spare their lives to get to us. It was no time for us to conserve ammunition in fighting them off. I clicked my rifle back to automatic, frantically fired crisscross at anything that moved before me, snatched off the pins and automatically hurled a whole boxful of grenades, and when the enemy jumped at me like black kangaroos from all sides, I threw away the rifle because they were too close to shoot, pulled out and wielded my bayonet at random not to allow anybody, anything, to come near me. Feeling a chaotic desolation that I was left alone in the middle of an insane massacre, I slipped into an escape shelter and, pressing my back on the dirt wall, gasping breathlessly, I touched the hair of whatever silhouette appeared before me, and quickly shouted "It's me, it's me!" in Korean if it was a crew-cut head. If it had long hair, I stabbed and stabbed and stabbed. But my bayonet kept stabbing empty air, and my hand, that had grabbed something a second ago, was empty too.

In the trench the enemy and the Korean soldiers bounced around like blind clowns, seeking each other and running away from each other; and a while later, the Vietcong main force passed through our line, and, like a pack of curs, rushed to the barbed wire defense barrier surrounding the company base.

I felt weak, my knees wobbly, and I collapsed, flopped down on the ground, staggering with exhaustion, my whole body sticky and numb. My consciousness turned blurry as fear throbbed up from my stomach to my choking throat, the fear that we would be individually checked off by the enemy after daybreak and the survivors shot one by one, for we had fallen behind the enemy line.

In all that chaos, I had a brief moment of solitary peace. Dark figures, both the enemy and friendly soldiers, rushed back and forth along the trench a few inches from me, but I squatted down and stayed motionless in the escape shelter, like a pupa in a cocoon, watching the passing shadows, a spectator. Temporary reprieve from the battle. The combat was inches away from me but I had retreated from the acts of war, hiding in my cocoon, listening to the dull sounds of the passing feet in the illusory quiet.

I wondered what Pyon Chinsu might be doing now. War is terrible, a horror. But he apparently did not know it would be this terrifying. I did not know this either.

I wanted to talk to somebody. Where was everybody? Sergeant Chon Hisik, the squad leader, Pong-Gyol, Piggie Chang, Lieutenant Choe Sangjun, the platoon leader, Sergeant Chi Taesik, Tap-Tap-Tap the radioman, Private Pyon Chinsu, the great painter of Charlton Heston, Corporal Kim Chaeo, the Yeller . . . they had been with me. Where were they now?

Then I heard Chon Hisik shout from the next escape shelter. Sergeant Chon was alive. "The radioman is wounded," he was yelling into the PRC-6. "Shell our position, sir! Concentrate the howitzer fire on our position. And fire!" He was calling in an indiscriminate shelling over our heads. "We're overrun and I think most of the enemy force is concentrated over here. There're simply too many of them. We can't fight them all, sir. No. No. I tried. But I can't find the platoon leader. I don't care if some of us have to die. I can't find any other survivors and we're going to die anyway. All of us. You've got to clean up this place. That's the only chance we've got to fight back the Cong, sir!"

Friendly fire began to shower us. I saw the claymore mines explode outside the company defense barrier through the barrage of dirt gushing up all around the trench. In the white flash of mortar shells, the Vietcong danced to their death. Armfuls of dirt poured down to bury us, to bury the enemy.

Hand-to-hand combat was over by the time the fire ceased to pound us, but I remained crouched in my shelter. Someone crawled toward me along the trench. I staggered up, thinking he was Chon Hisik. He raised his hand to strike, to stab me with something, with his bayonet.

"It's me, it's me," I shouted urgently, but it was too late. It was Pyon Chinsu. It was too dark to be sure of anything else, but I was sure it was Pyon Chinsu who stabbed me. I could not tell where he had struck but I felt an excruciating pain in my abdomen, and was thinking, *This is it, I'm dying now.*

12

I thought I must be at a vineyard somewhere on the Mediterranean until I realized that I was lying on the wet floor of a cold trench. I must not die here, I thought, sitting up.

My luminous watch showed it was 0225 hours. I could hear the sound of the battle still raging somewhere. I raised myself, reeling on feeble legs, and looked around outside the trench. The rice paddies were littered with fresh bomb craters and the battle was most fierce at the barbed wire fence of the company base. A wasteland. Devastated. I could not find any Vietcong around the trench; we had been isolated behind the enemy offensive line. I could not find Pyon Chinsu.

I flopped down again, despairing, and ran my hand over the wound. I had been wrong; I was stabbed in the left thigh, not in the abdomen. My trousers were soaked in blood, but the wound did not seem to be so bad. My left thigh was cut about an inch to the inside and blood squished under my testicles.

I pulled out the constriction bandage from my cartridge belt and staunched the blood, already thickly congealed. Staggering up, I picked up an abandoned carbine nearby, replaced the magazine and observed the combat situation again. Despite the bright moonlight, I could not see the base clearly because of the distance, but I saw that the northwestern barbed wire fence in the sector of the 2nd Platoon had been demolished, and hand-to-hand combat was going on at the helipad.

The forward trench was now out of the enemy attack range and I felt like a straggler. I started to crawl slowly along the trench to see if any other soldier was alive. Now and then my benumbed hand touched the lumpy flesh of dead bodies, but I did not feel anything at heart. My senses were paralyzed. I was beyond fear and pain.

The muzzle of a blunt M-1 rifle stuck out of the dark to thrust into my chest. "Who goes there?" Sergeant Chon Hisik asked in a low voice.

"It's me," I said, feeling suddenly weak from relief. "Sergeant Han."

Sergeant Chon's head emerged cautiously from the pocket shelter. His eyes flashed white by the flare. "Squeeze in here," he said, pulling me to his side. "You'll get your life wasted for nothing if you crawl around like that."

I squirmed into the escape shelter and crouched beside Sergeant Chon. He fished out a Chiclet from his cartridge belt and began to chew it passionately. He smelled of sour sweat.

"How's the situation going?" I asked, lifting my stiff leg and placing it in a more comfortable posture.

"Looks like the company base will fall," he said, chewing fast. "I overheard radio communication between the CO and Battalion HQ about ten minutes ago. Said the enemy force is estimated at about sixteen hundred. The Cong demolished the barbed wire fence and pushed in all the way to the water tank."

"How about here?"

"I don't know. Everybody scattered. Maybe hiding in the rice paddies or behind the bushes. There must be some enemy around, but I can't see any."

"What should we do?" I asked him. He was our squad leader. I needed someone with authority to lead us, me, in a strange situation like this. I did not want to feel lost. "Find the survivors and get them organized for a flank attack?" I suggested doubtfully.

"What the hell do you think we are? The commandos of Navarone? There're hardly twenty of us left. You think twenty of us can fight sixteen hundred?"

"But we should do something."

"I know one thing that we should do. You just hide here until daybreak and see what happens. *Then* we will decide what to do."

Hiding the flame with my helmet and cupped hands, I put a cigarette between my dirt-caked lips and drew a match. After a long drag of the tangy smoke, I said, "I'm wounded."

"Bad?"

"I guess I'll be all right. A bayonet—in the thigh."

"Oooo."

"You know who did it?" I said. "Pyon Chinsu. That bastard stabbed me."

"You're kidding."

"No," I said. "I think he mistook me for a Cong."

"That son of a bitch."

"Where is he now? Did you see him?"

"I don't have any idea where he's gone to. Maybe he's dead by now. I saw him crawl out to the rice paddies, ten minutes ago. Looked like he'd gone crazy or something. He won't live too long like that."

I nodded.

Sergeant Chon was somewhat relieved that I was with him in the narrow pocket shelter, and he fell asleep a while later, half reclining against the dirt wall and leaning his cheek on the barrel of his rifle. The Chiclet rolled out of his mouth. Hiding in the dirt hole like a deserter, I waited, and listened to the howitzers and rifles.

For four hours I watched the burning flares, as I had often watched stars in the summer nights of my childhood. Leaning against the wall, the rifle across my knees, vaguely listening to the distant noise of the blood hunt, I was absorbed in extremely incongruous rumination. Perhaps the human soul is purified and subdued to the state of tranquil peace if it faces crisis in total absence of salvation, or so I thought. Love, hate and all other emotions may be a futile waste of psychic energy when one has to watch the hours ticking off to nothingness in the stormy turmoil of death. What noble thoughts could a human being entertain at the moment of confronting the inevitable animal logic of war, the ultimate law of the survival of the fittest—that one should destroy and prey on the other for self-preservation?

Everything seemed to be so remote and elusive. The potential reality that some day my Vietnam duty would be over and I would return home and eat rice and kimchi sitting around the table with my family in a duct-floored Korean room—the distant reality that I would become an ordinary, normal human being again and mingle with others of the same species, to talk about everyday life and petty worries and worldly cares, when the war would be finally over, at least for me, and I would not have to wear this cursed military uniform any more—all these mundane future possibilities did not exist for me at that moment.

The killing I had witnessed in the trench, the animosity and violence of humans destroying one another with mechanical butchering devices—it all seemed to be a momentary insanity. Blood, the ecstatic thirst for blood.

I thought about Ernie Pyle sauntering on Normandy Beach, about the Dien Bien Phu battle where one of Nhat Tien's four sons had lost his life, about the famous lines of *Macbeth,* about Old Man Santiago and the great marlin and the boy, about the shoes I had sent home from boot camp at Nonsan, about the bandage Trau had stained with hog blood, about Corporal Lee Kwanil who had died in the dazzling afternoon at Hill 24, about the undulating hills covered white with snow during the January Retreat of the Korean War and the endless procession of refugees heading for the south, about the fantastic hip motions of Piggie Chang's girl, Pak Kwija, and about the tent chapel at Division Head-quarters. I remembered the four endless lines of bobbing helmets of the recruits returning to their barracks in stifling summer heat and dust after the PRI course at Nonsan Training Camp. I thought about the retreat bugle and the red color in the Korean flag. I wondered what victory meant, and defeat. I thought about dog soldiers dying in the mud and the shining stars on the generals' uniforms, about the send-off ceremony at Yongsan Railroad Station, about the faces screaming mili-tary songs in the night train, about the slogans urging the sacrifice of one's life for his country, about endless marches and medals, about flags, battle cries and brain-washing government propaganda, about the fox-holes on the rice paddy dikes that reminded me of crab holes, and about the Vietcong body whose legs had stuck out heavenward from the puddle.

And I remembered the rumor that they moved dead soldiers at night only, in and out of the morgue at the field hospital of the Southern Cross Unit at Nha Trang. Somebody said the field hospital would soon move its crematorium to a new location because too many ants were collecting at the present site.

"No wonder that place attracts so many ants," Master Sergeant Han Myongsun once said. "They roast the bodies all the time there, don't they? Imagine how nice it would smell to the ants."

I used to think death was a clandestine, religious concept. But in a war, human death was not even as serious as a pimple. Nothing was serious in war. Life, death, and all concepts lost their meanings, leaving only the faded sibilant sounds.

Daybreak. As the night cleared off, the soldiers who had been hiding gathered at the trench, one after another, like turtles lugging themselves up the sandy beach in spawning season. Lieutenant Choe Sangjun, the platoon leader, also emerged from somewhere and checked his men, busily crawling around. Sergeant Chi Taesik, the radioman, who had passed out when a bullet hit him on the shoulder, slowly regained consciousness and asked the gathering soldiers, "What's going on? Are they gone?"

We could not know when it had happened, but Sergeant Sin Taejin was dead. Sergeant Sin had fallen on his side and most of his torso was buried in the dirt thrown over us by artillery shells. Only his hips and legs, broken, crooked, twisted out of the surface. We found a shrapnel hole under his stomach. Written in thick black clumsy handwriting on the camouflage canvas of his helmet was, "Patience. Suk, Wait Till I Come Home." Sergeant Sin would have married Hisuk, a beautician at his hometown of Chunchon, as soon as he returned home.

Twenty-six of us, though covered with dirt and sweat, had survived the assault. The re-grouping soldiers sprawled in and near the trench and absent-mindedly looked around at the devastated land, smudged dark by smoke and explosion, and the dead bodies bobbing in the shallow water of the rice paddies. At the company base the fireworks of killing were still raging.

Pyon Chinsu showed up a little after six. His muddy face had swollen bluish, like a drowned man's, and his eyes were two glass balls barely hanging in the dark sockets of his skull. On the nape of his neck there was a scar in the shape of a leech where a bullet had grazed him but the bleeding had stopped quite some time ago.

He slid down to the trench like a desperate runaway seeking shelter. There was a fluorescent glint in his eyes. Pyon Chinsu seemed fearful that I might take revenge on him for his mistake of stabbing me. I moved over to him, lifting and dragging my leg with both hands, to let him know that I did not want him to worry absurdly on account of me. But when he noticed me approaching him, he shrank like a sea anemone.

"Don't worry, Private Pyon. I understand."

"Worry about what, sergeant?"

"Your stabbing me. That kind of mistake can happen in the dark. I don't mind."

"*Me* stabbing you?"

"Yes. You stabbed me," I said, keeping my voice low so that other soldiers in the trench could not hear.

"I never did that. What are you trying to do to me, Sergeant Han? Why do you say such a thing to me?"

Pyon Chinsu denied it persistently. It would be of no use to argue about it with him.

"When did you get that?" I asked.

"Get what?"

"That. On your neck. A bullet has grazed there, I think."

He quickly ran his open palm down the nape of his neck, then twitched spasmodically, his body freezing, his hands twisting. "I'm— I'm hit!" he said. Private Pyon had not noticed the blood up to now, but he suddenly bent himself back as if to recoil away from his own wound, gasping, "Oh, oh, oh." He gasped some more and wheezed, "I—I'm hit—on the neck!"

"Shut up, you fucker," Sergeant Chon growled, kicking Pyon's shin with his booted foot.

Private First Class Pyon held his breath like a young child trying to swallow his sob for fear of another blow from his drunken father. He kept looking around at us with panicked eyes.

At 0820 hours the enemy began to retreat to Hon Ba Mountain and the Valley of Death in the northwest. They fled helter-skelter, dragging or carrying the wounded and finishing off their hopelessly wounded survivors so that they would not leave any prisoners or information behind.

American gunships flew in and blasted rockets over the fleeing Vietcong. Chinooks landed on the rice paddies to pour out reinforcements. The soldiers who had survived the hours of nightmare rushed over the demolished barbed wire fence, howling and yelling and chasing after the retreating enemy.

"Let's go! Shoot them down! Shoot them all!"

At the platoon leader's howling order, the soldiers crouching in the trench leapt out to the rice paddies and splashed across the water, shooting at everything, shooting at nothing, just shooting.

Sergeant Chi and I stayed behind, because we were wounded; we only watched the frenzy. Like a child whose big brother showed up just in time to rescue him from a back-alley bully, the shouting soldiers pursued the enemy in a frantic ecstasy. Screaming so that the horror of mass death should never come back to them, screaming that this should be the end of all the horrors in the world. They ran breathlessly shouting, and the burning red sun sizzled in the sky, vibrating with the sputtering rotors of the helicopters, the shrieking human cries and blasting weapons. The nightlong battle was finally over.

The soldiers removed the enemy and friendly casualties from the demolished barbed wire fence. The cartridge shells, piled in small heaps around the trench, shone like gold sticks. The wound in my thigh began to hurt. The company commander mustered his men at the battered helipad for a roll call. As he called out the names one by one, the survivors confirmed their presence with tired voices.

The friendly losses numbered 18 KIA, including Sergeant Sin of our platoon, and 36 wounded; most of these casualties had been suffered by the 9th Company throughout the night. The enemy body count was 172, but we found no wounded survivors to take as prisoners and interrogate about the strategic purpose of the night's attack.

When the casualties were checked and the body count taken, Lieutenant Colonel Song Chigyu, the 3rd Battalion commander, arrived in his jeep, with the windshield down on the hood, to see firsthand the results of the battle. The company commander busily guided the battalion commander, showing the bloody bodies torn apart by howitzer shells, while the movie and still photographers ran around, under the direction of a glaring information officer, to document the deadliest encounter with the Vietcong by the White Horse warriors. The battalion commander inquired about friendly casualties with a grave expression and when he was told of the enemy body count, a misty smile rippled through his rigid expression of nightlong fatigue. To get 172 enemy at the cost of 18 friendly loss was a gratifying deal for any combat unit commander.

Several minutes later the regimental commander arrived in his jeep, with the windshield down, accompanied by operations and intelligence officers. The battalion commander repeated what he had heard from the company commander, and the regimental commander replicated the earlier facial expression of the battalion commander. About ten minutes later the division commander arrived in a Huey with his staff officers. The regimental commander repeated what he had heard from the battalion commander, and the division commander assumed the pleased expression that the regimental commander had displayed.

The division commander shook hands with the soldiers, congratulating them, and other commanders and staff officers did likewise with other nearby men, who blinked their idiotic eyes slowly, their faces dumb and uncommunicating, their heavy arms lolling down. The soldiers wanted to get somewhere right now and sleep, but the commanders had to keep them on their feet, at attention, so that they could lavish their excited and delighted congratulations on the heroic dog soldiers.

The loose fatigues looked bigger than ever on their haggard bodies. The filmy pupils of their eyes did not seem to reflect the nightmare they had just survived. They were too tired. The overnight hell had been absurd, astonishing and illogical. Too strange—yes, strange.

I limped along a dike toward the 3rd Platoon barracks, hanging on to Sergeant Chon Hisik's arm. The soldiers trudged home. Someone behind us argued indifferently with no one in particular about whether a howitzer shell travelled faster than sound: "If sound is faster, you'll have some time to escape the incoming shell. I don't know. Who cares."

The soldiers looked defeated, but then, what victory had they achieved anyway? They had survived a night. That was all.

I felt my wounded leg stiffening cold as if the blood had stopped circulating. "It hurts bad," I said, pointing at my thigh with my chin.

"But you have to thank heaven for your luck," Chon said. "You might have needed to practice the speech on the bus—'I lost one of my legs in Vietnam.' You know."

Then we heard the noise of a flock of quacking ducks from the brook down at the end of the narrow irrigation ditch. Tens of villagers were crowding along the dike to watch something that we could not see yet because the dike and the villagers blocked our sight.

"Something must be going on there," Sergeant Chon said. "Let's go take a look."

As we neared them, the villagers stepped aside to let us pass, cautiously watching us, some of them fearfully glancing at the brook. An old farmer with a white towel tied around his head gestured for us to take a look and pointed at the water, trying to explain something in fast Vietnamese. Among the clumps of weeds in the water, a corpse of a dead Vietcong was floating, face down, his lower half under the abdomen blown off, probably by a mine, the tangled lumps of entrails squeezing out of the torn underside and waving in the thick bloody water.

What the villagers were watching was not the remaining half of the body but some hundred ducks, in a noisy quacking swirl of flapping and fluttering, jostling to have a slurpy bite of the blood-oozing intestines of the shredded human being.

My stomach churned violently, but my eyes were helplessly fixed upon the wretched carcass, the squalor of that mashed filthy *thing,* the flesh of man chopped and eaten by a flock of tamed birds. The great *homo sapiens* launching flying machines to heaven to conquer space, the creator of Greek and Roman civilization, the mighty ruler of the universe—and here he had turned to prey for the river ducks in this blood-drenched reality.

Cold drops of sweat stood out along my spine, the horror injecting the freezing poison into every single pore as I stood there, shuddering, as if an imaginary vulture were pecking and biting and tearing off my fingers and toes and eyeballs with its metal beak. I was still alive, but that giant bird just kept tearing off my flesh piece by piece. I felt like collapsing any moment. My legs shook. When Sergeant Chon shouted, "*Xau lam,* you savages," to the villagers, they left the ducks to chew up the human body. Then Chon opened fire into the cluster of white feathers, and blood spattered from the exploding ducks, and I fainted again.

When my name was included in the list of 28 medevacuees to be sent to the Nha Trang field hospital among the 36 initially wounded, I was relieved that I could get away—get anywhere away from last night. One single combat with the tangible enemy was enough to make me abhor a war that once was an eternal state of boredom. Now I knew what it really was like, and I wanted no more of it. I wanted to be away. Other wounded comrades felt the same way. I could tell it from their relieved expressions as they climbed up into the trucks leaving for Nha Trang. An exception was Corporal So Ingi, whose right arm had been torn off. It had simply disappeared in a rocket explosion in the night.

Pyon Chinsu was also included among the evacuees. The wound on his neck had healed by itself, but he had been dogging the platoon leader's heels all morning, blubbering over and over again in a tearful and frightened voice, "I'm sure a shrapnel is stuck somewhere in my throat, sir. The flesh will decay from inside my neck and I will die in a few days if I don't get proper medical treatment immediately, sir. I know a shrapnel is stuck somewhere in my throat, sir."

Lieutenant Choe, who could not stand Pyon's nagging plea any longer, finally barked at Private Pyon Chinsu to get on the truck, swearing, "All right, you fucking bastard, go to the hospital and drop dead there, if that's what you really want."

When the trucks, loaded with the wounded soldiers in bloody fatigues and grimy bandages, arrived at the Ninh Hoa check point, the MPs had blocked the road with triple barricades and told us to return to the base because the highway to Nha Trang had been closed by the Vietcong during the night.

A tense atmosphere hung heavily over the company base when we returned to the barracks. The CO had just finished reorganizing two platoons for the upcoming combat mission, and these were now packing new supplies of ammunition and rations.

"What's going on?" I asked Sergeant Chon Hisik who was fastening the straps of his knapsack.

"The whole Ninh Hoa area is besieged," he said. "Combat is in progress everywhere. Damn."

The soldiers said the Vietcong attack last night had been a mere prelude to sound out our firepower prior to the major assault yet to come. While the attention of the whole division had been diverted to the 9th Company under attack last night, other VC elements and NVA units were suspected to have infiltrated all the villages around Ninh Hoa. Some of the enemy forces had mingled with the inhabitants of Lac Ninh plain, as well as of the Ninh Quang and Van Gia areas, to take them as hostages and establish a network of dispersed strongholds; these elements might launch an all-out attack on the division headquarters perimeter using the villagers as a shield. The plain of Lac Ninh, that had been "pacified" by the Koreans through a series of Bulldozer Operations, had fallen into the enemy's hands overnight. The companies that had gone out to Lac An on a reconnaissance mission in the morning were attacked and repulsed by a Vietcong ambush.

Sergeant Chon slung the rifle over his shoulder. "They say the area taken by the Cong is 4 kilometers long and 3.5 kilometers wide. The enemy has most of the villages around here and is dug in, probably determined to push a long-term action. A chopper spotted a regular NVA flag flying high in one of the villages. This fight won't be an easy one for us, because they've taken the town of Quang Ngai where they probably can secure enough rice to last them several months."

Only the wounded soldiers stayed behind at the company base under the command of the executive officer. The active combat force of the 9th Company left immediately after lunch for Lac Ninh plain where the noise of gunfire was growing more and more violent.

The wounded soldiers listened to the reports on the open command post radio. The situation became more and more intense and unfavorable. The friendly forces drew a circular defensive cordon, with Division Headquarters at the core, and exchanged fire with the scattered enemy at random spots, but it never was easy to search out targets among the inhabitants and eliminate them. The governor of Khanh Hoa Province forbade air strikes or howitzer shelling of the villages held by the Vietcong lest the innocent inhabitants be victimized, and even the commander of the ROK Army Field Operations Headquarters, who had flown in urgently by helicopter from Nha Trang, failed to persuade 1st Lieutenant Phuc Van Vien, ARVN, the mayor of Ninh Hoa, to allow the use of heavy artillery over Ninh Quang. The Voice of Hanoi encouraged the Vietcong warriors of Quang Ngai all afternoon to fight bravely unto the last man and wipe out the brutal Daihans, the mercenary running dogs of the American imperialists who were butchering innocent Vietnamese without any reason, political or otherwise.

By four o'clock in the afternoon the friendly forces had suffered 40 KIAs. The soldiers were infuriated and frustrated because their fire was restricted while they sustained an unlimited enemy barrage. Many of them suffered from the intolerable urge to just push into the villages and burn and kill everything in sight, the enemy and the inhabitants alike.

We received the order to move out, too. Only seven seriously wounded men were told to stay back. By the time we, the small group of wounded riflemen, arrived at Ninh Quang to join the main company force in action, the 9th Company had been helplessly pinned down on

one side of the railroad bed. The soldiers could not even raise their
heads because the Vietcong fired selective, perfectly-aimed shots whenever someone tried to move. An armored personnel carrier, whose side
had been splintered by enemy rocket fire, was abandoned at the foot of
the bank. Several Cobra attack helicopters swooshed up and down,
tearing and churning the water of the rice paddies with miniguns and
Browning 50 caliber machine guns, and the armored cars of the U.S. 1st
Cavalry were thrown in to help the besieged Korean troops from the
flank, the executive officer told us, but we could not even go near Ninh
Quang where the actual enemy was because of the civilian hostages.

Vietnamese workers were mobilized in the late afternoon to dig
foxholes for the wounded soldiers who could not do the digging themselves. Glancing at the Vietnamese diggers every so often with flashing
eyes, Pyon Chinsu said, lying on his stomach next to me:

"Look, sergeant. Look at them over there, at the Vietnamese diggers.
The Viets are digging graves. They're digging graves to bury us. Look!
Look at them over there, sergeant!"

Fastening the sling of his M-1 rifle, Private Yun Chilbok, the "Boar,"
spat a gob of chewing tobacco into the weeds. "This bastard is real bad
news," he said, pointing at Pyon with his chin. "Guess he's gone clean
crazy. What the hell did this fucker come all the way to Vietnam for
anyway? Hey, you fucker, go somewhere I can't see you and hiccup to
death."

Private Pyon, with a worried look, glanced at Boar and whispered to
me in a lowered voice, "You've got to stop them. Those gooks, you know,
they're digging our graves."

"No. They're digging foxholes." I said, "For us."

"But they're preparing our graves. They'll bury us there. They know
we will all die in this battle, and they will bury us there!"

As night fell, the breeze brought us a soft drizzle. Machine guns
grumbled somewhere once in a while. The American armored cars had
retreated into the darkness. In the sky blazing with flares, Hueys and
Cobras sputtered around. Small arms cracked at distant villages where
sporadic firefights broke out.

Other soldiers slept for about two hours by taking shifts in their two-
man foxholes, but I could not sleep a wink because Pyon Chinsu kept
gibbering all night. He muttered and grumbled on and on until dawn, and
I decided I would not spend another night with him in the same hole, no
matter what, because it was apparent now that he was off his rocker.

"You understand why I was so afraid last night, don't you, Sergeant Han? You can't help it when you're plainly scared. I couldn't understand where so many Vietcong just popped out of all of a sudden. When we used to go out on operations or patrols, we never saw any of them, did we? The Cong simply didn't exist anywhere around us. They were nowhere. I will never know where all those Cong had been hiding. There were so many of them last night. Boy, so many of them. They were all over the place, and I saw the bullets, thousands flying toward me. And I could hear the sound. The sound of all those rounds hurtling toward me. They sounded like so many gongs clanging. Did you hear that sound? You did? And my hands were so shaky I simply couldn't shoot straight. I felt my head would be blown off any minute. I was so scared. I felt something was running in my pants. I opened up when I saw the first VC and kept firing all night, but I kept shooting with my eyes closed because I didn't want to see all those bullets coming at me. Me. I kept firing so that nobody, no bullets would come near me. But I really didn't know that I was hit in the neck. I don't know who did it, but a piece of lead is stuck in my neck and I'll die soon, because my throat is decaying fast from inside. Why don't they send me to the hospital when my neck is rotting and decomposing from inside? It's too miserable to watch yourself dying with a decomposing neck. How can they send wounded soldiers out to combat? They shouldn't do that, really. They shouldn't send a dying man to fight the Cong. All the people in the world are plotting to kill me. Aren't they? I know it. I know what they're doing. I know what they're trying to do to me. You know it, too, don't you, Sergeant Han? Why do you think they chose me of all people to kill? I know. They don't like me and that's why they're trying to kill me. I know they plotted to send me back to this battle so that I would get killed."

The next day, one of the three Vietnamese agents who had been sent to Hon Heo Mountain to capture a Vietcong and get some information about the general scenario of the enemy attack, was shot in the chest in an ambush and died at the foot of the mountain. The other two returned to the AIU office at Ninh Hoa, wounded, without any helpful information to report. But the 8th Company fortunately captured all the six Vietcong scouts dispatched to Ninh Pung from the Valley of Death. Two of the captives were in Korean military uniform. The Army Intelligence Unit interrogated them and found out that the attack on the 9th ROK Infantry Division Headquarters had been planned two months ago, and the strike forces had been secretly gathering in the Hon Heo Mountain and Song Da Ban areas.

In the afternoon, the situation started to turn favorable for us at Ninh Quang, the village we were ordered to take back. The villagers fled from the Vietcong by two's and three's at first; occasionally dozens of them dashed through the dusk, splashing across the rice paddies to safety. I saw three of them shot to death by enemy fire during their desperate flight, but more than thirty of them made it. During the night, 80 more villagers safely escaped out of the village and provided us with valuable information about where the remaining hostages were held and where the enemy positions were. Surprisingly, only 14 Vietcong were occupying Ninh Quang.

Word got around early the next morning that the 28th Regiment had begun their move southward from Tuy Hoa, and the Tiger Division might also come down to our aid from Qui Nhon. On the second day the Koreans suffered 41 KIAs and 69 wounded, and confirmed 49 enemy KIAs and the capture of 20 small arms.

My plan not to share the same foxhole with Private Pyon did not work out. No one else was willing to accept him. Spending another night of disturbed sleep with Private Pyon in the sultry hole, I thought somebody really had to do something about this man; I suspected he might have succumbed to battle shock.

In the morning the 9th hit Ninh Quang. Following the meticulous plans Captain Kim Sanghyop had spent all night drawing up, we were organized into seven teams and assaulted all the enemy positions simultaneously at daybreak. But the enemy was already gone, leaving only the North Vietnamese flag—a yellow star on a red background—flying high on the pole in the village square. We heard occasional shots, but saw no enemy as we rushed to the town's center.

Although the regimental and division commanders made personal visits to the 9th to congratulate them for their first recapture of a village, the soldiers were downcast, as if they had taken a ghost ship. The villagers came to us with bundles of bananas and fiery country wine, thanking us, but few tasted their gifts.

At the fall of evening, I went to the platoon leader's foxhole and reported to him on Pyon Chinsu's state. I asked him to send Pyon back to the company base because he seemed to be mentally ill, but the lieutenant huffed at me.

"Shut up and go back to your position. That asshole is faking, faking everything, faking he's crazy, because he's too scared to fight. He's just dying to get out of here. Let him go crazy. Let that asshole fuck himself and drop dead."

That night I had to listen to his blubbering and raving again until dawn. His haggard face was ghostly because he had not slept for days, and his voice sounded like an echo trembling out of a hollow pipe.

"Did you notice the spiteful glances of the hostages this afternoon when we charged into Ninh Quang? They looked daggers at us because they think we're their enemy. I know why they glared at us like that. They hate us. They don't hate the Cong, but they hate us. Because they think it's our fault that this war is going on and on. Right? They think this war will be over the moment Daihans and Americans get out of this country, Sergeant Han. They think so, don't they? And what are we fighting and dying here for? If they don't appreciate it at all. Why do we waste our lives at a godforsaken place like this? They don't want to fight, and they don't want us to fight for them either. And why do we have to waste our lives for these people who don't want a war in their country in the first place?"

And then he suddenly began to talk faster as if he was short of breath. And short of time: "Why doesn't this war end quickly before my whole neck decomposes? I can't sleep here in this hole, Sergeant Han. If I ever fall asleep, these Vietnamese gooks will bury me here right away. They will bury me alive, and that's why I can't go to sleep in this goddamned hole."

He squinted at me, panting like a horse that had just finished a race, leaned forward, and whispered to me in a strange, covert tone. "I am afraid. I have a weird feeling that I may never hit any enemy if I shoot at them all day long. All the Vietcong are coming to get me. Every single one of them. Why do I have these strange feelings? Why am I like this? What has happened to me? Why should I be singled out to die in this war?"

On the fourth day we moved to a new position behind a small wooden church at Ninh Pung, dug in again, cleaned our weapons, and were resupplied with ammunition. The soldiers, having regained some confidence after taking back Ninh Quang without suffering any casualties, began to crack the usual jokes.

I felt I was going crazy, too, because Pyon continued to rave, even in daytime. White scabs were peeling off his chapped lips. He had eaten almost nothing for four days. He was plainly insane. I began gradually to pity him and occasionally responded to his endless incoherent monologues, reassuring him that there was nothing to worry about.

I had fallen asleep after a C-ration lunch, exhausted by the noontime heat, and was startled back to wakefulness from a short troubled nap. My hazy half-open eyes caught the quaint sight of Private Pyon uncomfortably squatting in the bottom of the narrow foxhole. He did not have his helmet on and broadly grinned at me as I opened my eyes and sat up, surprised by the foul stench of feces. Sweat drops glistened in the sunshine on his dark tanned forehead. Then I realized he was sitting on his upturned helmet, evacuating himself.

"What are you doing?" I asked, puzzled.

"Emptying my bowels," he said, grunting to push. "This helmet is really neat. You can use it as a wash basin or a cooking pot. And you can use it as a lavatory, too. It indeed is nice to have a helmet at a place like this."

I was frightened. I had a sudden premonition that Private Pyon would die today. Or tomorrow, maybe. Terrified, I decided I should do something about him immediately.

Leaving Private Pyon alone in the foxhole, I hastened over to the platoon leader and reported to him what had been going on in our foxhole the last several days. When I returned with the lieutenant, Private Pyon was busily digging in the bottom of the foxhole. I asked him what he was doing and Pyon said he had to bury the chamber pot quickly before the smell attracted VC.

Lieutenant Choe sighed. "I understand what you mean all right," he said. "I'll medevac him tomorrow."

But the enemy renewed their coordinated offensive at dawn and Pyon Chinsu was not evacuated. Highway 1, that had been cleared briefly yesterday afternoon, was blockaded by the VC during the night, and the noon reports from different sectors were very discouraging, including the report that Lieutenant Colonel Han Sangjun, commander of the 2nd Battalion, 29th Regiment, had been killed in action.

I overheard an officer recount the story of Colonel Han's death.

The Vietcong had been surprisingly strong, opening fire at unpredictable spots and at unpredictable moments. When his men were trapped next to a stream and would not move quickly enough to cut down the enemy fire and break out of the low grounds, Colonel Han had become infuriated by "the imbeciles." He kept screaming through a bullhorn from the CP down to the helpless soldiers: "Send those shitting cowards by the bombed shack over to that log bridge there and you, yes, you stupid, what the hell are you doing behind that tree? Move out! Move out!" But the colonel soon realized he could not fight the war with a bullhorn. Despairing and frustrated by all the shouting with almost no corresponding action on the part of the soldiers, he ran down to the stream, snatched an M-16 rifle from a cowering corporal, and rushed down the bank to wade across the stream, firing his .45 and the rifle at the same time toward the opposite bank like a mad man, calling the soldiers to follow him, "Come on, bastards, come on!" No John Wayne, the colonel turned into a beehive of bullet holes before he reached the water.

Under the circumstances, they needed every man available, including Pyon Chinsu, to fight back the enemy who seemed to be bracing for the second wave of an all-out attack.

13

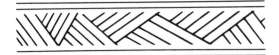

The radio man was eavesdropping on the command post's frequency with a backup radio. A fierce battle was in progress at the Loc Binh area where the U.S. 1st Infantry Division had encountered VC infiltrators early in the morning. The 29th Regiment managed to push out most of the enemy elements from the division headquarters perimeter after days of harrowing fights, but the reorganized VC units of Ninh Da and Ninh Pung showed an obvious intention to launch an intensified attack on the ARVN aviation corps north of Ninh Hoa. Refugees again swarmed out of the villages where minor, broken VC units were concentrating, and several Vietnamese looters, with furniture and rice from empty houses, were observed from recon choppers. The senior platoon leader, acting as the commander in place of the wounded CO, and the leader of the firearms platoon, the 5th Company, were also medevacked after they had been machine-gunned by an American helicopter whose crew had mistaken the Koreans for enemy.

Around eleven o'clock in the morning the TI&E staff officer visited our company with Bill Wildow, an AFP correspondent, and Vo Thanh Son, a Vietnamese free-lance cameraman on an assignment for the American CBS-TV network. The staff officer left the foreign reporters with 1st Lieutenant Lee Taehun, asking him to help them cover the vivid combat first hand, and then excused himself to fly out to Nha Trang to fetch the Korean war correspondents who were waiting at the Press Center for a helicopter to transport them to the battleground.

I went to the CO's tent, which was rigged up beyond a dike, where Captain Kim Sanghyop and the two foreigners were waiting for an interpreter, because Lieutenant Lee had summoned me to assist the correspondents cover the battle with my French and English. Lieutenant Lee complained vociferously that the TI&E staff officer had run away to handle the easier flock of Korean reporters, leaving these two foreigners to him. The colonel could not speak English well, but it soon became apparent that he was greatly pleased to associate with the foreigners who were working for a world-famous television network and a wire service. The captain did not talk much because he was too tired from days of non-stop combat. But the lieutenant voluntarily went through the long and painful task of explaining the whole step-by-step progress of the fighting, from the long-expected night attack by the massive enemy force, up to the present minor skirmishes going on at the outlying villages near the division headquarters perimeter. His gestures and diverse facial expressions were intended to embellish his limited English. He also presented the history of the ROK Army and the 9th Infantry Division, as well as his personal views, as a military man, on the similar political dilemmas of the two divided nations, Vietnam and Korea. He did not seem to mind me helping him out as an interpreter in the last half of his presentation covering the Korean War and the significance of the Korean participation in the Indochina conflict.

After the two reporters took several pictures around the captain's tent and jotted down some superficial statistics out of sheer politeness, Lieutenant Lee and I took them by jeep to the temporary regimental

Command Post installed in the yard of the AIU building in downtown Ninh Hoa. We drove along the dirt road. Foot soldiers and military vehicles hurried back and forth, like a swarm of ants carrying fragmented pieces of a dead locust home. We entered the small town of Ninh Hoa, littered with abandoned rolls of rusty barbed wire. The whole town was deserted, like the ruins of a city devastated by plague. The Vietnamese merchants were taking a nap, their goods spread on the ground like dumped garbage. Regardless of the combat going on everywhere around the town, the Vietnamese did not want to miss their daily nap in the heat of the day.

In the regimental CP tent, covered white with dust, the exhausted soldiers looked to be perspiring zombies, sweltering in the suffocating heat. When we entered the tent and introduced the reporters to the regimental commander, the tall colonel with the agonized eyes instructed his intelligence officer to give the correspondents a briefing on the battle and provide them with all the possible assistance with their coverage, and then apologized that he had to go out to Ninh Quang to monitor the situation there. He hurried out to his waiting jeep standing in the yard in the scorching sun with its engine running. The jeep disappeared trailing a swirl of rising dust. In the next tent a sallow-faced major, who had not noticed us coming into this tent, was yelling angrily over the squelch of radios and the howitzers firing near the northern bridge of Ninh Hoa

"They're accusing *us*? Thirteen villagers have been killed up to now in our engagements with the enemy who are dispersed all *over* this goddamn plain," the major screamed hysterically. "What the hell's with these Saigon guys anyway? What do they want—a written confession that we are lousy soldiers fighting a lousy war? We're shitting to fight it out in this damned situation, and they say they're coming up here for a supervisory inspection, eh? What do those fathead desk guys want us to do? Are we supposed to check every gook's ID card one by one before shooting them when the villagers are shooting at us like hell? It doesn't matter whether they're forced to by the VC or not when they're shooting at us. You're supposed to return fire, right?"

When the intelligence officer went over to the next tent and told him to pipe down because foreign correspondents were around, the major stopped yelling, squinted at us under the rolled-up flaps of the tents, and then walked away to the AIU radio room, still grumbling. The intelligence officer returned to the CP tent and very professionally briefed the reporters on the present situations, skillfully using a long wooden pointer while standing rigidly before the huge vinyl-covered board which showed the current happenings out in the field. The terse entries on the board, which was as large as a classroom blackboard, represented—in dry summarized capsules—the chaotic individual realities in the making, the ruthless blood hunt somewhere near us. I had a passing curiosity about what complex and disheartening tales of war might be hidden behind those brief but efficient narratives.

1042 8 Co attacked d. ambush by 1 grenade 5–6 rifle shots.

1025 AOP spot 2 VC at CP 140756. Van Ninh agent report—VC in hiding at VN armed with 2 60mm, 2 MSG, also AK. RCN report at 0740 VC sympathizer contact with 8 VC at BP 986703. 100 VC strong of 9 BN, 18B R infiltrate Phu Binh. Z11 Co join local VC H71 Co of Hon Heo, infiltrate Ninh Da, demand rice and meal from inhabitants. Dug in on bank by river. Friendly encirclement closes in, enemy resist with small arms and grenades.

0032 VC platoon infiltrate from NW. VN militia platoon on ambush at BP 943848 retreat to BP 943841.

Obviously displeased by the regimental commander's discourtesy, the foreign correspondents left for the 28th Regiment in Tuy Hoa by helicopter. I returned to my foxhole. I noticed Pyon Chinsu had turned mute in the meantime. Quietly gazing at me with his unseeing eyes, he kept smiling an empty expressionless smile—a happy idiot. Then he had another session of raving monologue at dusk.

After the medic made a round, checking the wounded in the foxholes, I sat down on the box of C-rations newly supplied to Pyon and me for the next two days and blankly looked around the field illumined by the mercurial moonlight. Frogs croaked noisily down at the rice paddies. Frogs used to croak this loudly in late summer nights in the Korean countryside. A single rifle shot cracked, then another, somewhere distant as if someone were practicing marksmanship. The shelling also regained its normal rhythm of booms, with measured intervals like the regular breathing of a man peacefully asleep. I was so exhausted by lack of sleep and Private Pyon's raving monologues, as well as paralyzing tension, that I could not even breathe freely.

Staring at me with his stupefied eyes, his chin resting on his knees, Private Pyon was talking to me, or to himself: "Did you see the hearses going to Nha Trang during Operation Bulldozer Four? Three-quarter-ton trucks with white bandages crossed on their hoods. The army hearses carrying dead soldiers to the crematorium at Nha Trang. Did you see those trucks? I saw four of them during the Bulldozer operations. When I die, I'll also be carried away by one of those three-quarter-ton trucks with a white cross on its hood. You know how they dispose of the dead, Sergeant Han? I know. I actually saw how they pack away the dead soldiers. They put the body in a bag made of waterproof cloth that looks like a folded poncho. The bag has two handles shaped like human ears at both tips of the top side so that you can drag it around easily. You put a body in it, zip it up tight, and load it in a truck. Like a bag of rice. One of the bodies kept bleeding for hours after it had been packed away in a bag, and I saw the blood seep out through the jammed zippers. You'll be surprised to see how much blood a human body carries in it.

"What's going to happen to me if the stupid guys at the 102nd Field Hospital of the Southern Cross Unit get mixed up about my dead body and send the ashes of somebody else to my parents? What will become of me then? Where shall I go? It may not matter too much where I go once I'm dead, I guess. If the flesh inside my throat keeps decomposing this fast—I can actually smell the decaying stench from my own throat—if the flesh inside my throat keeps decomposing like this, my neck will simply disappear and my head will fall off like a rotten apple. Can you imagine that, Sergeant Han? A dead body without its head would look really scary. I heard Americans are experts at patching them up, even bodies blown up by a mine or bombs. They groom the face of a corpse with elaborate makeup, dress it up with a new military uniform and send it home, frozen in a refrigerator coffin. That's what I heard they do about their dead comrades. Dead Koreans return home cremated and packed in small white boxes. It's a blessing not to die as a Vietnamese, though. The Vietnamese just leave the dead to the wild dogs after the battle. Even if one is lucky enough to be brought to the morgue of a field hospital, there's not much chance for his body to reach his home, Corporal Kim Chaeo said. You know Corporal Kim? He knows all sorts of things and he told me a lot of stories about the processing of dead soldiers. If a Vietnamese wife goes to the morgue where her dead husband is supposed to be and asks for his remains, they chop off a piece of any dead body at hand, the way they sell meat at a butcher shop, and give it to her. Really! That's what Kim said. What will happen to me if I'm mistaken for a Vietnamese when I die and my body is sent to such a place? That shouldn't happen to me. I don't want it to happen. I have to go home. I have to go before that happens to me. I'll go home by plane, because it takes only eight hours by airplane to go home."

He started to crawl out of the foxhole. I tried to pull him down by the cartridge belt, shouting, "What the hell are you doing? How can you get on an airplane in the middle of the night?"

"I have to go home by any means. If I fool around here too long . . ." He shook my hand off and jumped up to the dirt pile before our foxhole, and when he was about to leap into the dark towards the stream, an automatic rifle, an AK 47A, growled briefly somewhere and Private Pyon fluttered in the air like a bird hit by a broomstick, and tumbled down to the bottom of the foxhole, spattering hot blood across my face.

Pyon Chinsu was medevacked. I felt lonely, deserted, in the strange silence that surrounded me with chilly empty space, the empty space suddenly blank. The endless noise and annoying existence beside me had been removed. The pallid light of the waning half moon looked so cold over the quiet peaceful field. I even missed him. I could not understand why, but I did. I felt I had disappeared with him, and was sorry that I had detested him like an eternal punishment.

I could do nothing but watch him helplessly when they carried him away on a stretcher like a bloody bundle of torn rags. He was unconscious, bleeding in torrents, and smelled badly of feces. Every place I touched in the foxhole, after he was gone, was sticky with the blood Pyon had left behind with me. I performed my wobbling, halting physical motions the next day in a dazed state, suffering from a vague fear that I might have already died some time last night. Spending the whole day in stupefaction, it occurred to me that human consciousness, perhaps, stops functioning at times like a valve, like a machine that closes and opens automatically.

In the morning light I saw my flak jacket and fatigues had been smeared with blood while I had been screaming for the medic, holding Private Pyon in my arms. I clasped him so hard in my arms that I was afraid his skull might crack and his brains spill out on my trousers, but I could not let him go because I feared his life would slip out of his head, that kept butting and jerking on my chest, if I did not hold him tight enough. The black splotches of his blood all around the foxhole—it was a horrifying sight.

The day broke, the eighth day of the battle. Led by nine APCs, a combined unit of American and Korean soldiers, along with Vietnamese militiamen, assaulted Ninh Pung from the left flank. The friendly forces suffered 32 KIAs and 14 wounded, exacting 55 enemy lives. All day long, I crawled around on my stomach, opened fire whenever I felt I was supposed to, and swallowed so much dust my throat felt sandy in the evening, but I was little conscious of my own actions. Returning to the foxhole at nightfall, I thought about Private Pyon, who used to rustle sneakily in the dark to clean his thighs with tissue paper when he contracted gonorrhea because he worried he might die without ever experiencing sex; the soldier who had hiccupped all night because he was too scared of the mortar shelling; the young boy who promised all his comrades a free movie when we returned home and he got back his old painting job at Taehan Cinema. He was gone, leaving dark splotches of dried blood everywhere around me. He might die, I thought. He might have died already at the field hospital.

Sometimes it was wiser for one to live without knowing anything else but the primitive state of living itself. Pyon Chinsu had a premonition about his death and his secret knowledge frightened him. His raving monologue was a means for him to sustain his flickering life, the sole futile attempt he was capable of performing, the only way he could declare his yearning for home and peace. He lacked the animal strength and will power to survive in a strange country where all men were trained not to think but to kill, and all conceptual agonies were mental wastes.

I avoided looking at the corner where Private Pyon had been squatting last night, blubbering about the meat of dead Vietnamese soldiers. I feared I might see his pallid ghostly face, the skull with two huge, black, hollow eye sockets staring at me if I ever turned my glance to that direction.

The last phase of the hunt was finished at all the villages surrounding the division headquarters perimeter, and the battle was finally over. It was time for us to return to the base.

We trudged to the base along Highway 1, in two marching rows, mud-caked rifles slung over shoulders, carrying hastily packed knapsacks with straps or poncho flaps dangling loose. Neither the company commander nor the platoon leader forced us to maintain a gallant and vigorous gait or appearance to impress the Vietnamese farmers on the road. It was no time for pomp.

We had not washed, eaten real food, nor truly slept for fifteen days, and now we were returning home to piled C-ration boxes, canvas cots, sandbags, barbed wire fences, and bunker doors made with the planks torn out of ammunition boxes. But that dirt cave provided a sense of security and comfort. That cave was a cozy home, a womb to snugly crawl back into.

The soldiers marched slowly, their faces tanned dark, fatigues blotched with salty stains of dried sweat. Their expressions showed only one simple desire—to have a cool shower and undisturbed sleep for forty-eight hours straight. Passing by Ninh Quang and Ninh Hoa, we looked around the seedy huts of the outlying villages and the farmers now back at their homes. Women and old peasants watched us pass by, baring their gums, smeared red or black with betel juice, in identical broad grins. I suspected they were entertaining scornful thoughts: "We enjoyed our daily siesta thanks to your dirty work in the mud."

On the streets noisy cyclos busily roared around. The townspeople had watched one more of the countless battles in their 20-year-old war, and, as if just awakened from a short nap, they would have to continue their lives of cheating, prostituting—surviving. The foreign soldiers fought and shed blood to prolong the mediocre lives of a woman hunting fleas, her child playing with a cockroach on the road, and the old shopkeepers who did not seem to be suffering from any shred of guilt for their indifference about the war.

Passing by the 29th Regiment parade ground along the road from Ninh Hoa to Tu Bong, I saw the corpses of those who had died during this two-week battle. The tarpaulin bags containing the bodies, that had not been delivered to the crematorium because the road to Nha Trang had been blockaded, were lined up on the parade ground in orderly rows. More than 150 bags were there, attracting a swarm of flies with their nauseating stench. I dared not cover my nose, for I had a strange fear that the bodies might suddenly sit up and glare at me, hissing, "You don't like the smell of death, eh? Why don't you join us and see if you smell any better?" Some soldiers stopped, stunned, to watch the ghastly scene of the death bags, their faces disbelieving.

I recalled the black shadows etched so clearly in Private Pyon's face when it was illumined by the shaky flashlight while the medic was checking his bleeding wounds. All these dead bodies.

This could not be real.

Turning back to leave the parade ground, I imagined the tarpaulin bags unzipping themselves and the torn bodies pouring out, alive again and dripping.

The soldiers of the 9th continued their silent march toward Tu Bong. I looked back several times to see if the bodies were trudging after us.

14

A group of Korean and foreign war correspondents had flown in from Saigon and Nha Trang to follow up the battle of Ninh Hoa, and the TI&E staff officer gave an assignment to the 9th to "cooperate with one of the press guys." The reporter to be sent to our company, along with the 29th Regiment information officer, was planning to make a vivid combat documentary of the soldiers fighting the battle that had just ended. We could not understand this, or what our assignment was supposed to be, until the reporter arrived at our tactical company base.

Kim Chunok, a stocky and extremely demanding man originally dispatched to

Vietnam by a Korean daily newspaper, was, as we later found out, not much devoted to covering the news for his own newspaper. Instead, he spent most of his time taking still photographs and moving pictures he could sell to foreign news agencies such as Visnews or the Associated Press. The information officer even tipped Captain Kim Sanghyop that this particular news guy might be real bad news since he was not exactly a popular character among the Korean press corps in Saigon because of his professional infidelity. But the captain did not seem to mind very much if the war activities of the 9th Company were publicized by more influential foreign news agencies instead of a domestic newspaper with limited readership. Kim Chunok's first demand of the captain was to mobilize two platoons so that he could stage nice combat sequences at the rubber tree plantation in southern Ninh Hoa. The rubber trees planted in geometric patterns by the French colonialists would conjure up a spooky background with an eerie beauty for his intensely gripping documentary, the reporter explained. He apparently knew what he was talking about. He did not mind that, in fact, no action had taken place at the plantation during the battle because the erect trees with no under-brush offered little concealment for the Vietcong.

The soldiers, whose knees were still shaking from lack of sleep and prolonged battle fatigue, trudged down the whole distance of one kilometer along the rusty railroad to play actors for a staged war documentary. When we arrived at the plantation of tall gum trees, the reporter in Vietnamese paratrooper fatigues and jungle boots, with three cameras for black-and-white and color still pictures dangling from his neck, the movie camera slung over one shoulder and the heavy film bag on the other, explained the plot of the scenes he was hoping to film here to Lieutenant Chang Mingyu, the information officer for the 29th Regiment who had accompanied this extraordinarily busy reporter from Division Headquarters to this shooting location. Lieutenant Chang explained to Lieutenant Choe Sangjun, the 3rd Platoon leader, who was to lead the soldier actors during the filming, what the reporter had instructed him to do.

For the production of this "documentary film showing live combat action," Reporter Kim assumed the role of director; Lieutenant Chang was the prop man and prompter, while Lieutenant Choe and we, the foot soldiers, were the extras. There were no stars. Sergeant Chon Hisik and Piggie Chang staged, as directed, a colorful smoke screen with several red and green smoke shells at the entrance of the plantation and on the nearby rice paddy dikes to create an atmospheric, hazy backdrop. Normally they were used only for showing our position in the jungle to the supply chopper in the air. Then the reporter ordered us to rush out of the colorful smoke screen with a terrific battle cry and run toward his buzzing movie camera, firing our rifles like hell at the innocent rubber trees. This was the first time I had ever seen the smoke shells function as a misty shield the soldiers could hide in, like Hong the Magic Boy who used to suddenly appear or disappear in and out of the exploding cloud of smoke in an ancient Korean folk tale.

Kim lay on his back next to the light machine gunner and shot a long close-up sequence of the spent cartridges spewing out of the gun against the clear blue of the sky. "A good contrast of war and peace," he commented on his own work. He also took pictures of us crawling in the rice paddies like toads, half submerged in the water, supposedly infiltrating the enemy position in broad daylight.

Sergeant Kim Mungi and Corporal Kim Chaeo enjoyed themselves a lot, splashing across the watery paddies, chuckling and dodging imaginary bullets. They even made several novel suggestions to the director-reporter for intense dramatic effects such as using coffee to make blood stains.

"This movie is going to be shown in the Korean theaters, sir?" Corporal Kim asked the reporter naively. "Why don't you make my face appear big on the screen once in a while?"

The mock battle in the plantation lasted for more than two hours, but we did not know when the shooting would be over. We had not brought any C-rations with us, and I pitied myself lying dog-tired on the damp ground among the rubber trees. I felt the skin inside my stomach peel off and exhaust gas erupt from my throat. The reporter, still not satisfied by the takes he had shot so far, insisted the work continue without interruption for lunch back at the base, for he had to fly out to Saigon no later than 4:00 p.m. tomorrow afternoon to deliver "the material while it's still hot." He kept saying he would be through "in a jiffy," but I suspected we would have to go on splashing and rolling and yelling until dark, or until Kim exhausted all his film. He might even demand our cooperation to stage nocturnal combat scenes. While I was firing my carbine at the gum trees, prostrate in the afternoon heat, yawning, I wondered what my friends might be doing right now at home. It was Sunday. Pyongpil might be climbing Paegundae Peak with some of his friends. Chongsik might be boating at Tuksom resort with a

pretty college girl, passionately discussing Rilke and roses, as ever. But I
was out here, alone, abandoned and forgotten, belonging nowhere. I
had had this same incongruous sense of absurdity while passing underneath the barbed wire netting for infiltration drill under noisy machine
gun fire at Nonsan Training Camp two years ago. A mock war. A
fabricated danger. The untrue moments in one's life. And now I was
going through these untrue moments of a fabricated danger in another
mock war. Right here in the land where a real war had been going on
until yesterday, a few hundred yards away. For an infantryman, fighting
was a profession, his sole function. Killing was the job officially given to
foot soldiers. Now, here we were, playing fake actors in a fake war for a
fake documentary.

Kim, obviously unhappy with the scenes we had acted out so far,
dejectedly looked around the plantation, probably trying to divine the
illusive possibilities hidden among the gum trees. The soldiers waited
for his next instruction, watching the beads of sweat hanging on his
nosetip. Kim put down his cameras under a tree and went over to
Lieutenant Choe, the platoon leader, to give a general direction.

"Listen, lieutenant," the reporter said. "It just doesn't look real
enough. This time, tell a dozen of your men to run from that tree over
there to this tree over here with a horrible battle cry. They will hit the
dirt right here and quickly load their weapons and open up at the enemy
hiding over there. And I want to get some shots of the radioman urgently
calling in howitzer support, too. Let's have the radioman wounded in
the leg, so that we can have the medic in the picture. A combat scene
without a medic is a dud. While the wounded radioman is urgently
calling the FA, the medic dresses his bleeding leg. And I want someone
to burn that solitary hut over there with a flame thrower. I wonder if
anybody lives there. You go to that shack and check if anybody lives
there, lieutenant. And it would make a better picture if a VC runs out of
the hut to surrender, his arms thrown up high, immediately after the
flame is launched at the thatched roof. Can you bring a VC prisoner
from somewhere and keep him here until I finish this sequence, lieutenant? Maybe they have some prisoners at the regimental camp."

Lieutenant Choe mutely glared at the reporter for a full minute, it
seemed, his eyes burning with suppressed anger, and then said in a
quiet voice, articulating each syllable emphatically, "Listen, Mr. Reporter. Why don't you fuck all this nonsense and leave us alone? Do you
think I graduated from the Military Academy and came to Vietnam to be

an actor for this shit of a movie so that you can make money by selling junk films? If you want a combat scene, be here when a combat is actually going on." He turned to the soldiers awkwardly standing in the rice paddy as the reporter had left them. "Let's go home, you bastards," he said to us.

When the platoon leader called us "bastards," it sounded affectionate. While the reporter and the information officer were blankly gazing at the lieutenant, gaping, stunned by the quiet but contemptuous outburst, we slowly gathered our weapons and wiped off our wet, muddy fatigues. The information officer hastened to us and flared up at Lieutenant Choe.

"What do you think you're doing? Get back to the plantation and let Kim finish his work."

The platoon leader would not give in: "What the hell do you need these crazy news guys for, anyway?" he hissed. "Is this war some sort of candy bar or a newly developed farming tool to be introduced to a consumer market? Why do we have to make movies to publicize it? Why should we help that son of a bitch make this film and cheat people? At the company base, that bastard said he would take just a few brief shots and he'd be finished in ten, or fifteen minutes. You heard what he said, didn't you? 'Oh, fifteen minutes, at most,' he said, and I brought everybody down here, even some of the wounded, because I believed him. But look what he's doing to us. If that asshole wants an action movie so badly, tell him to call Burt Lancaster and Kirk Douglas."

We trudged back to camp along the railroad, led by the platoon leader.

Lieutenant Choe was summoned by the battalion and regiment commanders in the afternoon to be censured for his uncooperative and insubordinate attitude. When he returned to the base in the evening, Lieutenant Choe looked calm and subdued. He did not mind being punished when he believed he was right.

The first thing we had to take care of after returning home was evacuation of the wounded. The captain himself classified the wounded soldiers one by one, deciding who should be sent to Nha Trang or the division clinic or stay behind to defend the base from possible enemy attack. Among the 21 soldiers to be evacuated to the 102nd Field Hospital, 12 less serious cases were given the mission of convoying the dead to the crematorium which was located in the hospital compound. I belonged to another convoy crew led by Lieutenant Lee Taehun, the executive officer. Our convoy squad was assigned to transport sixty bodies to Nha Trang Airport before reporting to the hospital for medical care ourselves; there were too many bodies for the crematorium at Nha Trang to process, so sixty of them were to be shipped to the Tiger Division facilities at Qui Nhon. The convoy duty was assigned to wounded soldiers because they needed all the able bodied troops to defend the bases in case the enemy launched another attack.

We left the 29th Regiment parade ground for Nha Trang, three wounded soldiers assigned to each truck loaded with the body bags. We traveled along the endless road, bumping and jolting for one and a half hours, with the heavy canvas cover down despite the heat and the stifling stench lest the Vietnamese on the road should see the shame of the dead Koreans. In the truck the tarpaulin body bags were piled securely one on top of another, and a tag carrying the dead soldier's name, rank and serial number was stapled on each bag like a cargo identification slip.

Blankets of flies swarmed over us as we passed the Nha Trang dumping place, and I waved my hands desperately so as not to let them sit on my skin. When our sombre procession of four trucks passed through the swarm of flies and entered downtown Nha Trang, I lifted the back flap of the canvas a little to breathe deeply the fresh air of life outside and subdue my throbbing nausea. *Con gais* bicycled along the shore promenade lined with tall shade trees, fluttering the long tails of their soft-colored *ao dais*. Red-lipped prostitutes were having their lunch of roast rice, sitting on a rickety wooden bench by the doorless entrance of a roadside shack. Frail high-school girls sauntered down to the white beach, their conical straw hats and textbooks bundled with elastic bands slung over their backs. Several American soldiers were dredging the ditches along the airport wire fence, and two gorilla-like officers with fat bellies, shamelessly naked except for dark green shorts, drove away in a jeep to go swimming. Into that picturesque scenery drove the trucks heavily loaded with stinking bodies steaming with decomposing vapor.

Watching the green waves and white foam gurgle up the beach, I recalled the East Coast of Korea. I felt the salty breeze from the sea softly stroke the nape of my neck. I thought of the Korean autumn. I thought of the glorious tints of the autumn leaves on Sorak Mountain which might be blazing up now like the colorful fluttering garment of a dancing sorceress. But that autumn was away, far away from me.

We drove into Nha Trang Airport and parked the trucks near the hangars, off to one side, where they would not be too conspicuous. The wounded soldiers climbed out of the suffocating trucks and scattered into the shade, away from the corpses, to wait for a transport plane to come to carry the lifeless human cargo to Qui Nhon. I followed Lieutenant Lee into the passenger terminal for military personnel and bought a salami and cheese sandwich and a can of warm ginger ale from the sandwich counter. Washing the taste of morgue from my mouth with the ginger ale, I sat by a window and looked out at the black runway.

On the asphalt under the scorching sun outside the quonset terminal building, four Vietnamese boys, who earned tips by hailing taxis for foreign soldiers on R&R, were playing the game of throwing their coins into an empty can. Tinkle, *trrrrrrrrrr*. The sound of a coin bouncing and rolling away on the asphalt. Languid.

In the waiting room there were no Koreans except Lieutenant Lee and me, but six Vietnamese and about thirty Americans waiting for the afternoon planes to Ban Me Thuot, Pleiku, An Khe, Qui Nhon, Cam Ranh, Saigon. A Negro soldier with thick, primitive, pinkish lips was asleep by the grimy water cooler, sprawling on the three chairs lined up along the windowless wall. The white soldiers playing checkers, sitting around on their duffle bags, still retained their soft white skins and the green lustre in their eyes; they must be new here. A young soldier, a boy just out of puberty, standing alone by the door, holding a heavy M-14 that did not seem to belong to him, was blankly gazing at Brinks' PX quonset building behind the hangars. I talked to him. The boy soldier said he had been transferred here from West Germany 45 days ago and now was flying up north to Hue. He had a tranquil sadness in his eyes. Other soldiers of the United States of America were sitting alone, or by twos and threes, on the disorderly rows of benches, reading the *Stars and Stripes*, talking, or looking around, bored. The soldiers waiting for their planes to carry them back to the jungle after the brief in country R&R— what could they have enjoyed as the reward of their sacrifice in this war besides the slippery groins of the Vietnamese prostitutes in Saigon or Nha Trang?

A robust soldier with the shoulder patch of the 5th Special Forces and a dusty green beret, who had just flown out of Pleiku, was restlessly waiting for the plane to Saigon, every so often going over to the space call counter to check the waiting list. His jungle boots and M-16 rifle were caked with fresh red dirt. Next to this taciturn, bulky soldier with strangely melancholy blue eyes, a tiny Montagnard scout with dark tanned face and glinting mousy stare was sitting silently, hugging his huge M-1 rifle. Though traveling together, they did not talk to each other. Like eternal strangers. Where were they going in a hurry? To seek help for their comrades deadlocked in the jungle?

The eyes of soldiers who have encountered death face to face have no pupils, I thought. What was the Green Beret soldier thinking about behind those transparent green eyes?

Watching the soldier and the Montagnard scout sitting side by side, the tribesman probably no more than one fifth of the Green Beret in physical size, I was reminded of the biblical David and Goliath fable. And I pitied the American who was too big for this war fought by small people in small ways. Whenever I came across the Caucasian and Negroid soldiers who would fight and die for the Vietnamese but who were rarely welcomed or respected by this yellow-skinned dwarfish race, I felt I was watching the fall of a swaggering idol, a boastful giant who had never learned how to live outside his own world.

Nobody from any country had come to Vietnam for the sheer love of dying. The Americans were here for their national and strategic interests, the interests that made Washington send their young soldiers here. The Americans at home had begun to hate their own compatriots more than they did the ideological enemy. In this war, they were fighting against nothing but themselves. In this badly publicized war, that refused to recognize heroism, the Americans were the enemy of Vietnam, both North and South, as well as of their own nation.

During the Korean War in my childhood I saw many American POWs on Seoul's streets herded at gunpoint by North Korean People's Army soldiers to Mapo Prison. Their hands on their heads, the stripped GIs trudged along the road, their listless penes drooping pitifully. Those helpless penes looked so sad. But those soldiers at least were not abandoned by their own people.

On the wall next to the space call counter, someone had scribbled in large block letters with a red crayon: "Denton, Texas, 15,912 miles." At an American base on the road outside Nha Trang plank signs had screamed the names of hometowns among the rows of tents pitched in the barren field of swirling loess dust: Dodge City, Omaha, Albuquerque . . .

Among the numerous scribblings in tiny wriggling letters on the wall

of the airport bathroom, I found no obscene writings. In the Nha Trang
Airport toilet, the soldiers were chanting for home, instead of sex. From
the spot where my eyes automatically fell, I read these scribblings:

45 days to go home. Short.

36 days. Shorter.

34 days. Shorterer.

16 days. Shortest.

4 days. Anybody shorter?

On the plane home after this piss.

I left yesterday.

While glancing through the crumpled pages of comic strips in the *Stars
and Stripes* I had picked up from the littered cement floor of the waiting
room, I heard several young women burst into a laugh and that laughter
sounded very familiar to my ears. I knew for sure they were Koreans.
Four young girls, in blue or bright red slacks so tight that the outlines of
their panties were showing distinctly, had entered the passenger terminal. The tallest woman, who had dyed her hair blond, wore a thin
yellow blouse through which I could see her erect nipples and the faint
dark brown shade around them. They were a troupe of traveling show
girls, often publicized at home as "Korean entertainers actively working
on international stages," probably on their way to Cam Ranh Bay to strip
for an American audience tonight. A fat American in colorful Hawaiian
shirt and Bermuda shorts, doubtlessly the manager, waddled in after
the girls, puffing at his big stick of a brown cigar. The American soldiers
playing poker by the blinded window whistled at the girls, who waved at
them, smiling easy smiles. While the beefy manager was presenting
some papers and registering their names on the waiting list at the space
call counter, the four girls put their trunks down by the soldiers and
watched them play poker and yowl like howler monkeys. The four
women had not seen Lieutenant Lee or me yet.

I became suddenly restless. Perhaps it was because I believed the
land of war was a sanctuary for the male human species, but I always
felt ashamed and humiliated, like a boy caught masturbating, whenever
I saw Korean women anywhere in Vietnam. Maybe it was because all
the women I met in Vietnam were of the kind that brought disgrace and
infamy to my nationality and my personal self-esteem. I had heard too
many tales about the singers and dancers coming to Vietnam for "enter-

tainment activities on the international stage," which turned out to be no more than international prostitution. When I was having a lunch of cold noodles at a Korean restaurant at Cam Ranh one day, a skinny and overly friendly Vietnamese laborer from the American base pointed out for me a Korean couple strolling along the tarmac road towards the cactus field behind the restaurant, and explained that the Daihan *con gai* lived with a Daihan employee at an American construction company during daylight, and slept with an American *thieu-ta,* a major, at night. That afternoon, and whenever I read such blatant phrases as "Miss Pak, the Sex Bomb Directly From Korea" in the night-club advertisements carried by the English-language newspapers, the *Saigon Post* or the *Saigon Daily News,* I used to scorn myself, an infantryman at the bottom of an enormous structure who was contributing his infinitesimal bit, so these voluptuous girls could conquer the world with their vaginas.

"What do you know," said the shortest girl in a striped blouse, embracing herself. "They have a winter in Vietnam, too. I feel rather chilly today." The weather in January here was like that of a crisp autumn at home, but some Vietnamese on the downtown streets of Nha Trang, I had noticed, were clad in warm sweaters and jackets, or long-sleeved leather overcoats.

"Why don't you take Jason to the men's room and ask him for a good hug if you feel so cold?" the tall fake blond said in Korean, pointing with her chin at the manager who was coming over to them. "You'll have to sweat a lot because he's so big."

The girls burst into laughter. The five sat around on their trunks next to the poker-playing soldiers. Jason spat on the floor.

A Negro looked back at the tall woman over his shoulder and said, grinning, "Hey, honey, fuck me."

The woman responded spontaneously like a comedian's well-trained partner. "I'll give you a free one if your tool is big enough to make me happy. Let me take a look at your thing, uh?"

The Negro slouched up and opened his fly to fish out the dark brown rubbery tube. He shook it like an old broken hose a few inches before her eyes and said, "How d'ya like that? Will ya give me a suck? Uh? Uh? Will ya gimme a suck?"

The girl slapped it playfully, giggling. "Take it away," she said. "Smells so bad."

The girl in the striped blouse said, "You can't get in anywhere with that rubbery thing. Maybe all the workout you get is a sucking job, eh, you sucker?" Even her voice was like a soldier's.

I shrank myself so as not to be noticed by others, blushing hotly. I was suddenly reminded of the sixty dead bodies piled in the four trucks outside. Why had God ever allowed these whores to thrive on the deaths of my comrades?

Lieutenant Lee, his face red from anger, tugged at my elbow. "Let's get out of here," he hissed at me.

We sidled away from the laughing crowd and sneaked out like burglars to the black asphalt. Glaring at the trucks parked by the hangars, the lieutenant muttered, "I want to break my rifle to pieces rather than fight in this absurd war so that those whores can come to Vietnam and make money by selling their cunts."

When the arrival of the transport plane to Qui Nhon was announced through the loudspeaker in the passenger terminal, Lieutenant Lee called us. We scrambled up the trucks and drove out to the runway. Palm trees swayed in the sea breeze along the wire fence on the other side of the airport. The January sun of Vietnamese winter was parching the afternoon.

A massive C-130 Hercules slowly moved backwards to the end of the runway and stopped before a stack of steel beams near the hangars. One of the trucks, also slowly driving backward, approached from the opposite direction to the tail of the plane and stopped close to the end of the fuselage. The heavy back door of the transport was lowered to the ground. A second truck approached the plane's tail, and the remaining two trucks closed in as well so that the narrow square space formed between the trucks and the plane was blocked off from outside observation.

The lieutenant checked the gaps between the trucks to make sure that nobody could watch the transfer of the bodies. The drivers of the last two trucks rolled up the canvas back flaps and pulled out a cot. We rigged the cot aslant, like a slide from the tailgate of the truck down to the runway asphalt. The soldiers began to slide the body bags down the cot one by one. As each body bag slid to the asphalt with a thud, two American GIs in green undershirts picked it up by the ear-like handles and shoved it onto the plane. The tarpaulin-packed bodies piled up in the cavernous hold, and when the two trucks were empty, they changed places with the other two. Nobody covered his nose from the stench.

When the loading was over, Lieutenant Lee fetched a large Korean flag from the driver's seat of the leading convoy truck. Two Korean and two American soldiers held the four corners of the flag tightly and began to fold it ceremoniously. The lieutenant handed over the flag folded into a small triangle to the American senior officer of the transport plane. The two officers stepped back and saluted each other. The lieutenant, who often looked so ridiculous when he philosophised naively about everything, now looked like a solemn representative of noble humanity. The back door of the C-130 slowly craned up and the Hercules plane rolled out heavily to fly away to the north.

A few days after we had reported to the 102nd Field Hospital, Korean newspapers carrying blown-up headlines about our 'Victory of Ninh Hoa Battle' began to pour in through USAPO mail. The emphatic Gothic headlines of the civilian newspapers announced in pompous military rhetoric that the brave White Horse warriors had killed 580 Vietcong during the two-week period in Ninh Hoa area. Not a single newspaper reported that the Koreans also lost two hundred lives.

The news films we saw at the hospital repeated the identical stories in the identical manner, as if all the news had been mass-produced by the same copying machine provided by the government. In the news films that had documented the staged mock battles mobilizing soldier extras, in the obvious sequences Kim Chunok might have produced, smoke screens clouded up everywhere, the soldiers leapt over barbed wire entanglements with a "terrific" battle cry, and Vietcong crawled out of underground tunnels with their hands thrown up high. But no news film ever mentioned that any of us died during the raging battles. Not even a single word was wasted to discuss the warriors lost. Although they knew those news films were fabricated propaganda, the wounded soldiers did not mind. Applauding and laughing and yelling and beating the ground with their crutches, the soldiers enjoyed themselves and the movies, the comic adventures about themselves.

"Look at that! Hey, look at that boy running like a horse carrying that damned heavy AR! Whose son is that?"

"His folks at home would be mighty proud of him. 'I got a son who was in a movie, he-he-he-he!'"

"You're blocking my sight, boy. Take off your bandage, will you?"

When these "live on the spot combat reports" were shown at the Korean cinemas or on television, the ordinary people would never guess what pains we had gone through during the two weeks of "victory and glory." And they would never know that we died, or were maimed and crippled, or raved terrified in our foxholes, for they saw us only as the exciting heroes running around with blazing rifles. Truth was victimized for the creation of cardboard glory.

Nobody wondered why the war in Vietnam never ended if the Korean soldiers scored one victory after another wherever they went, wiping out all the VC there. So many Americans were reported killed and wounded day after day. Vietnamese and Vietcong also. But never the Koreans.

Watching our brave selves on the screen, I wondered what I should say to my friends about this war.

I spent a very monotonous three weeks at the hospital. I was physically comfortable because there were no patrol or ambush missions, but my heart was not easy. The steel beds and fluorescent lamps in the ward looked so strange, so outlandish, and the nurses and the army surgeons, who were lounging around in their impeccable white gowns, instead of dirty fatigues smudged with sweat and dust, looked like hypocrites who should not be allowed around combat soldiers. I hated the non-combat personnel at the hospital because I thought it was unfair that they were paid the same as we were, while we had to do all the fighting in the jungle, getting killed or wounded all the time, and they stayed safely behind just watching the show. The wounded soldiers looked like prisoners, the hospital soldiers their guards.

The sight of the casualties—the wounded or the dead—had more impact on me at the field hospital than in actual combat, perhaps because I could watch them objectively at a distance, as a third-person observer here, instead of lost in the chaotic action. It seemed a monstrous worm was squirming among the gory bodies and the mutilated soldiers that were transported like unpacked meat to the field hospital. The hospital looked like a terminal.

A rumor would get around for a few days that a bloody battle was raging somewhere. Then, one day, the wounded and dead soldiers, wrapped in bloody bandages or packed in body bags, were flown in by helicopters, and the surgeons started their work, patching up the tattered human beings as if they were broken machines. For them, amputating live human limbs or disposing of the charred bodies was a job not a bit different from overhauling an automobile.

In the ward where twenty steel beds were lined up in two rows along the plank walls, I was often awakened at night by nightmarish screams and agonized groans. I dreamed almost every night, but never, not even once did I dream about the body chewed by the river ducks. Very strangely, the most shocking experiences I had gone through were never reproduced in my dreams; maybe something was wrong with my subconsciousness, but it totally failed to respond to those shocks, contrary to psychoanalytic theories. Nor had I ever seen Hai or the Tuc My beach in my nightly dreams. Instead, I usually dreamed about such incongruous and absurd things as a swallow fallen to the ground from its nest under the eaves at my childhood home at Sosa, rubber balls floating down the muddy stream at Mapo during the rainy summer seasons, a bus skidding sideways on a snowy slope, a blind man playing with a mute blackbird, and a Soviet military helicopter hunting white polar bears in Alaska.

During the daytime, the recuperating soldiers would congregate in the shade and talk about the war that seemed to be an incident happening in another world now because they had a temporary reprieve from it. They languished away their healing hours, talking about the combat in which they had been wounded or going to the crematorium to watch "how the dead guys are roasted."

They were only fifty miles away from the active combat zone, but the war seemed to be a fairy tale to them as long as they were here. Life at the field hospital lacked reality, the only reality—war. I had absolutely nothing to do but wait for the time to sluggishly elapse until my thigh would heal, so I climbed the hillock behind the crematorium once or twice every day and, sitting under a thorny tree with a vacant mind, watched the yellow smoke curling up from the black chimney, the sea dozing beyond Nha Trang, the white giant Buddha, and the Phantom jets flying out on a bombing mission.

About two weeks after I had been hospitalized, a short bespectacled medic came to our ward looking for me. He said, with a knowing smile, "A visitor is waiting for you at the meeting point."

"The meeting point? Where is that?"

The 102nd Field Hospital did not have any interview room or other established facilities where patients and visitors could meet; nobody had expected any families or friends would visit the patients hospitalized here. The meeting point, the medic explained, was the barbed-wire fence behind the Seventh Ward where visitors would wait to meet the hospitalized soldiers. The meetings were usually arranged by the MPs at the gate; the recruits at boot camp, where personal visits were absolutely forbidden during the six-week training period, used to meet their families this way, paying some cigarette money to the MPs at the main gate for making the rendezvous arrangements.

I thought Sergeant Chon Hisik had come to see me, for he was always the first one to pay a visit if anybody was in distress. But the visitor was Hai.

As I approached, her fretful gaze was fixed on my face all the time, as if she was afraid I might disappear like smoke if she averted her eyes from me even for a moment. Gripping the barbed wire defiantly with her tiny pale hands, she said nothing, merely stared at me, but her expression told me what she could have never expressed in her halting words. Her lips twitched, very slightly, as she glanced down at the bandage tied around my thigh, beneath the torn leg of my trousers.

"How did you find out I was here?" I asked, with exaggerated gestures. I could not think of any dramatic words for the occasion.

"*Ha-si* Chon tell me go see you," she said. So, this was a visit from the sergeant after all, I thought.

But I was dazed just the same by her unexpected visit. Her visit was a bewildering surprise, for I had never even dreamed of anything like it. I had not written home about my accident because I thought it would not do anybody any good, so no one outside the 9th should have known about my hospitalization. But she was there, outside the unromantic barbed wire fence.

Then, as if from a delayed reaction, I felt a gradual sadness stir in my mind like an autumn breeze. There was no reason why I should be sad, but I was.

It was true I was delighted to see her, but I also pitied her guileless heart. She made me feel pity and sorrow out of guilt, because I thought I did not love her, yet. For me Hai was a refuge, a passing affair in a war zone, but she seemed to see me as an ultimate hope or an object in her belated adolescent quest for love. Perhaps Hai expected too much from a relationship that was, on my part, neither innocent nor honest. I was not ready to fulfill her hopeful expectations. What I probably wanted— or needed—was a psychological pastime, and I wanted to be with her because there was no other woman available. I tried to convince myself that a true love between a prince and a prostitute was sheer imagination. I was not willing to love Hai. She was just a straw that a drowning man would try to hang on to. She was not to be the woman for my lasting love, because a straw cannot save a drowning man.

Despite all these logical dissuasions by my mind, my indiscreet heart brimmed over with a sudden gratification at seeing her. She was out there, on the other side of the barbed-wire fence, and she was there for me, for me only. I wanted to climb over the barrier between us to be nearer to her, but I could not move my leg freely yet.

On the day when I was released from the 102nd Hospital, I went to the ROKF-V Field Forces Headquarters in downtown Nha Trang and waited for the mail truck, which also served as a regular shuttle bus for soldiers traveling individually between the ROKF-V Nha Trang Headquarters and the 9th Division Headquarters, from where I could easily find transportation to the company base. But the mail pickup for the White Horse Division was canceled that day because the mail truck had been mobilized by the 28th Regiment for a special civic activity at Tuy Hoa. I went to the switchboard, barely managed to reach the company CP, and explained to the clerk that I would not be able to report back to duty until tomorrow afternoon because there was no transportation available.

It was still morning when I left the ROKF-V Headquarters. I loitered around the town, peeking in the shop windows, talking to the children in Vietnamese-English when they followed me on the streets chanting, "Gimme chop chop, gimme cigarette, okay, okay," and smiling at every strange passer-by, because I felt so good about the whole world. Death and danger waited for me back at the base, I knew, but I was nonetheless happy and delighted to go back to my old buddies.

During early lunch at a Korean cold noodle house I decided to go to Tuc My to see Hai. Of course I could go to the Southern Cross Unit for a bunk and meals until tomorrow, but this opportunity was too precious for me to lose. I did not hesitate to take the risk of traveling by a dangerous local Lambretta mini bus. My leg was still stiff, so it took almost forty minutes for me to walk from the highway, where I got off the Lambretta, to Trau's house, limping uncomfortably all the way along the dirt road and the rice paddy dikes. I felt giddy and my stomach was somewhat turbulent, but I welcomed even fatigue and cold sweat as pleasant blessings; they were natural symptoms for a patient recovering from three weeks of confined life at the hospital. Even the farmers seemed to be friendly today, and I waved at everybody I met on the dirt road to the seaside village.

Trau was so delighted by my unexpected visit that he scurried around the house cheerfully, showing me the live bullets, a military map, broken binoculars, and a jeep's hubcap, all that he had collected during the last two months. And he opened two C-ration cans he had specially saved for me—fruit cocktail and beans—because he knew they were the ones I liked best. But it was Hai's silent smile and the unspoken joy and excitement glittering in her eyes that made my every single limping step to get there today more than worthwhile. Hai hastily steamed rice so that I could have an early supper she cooked herself and still get back to the base in time. When I told her I did not have to go back until the next afternoon, Hai's face brightened. So did Trau's. Hai also prepared kimchi for a side dish, but the cabbages were not pickled enough to taste like anything at all. I had to pretend the insipid cabbage slices were the most delicious kimchi I had ever tasted in my life. That made Hai happy, and she kept asking me, "More? *Beaucoup* more?" My overly convincing pretense ran short, however, as my stomach could not take too much of the flat, raw vegetable.

Trau, who always had been tactful, left home immediately after supper, excusing himself with the explanation that he had to go to see a friend at a neighboring village and might not be able to make it back home tonight. While Hai was washing dishes, I smoked at leisure, lying on the bed, watching her long black hair, thinking, yes, this is what married life is like, I guess. My heart relaxed, and time seemed to have slowed down its elapsing flow.

We went out to the beach after dark and sat side by side on the sand to watch the stars blinking like tiny distant electric bulbs. We softly exchanged pleasant talk about what seemed impossible to express through the smatterings of childish idioms in French, English, Vietnamese and Korean. We talked about the *Daihan mua dong* season, when the whole Korean countryside turned as white as paper, and about the bad, bad *xau lam* war that made *beaucoup* people die and cry and suffer, and about the *ngoi sao* twinkling in the *bau gioi* like *beaucoup beaucoup* gems, and the warmth in the heart you would feel when a caring person was sitting next to you.

I gently pulled her towards me because her eyes glimmered with the starlight in the blue darkness. She was in my arms, so helplessly petite and softly feminine, surrendering with her whole being. She responded like accompanying music to my hands, that slowly undressed her, not hurrying, not fearing anything, not demanding. Her small and pointed breasts were aroused, hard to my touch, and her abdomen was small and smooth like breathing silk, and we lay side by side on the cooling warm sand, naked, and I moved slowly, inhaling the exotic scent of the Vietnamese soap enveloping her whole undulating body, her bare skin, and I submerged into her fragrance, deeply, peacefully, quietly, stroking, rubbing, kissing, smelling her hair, brushing her ear with my nose, and we were so deep inside each other that the world around us had disappeared into silent nothingness.

Our movement over, I rolled down from her elastic moist body, and the sand grains, still warm from the buried heat, crusted on the perspiring skin on my back and chest, and she rested her cheek on my stomach, her soft hair covering my abdomen snugly like a small blanket, and she sang "Saigon Dep Lam," my favorite Vietnamese song about the beautiful city of Saigon, in a soft quivering voice, writing something on my sand-covered chest with her slim finger.

We walked back to her house, naked in the moonlight like the first human beings on earth, Hai carrying the clothes in her arms, I holding her slender waist with one arm and carrying my blunt boots in the other hand, and we snuggled to each other in her bed, stroking and rubbing and smelling all night, and we became one body three more times until we finally fell asleep in oblivious peace and pleasant exhaustion when the southern window started to show dawn faintly.

She cooked the breakfast while I was still asleep. When I woke around eleven o'clock in the morning, she had set the dishes on the small plank table that Trau and I had made one Sunday with ammunition boxes, and was back in the bed, naked again, next to me. Leaning her cheek to my shoulder, she whispered to me that Trau had gone out again after his hasty breakfast and would not be home until late.

Waiting on the deserted Highway 1 in the late afternoon for the mail truck to go back to the base, I remembered Hai's smooth legs, her glossy black pubic hair, the starlight on the beach, and the tasteless cabbage of the imitation kimchi. And on the truck, scampering along the highway to Ninh Hoa, I was overwhelmed by a strange sadness—the same sadness I had felt when she was gazing at me with her tearful eyes on the other side of the barbed-wire fence at the meeting point. I felt sad and empty, as if I had just lost a woman I had been cherishing dearly in my heart. I was sad because I felt I was cheating a woman who trusted me.

15

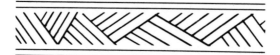

squeezed the carbine cartridges, slowly, one by one, into the long curved magazines; we bound two magazines together with a green packing tape, the open tops facing different directions so that we could quickly reverse them and fire another burst when one magazine was spent in close combat in the jungle. The yellow rounds were cold and smooth to the touch of my fingertips. The shiny black magazines felt pleasantly heavy. The bullets were solid, formidable, apt symbols of protection and survival. Why did I always feel a quietly throbbing excitement and gratification whenever I felt the sagging weight of the rifle in my hand?

Ten thousand strong were being mobilized for Operation White Horse One, the target of which was Hill 729, Khanh Hoa Province, the fearful Hon Heo Mountain that had been dismally waiting for our coming all these months.

Pyon Chinsu did not join the operation; he had not come back from the field hospital. Some suspected that he had been shipped to Korea from the 102nd Field Hospital, never recovering from his mental derangement. Corporal Kim Chaeo, the herald of all sorts of bad news, brought us the doubtful information that Private Pyon had been paralyzed from his waist down and discharged from the army through the 30th Reserve Division in Seoul. But there was no way to confirm the authenticity of the rumor that he had become sexually impotent due to his partial paralysis. All rumors about Pyon Chinsu sounded plausible.

I could not blame the soldiers for treating Pyon Chinsu like an old joke that had nothing to do with us any more, for I had also submerged myself in the oblivion that enabled all of us to survive by forgetting somehow the war we were fighting in. The gruesome sight of Pyon Chinsu being carried away on the blood-spattered stretcher during the Ninh Hoa battle kept recurring in my mind like an endlessly repeating sequence of an avant-garde movie, along with the appalling images of the night when the Vietcong swarmed to their death under the bright full moon. But those gory incidents also lost their impact in a few weeks, slowly fading into the mist.

The morning was dreary. A dusty wind had been whirling on the plain throughout the night. The company bases of minor strategic importance had been abandoned; a limited force of the remaining troops had to defend the area after the main contingent moved out. Heavy shelling had continued all night to scare away enemy elements hypothetically on the move in the lower hills. Well into the evening, helicopters had sputtered around to deploy the troops to new positions for an effective, coordinated future defense of Division Headquarters.

The operational information and messages were delivered to the Company CP from Division G-2 and G-3: Weather, partly cloudy and occasional rain in northern Khanh Hoa in the evening. Flight feasible. Northeasterly wind. Velocity 10–15 knots. Sunrise 0707 hours. Sunset 1838 hours. Moon rises 1102, sets 2314 hours. Visibility 10 miles. BMNT, EMNT 1926. Password: One blood—one nation.

Its barrel and action newly oiled and shining black, I leaned my carbine against my cot and gazed at the pile of cartridges forming a small mound before my knee. Three hundred rounds. Three hundred glinting brass casings. Lethal bullets and gunpowder were not merely the means to liquidate the enemy; they were the precious guardian spirits protecting my life in the jungle.

I scraped the remaining cartridges into the holders of my web belt, laced my jungle boots tight, fastened the sleeves of my fatigues with black rubber bands so that no loose flap of clothing would trigger a booby trap in the jungle, clipped the chin strap of my camouflaged helmet, slung over my shoulder the knapsack filled with enough combat rations to last three days, picked up the loaded rifle and locked the safety catch.

Leaving the bunker, I looked around the base to which I would not return for a month, or forever. The company CP squatted in the dark like a giant toad, and the zigzag network of trenches wormed around among the bunkers that humped up here and there like grave mounds in Korean cemeteries. The fully armed soldiers, who looked like a herd of gorillas in the fading darkness, gathered around the company bulletin board.

The contingent from the 9th Company was to rappel into the target from the air because the selected assault zone was thick with tall hard trees whose bark was so fire-resistant that even napalm could not burn them down to clear a landing zone.

When we arrived at the rendezvous point at 0640 hours, the troops of the 7th Company, who had arrived earlier, were waiting for their choppers. They were huddled in clusters around soaring bonfires like flocks of shivering wild ducks. The dawn of the jump-off was wet and chilly even for this subtropical country. A while later we lined up like a queue of free loaders before a food stamp office, and climbed aboard the UH-1Ds, their blades pulsing overhead.

Reeds and grass leaned down to the ground, churned by the fierce wind of the main rotors, and when all the soldiers with their knapsacks and weapons were loaded amid the deafening noise of the running engines, the twenty helicopters lurched up, one by one, faltered momentarily a few yards above the ground, and then raising their tails, suddenly spurted forward after a roaring engine scream. The buffalos, that had been roaming around in the field, stampeded across the rice paddies, startled by the flying noise.

We flew low, like swallows skimming over a lake's surface, gliding toward the dark mountain. The choppers began to slide up diagonally along the slope, still clad in the placid milky beam of early morning. Soon the red molten lump of the sun rose from the Dong Hai Sea. I saw the jagged shadows of Huey attack helicopters in tight formations, by fours, falling on the dazzling white clouds down below. Soft spectral colors sparkled around those airborne shadows. The choppers flying beneath us created perfect spinning circles with the yellow stripes painted at the tips of their main rotors. To fly across the blue morning space was an act of beauty in itself.

Flight quickened all the metabolic rhythms of my body—heartbeat, pulse, breathing. I thought I could actually hear the blood rushing faster in my veins. Overlooking the green undulating peaks and ridges, soaring higher and higher in the sky like a majestic eagle, watching the earth falling off, away, away from me, I was briefly lost in the world of forgetfulness; I did not know where I was going, and what for, because I had fallen into inexplicable rapture, flying, soaring, soaring high into the unknown world of blissful solitude.

When we reached the landing zone, the helicopters halted in the air. I could not see any ground among the dense foliage of the virgin forest clothing the world totally in dark green. A bundle of rope, one end tied to the pole behind the cockpit, was hurled down from each side of the chopper. The 50-meter coil of rope floated some distance down like entangled string snakes and then straightened with a shaky jerk to stab into the green carpet of foliage like a long syringe. The soldiers tightened their knapsack shoulder straps and slung rifles upside down over their necks.

In our chopper, I, the second sergeant, and Chi Taesik, the radioman who had returned from the field hospital three weeks earlier, were in the first team to go down the 40 meters to the ground by the rope. I fastened the helmet strap tight under my chin and stepped down on to the landing skid, leaning back to maintain the balance of my body, winding the knotted rope around my arm and thigh. Between my pincered feet the lone white rope hung down like a thin endless tail, waiting for me to span the infinite vertical space. By this rope I had to go down there, not knowing what was waiting among those trees. My palms and wrists began to hurt.

"Let's go!" Sergeant Chi shouted to me above the floor of the hovering helicopter.

I pushed off the landing gear with my soles. My whole body swung and dangled high in the empty sinking air. The sky was suddenly filled with desolation and deaf silence. I could not even hear the roaring engine of the helicopter overhead, as if I were confined in a hanging transparent globe. I had an illusion, however, that the soldiers in the chopper could distinctly hear my breathing and heartbeat—*thump, thump, thump, thump, thump.*

I descended, slowly, automatically, hand over hand, my knees clasping the rope. My knapsack kept sagging downward like an anvil. I kept climbing down but my swaying feet touched nothing but the empty air. I felt a sudden despair that I was abandoned, all alone in the vast open space which existed only in concept, not in reality.

The eight of us from the first chopper kept climbing down the ropes, swaying like spiders at the ends of gossamer silks. Oddly, I felt a chilly loneliness up there rather than the fear of being helplessly exposed in the open air, an easy target. And I thought, What am I doing, hanging here by a rope? What had brought me here? And I wondered if my college classmates had been all hired by now. In Seoul competition for employment by major companies was growing more severe every year.

I kept going down, the rope was endless.

I felt I had covered an infinite space, when the tip of my jungle boot finally touched leaves. From sudden relief, sweat poured down my face and streamed down my spine.

As I burrowed some distance into the thick foliage, the sky overhead glittered in small blue pieces in the mosaic patterns made by dark green shade and white and golden spangles of sun. And when I climbed a little further down, I could not see the sky or the helicopters any longer because the leafy ceiling totally blocked my sight. There were so many trees, so thick, so big, so high, that I could not see the ground yet. Nor could I see the other seven soldiers in the first team. Sergeant Chi should have landed somewhere within three meters from me because we had come down from the same chopper, but I could not find him either.

I swung my legs several times and managed to grab a bough with my feet. I put my arm around the tree trunk, precariously standing on the bough and tugged the rope three times to signal the next soldier to rappel down. My eardrums started functioning again and I heard the remote whir of the helicopter engines from the invisible space. The rope whipped a couple of times and then jerkily wriggled up to disappear through the dense leaves like a thread of noodle sucked up with a slurp.

Under my feet, the primitive quiet was deep and dark green. Thick tendrils and heavy branches sagged down to hang motionlessly all around me like the botanical world in a Henri Rousseau painting.

Nobody, nobody was there. There was nobody in the mystical woods. Except me.

I decided to catch my breath before shimmying down to the ground. Perched on the bough like a squirrel, hugging my knapsack and rifle in my arms, I sat, cozily surrounded by wide glossy leaves, hidden in the ancient silence, out of anybody's reach. An unexpected exultation penetrated my heart. I relished a private moment of peace, all mine, all by myself—something like the warm comforting bliss during a night flight over thick piling layers of cloud glimmering in moonlight. There would never, never be a war around here, I felt. I wanted to take a nap.

Perching on the bough, hugging the knapsack in my arms, shrinking my shoulders, shrinking myself like a ball, like a fetus, I listened to the peace in the forest, and watched the mystery of the trees that had never suffered human existence, no artificial disasters, and I thought myself a fetus squatting in a soft watery womb, a fetus snugly fit into its own niche, into a corner never to be violated by any other human. A lone bird twittered lazily nearby and I thought about the beginning of all beginnings.

Then I heard Sergeant Chi Taesik calling me in a hushed, careful voice from under the leaves. "Sergeant Han." He called from below.

I did not answer, I did not want to. He waited a moment, then called again, "Sergeant Han. Where are you? We're all down here except you. Where are you, second sergeant?"

The mission assigned to our platoon was to land on high ground near the summit and blow up the trees with TNT to clear the woods and secure enough open space to build a helipad. The landing spot would serve as an operational artery through which the ensuing forces would pour in to seek and eliminate the VC regimental headquarters hidden in the heart of this mountain. When their headquarters was destroyed, the fleeing enemy elements would be rounded up by the 28th and 30th Regiments' troops who in the meantime would have encircled the target areas.

It took not two easy days, as G-3 had planned, but a painful six days to clear the helipad with TNT because the trees, probably hundreds of years old, were hard as rocks. The Tac CP kept nagging and pressing us to hurry. We were frustrated because it took so much time to remove the trees, one at a time, while the forty of us, completely isolated on top of Hon Heo Mountain, had to defend ourselves too, regularly going out for a patrol against any possible enemy approach. Since we had to stay at the same place for days, we were soon surrounded by splinters of trees and piles of crumpled C-ration cans that created a tornado effect. I had always to watch where I was going lest I should step on the feces hidden under almost every small heap of leaves. Even without the higher commanding officers haranguing us to hurry, we wanted to finish the clearing job quickly and escape the encircling dump of trash and feces.

In a few days everybody began to smell like musty wet rags rotting in the humid monsoon season. Fatigues were drenched in sweat every day, blown dry by the cool jungle air every night, then drenched again the next day. I could feel chips of woods and leaves and small clots of dirt whenever I ran my fingers through my hair. Sweaty dirt peeled off my skin if I rubbed it with my fingers. But we could not afford the luxury of washing ourselves with the precious water supplied from the air every other day. When the choppers flew in and hovered 20 meters over us to drop the five-gallon cans containing potable water, we hid under the fallen trees to survive the "bombs." Crouched among the mutilated trees, we slept.

The sky widened in proportion to the open space on the ground littered with battered trees. A UH-1D carrying mail and other supplies finally made a somewhat dangerous vertical landing on the sixth day, lurching precariously into the perpendicular hole surrounded by tall lush woods. The 10th Company was brought in the next day to take over the job of expanding the helipad and to relieve us for combat duty. Finally then, in the second week of the operation, we joined the search and destroy sweep already in progress in the southerly sectors. We climbed down the mountain and began the search for the enemy.

It rained now and then. On the ground ripe fruits had fallen from various trees and decayed among decomposing leaves to form a squishy dark layer, thickly covering the dirt like wet padding. The whole jungle was pungent with the cool humid smell exuded by decaying plants. The soldiers trudged through, single file. The thick tendrils and branches knitted, crisscross, into a huge awning over our heads. Only when we reached a napalm or howitzer shell crater on a ridge did we see the sky. The soil in the valley had not seen sunshine from ancient days and had been so soaked in moisture, under these eternal shadows, that we could not dig foxholes unless we were ready to spend a night sitting in a pool of percolating water. I had a strong urge to pick up a handful of the black corroded soil and eat it; I was almost sure I could digest this dirt.

Our advance was depressingly slow. The soldiers moved quietly through the woods, their dog tags and the stacking hooks on their rifles wrapped with cloth so as not to make any sound. The loose flaps of their fatigues were likewise bound with strings or rubber bands to prevent accidental detonation of booby traps. The lead soldiers wielded their machetes to clear a path whenever dense undergrowth and wild vines blocked our way.

The enemy tolls mounted in the second week as we reached the VC positions. The encirclement closed tighter, with the main forces sweeping up the ridges and gorges while the 29th Regiment companies, airlifted to the summit, pushed the enemy downhill. Pressing hard from both sides, we suffered few casualties. Seven had been reported killed so far, by snipers or poisoned arrows and other booby traps, while two scouts sent out by the 6th were severely wounded when a rifleman mistook a startled boar for a fleeing VC and hurled a hand grenade in the wrong direction. But genuine Vietcong guerrillas were also being captured or killed all over the encircling cordon as they recklessly tried to break through.

Whenever Captain Kim Sanghyop tried to get through to the battalion CP to report something, Sergeant Chi Taesik's radio kept screeching with calls from other units noisily filing their combat reports. The 29th Regiment had already captured more than a hundred firearms and eight prisoners, and killed 127. Enemy casualties kept increasing, the jungle seemed to sizzle with soldiers yelling and killing and laughing and hunting with abandon.

For the winners, war was a breathless joy and excitement, an ejaculation of male ecstasy. The radios reverberated with ceaseless triumphant cries that sounded like clarions. They were jubilant. The combat units enthusiastically pursued their enemy, the individual companies competing with one another in killing. The commanding officers repeatedly inquired of subordinate officers how many more they had killed; they were anxious to know. Amid this feverish atmosphere, one of the company commanders was reprimanded by his battalion commander because he had not kept his radio open for emergency communications; the company commander had switched off his radio, annoyed by the frequent demands for latest reports.

Victory was a fever. The exultation of the 9th was a near insanity when they located the VC 85B Regiment Headquarters and were given the order by the Tac CP to level it.

The enemy regimental headquarters was found by the five-man squad led by Sergeant Chon Hisik, who had been promoted to a sergeant first class three weeks earlier. We waited on this side of a suspicious ravine, concealing ourselves behind rocks and trees, while Sergeant Chon's search party crossed the stream first and checked the area to see if an enemy ambush was lying in wait for our crossing on the other side. Chon and his team vanished into the woods quickly, like water into sand, and reappeared a few minutes later. Sergeant Chon silently signaled that the coast was clear and we could safely cross the stream but had to keep quiet. Then they trickled into the jungle once again to continue their search further up the slope. We began to cross the rapid current, stumbling and reeling in the sweeping water that felt icy through our clothes, hanging to the rope rigged across the stream by Chon's squad. The smooth rocks in the noisily tumbling water were so slippery the men kept falling in midstream. We were exposed to sunshine for the first time in days, and the heated helmet felt pleasantly warm on my crown after the humidity of the dark jungle.

When the whole company had crossed the wild creek, we waited for fifteen minutes to check the surrounding areas, and then moved out, following the signs left by the scouting party. Broken branches or pebbles arranged in the shape of an arrowhead indicated the paths. We scrambled up a dry rocky creek bed for about five minutes; Sergeant Chon and his party were waiting for us, hiding behind yuccas and other tall tropical plants with broad fan-shaped leaves. He signaled for us to keep low and silent.

When I crawled over to him, Sergeant Chon pointed ahead and said in a muted voice, "It's over there. The VC regimental headquarters."

There was a small waterfall in a secluded deep gulch that would never be detected by aerial observation through the lush canopy of foliage, and by the stream flowing down from the waterfall we saw four bamboo structures resembling the watchtowers at Korean watermelon farms.

"Are you sure?" I said.

"A VC prisoner gave the exact map coordinates this morning. This is it."

These establishments had no walls, and the elevated platforms with bamboo ladders looked like the countryside pavilions where village elders gathered in Korean summer evenings with folding fans and refreshing fruits to chat with friends and forget the heat. There were also a pigsty and a chicken coop in a large pit with a grass roof near a slope. At first I could not believe these shoddy structures were the VC regimental headquarters that I had heard about so often. This was a picnic ground.

Sergeant Chi Taesik reported by radio to the platoon commander the exact location of the bamboo huts. Lieutenant Choe Sangjun hastily rushed up the creek bed and joined us. The lieutenant dispersed the soldiers to attack positions forming a wide circle around the bamboo structures. Following the platoon leader's hand signals, we crept closer to the potential enemy positions, holding our breath. The deep green silence was broken only by the falling water, occasionally cackling chickens and grunting pigs. We made no visual contact with the enemy. Lieutenant Choe waited for a minute longer and then climbed up a flat rock by the murmuring stream. He raised his left hand high.

"Open fire!"

The volley at the invisible enemy shook the ground with a rolling thunder, that turned to a drone of a stormy shower beating on a tin roof, and the partitions and roofs, woven with palm leaves and reeds as well as the bamboo poles and cushiony rush mattings, splintered to dust and fragments, battered by the pouring bullets. We exhausted whole magazines at the trees, the dark holes around the undergrowth, the sunken pits, the rocks hidden behind the waterfall, and anywhere we thought the enemy could be hiding. My nostrils were queasy with the sickening sweet smell of gunpowder; white bullet marks splotched the dark gray surfaces of rocks and spewed puffing dust in a disorderly pattern.

There was no apparent enemy resistance against the first volley, and the lieutenant ordered us to cease firing. We emerged from our hiding places to cautiously approach the bamboo huts.

The enemy was not here. The enemy was nowhere. We searched and searched, but the Vietcong were long gone. It was obvious they had abandoned this headquarters in the first phase of the operation.

The soldiers destroyed everything in sight with their rifles and hand grenades. The huts were torched, leaving only piles of burnt bamboo. Explosions echoed violently in the caves nearby and white smoke belched out of tunnel entrances that had been camouflaged with withered twigs. All the Vietcong supplies that were found were systematically destroyed. Medicine boxes that had been neatly classified and piled in an underground warehouse were pulled out and hurled against the rocks. Countless bottles with handwritten labels shattered into shiny glass fragments, the liquid staining the rocks and the ground with exploding imprints. Corporal Song Pyongjo, the AR gunner, dragged out an armful of cooking pots from a tunnel, dangled them in a row on a drooping branch with fishing lines that VC used for rigging booby traps, and then opened up his automatic rifle at them, ratatatatat, laughing. Some soldiers put on colorful transparent panties and black brassieres over their dirty fatigues and demonstrated their individual versions of the Monroe walk on a flat rock, like beauty pageant contestants. Corporal Yun Chusik found several rolls of silk and draped them across his chest like a pirate decorated with a sash.

Among the spoils found in the secret caves and tunnels I saw blood-stained cartridge shells, American automatic rifles and M-2 carbines captured earlier by the Vietcong and now recaptured by the 9th Company soldiers, U.S. military supplies, contraceptives, GI diaries, family photographs, Ho Chi Minh sandals, bamboo spikes, nails, and a broken rocket launcher.

Corporal Kim Chaeo emerged from the cave above the pigsty with a box of rum in his arms. "Look here, lieutenant, sir," he called cheerfully. "The Cong must have saved these for some victory celebration."

"Let's have a celebration for *our* victory," Piggie Chang said. "I think I haven't had a drink for centuries."

Corporal Min the Butcher said, grinning, "Nowhere in the combat manual can I find a passage mentioning that we might have a free drink thanks to the Cong."

"Why don't you butcher a pig over there?" Private Chon Chilbok said to Corporal Min. "We will have a roast pig for the rum party."

"Yeah, let's have a celebration with a piggie!" Piggie Chang cheered.

Several soldiers, led by Piggie Chang, rushed to the pigsty. Sergeant Chang Taejun ordered Corporal Min Chonggi to kill a pig, because butchering was his specialty after all. "The Butcher" fitted the notorious bayonet on his rifle, strutted into the pen, aimed his bayonet straight at a pig in a perfect combat posture, and attacked. The stabbed pig squealed, blood gushing out from the impaled belly. The soldiers cheered, then scattered to gather twigs and logs to build a fire.

"I never knew the Cong were such friendly chaps," Private Kang Chiu said, sharpening a branch to use as the skewer. "They might have been planning to throw a feast to welcome us with all this rum and pigs and chickens."

"Hey," someone called Corporal Chae Mugyom. "You go over to the chicken coop and wring the necks of a couple of fat hens. I really like roast chicken, you know."

Corporal Chae leaned his rifle against a tree and rolling up his sleeves, was about to enter the coop. Chon Hisik, who had been reloading his magazines by the twig gate, stretched his arm to block Chae's way. Chon pointed at the chickens with his chin and said, "Don't touch them. They're mine."

I glanced back at him over my shoulder, as I took my jungle boots off to wash my feet by the stream, for I thought his voice sounded too serious. I swallowed a sudden fear, because I noticed an icy glint flash through his eyes.

Corporal Chae stepped back, puzzled and frightened. Several soldiers, abruptly turning tense, silently watched Sergeant Chon open the twig gate and sit down on the ground. He raised his knees and fitted them into the armpits to assume the sitting posture to shoot a fixed target. I had never seen such a perfect shooting posture, not even from a PRI instructor at the boot camp. He locked a new magazine into his carbine chamber, loaded the lead cartridge, opened the safety catch, wound the sling tautly around his arms, placed his right cheek slowly on the stock, and then with a careful aim, squeezed the trigger. One single shot rang out and one chicken, a sudden lump of blood and tangled feathers, bounced off the fence and fell to the ground, a pulpy mush spilling onto the dirt. He aimed again while the startled birds flitted around in a frenzy, and slowly pulled the trigger. Another hen, that had been fluttering back and forth cackling noisily, turned to an instant clot of mashed bones and blood-spattered feathers. One by one, he shot and killed all twenty-four chickens: methodically, never hurrying, never flinching, never looking back at anybody, totally absorbed in his work. He was an outstanding marksman who had won the first prize of fifty dollars at the battalion shooting contest in February, and he did not waste one single bullet in executing the helpless birds.

Other soldiers blankly gazed at him, stunned.

Practicing marksmanship with chickens as live targets might not have been such "a big deal" for other soldiers in a combat zone where even human lives were wasted for absolutely nothing, but I had a reason to fear that incident. I was the only one, except Sergeant Chon himself, who knew what Sujin had written in her last letter to him. Since that letter, he often brooded for hours without a word or behaved very strangely at times, as if hoping something terrible would happen to him. At times he would tell me light-heartedly, "There're as many girls around me as shrimps in a whale's stomach," and even hummed pleasantly to convince me that he really did not care. And he continued to play practical jokes on his buddies, filling the Butcher's canteen with urine that did not taste much different from the tepid ordinary water with salt tablets dissolved in it, writing fake love letters to the platoon leader signed by the *con gai* working at the Division PX, replacing the strings of Sergeant Oh Ujin's guitar with rubber bands, cheerful as ever, teasing everybody around, laughing. But I shuddered whenever I saw this burning anger in his eyes. I knew well what anger could do to him—and what he could do in anger, and I feared that Sujin would be dead a few days after Chon's return home.

He slung his rifle over his shoulder, dusting the seat of his pants, and when he turned from the dead chickens to me, his face brimmed over with a surprisingly innocent and bright smile, like a child who had just won a big teddy bear from a shooting game at a country fair.

Since we did not have any more work to do, except the destruction of the empty enemy stronghold, the rum party was soon in full swing by the waterfall; the soldiers sang "The Camellia Maid" and other popular or folk songs, all at the top of their lungs, while cooling their feet in the water, their lips oily with pork fat, and all the while tapping their helmets with bayonets for the musical effect.

Sergeant Kim Mungi discovered a Vietcong latrine under a tree near the underground medicine storage, and opened a 'perfect aim crap-shooting game.' The VC toilet was totally hidden underground without any visible structures standing above the ground. The pit was completely concealed by a raft-like log lid and dirt covering; the only visible part was a square hole barely large enough to allow a clenched fist to pass. The soldiers, after paying a dime for the entry fee, stripped their behinds and aimed at the hole to win a bottle of rum, the prize for the soldier who dropped most lumps into the square opening without leaving any smear on the wooden frame. When a lump would drop into the hole with a perfect aim, the spectators cheered, applauding. If someone kept grunting without much success at producing "the grenade," Kim

Mungi would shout like a baseball umpire with an exaggerated sweeping motion, "Strrrrrrrrike! Out! Out!"

While the rum party and the crap-shooting game were going on, Master Sergeant Han Myongsun found an old movie projector and one reel of film in a tunnel near the waterfall. We had no idea where the Vietcong had captured it, but the projector was a Bell & Howell. The platoon leader checked the film and said, "Hey, this film got a *con gai* actress in it. Maybe this is an official NVA porno movie to help the lonely Cong masturbate in this godforsaken jungle." He told Sergeant Chon Hisik to prepare for a VC movie show in the evening, "but run it proper, not backwards this time. And the show is for free. Pass the word."

After supper the 3rd Platoon soldiers watched the Vietcong movie on a gray silk screen draped from a branch, its bottom weighted down with stones. We could not hear the dialogue too clearly, and the background music was full of unintended trebles, like a 30-year-old record played on a rickety phonograph at a wrong speed, but the story was simple enough for us to follow. A sick Vietcong fighter, hungry and lost, staggered into a peaceful village with buffalos and chickens and singing children, after a painful and weary journey. And a sympathetic family, including a young beautiful and compassionate daughter, devotedly nursed the distressed man until he recovered his health and returned to his comrades to continue his struggle for the National Liberation Front.

Imitating the over-emotional voice of a silent film narrator, Piggie Chang now and then interjected his personal interpretations into some dramatic sequences in the 20-minute VC odyssey, raining with scratches from the beginning to the very *Fin*: "Oh, the moon is so miserably beautiful and this miserable Cong is hungry for food, hungry for home, hungry for cunt. I have been fighting for the National Liberation Front for seven years and my legs are tired from too much running. How sad is my cock that hasn't been in any *con gai* for over nine months. Oh, help me, Uncle Ho, oh, *quo vadis*, Uncle Ho!"

Leaning against a tree in the dark, I watched Sergeant Chon mutely operating the projector, once in a while lightly tugging at the film to feed it into the sprockets.

I did not know what kind of a girl Sujin was, and how deep a love they had shared. Piggie Chang told me that Sujin used to come to visit Chon at least twice a week during the combat training period at Yangpyong, but Chon himself rarely said anything to me about her until that night when he brusquely handed a letter over to me in the dark. I read it by flashlight, lying on my cot in the bunker. The letter was self-explanatory. She had married last month.

My husband (this word sounds as strange to me as it may to you) he's a friend of my brother. I used to know him even before I met you at the park, and to tell you the truth, I occasionally met him even while I was dating you. I won't mind how badly you'd think of me, because I've made up my mind to accept certain things to come. It may not matter to you any longer, but I married him not because I loved you less. Only—you were too far away while he was always beside me. And you may be partly to blame because you didn't have me when you had a chance to that night. You should have taken me before you went away. I burnt all your letters two weeks before my wedding. And those little packets of coffee you used to send me. The tin foil shriveled in the fire and the coffee boiled like molten toffee for a while, the brown clod turning to black soot. I thought about keeping your letters but changed my mind. The idea of secretly keeping your love letters seemed so hypocritical after what I've done to you. It's nothing more than an act of deceiving myself. To say a lot of sad words to you, or to send back the letters to you—those things somehow seemed to be sheer melodramatic deceptions, a selfish consolation for myself. Marrying someone else without even telling you is a betrayal, I know, so I won't try to beautify it with any pretentious verbal sentimentalism. I can't expect or imagine, or even hope for a beautiful goodbye between us.

The letter was not signed. I gave it back without finishing it.

"She says the bridegroom was very happy to know she was still a virgin," Sergeant Chon had said that night in the dark in a strangely subdued voice. "I didn't touch her even when we slept together at Yangpyong Inn because I wanted to keep something precious for our marriage. Wasn't it indeed a nice wedding present of mine for the bridegroom?"

Since then he did not mention Sujin in my presence ever again. But I knew how deeply he still loved her. I recalled how he used to collect the small packets of coffee from C-ration boxes and, once in a while, send them to Korea in a big pouch. I often wondered if he was sending them to a small coffee shop run by someone he knew, for real good coffee was scarce back home. The letter had revealed where all those packets had gone. Chon had told me once about the romantic lonely nights his girl used to savor by candlelight with a cup of hot coffee.

Chon found it very hard to believe that Sujin had really married someone he did not even know, and he pretended everything was all right, but his reaction to the shock would show sometimes in a very violent manner. About two weeks after he received the letter from Sujin, Sergeant Chon and I stayed overnight at the enlisted men's quarters of the Field Army Headquarters downtown in Nha Trang because our supply truck had to wait until the 100th Logistics Command started issuing new camouflage fatigues the next morning. While we were drinking about the fifteenth bottle of Ba Muoi Ba beer at a Korean cold buckwheat-noodle shop, he blurted, "I will sleep with a whore tonight. You coming with me?"

I was afraid of venereal diseases and Vietcong assassins rampant at the brothels maintained for American or Daihan soldiers, but I decided to go with him, somewhat reluctantly, because I could not let him go alone in that condition. He was much more drunk than usual. Sergeant Chon led the way. Chon had never slept with a prostitute, or any other girl, as far as I knew, but he must have asked his friends how to get around the Nha Trang brothel compounds, for he seemed to know the back alleys as well as he knew the lines in his own palms. My hazy drunk eyes tried to register the landmarks in my memory so that I would be able to safely retrace my way back out of this alley later, but my fogged vision left no clear imprints of the noisy streets, the sloshing muddy puddles, the barbed wire thrown around some important-looking buildings across the road and Negro soldiers yelling, and then we were already in the middle of a smelly and filthy district that I recognized at one glance as a typical prostitution town.

Colorful signs swayed like cackling witches in the dark alley lined with bamboo fences, where stupor brimmed over the world, densely enveloped by opium smoke, marijuana smoke, grass smoke, smoke, teeming with spermous smells excreted by bodies in spasms, gasping in the steamy turkish baths, in the grimy sweaty beds, in the musty whorehouse cells and the splashing bathtubs in cheap hotels. I saw lamplights as faint as kerosene lanterns in a misty harbor. I thought I heard a wailing young female voice yearning for bygone love in a

throbbing dying song. The "taxi girls," whom anybody could ride for the
fare's worth, their faces thickly made up like Japanese kabuki actresses,
snooped out of the plank shacks, beckoning at the males.

Sergeant Chon, who had been reeling ahead of me into the flesh
market, swung back towards me, staggering like a rolling ship, and said
with his twisting tongue that seemed to keep rolling back to his throat,
"The *con gais* working at the turkish baths here give you a hell of a
sucking job, Master Sergeant Han told me. You just go crazy in their
mouths." He burped. "You know something, Sergeant Han? At the
turkish baths at Samgakchi in Seoul, the Korean girls give world-famous
sucking jobs to Yankee soldiers and foreign tourists or businessmen
visiting our glorious capital city. Did you know that, Sergeant Han? The
master sergeant told me that. Do you know why the earth keeps
revolving? Because it's dizzy when everybody is sucking everybody else.
That's why. Let's go and get ourselves sucked. Come on. Follow me."

He waved at me, turning back to the alley. We picked a two-storey
frame structure at random and entered.

The top-heavy shanty, loosely built with nothing but plank boards
and scantlings, looked so shabby and precarious I felt the whole house
would crumble down if someone shook it hard enough. I followed
Sergeant Chon into the dirt-floored hall where a lone electric bulb was
gleaming dimly in the fog of cigarette smoke. Six or seven young girls, in
miniskirts or naked except for black or red brassieres and panties in
matching colors—two of them with bare breasts—were sitting on the
wooden benches along the three plank walls like displayed meats at a
slave market, waiting for the customers to come and rent them, the
women leisurely smoking, beaming idiotically, or opening their legs and
pointing at the secret fold in the groin.

"You can have one too, Sergeant Han," said Sergeant Chon, checking
the girls one by one with his bleary eyes. "I will pay for your whore and
the magnificent sucking job and everything. Comrades-in-arms should
go everywhere together—to death and to whorehouse alike."

A dark-skinned girl, whose black triangular panties and big brown
nipples were seductively visible through her thin pink slip, emerged
from a dark corner, went over to Sergeant Chon, lifted her slip and
pulled her panties down to show what she had in store for him. "You
sleep with me?" she said. "Okay?"

"Sleep with you? I didn't come to this fucking whorehouse to sleep. I
came to vum vum!" He roared with a laughter.

"Vum vum okay," the girl said, giggling. "Vum vum namba one."

I did not feel like having a girl at such a filthy and humiliating place, but as long as I was in the house, I might as well choose a whore to be with and wile the time away until Chon was finished with whatever he wanted to do, I thought. I did not want to have any unnecessary argument with Chon; I just hoped everything would be over quickly so that we could go back to safety at the EM quarters. I picked a very short girl with black straight hair billowing down to her fat hips. The short girl with fat hips and I followed Chon and the dark-skinned girl in black triangular panties up the shaky squeaking stairs. The two girls led us to a room partitioned off from other rooms by long plank boards. The four rooms upstairs had no walls except these loose planks, and one could hear and see virtually everything that others might be doing in the next or opposite rooms. And each room had two beds side by side, separated only by thin transparent mosquito nets.

Lifting the grimy mosquito net rigged on wooden poles, Sergeant Chon crept into the bed on the left with his prostitute, who kept jabbering something in Vietnamese without caring if anybody was listening or not, and the girl, kneeling on the bed without any coverings, turned off the electric light dangling in the air between our two beds. I was dragged by the hand into the bed on the right by the short girl who asked me one question after another without waiting for my answers, "You like vum vum? You like Vietnamy *con gai*? Daihan *con gai* vum vum namba ten? You like Vietnamy?"

While I was taking off my clothes hesitantly, the girl with fat hips slipped out of her scanty clothing quickly and lay in the bed, immediately opening her legs outright, so matter-of-factly, so publicly. Although the light was out, red and blue lights flickering on the signs outside trickled into the room through the bare windowpanes, and I could plainly see the dark hair in her groin, and the whitish thighs, and her breasts that looked like swollen pancakes.

In the other bed, Sergeant Chon had already begun to swim on top of his girl; I could see them through the two sheets of the flimsy mosquito nets. I awkwardly crouched in a crawling posture over my whore, withdrawing more and more from the urgent reality as I remembered the dreadful rumors about the latest venereal disease called "the Vietnamese shower VD," that was known to be widespread among the Vietnamese prostitutes in big cities. "If you contract that disease your 'fountain pen' will leak in all directions like a shower head," Master

Sergeant Han Myongsun used to warn the soldiers whenever they discussed a visit to the brothels.

As I did not make any more moves, suspended in the air like a turtle-shaped bridge, the girl wrapped my hips with her expert legs and pushed herself up several times. I was frightened, for my initiative was stolen and I did not know how to get it back. Although I had not told Sergeant Chon yet, this was the first time I had ever been with a prostitute in bed, and it was by no means an ideal situation for a sexual experience. I could not have an erection. The small girl stroked me with her tiny hand for some time, but I could not shed my vivid sense of those creepy, darting millions of VD germs spreading through my whole body from the groin to the thighs, spreading out in all directions to the abdomen, to the chest, into the stomach, to the neck, into the brain, into every part of my anatomy.

"You like suck better vum vum fuck?" the prostitute offered when she noticed I was not ready. She probably did not want me to use up all her business hours for the night. "I namba one suck. I suck you erection. Okay?"

Frightened, I refused.

She was on top of me this time, but soon realized nothing would work to get me aroused. She gave up with a quick professional resignation. She must have had many similar experiences. She slid down from me and cautiously watched my face for a while, lying prone on her side with her cheek propped by her hand, her other free hand still playfully stroking me. I felt relieved when she no longer tried to lead me into the act.

The girl in the other bed kept moaning and panting loudly, at times uttering some unintelligible Vietnamese words that sounded like orgasmic ejaculations. The girl in my bed, giggling, occasionally asked or said something through the mosquito nets to the gasping girl squeezed under the heavy bulk of Sergeant Chon. Blankly gazing at him pant and pump only an arm's stretch away, I felt an odd sense of guilt. I knew this was the first time for Sergeant Chon, too. I waited for him to be done with the first sex of his vengeance, or whatever it was, so we could leave this sordid place as soon as possible. To distract myself, I tried to visualize a beautiful snowscape of the rice paddies in Kangwon Province where I had spent a winter in my college years, a long, long time ago. The girl lying beside me with her pancake breasts and fat hips nudged me, giggling. She pointed at Sergeant Chon, who was still violently absorbed in his thrusting motions. I noticed he was crying. Not sobbing silently with restrained emotion but wailing aloud, grievously, like a bereaved mourner. The two girls giggled happily, chattering to each other in excited voices, probably thinking Chon cried because he could not hold his exploding orgasm any longer.

I knew why he was crying. He was mourning his virginity that was wasted in this filth, as everything else he had possessed was wasted in this country, in this war. And I knew that he was dying inside. Ever since then, I felt an acute sense of responsibility, that I had to protect him.

On the third day
after we destroyed the VC regimental
headquarters, the 9th Company soldiers
meandered all morning in jungle of various
shades of green and brown and grey,
through a labyrinth of glossy broad leaves
and long leaves and pointed leaves and
thick strong runners and vines climbing up
and down the trees or hanging from the
branches, everything motionless in stagnant space and suspended time. In the
afternoon we arrived at a gulch where
crags and rocks piled up high on both sides
along a small stream as if the whole area
had been swept by a mountain flood. The
company commander ordered us to halt.
The captain decided that this topography

represented the typical terrain suitable for underground VC shelters that needed multiple secret exits for emergency egress.

"Looks like some rat holes are hidden under those rocks," the CO said. "There must be some rats, if there are holes. Get ready for a mole hunt."

Captain Kim Sanghyop deployed his men to form a wide circle around the suspected tunnel zone, shot up a yellow smoke screen to notify the battalion command post of our location for underground search, and selected fourteen soldiers to organize two-man mole hunter pairs to assign to the most likely seven entrances. While the selected fourteen, including me, were taking our clothes off to prepare for the hunt, the assisting soldiers climbed to the tops of the rocks following the captain's hand signals and dropped hand grenades into the suspicious holes and crevices. Nerve-wracking metallic sounds of explosions vibrated under the rocks, and the burning gunpowder, as it always did, made my stomach queasy with its repulsively sweet odor.

The soldiers shouted to the gaps among the rocks for the Vietcong to throw away their arms and come out with their hands up, but there was no response from the enemy. The soldiers opened up into the holes and waited for a while more. When the enemy still did not react, the captain signaled for us to go down. Three pairs of us would climb down.

I took my clothes off except my flak jacket, fastened three fragmentation grenades on my chest, removed both canteens from the cartridge belt and clipped a flashlight on it in the back, released the safety catch and set my M-2 carbine at automatic, and then began to climb down the dark gap among the jagged rocks. The smell of mushrooms or decaying logs wafted up from the dank bottom underneath. Once in a while, a rifle shot or two rang out spasmodically somewhere under the rocks, and then everything fell silent again.

Private Yun Chilbok, who had been assigned to my team, followed me close behind, and I climbed down about five meters, pushing the rock walls outward with my hands and feet as when climbing down a chimney until I landed on the quiet, humid dirt bottom. Private Yun stepped down behind me with a careful thud shortly after, but I could not see anything in the sudden dark. I gasped, because I was feeling suffocated by the stuffy humid air and the depressing space sealed by darkness. I felt I was diving to the bottom of a pit filled with mud.

Leaning one shoulder against a jutting rock, I took a long deep breath and then fumbled about the ground to see if there was a tunnel leading anywhere. I was not sure if Yun was still behind me, because I could not hear his breathing. I hesitated for a moment, not knowing which direction to take, for a rather wide space was open before me; the wet cool air grazing my skin told me there was a spacious cavern in front of me. Aiming my rifle forward, ready to fire with one hand, I unhooked the flashlight from my hip. I switched it on, swung the beam around the dark open space once, thinking, I was right, there *was* a cave, and quickly switched it off so as not to give any chance for the enemy, if there was any waiting in the dark, to fire at me.

The moment I switched my flashlight on again, the straight beam streaked out like a laser lance across the underground darkness and caught the pallid and frightened face of a haggard, terrified Vietcong, who, dazed by the sudden blinding light pouring over him, just stood there like a strange primitive mural, stiffly hiding in a narrow crevice in the opposite wall, perhaps fifteen meters away from me, perhaps ten or less, standing on a small ledge like a wax statue, awkwardly holding with both hands an AK 47 assault rifle that looked like a hugely magnified spider leg, his startled eyes dilating, expanding as big as fists, as big as baseballs, and I pulled the trigger although I was not aware of it when I did it, wriggling my knees to hide myself behind the jutting rock for cover, and the flashlight fell and rolled on the ground, and I kept firing breathlessly, actually holding my breath, gripping my rifle, until I consumed the whole magazine. Everything in the ensuing moments was swept away in one short flicker, like lightning consumed instantly by stormy darkness, the whole world frozen, motionless. There must have been the shots and their echoes in the sealed space of rocks, because I saw flame at the muzzle, though I heard nothing. Hastily I pulled out the magazine, turned it upside down and inserted the other end into the chamber. Somebody—Private Yun—picked up the flashlight and switched it on, and quickly turned it off, but during that one short flicker of light, I saw him, the enemy, sticking to the wall like a bat, his enormous eyes glinting blue, blood dripping from his mashed lips, red spattering the rocks, all over his body, bleeding somewhere heavily although I could not see his wounds clearly, and he was falling down like a tall jelly post. That was not a man, I thought, that could not be a human being, with one arm hanging loose, torn at the shoulder, his abdomen and thighs pulped and churned to a bloody gore, and I emptied the other magazine like a mad man, not knowing why I had to shoot any more but just doing it, possessed by fear, and the shredded body, that might have absorbed all 32 rounds I had fired towards him, was collapsing, like a sinking ship, slowly collapsing to his death.

Just as I had heard so clearly the thud of the Vietcong falling to the ground during the night battle in Lac Ninh plain, I heard this Vietcong fall on the damp ground with a thud. I screamed to God, although I was a hardcore atheist with a complete theoretical rebuttal of all arguments advocated by St. Thomas Aquinas, and I screamed again and again to God because I was overwhelmed by primitive terror, a terror that was strangulating me, and I kept screaming, and the scream tore out of my brain, and I was suddenly seized by a choking fear that the falling Vietcong might leap to my neck with a bursting supernatural power and shred me with his bare hands, shred me the way I had pulverized him, so I plucked off the hand grenades from my chest and pulled off the safety pins and hurled them one after another towards him, screaming.

I wanted him to vanish without trace because I did not want to believe he had ever existed, because this, all this, what had happened before my eyes a moment ago could not have really happened to me. And after all the grenades had exploded against the opposite wall with deafening thunder, I crept up the tunnel, sobbing and blubbering.

I was scratched on my arms and knees and shins from wriggling and climbing up between the piles of jagged rocks, and I wondered what my mother was doing now, and I wanted to love somebody and I wanted to sit by a bonfire and listen to a friend croon a quiet song, but I had just killed a man and I was a killer, and I felt I would never see the sunlight again even if I kept climbing up the rocks for years.

I scrambled out of the rocks, stumbled down to the stream trickling through the fallen trees and vomited loudly and violently until my entrails, entangled and sour, seemed to spill out of my throat. Beside me down at the stream, Corporal Kwon Yongjun was washing his fatigues that had been drenched with blood during his desperate combat a minute ago with a Vietcong in the underground tunnel. The two aluminum identification tags hanging on his neck glittered white reflecting the sunshine. Corporal Kwon retched a few times, too, and, when finished with washing, he brushed his teeth and gargled his mouth with salty water before going over to the medic to ask for some medicine to ease his stomach. The blood stains were still distinct on his wet fatigues like the spots left by gum sap.

I washed my face several times and vomited, over and over again, until my stomach felt like an empty bag. But the throbbing nausea would not go away. My head kept swimming, and I felt my brain had slipped out of its skull and was floating outside my head, spinning, the grey and white mush scattering in all directions. I shuddered with an odd feeling that a thick slimy vine would slither down from heaven like a giant serpent and noose my neck with its tail and haul me up high into the air, and leave me dangling up there until I choked and withered. My senses hazed into foggy chaos, and the trees and the rocks and the stream and the sky, everything around me looked like blurry images projected upon a thin transparent screen.

Seven Vietcong were killed and two were captured alive in the underground tunnel complex where I did my first extermination of human life. It had been only half an hour since they had finished the mole hunt, but several soldiers were already joking about the death game they had played under the rocks, boasting how they had got one. While Sergeant Chi Taesik, surrounded by the captain and the platoon leaders, sent radio reports to the battalion CP, the soldiers chattered about the one-on-one fighting as excitedly as if they had just sold a worthless thing to a gullible country gentleman at a traveling market.

"When you receive a medal, you see, you have to stand at attention throughout the ceremony," said Corporal Song Pyongjo, oiling his automatic rifle. "This time we will have to remain standing stiff until we get cramps in our legs waiting so long for our turn, because so many of us will be decorated."

"The battalion commander's got cramps in his cheeks from grinning so much lately," said Master Sergeant Han Myongsun, chuckling at his own witty analogy. "He's been too happy these days because the companies under his command are doing so well in this operation."

Private Yun slouched over to me, his M-16 slung upside down over his shoulder, holding an empty C-ration can out before him like a beggar carrying an alms bowl. He sat down beside me on a crag and stared for a while, then said, "How do you feel?"

I looked at him with my foggy eyes. I felt my eyeballs were wrapped with a thick opaque layer of film.

"I didn't feel too good," I said, honestly. "I threw up."

He unslung his rifle and put it down across his lap with a knowing grin. "I guess everybody feels that same way, Sergeant Han," he said. "My stomach was terribly upset too when I killed my first Cong at Ninh Pung. That feeling won't go away for several days. But you will get a medal too, anyway."

I said nothing. He closely studied my face as if he was looking for a clue in my expression. Conscious of his stare, I nodded blankly.

"I killed a man," I said.

"You sure did, and a clean job it was," he said. "We dragged out all the VC bodies out of the tunnels, except the one you disposed of. You really got rid of him good, I guess. Blown to pieces all the way. I've never seen a body so shredded." He chuckled. "But I could verify the enemy KIA for you, after all."

"Verify? How?"

"I saw it all, sergeant, didn't I? I watched all that was going on with these two naked eyes. I was just behind you, remember? You seemed to be shouting a lot but I couldn't hear you too clearly because of all those explosions and rifle shots and all. Boy, you really gave him a clean blow job. Grenades and all. I had to bring this out of the tunnel and show it to the CO to verify the body count. You can keep it if you want a souvenir."

Private Yun offered me a can. I looked into it. The jagged top had been gashed open with a bayonet. Inside was a piece of mangled meat. I leaned backwards, trying to avoid what was obviously intended for me.

"What is that?" I asked.

"The left ear, of the Cong you killed," he said nonchalantly. "I cut it off after you climbed out of the tunnel. You have to present the left ear of the enemy if you want to prove you killed him. It's evidence you need to get a medal, you know."

And I began to vomit again.

For three or four days I ate almost nothing but a few crackers. If I opened a C-ration can and there was meat inside—ham or beef or turkey or any wet brown lump—my throat became so dry I could not swallow. When I managed to fall asleep at night, I was haunted by the nightmare of the Vietcong repeatedly collapsing and rising and collapsing again in the dark cave, and when I woke up, drenched in cold sweat, my stomach tumbled with a million worms in it. In the appalling silence of the jungle, I would tremble with the strange fear and belated discovery that it was not the Vietcong but I who had died in the dark. For I felt deprived of human status because I had destroyed a stranger's life through the most bestial act. The excuse that it had been sheer reflex could not justify my doing it.

I had seen many deaths with my own eyes, but until I actually caused one myself, it had never struck me with such staggering impact. All the deaths I experienced were so sudden, so chaotic, so noisy and destructive. About death, I now saw a truth that I would have rather not known. Death was never mysterious or majestic or even tragic, as I had imagined. To die well requires more spirituality than to live well, Montaigne had said. But I never saw anybody who died a formal death, or who left his last words properly. All the deaths I saw were unpredicted, inexplicable, unjustifiable. Simple extinction, extermination. That was all. And now, I had become an agent of one such absurd and dehumanized elimination. I, the self-styled intellectual, who belonged to the primates, was a murderer.

I felt a giddiness that a recovering patient might feel on his first day out in the sun, as if suffering from a mental hangover, my soul extinct and severed. The physical frame, without the mind, shuffled around. I could not know exactly where I was during those days. Whenever I recalled myself pulling off the pins and hurling the grenades at the Vietcong, who was already falling, dying, I could not breathe. Meanwhile in my empty echoing skull, conflicting thoughts popped and clashed with one another like the gingko nuts in a raffle wheel. I was ashamed that I had killed a man.

All the eloquent clichés in war movies did not help me a bit in convincing me of the justice of what I had done. I could never overcome my humiliation and contempt for myself. A young man at my age should be dating a girl, discussing Shelley with friends over a drink, going to the movies with family on weekends, taking examinations to get a job somewhere back home, but I had become a monstrosity who could tatter a human to mangled fragments with explosive metal. I could not understand why mankind should be categorized as *pri*mates when they slaughtered one another in mass killing sprees between large, forced organizations. How could killing be a virtue in any sense? The logic advocating mass murder was that violence could not be dissuaded by reason, that the only practical answer was defending oneself and avoiding passive death amid the human bestiality by doing the killing yourself. Beating, biting, shooting, blowing to pieces. Individual justice was not practical in war; individual justice could not be realized in or through war. War was mass action and mass thinking. Man was the most cruel animal on earth, who could actually kill out of theoretical hatred or ideological differences, not out of simple necessity for survival. Man was capable of inventing the guillotine, of dancing a killing feast in the moonlight.

Whatever arguments I might develop in my head, the proposition that I—*this* I—had killed a man could not be rewritten. I, who had arrogantly entertained the puerile fantasy that I would study the war as a metaphysical phenomenon, killed one human being like an animal, shredding him into splinters of bones and meat in the most savage way. The abstract concepts of triumph and defeat and glory had completely vanished from my mind, leaving only the huge stains of unforgivable acts.

I was an executioner, the savage brute wielding a throat-cutting ax, hiding his face in the black hood. Now, the deed done, I could not judge or decide anything. What other definition but execution could I apply to describe killing a staring man face to face. If someone asked me why I had killed him, I had so many things to say, but I could find no argument with which to convince myself of its justice.

I was awarded a decoration for killing that Vietcong. The medal of murder for my exemplary heroism and valor. Someday, I thought, someone would come to seek me out for revenge, for no man is given the right to kill another man in any circumstances.

In three months I would go home. Yet I had lost home, I had been banished from it. Where could I return to after having gone through this? Where was the home I was supposed to return to? How strange and remote. Who could believe one single year could be such a long time? I was a grotesque. I wanted to squeeze into a secret narrow chink like a bedbug and just die there away from the world, without suffering in this emotional wasteland any more, never returning to my capsized reality. I wandered about the jungle like a ghost. My spirit had withered away into nothingness.

"Get me a stick," Captain Kim Sanghyop hollered.

I was startled by the sudden shout; he sounded so spiteful and menacing that I sensed another interrogation of the prisoner was forthcoming. I looked back at the CO, who was replacing his canteen into the casing on his cartridge belt, sitting astride a jutting rock shaped like an eagle's beak. We had just finished lunch and I saw that the captain was going to interrogate the Vietcong prisoner before leaving for the afternoon patrol. It was the fourth day after the killing in the caves.

The two Vietcong prisoners had been captured in the underground tunnel complex of Caterpillar Gulch. One of the prisoners was a woman and she could escape physical punishment, but Huong was severely beaten during repeated interrogations. Of the nine Vietcong who had been killed or captured in Caterpillar Gulch, all but Phan Thi Dap, the female prisoner, had been armed with automatic rifles; but no arms cache was found near the regimental headquarters. The captain naturally suspected there must be a secret place, safely away from the headquarters, hiding enough weapons to supply all the VC elements on this mountain. He had decided that, with just enough torture, the captive would confess the secret location, and the 9th might catch the biggest fish in the whole operation. Who cared about the old Geneva Conventions of 1864 anyway, when neither North nor South Vietnam respected even the Geneva Agreements of 1954?

Piggie Chang twisted off a thick branch from a tree near by and trimmed off the leaves and twigs with his bayonet to prepare a cudgel. The captive, whose face was swollen puffy and bruised black and blue all over from two days' beating, was suddenly frightened again, his terror-stricken eyes flashing to study the expressions of the captain and other soldiers to see if this stick was meant for him. From his disfigured face, fear exuded.

I pitied him, his small crouching body that would have to go through another session of punishment. This Vietcong prisoner looked so weak and miserable when first captured that I doubted this was the same enemy we feared so much all the time. Huong was in loose black garb, the Vietcong uniform of *calico noire,* wore Ho Chi Minh sandals made of a sliced car tire, and carried a canteen made out of a hollow bamboo block; the emergency food found in his cloth bag were snails, dried caterpillars, a half-rotten fish and some rice.

Captain Kim snatched the stick from Piggie and stabbed Huong's stomach with it, asking where the rifles, the carbines, were hidden.

"*Sung truong?*" A stab. "*Cac-bin?*" Another stab.

I could not read Huong's expression well because his face was shapelessly disfigured, but I knew he was clenching his teeth. I saw his jawbones gritting.

"*Toi khong biet.*"

Squatting under the rock shaped like an eagle's beak, his hands tied behind his back, Huong once more repeated the same answer, "I don't know," and stared with hostile eyes at the female Vietcong, Phan Thi

Dap, who was watching him from under a tree across the stream with an indifferent expression. I was not sure if that glare was an expression of his anger for the punishment given to him alone, or a warning that she must not confess anything to the Daihans.

"Where is *sung truong?*"

"*Khong biet.*"

The stick landed on Huong's back with a blunt thud. The prisoner fell on his face, groaning. I had been often surprised to see how much punishment the human body could take in demanding terrain, but it made me panic to watch Huong's small and debilitated body endure these beatings for days. I believed he really did not have any information valuable to us. It was irrational for him to undergo such painful and harsh torment for whatever meager information he might be withholding. Huong said he had involuntarily lived as a Vietcong guerrilla for three years because he had been kidnapped and forced to join them. If what he had been saying to the captain was true, he was not even a regular Vietcong, but an innocent kidnap victim.

"*Sung truong!*" A blow on the shoulder. "*Sung truong!*"

"*Khong biet. Toi khong biet, dai-uy.*"

"You *khong biet* too much, bastard!"

The stick swished in the air and landed on Huong's knees; the captive rolled on the ground, cackling in his throat, his eyes turning white epileptically. Thus the interrogation continued until the soldiers had to deploy for the afternoon search for the arms cache the captain believed was not far away.

The platoon leader gave me the guard duty so I would stay behind at the temporary CP, because he noticed I was weak from not eating too well, still suffering from shock. This left me with the captives all afternoon. The other thirteen soldiers, who had also been exempted from the afternoon patrol, tried to put various nonsensical questions to the Vietcong. They were curious and intrigued because this was the first time they had ever seen captives. With the Vietnamese handbook in their hands, they looked up the necessary words.

"Hey, *xin cuu toi,*" said one: Please help me.

"*Chung toi la linh Daihan,*" someone else shouted: We are Korean soldiers. "*Toi la ban.*" I am your friend.

"*Quay lung lai.*" Turn around. "*Lui lai.*" Move back. "*Dung lai.*" Stop. "*Tien len.*" Advance. "*Dung lai. Gio tay len.* Hey, what should I say in Vietnamese to tell them to drop their hands?"

"*Ong manh khong? Ba manh khong?*" asked Kim: How are you, mister? How are you, miss? "*Toi ten la trung-si nhat Kim.*" I am Sergeant First Class Kim.

They had a lot of fun with this baby Vietnamese; for most of them this was the first and probably last opportunity to ever use their knowledge of the language, besides the short shouts during combat.

Sergeant Oh Ujin, who spoke Vietnamese rather well out of his need to speak it (because he had fallen for the *con gai* selling American cigarettes at a small Ninh Hoa shop), was also with the guard team and provided us, especially me, with much help in communicating with the prisoners. Since they hoped to be friendly with us, probably to win some sympathy from the soldiers when the captain was not around, the two Vietcong were more than willing to answer any personal questions we asked as long as we did not demand the location of the secret arms cache.

Huong Quynh Hoa, twenty-nine, a farmer, had been kidnapped by two Vietcong at night three years ago on his way home from the tool house at Ben Ghe, taken to a camp in Death Valley on Hon Ba Mountain. Since then he had endured very long and helpless days. After four days, weapons training, the Vietcong drill instructors were annoyed by his obtuse awkwardness in handling machines and weapons. On the sixth day of captivity, he was summoned by a VC cadre and taken to a small shabby hut in the woods with four other disqualified men. Here they did farming work under constant surveillance by Vietcong guards, eating nothing but two rice balls a day with smelly fish and salt. Cultivating vegetables in the desolate woods every day, they were gradually reduced to gaunt skin and bones because of overwork and accumulating fatigue. He had looked like a starved beast, his hair grown long over his shoulders and tumors swelling all over his body. Six months later he was taken back to the camp and made a Vietcong fighter. Probably they needed more men, he thought, since the Daihans had moved into their sector. He was taken to Phu Cat where he was given the duty to watch for any Vietnamese or Korean soldiers invading the Vietcong's area.

It was obvious by then that he would be executed by an ARVN firing squad if he returned home because he had been with the Vietcong for half a year; he had no choice but to stay with the VC fighters and obey their orders. When the sun was good and a drowsy breeze stirred peacefully in the valley, he would perch on the lookout platform high in a tree and gaze down at the lone path leading from the jungle out to the plain. He had heard that the Daihans belonging to the Tiger Division, who had tramped through this region once, would come back soon, and he thought it would be his last day if those notoriously cruel Daihans returned. Daihans were always half drunk, they said, and killed everyone in sight without any questions asked. Perching in the tree, thinking about Daihans, gazing at the lone path, he continued to die every day. He died yesterday, he died today, and he would die again tomorrow. In imagination he kept dying over and over again.

The rumor had been in circulation for months that the Chinese Army would come to help the Communist Vietnamese liberate the people in the South, but they never came. He had heard so often the hopeful story that the North Vietnamese Army and Vietcong units would join forces and wipe out all Daihans and Americans in this area, but the Tiger Daihans stayed, growing stronger each day.

The Vietcong propagandists said American airplanes were made of wood and paper, but he could not understand how the wooden planes shone so, like silver plates in the sunlight, and poured down so many bombs. And he found in the jungle the leaflets scattered from the air, and these leaflets sometimes carried a picture of an enormous and mighty airplane with an explanation underneath in the Vietnamese, Korean and English languages, saying, "This is a B-52 bomber used by the United States of America, a strong ally of Vietnam. One single plane like this carries 29,700 kilograms of bombs. It can hit any target accurately and kill all the living things in the target area." It was too dreadful a monster for an aircraft made of wood and paper.

He was hungry. Even salt was precious. Sometimes he had to chew and swallow raw rice. Whenever the word got around that Daihans were out on a long distance reconnaissance again, Vietcong fighters had to eat raw rice because they could not build a fire, even in the secret underground General Hoang Cam stove, lest the leaking smoke should pinpoint their location to the cruel Daihans lurking somewhere in the dark jungle. If they really could no longer stand raw meals, they had to wrap soaked rice in a vinyl bag, bury it in the ground, build a fire upon it, run away to safety, and then return to the spot in a day or two to dig out and eat the cooked rice.

He wondered then if Daihans really killed Vietcong on the spot without even asking questions. Would they really shoot him down on sight, if he went down to the plain along that lone path with a white flag? He could not know. And he sometimes imagined himself actually going down the valley with a white flag hidden under his testicles. He could imagine as much as he wanted to, the Vietcong guards could not look into his head, but he had to be extremely careful when he slept alongside Vietcong fighters not to speak about the white flag in his sleep.

He missed his wife and four sons. His wife was as beautiful as an exquisite jade doll and as small as a child herself, but gave birth to a son every year—four sons in a row!—until he was kidnaped by the Vietcong. She was pregnant again at that time, and by now that fifth son should be three years old. They had wanted to have a daughter this time because little girls were so lovely, snuggling up all the time like cats, but Huong was sure the fifth child was a son, too. He wondered what his wife was doing now with all those children. He was worried about how she could support the whole family by selling betel nuts and bananas at Ben Ghe market. He sometimes wanted to sneak down the mountain and go to Ben Ghe market or his old home by the tutelary shrine to see his lovely wife and lovely children, but the comrades were constantly watching one another. If he was caught anywhere outside the perimeter without official authorization, he was as good as dead. Or he might be caught by ARVN or Daihan soldiers and be executed in public. A public execution would certainly bring harm to his family. If he hid somewhere with her help, the VC comrades would certainly come down to the village and execute his wife and all five children in retaliation. He would run away with his family to a remote place where the VC would never find them if . . . if . . .

He was lonely. He was hungry. Weary.

He was afraid that someday he would be captured by the enemy and die like a dog, brutally mangled and chopped, as some comrades said. If he had to die, he wanted to be executed by Vietnamese or Americans, or even by Vietcong, but never by Daihans. Daihans might really cut his fingers and toes one by one, and, as the VC propagandists said, skin his legs with a razor blade while he was still alive. Once he had seen his comrades go down to a village and cut the wrists and ankles of a child with a straw-cutter to terrorize the villagers. In this execution, Huong had been given the mission to find a cutter, any cutter, in the village, so he did not think he had done much wrong himself except watch the whole process. And it was a terrifying sight to watch. They said Daihans were far more ruthless and terrible. Were those stories really true? Or were they simply fabricated tales like about the paper airplanes?

He kept thinking about the white flag. The enemy planes dropped leaflets and broadcast from the air claiming that the Allied Forces would guarantee safety and welfare to the returnees. They would even offer rewards if the defectors brought weapons. The VC comrades and guards and propagandist cadres said everything those leaflets and airplanes had said were lies. The leaflets said the National Liberation Front was cheating the people so that Communists could take over the whole country. He could not believe either side. Someone must be telling lies, but he could not know who was. He was so confused now he was never sure what would really happen to him if he went down the mountain with a white flag. Unless he actually did. He did not have the courage to go down the mountain without any definite plans. Yet he thought it would be a good idea to carry a white handkerchief with him just in case he was captured by the Tiger Daihans out on an operation. Dozing in the silent sleepy sun high in the treetop platform, he kept thinking about that white handkerchief.

Two and half years after he had been taken by the Vietcong, Huong was transferred to Ninh Hoa area in Khanh Hoa Province. He was given the same old job as a look out to watch this time for the White Horse Daihans instead of the Tiger Daihans, perching on a treetop platform at the entrance of Caterpillar Gulch on the ridge of Hon Heo Mountain. He spent the days and nights in the tree, thinking about the handkerchief.

Three weeks after he had been transferred to Hon Heo Mountain, he went down to Route 1 with three other Vietcong comrades to collect the toll from vehicles passing the old VC checkpoint near Lac An Village. But they could not even reach the highway; they met a Daihan ambush at the foot of the mountain near Tu Bong and had to flee back to the woods. Until several months ago they could openly block the road and collect tolls in broad daylight from Lambretta mini-buses and other civilian vehicles, but things had changed drastically in recent weeks. Now they had to go down the mountain only after dark to avoid encounters with the White Horse Daihans, and it was not safe at night either. After the Daihans had occupied the Lac Ninh plain area, Nhat Tien, the oldest and most influential elder in this area advised the Vietcong fighters not to visit the villages during daytime because it was dangerous. The Vietcong had to make a concession to Nhat Tien. They would not have any Communist nationalist fighters permanently stationed in the Plain if the villagers would regularly provide the VC with rice and other essential necessities. Some other villages flatly refused to pay tax to the National Liberation Front because they were convinced that the Vietcong would eventually lose the war. If any refusal was strong enough to influence other villages, the comrades had to resort to demonstrative and very effective terrorism, burying several villagers alive in a pit or breaking a randomly selected farmer's neck with a shovel blade. Then the villagers turned immediately obedient and meek.

Lately they could not go down to the villages even at night. Four thousand Vietcong and NVA forces had concentrated in Hon Ba Valley several months ago to attack and annihilate the Daihans in Ninh Hoa area, but this massive offensive failed. As an aftermath of that bungled offensive, Daihans established such a strong influence in Khanh Hoa Province that the Vietcong in that sector found it harder and harder to reach the populace. All the villages were eventually controlled by Daihans, and one night a few weeks ago, five comrades who had gone down to a Dong Hai seaside hamlet to get some fish were all killed by a Daihan ambush squad. Supplies ran short and the comrades turned to stray buffalos for their main source of food, although buffalo meat was too tough to chew and tasted so terrible. Then the tenacious Daihans began to butcher the roaming buffalos with howitzers to deny the VC this important food source. Night after night the shells kept flying in, and the comrades had to sleep in caves or under protruding rocks to avoid the random shelling. And when they ran out of food, the comrades sometimes had to hunt mountain turtles, frogs, lizards and snails.

Finally, after all the persistent rumors about the impending massive enemy operation, thousands of Daihans poured onto Hon Heo Mountain. The main force of the VC 85B Regiment had already escaped to Hon Ba area in small groups moving at night when it had been repeatedly confirmed through intelligence channels that the Daihans were planning a surprise attack at Hon Heo. But almost 500 fighters, who had to stay to maintain the stronghold, were trapped by the overwhelming force—10,000 enemy troops. They tried over and over again to slip through the enemy encirclement that was closing tighter every day, and when they decided to give up the futile attempt to breakthrough, Huong and eight other Vietcong comrades hid in the underground tunnel complex in Caterpillar Gulch, the camouflaged secret shelter they had constructed for an emergency like this. But this shelter was not safe enough for them to hide from the Daihans who literally left no stone unturned in their hunt.

Phan Thi Dap, who had been captured by Private Yun Chilbok in the same cave where I had killed my Vietcong, was a surprisingly beautiful girl whose chestnut skin showed no sign of hardships. After I had scrambled out of the rocks in blubbering confusion that day, Private Yun continued searching the dark cave with my flashlight and found her lying flat on her stomach behind a rocky corner ten meters deeper into the tunnel, her head covered with both hands.

As she emerged from the cave and was brought by Private Yun to the shade of a tree where Huong had been already undergoing preliminary interrogation by Piggie Chang while the officers were still down at the rocks waiting for the rest of the soldiers to finish the mole hunt and come out, the soldiers cheered and clamored that they should strip her for a through body search. While other soldiers were watching in breathtaking anticipation and excitement, Private Yun removed her clothes one by one, like an assistant stripteaser, smirking, and pretended to search for a concealed weapon behind her ears, under her armpits and between her breasts. She just stood there under the tree, like a petrified Egyptian maiden, embarrassed but not blushing, her disconcerted eyes looking around the laughing and yelling soldiers. She made no attempt to cover her breasts or groin with her hands, or save herself from the public shame. She remained totally exposed.

"Hey, Boar, search that hair down there," Piggie Chang croaked in a choking horny voice, squinting at her pubic hair accentuated so emphatically in a black triangle on her white-skinned groin. "Who knows? She might be hiding a bazooka in that tunnel."

The naked body search was not exactly a necessity that day although there were rumors about the female Vietcong who carried lethal poison darts concealed in their genitals. Nobody knew how but said it was true. Actually these soldiers simply wanted to see a naked girl. Some wanted to see for sensual delight. Some were just enjoying themselves with the whole joke. Watching the slim and tender figure, the pinkish breasts hesitantly rising from the soft chest, and the smooth hips curving down like a swallow's shoulder, some soldiers might have indulged in a more romantic feeling even though she was a Vietcong captive. They desired the embrace of that white-skinned girl with long black hair swaying softly, and to forget this war, this jungle, forget everything they did not want to remember. What they wanted from her was not slimy grunting sex, but warmth and comfort and peace. That was what I wanted from her, if I could want anything from that captive.

When he came up from the rocks and saw Phan's petite, pure body, even the captain admired it in passing: "These Cong rats sure have some aesthetic eye. They know how to choose women, at least."

The exhibition abruptly ended when Sergeant Chon Hisik was awakened from his nap by the boisterous laughter and cheering shouts of the soldiers. He slouched up from his shade under a rock and came over to the tree surrounded by the crowding spectators. He stepped out towards the prisoners, his scowling face as angry as when he found someone sitting on his dumbbells, and the soldiers suddenly turned quiet, already starting to disperse; they knew Chon was in a foul mood, and when he was like this, they had better stay out of his reach and sight.

"The show is over," he said, picking up Phan's clothes. That was enough to make the soldiers hurry away. Chon handed the clothes over to the female Vietcong and said, gesturing for her to put them on, "*Mac quan ao.*"

In a few hours, she was dubbed 'Miss Vietcong,' and the soldiers would approach her to offer food and make small talk to listen to her voice, to listen to a feminine voice. Phan Thi Dap was a guest rather than a captive; the sun-tanned tough-talking soldiers might have been reminded of the soft voice and warm breasts of the girls they had left back home while listening to her talk. And they envied Sergeant Oh Ujin, who could talk freely with her in Vietnamese, and Private Yun, who pleasantly joked with a gloating smile that he would not wash his right hand until the operation was over because that hand had honorably touched Phan's soft skin all over.

Phan Thi Dap, who also had been kidnaped by the Vietcong and undergone incredible hardships in the jungle until she was captured by the Korean soldiers at the age of sixteen, totally revised our prejudiced notions about the female Vietcong combatants. Perhaps this girl was too beautiful to be our enemy, and we had a blind faith in her the way a man madly in love with a worthless woman would swear, "She's not that kind of a girl," no matter how hard his friends might try to disabuse him of his senseless trust. We simply did not believe anything she had told us about herself in her own words, because we did not want to, because we believed she could not be one of the real Vietnamese Amazons, whom we had heard so many horrible stories about.

Female Vietcong were different from any other group of women involved in armed conflicts elsewhere on earth, we had been often told.

They were aggressive and vicious. The young Vietcong girls, usually forcefully recruited at an early age, worked as nurses or clerks at the headquarters or dispensaries. Sometimes it was one of the major duties for them to sexually entertain the male VC fighters who had to live in the jungle for months at a stretch. Some of them infiltrated American military bases disguised as civilian workers or moved into the brothels with intelligence missions. When VC agents working as cyclo or taxi drivers in big cities would bring unsuspecting soldiers on R&R to their lairs, the female VC prostitutes took the prospective victims to their beds, a poisoned sting or a razor blade taped on their soles; these soldiers would be invariably found dead the next morning with their penes severed. Some female Vietcong would also disguise themselves as innocent country women, carrying fruit baskets or herding pigs, and haunt the enemy military installations to spy on movements of manpower, vehicles and equipment. They dug foxholes and built bunkers along with the men. When it was necessary for them to move to a new location to avoid intensified enemy bombing or shelling, they would trek through the jungle for days at the same pace as the men. They could survive for months, or perhaps years, with nothing but rice and fish and salt, the way their men did; they could hunt linsang with bow and arrows, and they even ate lizard meat. Often they were mobilized in combat to carry ammunition and supplies for the fighters; they joined the fighting if ordered to, evacuated the wounded and, in retreat, they gathered the abandoned weapons and carried them to safe hiding places. They buried dead comrades.

The intelligence unit once reported that the Vietcong had started to organize combat units solely consisting of female fighters. Six weeks earlier an ARVN special forces company had been ambushed by a female Vietcong squad at the cactus-filled sand field near Tuy Hoa Airport. Not a single female Vietcong survived the firefight; they had picked a wrong target.

But we believed Phan Thi Dap was not one of them; Phan was too young to have been gang-raped by the Vietcong in the jungle, too beautiful, too feminine to shoot at us as our enemy.

On the sixth-day the 1st Platoon excavated 67 hidden rifles from a secret pit camouflaged by a dirt-covered trapdoor only five meters away from where Huong had been captured. Among the spoils was a very small Polish revolver with a bluish black glimmer, that was so beautiful and shiny Lieutenant Choe Sangjun decided to keep it himself as a war souvenir without reporting its capture to the company commander. These weapons were discovered because Huong finally confessed; he could no longer endure the repeated beatings. I was wrong to have pitied the prisoner, believing he was innocent and really did not know anything about the buried weapons. He had known the exact location all along. Squirming his savagely bruised body uncomfortably at times, his left knee swollen enormously from the broken shinbone, blood and nasal mucus crusted like a scab of filthy grease all over his face, Huong now and then glanced with forlorn eyes at the captured articles that the Daihans had tied into bundles with creepers for easier transportation. As three soldiers were piling them up at one place to open the space for a transport chopper to land, Phan Thi Dap, with an indifferent and detached look, watched the bundles of dark rifles, hand-assembled grenades or rockets made of shell fragments and flashlight batteries, knives with honed saw blades fitted into handles made of flattened cartridge shells, Molotov cocktails, rattraps for future use as booby traps, dud shells the Vietcong had salvaged to dismantle later and reassemble to make new bombs, buffalo dung packed in vinyl bags, rubber strings and several hundred rounds of live cartridges.

Private Yun Chilbok,
sitting under a tree near the two captives,
was cleaning his fingernails with the
pointed tip of a broken twig. Sergeant
Chong Sangchol and two other soldiers of
the 1st Platoon finished piling up the captured articles by the stream and went over
into the shade for some rest. Sergeant Oh
Ujin was writing a letter, his rifle leaning
against his shoulder, using the knapsack
on his lap as the desk. It was a familiar
languid scene during a lull; we were waiting for a helicopter to fly in and carry away
the spoils and the two prisoners.

When Boar offered a C-ration can to
him, Huong quickly pawed it with his
pincer-like hands, repeatedly thanking

him in a hurry, "*Cam ong, cam on, binh-nhat, cam on,*" bowing servilely
over and over again; he was starved because the captain had forbidden
us to give him any food except water for two days until he confessed the
location of the secret arms cache. Huong belatedly tried to win the
soldiers' favor, a flattering smile constantly disfiguring his already
shapeless face. He did not know he was to be lifted out of here this
afternoon, and probably had decided to please the soldiers by any means
as long as he was in the hands of the Koreans so that he would be spared
any more punishment. Now that he had given them the information
they wanted, he was totally worthless to the soldiers, and he apparently
knew that he could be finished off here by any soldier's whim. But
officially he should have been transferred to the prison camp within
twenty-four hours of his capture because combat units were not allowed
to hold any prisoner for longer than a day; the intelligence people
wanted to have the prisoners as fresh as possible to gather hot, lively
information for faster facilitation of the overall operation. Captain Kim
had not made any reports to his superior officers about the capture of
these prisoners until the secret pit was found through the forced
confession so that his company could write up the biggest catch of the
mission. War was not fought by the set rules—this was the basic rule I
learned about war here. How could anyone expect logic and justice in a
war? In Vietnam nobody respected or fought by logic, because rules did
not win the war. The enemy did not fight by the rules, and all wars
were, in fact, phenomena arising from violated rules. How could anyone
make it humanitarian when war demanded annihilation of the enemy?
The hypothetical argument that a war could be fought, possibly, in a
humanitarian way was one of the most ridiculous philosophical and
political errors in human history. Brutes, not idealists, fought wars. If a
war could be a humanitarian effort, a fair game to be conducted justly
and by mutual consent, there would be no war of any kind in the first
place.

When Private Yun opened his canteen to drink some water after
consuming two cans of ham, Huong quickly thrust out his C-ration can,
that had been emptied in a matter of seconds, simpering apologetically.
"Look at this gook asking for some water," Yun said. "This Cong doesn't
know the law of the jungle—that you may offer your wife to a buddy, but
never precious water. And he isn't even a buddy."

Huong did not understand what he was saying and probably inter-
preted Yun's laughter as a sign of the fast-developing friendship between

them, for, after drinking the water from his can, the prisoner went on to ask for a cigarette, "*Dambai, dambai.*"

That was too much. For Koreans smoking had a certain ceremonious element, and proper smoking habits were among the basic manners one had to learn as a part of growing up: "Don't ever smoke in the presence of your elders; don't ever ask for a cigarette or light from any person older than or superior to you in any way." Private Yun kicked Huong in the ribs, growling, "How dare you ask for a cigarette, too? I gave you food and drink, eh? If you told us right away where the weapons were hidden, you could've saved us a lot of trouble. But you didn't, *xau lam.* And you still want a cigarette, eh? Eh? Eh?"

Huong crept away, covering his head with his hands, terrified again, looking around at other soldiers to plead for a sympathetic intervention, or perhaps to surmise what he should expect next. But there was no more punishment for him. Private Yun Chilbok sat down in the shade again and continued to clean his fingernails.

Watching Private Yun "Boar" Chilbok, I often thought the army might need a lot of men like him to win a war, this war or any other. He certainly contributed a lot more to the war than I did. He was born at a remote village in the Chiri Mountains, and he saw a 500-won bill and trains for the first time in his life when he was drafted and brought to the boot camp at Nonsan. He liked the army so much from the first day at boot camp, because the military system gave him free meals and clothes and boots and even soap and a toothbrush. On top of all this, they even paid him a monthly salary. Though the meager monthly pay amounted to no more than 30 won, or about a dime in American money, he was really impressed by an army that was willing to pay him anything at all while he was doing absolutely nothing but enjoying himself playing a real soldier with a real rifle and all. He could not understand why the city boys did not want to go into the army and hated the exciting army life so much; for Boar, military service was not a compulsory duty but fun, a lot more fun than digging the rocky hills to raise measly crops and starve all year round. The army even taught him how to use a rifle, and allowed him to actually fire the marvelous weapon for target practice. He was born with all the qualities to make a good mercenary, and when he finished basic training, he was ready for an army career. He heard from his comrades that if he went to Vietnam, "You'll be treated like an American soldier, the American government giving you a monthly pay of forty dollars a month, and you can experience a real war in a foreign country." He had never dreamed in his childhood in his godforsaken mountain village that he would ever see a day when he might be paid as much as forty dollars a month, and in the American money at that. In my mind he was often associated with primitiveness and savagery, which were probably the most fundamental and desirable qualities in a man facing a war anywhere.

He consumed everything in the C-rations; he did not mix the coffee with water and then drink it, but tapped the powder into his mouth directly from the packet and chewed it like a regular meal. He might have even swallowed the carton box and casing, if he could have digested it. When canned kimchi would arrive as gifts from some charity organization or a big business firm that apparently enjoyed a considerable profit and prosperity owing to the Korean involvement in the Vietnam war, most soldiers would fall sick from eating too much rice with the appetizing kimchi pickles, but never, not even once had he fallen sick from eating anything, anything in the world, as if his stomach were an iron-chopping machine. Whenever I saw him chew away a whole clove of uncooked garlic or swallow a chunk of raw pork, I often felt he and I belonged to different species. In fact we did. He would never waste his mental energy on dissecting and analyzing the war like a specimen under a microscopic lens; when he saw a war, he fought it, and that was all. He was a perfect combat soldier, while I was an illegitimate child of battle.

Huong yawned, probably feeling drowsy from the hasty meal after a long hunger, and wiped tears from his eyes with the back of his hands, which were bound with a rope. Private Yun seemed to be bored because he had nothing to do after cleaning his fingernails. He snooped around for a while looking for something to do, and then went over to Huong. He stared into the Vietcong's frightened eyes for a while. He chuckled. The prisoner turned wary.

"You look so miserable, boy," the private said to Huong in Korean. "Too bad you'll get another good beating at the prison camp, because they'll get really mad when the MPs find out that you told us all about these *sung truong.*"

Though he did not understand what the private said this time either, Huong simpered when he decided the Daihan was laughing because he must be in a good mood.

"Look at this son of a bitch smirk like an idiot," said Private Yun. He suddenly pulled out his bayonet and stuck the blade across the prisoner's throat. "How would you like it if I slit your throat open?" Then he drew a line across Huong's chest with the tip of his bayonet. "Or should I open your heart and scrape out your guts with this bare hand?" He showed his cupped hand to the captive, and then playfully asked him in broken Vietnamese if he wanted to die, "*Muon di chet?*"

Huong looked down at his chest with astonished wide eyes, his bruised face further distorting, like an emaciated Boris Karloff. He studied Boar's expression to determine if the Daihan really meant it, or if he was merely kidding. Private Yun made an intimidating face. Then the prisoner looked around at us to get a hint. The soldiers feigned serious or gloomy expressions. Now Huong was sure that Yun really meant to kill him. Then, very strangely, he showed the most peaceful expression since he had been captured, a faint shadow of a relieved smile lingering about his torn lips. Slowly, but resolutely, he nodded his head. His face gradually filled with an aloof detachment: total resignation had led to peace and comfort. He blinked like a stupid bull twice and then nodded again, this time more urgently.

"*Cam ong, cam on ong,*" he said.

"This bastard really wants to die, I guess," Private Yun said to the watching soldiers and replaced the bayonet in his sheath, laughing.

Huong's expression showed conspicuous disappointment.

The two captives were evacuated to the prison camp. Another week passed. The sky was as mild as the crystal water of a mountain lake. The cool breeze slithered up through our sleeves like a pet snake and tickled the hairs in our armpits. When we came out to a bald ridge overlooking the distant Dong Hai sea, the captain said we had better enjoy our hard-earned rest here because "all the enemy must have been washed out of Hon Heo Mountain by now and we have nothing more to do on this mountain."

The CO did not think it was necessary to keep driving his men hard any more, so he told them to make camp for the night while one squad went out to patrol the area for a regular safety check. The captain thought one squad was enough for the job, and that job was given to the 2nd Squad, 3rd Platoon. We did not mind at all walking around for one more hour in the jungle. The operation had been going on for almost a month, and now we were in the final phase of the second sweep before pulling out; we would return to base in several days, and then, two months later, we would finally be shipped back home. As cheerful as schoolboys in a dormitory preparing to go to their country homes on the eve of a summer vacation, the soldiers hummed and chattered and laughed and kept saying, "*Choi oi.*"

Our hearts seemed to be refreshed by the mountain breeze, cool as a Korean autumn, and the rocks were pleasantly warm to the touch. As if we were out on a picnic, the nine soldiers, forming a short line, strolled zigzag along the path meandering through rocks and shrubs, teasing one another, talking about the things we would do first when we returned to Korea, shooting at the enormous lizards that looked like baby crocodiles crawling on the boughs or sticking to the tree trunks. We were far away from the main force now and did not need to go any farther, but nobody minded some more extra work.

Sergeant Chon Hisik was leading us along the path going down the ridge, slashing off the drooping branches blocking our way with his machete. Sergeant Chon was always in the lead out on a patrol because he was the squad leader, and I had to watch out for him all the time; since being jilted he seemed to take more risks than he needed to, always volunteering for duty that might endanger his life, as well as ours. When we arrived at the edge of the jungle bordering the slope covered with the reeds that rose as high as our chests, Sergeant Chon studied the terrain for a minute to decide in which direction we should turn, and then pointed to the west.

"I see a narrow path down there. Follow me."

He turned, stretching his hand out to push away some tendrils with the sweeping motion of drawing a curtain. I heard a sharp metallic sound, a treble, a short twang, as if someone plucked a thin taut wire and quickly let it go. Sergeant Chon stumbled, dropping his machete, tripped by something, a booby trap, and weakly slipped sideways, like a baseball player sliding into home plate in an instant replay, and then spun once, very fast this time, his arms and legs floundering helplessly like the limbs of someone pushed off a diving board, and he soared into the air about three meters high, his leg, one leg, being dragged up by a rope, like a giant fish flipping over the water, caught by its tail, and his whole body dropped down listlessly.

His helmet dropped and rolled a few turns on the ground and the rifle slung over his shoulder slipped down and dangled down by his armpit, and he swung in a big arc, a heavy pendulum. Very slowly. And I saw his leg was snared in a noose skillfully camouflaged with some vines. I did not know where they had come from, but five or six bamboo darts had deeply impaled his throat and chest, where several strands of blood were dripping to the tall grass; he had triggered a complex booby trap system, a catching noose and poisoned darts hidden in the tendrils. His left arm was torn off, gone from the elbow down. Stunned, we blankly watched him swing in the air like a suspended heavy punching bag.

I felt I was suddenly suspended myself in a vacuum. His mouth gaping, his dazed eyes wide open and gazing at us, he seemed to be trying to say something but was too surprised and frightened to get any words out of his stuffed throat. Somebody started to cry. Sergeant Chon was not dead yet because he was croaking deep in his throat, desperately trying to sustain his breath, to keep breathing through his mouth, and then, like a beheaded shark, he twitched his severed arm, once, just once for the last time, and his whole body drooped lax. Slowly swinging, hanging upside down, he struggled no more. Sergeant Chon Hisik was dead.

The soldiers cut the rope off with Chon's machete, pulled his body down, wrapped him in a poncho quickly so that they would not have to see his dead face, and tied him with the vines like a mummy. Sergeant Chi Taesik called in a chopper to carry the body out of the jungle. All this while I was sitting on the grass, still stunned, gripping Chon's dog tags in my sweating palm. I, the second sergeant, had to take over the lead and give the order to the men as to whether we would continue the patrol—that was out of the question, of course—or go back to join the main force, but I was just sitting there, dumb, like a child gazing at soap bubbles. I could not decide anything. I could not feel anything. I could not even think. My mind was a vacuum. Like everything else around me. Everything floated around in that vacuum.

Sergeant Chon and I had not been close friends—I had never had a close friend in my life—but watching the soldiers packing his torn body with a poncho, I had a vague feeling that he might have been someone close to me after all, and I kept thinking about him, about someone who had wept on top of a Vietnamese whore, someone who had been so happy running the movies backward, someone who had shot down the helpless chickens one by one in perfect shooting posture, someone who had worried so much about the dirt in the folds of his navel.

After a whole month of deaths and nightmares in the jungle, the operation in Hon Heo Mountain was over and we returned to our base. The soldiers streamed down to the plain and flew across the green fields in the ugly Chinooks that looked like huge metal coffins. In the Xuan My rice paddies Vietnamese farmers were harvesting their crops, and a

Vietnamese soldier scooted along Highway 1 on a Honda motorcycle with a *con gai* hanging on his back. Sitting by a tiny window, with my soul shredded to pieces, I looked down at the beautiful countryside, as we flew home to the base. We were returning home after destroying an enemy stronghold, according to various reports to higher commands. But we were not the final winners. Tomorrow, maybe right now, the enemy who had been hiding somewhere underground we could not reach, might be crawling out and the scattered Vietcong would gather again to claim their old shelters. In less than a month Hon Heo would be again marked as an enemy territory on our strategic maps.

The sky and the sea and the plain were beautiful nonetheless. The way home was always beautiful.

Back at the bunker, I packed Chon's belongings to send them to his family. A plastic insect repellent container, unopened C-ration cans, a bundle of letters, a long piece of rubber band, wornout fatigues, the new field cap he had saved to wear when he went home, postcards carrying the photographs of Nha Trang beach lined with palm trees, a razor, the Parker ball point (still in its case) he had bought for Sujin at the Division PX, a pair of rush-woven slippers, a tube of eczema ointment, several pairs of socks in different garish colors, a half-filled bag of C-ration coffee packets he had been collecting, and the empty cot. Sergeant Chon Hisik ceased to exist.

When we returned to the base after the operation, Pyon Chinsu was back in the bunker waiting for us.

I could not fall asleep. Lying on my stomach, I watched the others in their bunks. They wore clean dark green underwear, dog tags dangling from their necks, most were sound asleep, their faces, peaceful, not even worrying about guard duty. I wondered how these men could sleep so deeply and with such abandon.

What would I see at the core of these soldiers if I peeled off all the military pomposity and foppery and the puerile war-game accessories: the shoulder patches, insignias, uniforms, infantile army songs, parades, and the extravagant barrack platitudes such as "triumph," "invincible defense power," "heroism" and "comradeship"? A Persian poet sang that the lion painted on a flag roared when the wind blew. Who would be able to penetrate the blown-up images to be fabricated by the swaggering soldiers. The truth would vanish into the exaggerated war stories, embellished and dramatized when they returned home. Even Private Pyon Chinsu, wrapping himself like a mummy, would tell his folks about the exciting shootings, helicopter flights, the beautiful *con gais,* the ambush or listening post or reconnaissance missions, jungle operations and all other specious nonsense that might mislead adventurous imaginations, but he would never tell anything about his hiccupping fits, all his shameful begging and pleas for exemption from the combat missions, or what he had done in the foxhole during the Ninh Hoa battle.

"What plans do you have for your civilian life?" Pyon said to someone lying on another bunk in the dark.

"I will sell everything I got in Vietnam and open a small rice wine house with that money somewhere at Yongdu-dong. How about you? You're going back to the cinema job of painting the billboards?"

"I think I'll go crazy just thinking about home. Pokju will be waiting for me, bathed clean and her legs wide open in a real heat."

Corporal Kim Chaeo said he would go directly to a Kwangbok-dong brothel to buy a hot delicious whore and unload in her all the sperm he had saved for a year. The first thing Piggie Chang wanted was a burning shot of soju with a gooey pork rib. A soldier from the back said he would travel all over the country and fuck all his pen pal girls, one after another. Sergeant Chong Sangchol wanted to go to his hometown, first and above all, to see his parents and visit his grandfather's grave. Sergeant Cho Mangil, the medic, was dying to drink a whole gourdful of cool water directly from his village well, not mixing salt tablets or anything in it. The sergeant also wanted to catch a nice cold and experience something really Korean, because it was nearly winter now back home.

If I had a right to choose a war to fight, I might have chosen a war in the old times, a war in which they used to fight with swords and bows and spears, a war in which I could see the purpose and motivation of the whole conflict more clearly. I wished I could convince myself of the reasons, even one single reason, why I had to fight somebody else's war in somebody else's land. I would have liked it a lot better if I could fight for myself, my family, my friends, for someone, anyone I knew, without the need to despair in constant scepticism. What had I gained? What would be left of me after this senseless war?

The whole nation experienced and fought the Korean War together, but in Vietnam the war only existed for us who actually fought it among total strangers. This war was nobody else's business. In the Korean

War, all the refugees streamed endlessly in the same direction. In Vietnam even the Vietnamese did not know where to turn, who to trust, and whom to fight. In my childhood war, everybody around me was in the same war. But in Vietnam we fought alone, by ourselves.

Lieutenant Choe
Sangjun told us that the 3rd Platoon would
leave on a special mission at daybreak, but
he did not elaborate. His order was too
short to be good news.

Piggie Chang asked the lieutenant what
kind of a mission and how long we would be
out on it. "We have to start packing now,
sir," Piggie said. "We can't decide what to
pack and what to leave behind unless we
know the nature and duration of the
mission."

"Pack everything you will need in the
jungle," Lieutenant Choe said, his expression tense. "But don't pack C-rations.
Special rations will be supplied to you
later. One more thing. Those who carry

small arms other than the M-16, leave your rifles home. You will be given new rifles."

That was all. We were not too happy about this order. Something serious was brewing. We, the 3rd Platoon, were sitting on top of it. Intelligence reports said the enemy elements were again concentrating in the 9th Division tactical zone, presumably in preparation for a coordinated attack, on a much larger scale than the Ninh Hoa battle, to be launched around the lunar New Year's Day. The enemy had again infiltrated Hon Heo Mountain in force. But we felt a more substantial threat from Song Da Ban Valley by Hon Ba Mountain where no friendly forces had set foot in years. The Korean infantry division had precariously positioned itself between Hon Heo and Hon Ba, the two enemy horns zeroing in at us. The White Horse had grabbed one of them— although not for long—but the other horn remained strong and untouched. The beast had to use its horns, sooner or later. We could easily guess that our mission was related to either Hon Heo or Hon Ba. We also knew this was going to be our last combat mission before returning to Korea.

We packed socks, soap to smear on our soles to prevent blisters, big green towels, toothpaste, tissue paper, spoons, cigarettes, bayonets, blankets, bandages and the other usual items. Late in the evening we were supplied with dehydrated food specially flown in by a Huey. The freeze-dried stuff was so light-weight and flat that each person could easily carry sufficient food to last a week. This was the first time we had ever seen these special kind of rations. The company commander explained to us how to "cook" the freeze-dried rations. The captain ripped open a plastic bag and showed us a handful of the contents that looked like dust dyed in batik colors. When he poured some water from his canteen on this small heap of colored powder, steaks and beans and all sorts of meals were instantly ready for eating.

"By God, nobody can beat the Yankees as far as military supplies," Captain Kim exclaimed. But the captain did not explain to us the reason why we were supplied with the dehydrated rations instead of regular C-rations. We just presumed that we were going to some place where we had better not expect any resupply for at least a week.

We were issued sixty rounds of M-16 cartridges for each soldier, and we did not like this either. Once we were engaged in an action, sixty rounds would be spent in a matter of minutes—or in seconds when fired on automatic.

The next morning at 0600 hours, the 3rd Platoon was assembled outside the CP bunker, and the commanding officer armed everybody with M-16s. We loaded the rifles and fired ten rounds each to check that the weapon operated perfectly. We were not resupplied for the ten bullets spent firing into the empty sky. I preferred to keep my own M-2 carbine that had become a part of me as we had been working together for almost a year, but the CO wanted everybody to carry the same rifle for a possible interchange. We did not ask what he meant by "possible interchange," we knew he would not answer anyway. The new fully automatic M-16s did not look like weapons capable of firing real bullets and killing anyone; to me, those black rifles seemed to be like imaginary space guns in American comic books. Their shape was too contrived and playful, especially the handle on the top, and the whole thing was too light to convince me it could actually damage human targets. Corporal Song Pyongjo also preferred to take his own automatic rifle, but the platoon leader said laconically, "No. Everybody M-16." Song felt his 11-pound "old pal" was much more dependable than this "toy gun" that weighed only 7.6 pounds when loaded with a 20-cartridge magazine.

Led by the captain and the platoon leader, the 3rd marched at sunrise for 20 minutes and arrived at the temporary landing zone. An ugly H-47 Chinook, that looked like a huge mechanical dragonfly larva, was waiting for us. We loaded our knapsacks and weapons aboard, and sat down in four rows beside the helicopter. The platoon leader reported to the CO that we were ready to leave for the mission, and the captain stood before us with his hands akimbo and his feet planted apart. The company commander finally explained to us what our mission was all about:

"In twenty minutes, you will be lifted to the entrance of Song Da Ban Valley by Hon Ba Mountain for a long-range secret reconnaissance mission. You may have noticed lately the foreboding intelligence reports about clandestine movements of the enemy in this area. We know a large number of enemy troops are actively operating and preparing for an action in our TAOR, but we have so far failed to gather accurate information about the enemy's intentions and the scope of their current activities because we lost many Vietnamese agents during the Ninh Hoa battle and our intelligence network was substantially impaired. But the Division G-2 analyses reached the conclusion that the new enemy stronghold is not located in Hon Heo because it is geographically isolated by the Lac Ninh Plain and also because that mountain is too well known to the friendly forces after the division-scale operation in that area. Air observations have confirmed indications that an increased number of separate enemy elements have been concentrating at Hon Ba Mountain in the past several weeks. Therefore, your mission is to go to Hon Ba Mountain and search out the enemy concentration point.

"From here you will be airlifted to the first designated location and then you will go to the second designated location on foot. There, you will change to VC uniforms, which are already loaded in the helicopter, and then advance into the Valley of Death for a long-range reconnaissance to seek out the enemy headquarters. Your mission is top secret. Even the other platoons in our company will not know, until your hopeful safe return, where you have gone and for what purpose. If you encounter a smaller unit of the enemy before the mission is accomplished, avoid an exchange of fire by all means, lest your location and movement should be discovered by the enemy main force. If engagement is unavoidable, finish it quickly and cleanly—and silently. You must not leave any such enemy alive. Any survivor signifies your death and the ultimate failure of your mission. When the elimination is finished, withdraw from the point of the encounter immediately, leaving absolutely no track. You must not be seen or heard by any enemy until your mission is completed. I repeat: Your mission is to search the jungle and locate the enemy position. That is all. No more. When you find the enemy position, you will withdraw and be extracted as soon as possible, and then the whole division will be thrown in for an intensive operation to wipe out the VC footholds and thwart whatever attack plans they have for the rumored Tet offensive. Since your mission is of the utmost importance, I don't want any of you to be captured by the enemy. Lieutenant Choe will see to it that the enemy gets no prisoner. I wish you all good luck. Any questions?"

The Chinook took us to the first designated location, a weedy barren field about two kilometers southeast of Hon Ba Mountain. Before we got off the helicopter, the platoon leader distributed to us the Vietcong uniforms piled behind the pilot's seat. We strapped the *calico noire* outfits and the *non* hats on our knapsacks, and advanced through the thriving shrubs and reeds toward the foot of the mountain. We did not change to the Vietcong uniforms yet so as not to be mistaken as the enemy by any ARVN or American troops who might by chance be out on an ambush mission.

When we had marched three kilometers and arrived at a rocky gulch, we took off our fatigues and changed to the loose black clothes and conical hats. We kept our jungle boots on; nobody would be able to walk a mile in the crude Ho Chi Minh sandals. The knapsacks we camouflaged with broad leaves and twigs; we carried cartridge belts and canteens inside the loose jackets. After checking the disguise of the soldiers one by one, Lieutenant Choe gave us his own instructions:

"Now we are going to search every inch of Death Valley until we locate the enemy's heart. We are not supposed to pull out from this mountain until the mission is accomplished, so you'd better walk fast, think fast, and find the enemy fast, if you want to go back to the base fast and start packing for the voyage home. Remember this—our platoon will be exempted from the next operation as a reward for this special mission, so this may be the last piece of action we're going to see before our return home. I hope the 3rd Platoon will not suffer even a single casualty so every one of you will be able to make it to the reunion party I plan to throw for you at Hanilgwan Restaurant in Seoul when we go home."

He paused for dramatic effect.

"From now on, we will have to move constantly and silently—more silently than the VC snipers do. Now, start moving, and keep your eyes peeled."

We usually christened the hills, valleys, slopes or caves in a combat zone with the names of famous actresses and their celebrated anatomies. These humorous, obscene names were much easier to remember than the original Vietnamese names. Many locations were dubbed "the Valley of Death." If a fierce combat had taken place and the friendly forces suffered several casualties somewhere on a mountain—it did not have to be a real valley, any place on a mountain with trees and rocks was eligible—the soldiers would immediately name it "the Valley of Death." If a gorge was too rough to climb, it also became a "Death Valley," and if they just did not like some place in the jungle and could not think of a better name, they called it "the Valley of Death."

But the Valley of Death on Hon Ba Mountain deserved its name. It was a grotesque place.

The American troops had conducted a defoliation operation over this valley before the Koreans moved into the Ninh Hoa sector to intercept the Hon Ba-Hon Heo route. All the trees were dead from chemical spray which had left nothing but a brown botanical cemetery, a wasteland of exposed grey rocks and dark brown tree skeletons.

We started climbing the mountain with the lieutenant positioned in the center of the leading 1st Squad's diamond formation, which was followed by the other three squads in a long file like the twisting tail of a kite. Reporting our position occasionally to the company relay station by radio, we climbed the ridge. At first the advance was very slow because we had to avoid the regular path so as not to be observed by enemy snipers or lookout posts; we had to cut through the dense woods, opening a new path with machetes while guarding all directions at the same time to spot the enemy before they saw us.

When we had passed the suspicious area where the VC lookouts must be located, we began to climb along a faint path that was probably used by the enemy to go down to the "populated zone" for supplies and information. No birds sang in the damp, ghostly woods that seemed frozen in chilling terror, and there was no wind to stir the leaves. We were so few and so isolated—forty-four men, dressed like Vietcong.

Sergeant Chong Sangchol, the 1st Squad leader, raised his hand high to signal a halt. The platoon leader hurried to him. "What is it? What is it?" Sergeant Chong pointed at the ground and the lieutenant picked up a square plank with two rusty spikes sticking up. The spikes had been elaborately concealed by the grass among the writhing thick roots of a tall tree. We knew what those spikes were for; it was one of the basic Vietcong devices. If anybody stepped or sat on it, the five-inch spikes with sharp points would pierce the sole, and there was no way of removing the spikes because they had barbs on both sides spreading downward, like a tuna-fishing hook. The spikes were coated with urine that would cause tetanus. This primitive implement was one of the hand-made weapons with which the VC usually fortified their strongholds in the jungle.

While the soldiers were examining the crude but unforgiving Vietcong weapon, passing it from one soldier to another, Lieutenant Choe said in a hushed voice:

"I think we're on the right track. If an enemy stronghold is located on this mountain, as we believe it is, more of these things and more intricate booby traps will be found on our way. We must be careful from now on. All right, 1st Squad, move out."

About an hour later, we found several crow's foot prongs. One of its four spikes would always stick up to pierce a victim's sole whichever way it sat on the ground. This device had been used by Oriental generals in ancient times to thwart an enemy's fast movement in approach or assault—in Korea Admiral Yi Sunshin used the same device in his land battles against Japanese invaders in the 16th Century—but the Vietcong used this old simple device against their foes who were armed and equipped with everything powerful and modern. The crow's feet, coated with buffalo dung or other poison, certainly were deadly.

The platoon was extremely tense, painfully alert for a suspicious string or thread that might trigger something to blow them up and expose the location to the enemy while, at the same time, we could not neglect guarding ourselves against the snipers or lookouts or ambush squads that might be lying in wait around the next bend. We moved at a snail's pace, like old women hunting for needles lost in the grass. When the lead squad was too exhausted from the constant tension of looking out for each step, the next squad took over. We were nervous and irritated at having to constantly look for the invisible nails and spikes, but we had no choice. In the jungle you had to fight on the Vietcong's terms.

Pyon Chinsu was three people ahead of me, next to Corporal Song Pyongjo, the AR gunner now reluctantly armed with "the toy gun." Pyon looked like an ox on its way to the slaughterhouse, his legs wobbly, as if he was not sure where he was going. This time he had not attempted any futile and obvious tricks to drop out of the reconnaissance mission. The whole thing had happened so suddenly and quickly that he simply could not try anything. Or, perhaps, he had given up because he was aware by now that nobody would be fooled by his petty schemes any longer and that no one was to be exempted. His buddies were all so used to his "crazy stuff" that nobody paid any attention to his quaint talk or behavior. In the 9th Company, Private Pyon was like a problem child nobody in the family even cared about.

When he was evacuated to the 102nd Field Hospital, he kept pestering the surgeons persistently, insisting he was a mental case. They were annoyed enough to re-evacuate him to the Dove Medical Unit in Vung Tau for further examination to decide if he should be really sent back to Korea and released from the army. They should have done that—let him go from the war. But he was back at the bunker when we returned from the Hon Heo Operation. The surgeons had sent him back to us, having decided he was a coward faking insanity. And now he was with us, in the jungle, trudging despondently after the AR gunner.

It took more than three hours for us to climb over one low ridge. Everyone was mentally exhausted already because you could not relax a single moment. The tension was oppressive. I wanted to scream.

After lunch, our squad was in the lead. Barely ten minutes after we had taken over the point, the soldiers at the head suddenly stopped. Everybody stopped, like a train stranded on a destroyed bridge. The silence surrounding us intensified. Several ahead of me whispered to one another, and Sergeant Han Taesam, the squad leader, called the medic and the platoon leader in a hushed voice. Like everybody else behind me, I craned my neck to see what was going on up front. The lieutenant and the medic hurried to Sergeant Han, and the soldiers mumbled here and there. The sergeant pointed down at a pit in the middle of the narrow passage between two rocks. It was a perfect trap; anybody passing here would use this narrow passage or cut through the dense thicket behind the tall round rocks. The lieutenant, the medic and Sergeant Han knelt down around the pit and stooped to look into the hole.

"Take defense positions!" the platoon leader hissed at us, looking back over his shoulder. There was a sudden urgency in his voice. "Spread out and take defense positions!"

I quickly squatted behind a tall tree and checked the suspicious spots around us. Then I glanced over at the front where the medic was reaching down to touch something. When our eyes met, Sergeant Han beckoned at me; I was his second sergeant. I went over to the pit between the two rocks and Sergeant Han Taesam gestured for me to take a look.

Yun Chusik had fallen into the pit. To his instant death. The rectangular opening looked like a perfect earthen coffin, with Yun's body sprawled in it lengthwise, face down. Broken twigs and dirt, that had been used as the lid concealing the trap, were piling onto his back. Dozens of bamboo spikes, planted at the bottom, impaled him and stuck out of Yun's sides and neck. The sharpened bamboo tips, the dead lump and the walls of the pit were smeared or sprinkled with blood. His body was ragged and drenched in red but I saw a cigarette butt still wedged behind his ear like a carpenter's pencil. He had saved that cigarette butt for one more puff later. He always did. Private Yun, "the Ancient Car," saved everything for future use, and never threw away a cigarette unless he had smoked it to the filter.

The lieutenant stooped further into the pit to reach Private Yun's body, snatched off the dog tags from his bleeding neck, raised himself, and, dusting his hands and knees, told Sergeant Han Taesam, "Bury him quickly."

It would be too much trouble to unskewer Yun's body from the bamboo spikes and then bury him somewhere else. That would take too much time, and the lieutenant thought we could not bother about protocol on this mission. So Yun Chusik was buried as he was, stabbed all over by the bamboo blades, in the Vietcong uniform, deprived of the final privilege of fighting his enemy face to face in his last moment. His rifle, his knapsack, and the cigarette butt wedged behind his right ear were buried with him.

The soldiers were mute, their expressions dismal, because they had lost a man on the very first day out. And because they did not know how long the mission would last. Three soldiers from the 2nd Squad shoveled dirt into the pit to bury Private Yun.

Aerosol insecticide cans had been issued each soldier every month. Nobody knew why Yun had preserved these aerosol cans so carefully. He kept them deep in his personal locker, like a family heirloom, never using them, braving annoying mosquitoes and all sorts of other pestering insects. Everybody in the bunker teasingly asked him why he was saving the aerosols—to use as a deodorant on his wedding night? When another can was issued the next month, he put this new can into his locker and finally took out the old one and began to use it. But sparingly. Whenever he went to sleep, he would spray two or three small puffs around his cot, as if spraying some spice over his food. Naturally, his aerosol lasted longer than two months, and the cans began to pile up in his locker.

Nobody knew why he saved everything, and why he collected all sorts of used things so passionately. He saved even typing paper which had been used on one side, and his locker was bursting with a full inventory of expendable supplies. At every inspection, Master Sergeant Han Myongsun would blow his top about the locker which looked like a miniature junk shop, and tell him to get rid of all the rubbish within thirty seconds. He'd begin to count: one—two—three . . . Private Yun's collection would disappear for several days but soon he would start to smuggle items back into his locker, bringing one secret bag after another on his way back every morning from a night ambush. Sundries jammed his locker. Why had he collected all those can openers, buttons, shoe laces, used razor blades, screws, insect repellent bottles, and the cartridge shells?

Private Yun was from a very poor family, and he sent almost all his monthly pay home because his parents and siblings needed the money so badly. Most soldiers did not like the government policy which forced the soldiers to send most of their pay from the American government to Korea, but Yun sent home more than he had to. With the little money he saved after sending 40 dollars home every month, he hoped to buy a Canon camera to take home as a souvenir of his adventure in Vietnam. But he never had been able to save enough money to buy the camera; he had barely managed, up to now, to buy a tripod and a strobe to go with it. He had planned to buy the camera with his last combat pay, which the government allowed private soldiers to spend freely in Vietnam. In a week or two the Defense Ministry would mail Yun's parents his belongings—a box full of can openers, rubber bands, used razor blades, buttons, shoe laces, screws, insect repellent bottles, cartridge shells, white plastic C-ration spoons, and a tripod and a strobe without the camera.

We transplanted some grass on the site where Private Yun was buried and camouflaged the whole place so that the enemy could not detect, for some time, any signs of our passing. Then we continued our march.

The weather was so sweltering that the dark green color seemed to drip from the leaves like molten toffee. As we were preparing to camp by a stream in a secluded gulch, lukewarm rain began to fall through the dense foliage. The rainwater felt as warm as a bath, perhaps because the leaves had been cooked by the heat all day long. Nobody had brought a tent. Long-range reconnaissance was no camping trip, as the platoon leader had told us. The lieutenant even forbade us to rig a poncho between rocks or trees to provide ourselves with a shelter from the steady downpour. The glossy poncho would be too visible, even in the dark, the lieutenant said, because the rain on the water-proof surface would reflect the faintest light.

The soldiers opened the plastic ration bags and just held them out to the rain to rehydrate their supper, and after burying the leftovers and plastic bags in the wet ground, they tightly tucked in their clothes and sought shelter under a tree or between rocks to pass the rainy night.

I skipped my meal. The freeze-dried food made me feel cheated. I did not like the idea of taking the essence only, eliminating all the natural flavors. Besides, I was not feeling too well in the rain, and found myself haunted by an overwhelming fear that this mission was going to be costly and that I would be included in that cost. I might not make it—this nagging fear kept buzzing in my ears.

I was in the same night watch shift with Private Song Namil. Crouching behind a leaning rock with Private Song next to me, I stared into the rainy dark and tried to count how many more night watches, if I survived them all, I had to be on until my return home—my return to freedom and civilized life.

I recalled the night watches at the Korean "front line" in my earlier soldier days back home. Each sentry had to stand guard for one hour every night at one of the five "vital" positions surrounding the barracks—the main gate, the rear gate, the ammunition dump, the open brook, and the CO's quarters—and there were also three "mobile" guards who were supposed to patrol around other "strategic" positions to intercept the imaginary enemy infiltrations. Nobody liked the guard duty, especially in cold winter, and the soldiers naturally wanted to cut the shift short. So they did. Usually, there was one official clock for a barrack, and this one timepiece determined the shift hours. Wrist watches were rare among the poor front-line soldiers and not many bothered to carry them. Each shift would turn the official watch five or ten minutes forward to shorten their duty hour. When the last shift went out the watch was usually more than an hour early. That was why everyone hated the last shift, but nobody complained much; everybody was doing it. I recalled those long sleepy hours of the last shift, thinking, I could not do that tonight because most now had their own watches. Soldiers who used to be paid almost nothing—a mere ten cents a month—by the Korean government because they were draftees serving their compulsory military duty for two and one-half years, now, as volunteers for Vietnam combat duty, were earning 40 dollars a month.

I gazed at Private Song's dark contours squatting behind the wet rock. Song never wore socks. He had such nasty athlete's feet that he dreaded wearing socks. Instead, like Russian soldiers, he kept his feet wrapped in cotton cloth. He was a twenty-four-year-old man of few words with a long horselike face. They said he had deserted once and been to the monkey house, but nobody knew anything much about that incident except for what was recorded in his personnel file. He never talked about it. He rarely talked about anything. But tonight, he wanted to.

His voice subdued, he talked about home. But I was not much interested in his recollections at that moment. Private Song continued to reminisce about his childhood in his hometown; he kept talking without caring if anybody listened or not. The rain had been thickening since midnight and I could hear the big individual raindrops spattering on the leaves. I was sitting on a folded poncho, feeling naked, the sticky insect repellent on my arms almost washed off by the rain. Song was smoking, hiding the glow with his wet hand.

"When this mission is over, Sergeant Han," he was saying, "I will go directly to the PX, and I will buy my sunglasses."

I said, "Sunglasses?"

"Yes. Nice U.S.-made sunglasses."

"What for?"

"I will wear them, of course. On the day we arrive in Pusan back home. When I get off the ship, I will wear the sunglasses."

I smiled silently in the dark, thinking, how small a man's ambition could get in some situations.

"I bought an Asahi-Pentax camera, too," he said, crouching into a ball like a porcupine. "I bought it last month. I will have it slung on my neck, when I get off the ship. With the sunglasses and the camera, I will look like a somebody."

I did not respond to that because I could not find an appropriate response, and I was now wondering if that Asahi-Pentax camera would fit with the Canon tripod and the strobe Yun Chusik had bought.

"In a month or two we will return home," he went on. "If we survive five or six more weeks, we will be on the ship going back home. My family, my friends, my girl—they will all be waiting for me at the Pusan pier. They'll come to the port to welcome me home because Pusan is very close to my hometown, Taegu. Almost every night in the past several months, I imagined myself getting off the ship at Pusan port. I practiced over and over again how to go down the ramp from the ship to the waiting people the most impressive way. Now I got everything worked out how to do that, down to the smallest details. I will go down the steps very slowly, all dignified and stately, like a real big shot, like a bridegroom entering the wedding hall. People wave flags down there and they sing marching songs to the music played by the army band. They will cheer until their throats turn hoarse, everybody looking up at us, the triumphant heroes home from the war. And I will walk down the ramp, one step after another, slowly, very slowly, with my sunglasses on."

I said nothing, listening.

"Maybe I will have a cigarette in my mouth," he said, imagining. "I don't have to light it but I will have a cigarette in my mouth anyway. Maybe it's better to light it. The smoke may look good. I don't know." He was trying to revise one detail in his imagination. "I can puff a little smoke, you know. Just a little. Maybe I will pretend I am thinking about something very deeply while I am going down. Like a philosopher or something." He paused as if he was examining the scene he had just painted in his imagination. Then he continued to embellish. "And I will buy a ring, too, with all the money I can save. I heard they sell diamond rings at the PX. When I walk down the ramp, I will wear the ring on my finger. This finger." He showed me. "When I'm almost down on the pier, I will hold the visor of my cap with my hand, like this, and then look around at the crowd down there, all the way around, so everybody down at the pier can see my diamond ring glitter in the sunshine. My parents and friends and relatives, and everybody will start asking questions. They will cheer for me, shaking my hand, and say all sorts of nice things to me. But I will say nothing to them. Without any word, I will just look around, with a very serious expression. And then I will slowly raise my hand again and hold the visor of my cap so that the diamond ring will shine before their eyes."

His voice was as grave as if he had already landed in Pusan.

"And when I return to my hometown, Taegu, I'll go to the biggest and cleanest public bath house in town. There, I will hire a dirt remover and give him a fat tip of 200 won and tell him to scrub out all the dirt I had collected on me for one year in Vietnam. I will ask him to scrub and scrub until the white skin underneath will come back to the surface. And then I will go to the barbershop in my old neighborhood. I think the barber will remember me. I used to drop by the barbershop every week while I was serving at the 2nd Army Headquarters in Taegu before coming to Vietnam. He will ask me where I've been because he hasn't seen me for a long time. 'Where have you been for a whole year?' he will ask me. I won't tell him anything at first. If he keeps asking me over and over again, I'll just tell him, 'I was away.' And I'll pretend I've fallen asleep while he's giving me a shave."

He sucked at his cigarette again, hiding the glowing light with his wet hand. The blood in the fingers of his cupped hands loomed red when the cigarette glow flared up.

"I'll go to the best restaurant in Taegu and eat pickled radish chops to my heart's content," he said. "After the dinner, it's time for me to go to meet my old friends at the wine house where we used to hang out. My friends will be there waiting for me to buy a drink to welcome me home, and they will want me to tell them about all the things I saw and did in Vietnam. Maybe we will drink and talk all night, but I'll never even say a word in their presence about Vietnam. Because this is my war, and they have no right to know anything about it."

He crumbled the cigarette stub with his fingers; the light had been already extinguished by the rain.

"What would they understand about the war and life here even if I told them?" He sighed. "April, May, June, July, August, September . . ." He counted on his fingers. "It has been ten months now since we left home."

Then he began to sob quietly.

Sergeant Kim Mungi
seemed to have somehow sensed it approaching. I often wondered how anyone
could know it was coming, but it seemed
they knew most of the time. Did some men
have an instinct?

Kim was leading the 4th Squad right
behind me, while I had to follow my squad
at its end as the second sergeant. The 3rd
Squad, led by Piggie Chang, was in the
lead of the whole platoon. Sergeant Kim
and I had spent many hours together, but I
never knew he could get so talkative. We
were on equal terms with each other. He
outranked me but I was three years older
than he was; he was a professional soldier
and his promotion was much faster than

the draftees'. He was not a very prudent man, but he tried all the time not to talk too much, for he had learned at a very early age at the orphanage that talking too much brought nothing to him but an occasional nosebleed.

But he was a different man today. His voice sounded so hollow—like the voice of a hidden man speaking for a wicked marionette in a puppet play—that I was taken aback by the chilly feeling on the nape of my neck, and instantly glanced at him over my shoulder. He was grinning like a half-witted person, his unseeing eyes swimming in the blank vacuum. I had never seen such an idiotic expression on his face. He had never shown fear in previous combats, but now his face was distorted and twitching with anxiety behind the dumb grin. The strangest thing about him this morning was that he talked so much; he talked almost nonstop as if he wanted to tell his whole life story. He prattled on and on while eating his lunch. Kim's endless, breathlessly, urgent monologue reminded me of Pyon's terror-stricken monologue in the foxhole at Ninh Hoa. Sergeant Kim could not stand even one single moment of silence, it seemed. If there was a pause, however short it might be, he was restless; he seemed to fear that he might have a heart attack from the frightening silence. He talked about only one thing—his pen pal writing, and nothing else.

"Sure, lots of boys envy me because I get letters from twenty girls a day," he said. He probably had far more pen pals than anybody else in the whole division. "But it also takes hard work to keep so many girls writing to you. It needs work and skill, as in anything else. If you write to so many girls all the time, you often get mixed up, and you have to be constantly alert not to make any stupid mistakes. And that needs something more than a good memory alone. I think I am a born pen pal because I enjoy all the hard work. For me, any work involving pen pals is fun."

He bound all the letters he had received from girls into a book every month—ten volumes of them so far—and he maintained a separate ledger in which he kept orderly records on his correspondents. Every day he made new entries in the ledger about the letters he received and read immediately so that he could maintain a "comprehensive picture of the overall pen pal flow."

"There are certain effective and fast ways to get many new pen pals. You try it my way any time you want if you really want a harem of girls writing to you. The easiest way is to use the pen pal columns in the popular magazines like *Humor, Arirang,* or *Old Stories and True Stories.*

You know, those magazines sent by the Defense Ministry to the army units at the Korean front line or Vietnam's combat zones. Everything is so simple. Really. You just have your name and address printed in one of those columns. Soon you will receive a heap of letters from girls all over the country. They just go crazy for the heroic soldiers fighting a war in a foreign country, you know. That's why you shouldn't omit 'ROK Forces in Vietnam' in your address. The girls love the military look in the address with all those abbreviations and pompous designations. And the US APO number also is sure magic. It looks so exotic and impressive because the 'US' gives a nice ring to it—as if we're a part of the world's strongest and biggest nation. Many girls like that."

He kept pausing to resupply the oxygen that was running short in his system.

"I have received so far a total of 2,647 letters from girls and more than three hundred letters will be waiting for me at the base when we go back in two or three weeks after this reconnaissance mission."

He regularly exchanged correspondence with twenty-eight girls. Three of them were in Seoul, and the rest lived in the southern Chollado Province where his home was. Many Chollado girls had become his pen pals when he contributed a short "Reminiscence of a Soldier in Vietnam" to *The Cholla Daily News*. Newspapers and magazines enthusiastically carried anything written and contributed by the Korean soldiers stationed in Vietnam. After the newspaper ran his piece, letters poured in to him, 267 of them, all from girls.

He had received photographs from a total of forty-seven girls so far, and among those girls, the most beautiful, in Sergeant Kim's and anybody else's eyes, was Ko Changhi, who worked for a department store in Seoul. The runner-up beauty was Yu Talhi, a member of the Mokpo Broadcasting Station chorus. I saw Ko Changhi's picture when Sergeant Kim showed it around to everybody, and this young woman in her mini-skirt was, indeed, unbelievably beautiful. Everybody in the company instantly fell for her, and during operations the platoon leader would joke, "Hey, Sergeant Kim, let's have a breather and take a look at her picture. This war might look a little better then."

When the 29th Regiment announced they would sponsor a photographic beauty pageant, six hundred odd soldiers applied for the contest. Their pen pal girls' pictures were posted on panels erected in the regimental parade ground. Everybody in the 9th Company, from the commanding officer to the radioman, believed Ko Changhi would win the crown made out of a shredded milk can. She did. And Yu Talhi of the broadcasting station's chorus won the honor of Miss Slender.

"You must be careful not to get confused about what you say to which girl in the letters you send. To keep track of what you write in different letters—that's demanding work, too. And when you want to receive more frequent letters from a particular girl, you tell her a small lie: that you've been wounded in action. Then, the girl will write you every day. I learned that trick from Sergeant Oh Ujin, and that trick always works."

As he kept talking on and on, the platoon leader came over to him and said, "You better shut up, or you'll get us all killed."

Kim lowered his breathless voice a little, but did not stop talking. "And there are some bitches who ask you to send them money because they heard we are paid well here," he said. "There are some girls who ask you to buy and send them perfumes and other cosmetics from the PX. You'd better terminate relations with those girls before they do you damage. There are some naughty girls, too. One girl, who used to write me, often copied all sorts of obscene passages from novels and magazines and sent them to me. I enjoyed reading them, but you can't expect a lasting relation from such a girl. Too much open sex is a danger sign and you have to watch out."

He talked faster and faster after lunch, until he almost gasped because he tried to say too many words in one breath. He was choking from his own words.

"Even if I have to write ten letters on the same day, I never run out of new things to write about. Don't just say 'This is a windy day.' Everything becomes a poem if you make it one. You can say 'This is a windy day' in a poetic way too. Like this: 'Westerly wind blows. The palm trees sway to the east. Easterly wind blows. The trees sway to the west.' There. You already have four lines of perfect poetry. I always write long letters, sometimes running ten pages or more. People like to read long letters because long letters show the things in our mind more deeply. And use soft girlish words like 'love' and 'dear' sparingly. Tender affection works most effectively when it is expressed rarely, because rarity makes it precious. You'd better believe me because I'm telling you all this from my personal experiences."

He was warned two more times by the platoon leader to be quiet. The lieutenant was so infuriated by his endless prattling that he even punched the sergeant once in his stomach. But Sergeant Kim kept talking and talking until the platoon leader had to give up silencing him.

"When I first came to Vietnam I had few pen pals," he said. "I simply could not find the girls to write. And one day I found an interesting letter among 'the consolation letters.' You know those letters—the letters students are forced to write in their classroom to the soldiers. This particular letter from a grammar-school child mentioned, in passing, that her father was always complaining because there are too many girls in the house. So I hopefully believed that I might get to know one of her older sisters if I kept writing to this little girl. So I wrote a long letter about the bright moon over the jungle and the exotic beaches with palm trees and the sadness after a bloody battle. Then I casually asked her to send me a picture of her family. She did send me a picture—of her mother and a younger brother. She had no sisters at all. I asked this nine-year-old girl whatever had happened to her sisters, and she replied she had lied to me, because she wanted to receive a letter from a brave soldier at war. She believed a soldier would write her back if he knew she had many sisters. She got me hooked, all right. That's how a child's psychology works these days, you know."

Reaching for his fly to urinate, Sergeant Kim Mungi stepped aside a little to let the soldiers behind him pass by, pushing off the sagging branch that was getting into his eyes. "Maybe some day the military experts should consider including consolation letters in our C-rations," he said, and a shot rang out. Sergeant Kim fell.

The soldiers halted momentarily to determine where the sniper's shot had come from. They quickly looked around, checked the ground to see if there were any booby traps or crow's feet, and then took cover.

It was silent.

After we had waited quietly for a full minute to check if any sniper was around us, the lieutenant signaled at me to go over and take a look at the fallen sergeant. I crawled over and examined Kim's dead body. A bullet had spun into his chest and torn out of his back. His penis was drooping on his fly like a withered cucumber, urinating. He had not been circumcised yet.

Then I saw the rattrap nailed to a tree about one meter away. The rattrap was securely fixed on the bark, about 1.5 meters high from the ground, and a sturdy hemp string was connected between the rattrap and the branch Kim had touched so that the string could trigger the rattrap to hammer a nailhead, the nail ingeniously rigged to strike the percussion cap of a bullet wedged into the wooden board of the rattrap. The spent cartridge shell, still in the board, was accurately aiming at my chest.

"It's not a sniper, sir," I reported to Lieutenant Choe in a loud whisper. "It was a booby trap."

The platoon leader sent out four scouts to check if any enemy was lurking near us, and the rest of us scraped the blood from the ground and buried Sergeant Kim Mungi's body behind a rock. The scouts returned to report that there had been no enemy in the vicinity to hear the shot. We moved out again and kept moving, without any definite purpose or destination, leaving a thick red track of grease pencil on the lieutenant's map. We simply kept going, not knowing where to go.

The dense foliage ended and the open sky burst into the jungle. Yellow reeds as tall as our chests stretched out about one kilometer before us. We looked far down at the greenish blue waters of Vung Ro Bay. The open space relieved our depression but we found it hard to breathe, stifled by the heat radiating from the reeds. We quickened our advance to traverse this open area fast so as not to be observed by any enemy on higher ground. The yellow color of the *non* hats blended well with the reeds, and I tried to reassure myself that the enemy might mistake us for their comrades.

We reentered the dusky jungle in the afternoon. Even the rugged boulders looked dark green, wet by the night-long rain, and the soldiers mutely advanced through the woods of brown and green. There were no clear paths in the jungle; it seemed nobody had passed here in the past ten years. We found no booby traps or crow's feet either, so we were somewhat relieved but annoyed, for we must be wasting our time in this forest. This safety also meant that we would never find any enemy position near by.

In the woods where the foliage formed a dense green canopy, we came across a small brook gurgling through the rocks, and the soldiers refilled their canteens, adding salt tablets or purifiers. Flowing water was safe from any natural or artificial poisoning. I drank some directly from the brook. It tasted cool but strange, because I had been conditioned to the salted water for almost a year. I worried that the pure water might cause diarrhea because my intestines would be upset by the unadulterated liquid.

We camped that night near the water source. My mind was lulled by the trickling as I watched the water tumbling over the stones. After a relaxed supper, I gathered leaves to make a soft bed on the damp earth; I did not have guard duty that night. Snugly lying on the leafy bed, I watched the soldiers still having their supper or smoking or brushing their teeth. Some silently cleaned their rifles in the thickening dark, picking or scraping out dirt and leaf crumbs from the muzzles or cartridge chambers with broken twigs. And then they slept.

We arrived at the Valley of Death in the afternoon of the fifth day. It was a grotesque landscape indeed. Over the whole defoliated, devastated valley, ghostly dark skeletons of burnt trees poked upward to the empty sky like long, gnarled fingers spreading out from the bony arms of witches buried en masse. The rocks and dead branches were leaden, and even the weather was bleak. Maybe the whole world would become a place like this when a nuclear holocaust wiped out all living things.

On the sixth day, we moved out of the defoliated area and took a charred path serpentining over a ridge. A mine exploded. Somebody screamed. I threw myself behind a collapsing pile of loose gravel and sprained my wrist. Stones flew away in all directions, and the explosion echoed here and there in the valley like rolls of thunder. A panic flashed through my mind. This is it, I thought, this noise finally exposed our presence to every Vietcong in this valley. Sprawling over the gravel, I wondered who had stepped on the mine.

We knew it was either Corporal Min Chonggi, Corporal Song Pyongjo, or Corporal Chin Sunggak who had touched off the mine. Pieces of broiled or blood-drenched flesh hung or stuck here and there on rocks and branches, and we could not know at first who were the victims until each squad finished checking their men individually. All three of them had been blown to unidentifiable ragged shreds.

"The enemy must have heard the explosion!" shouted Lieutenant Choe, lying flat on a rock. "But they might not know the location of the exploded mine unless they are somewhere very close. So everybody hide, stay tight. Just don't move."

Gripping our M-16s, we carefully looked around to check the surrounding areas, hoping no enemy would be found. Hoping no enemy was observing us. We waited for a long time amid the heavy silence. My vision turned hazy. The sky and the rocks and the trees flickered and dimmed to blurry shapes, losing their individual identities. I was terribly lonely.

Then I heard a moan.

I looked back and saw Sergeant Sin Kyusik, who was sitting helplessly before a rock five meters away from where the mine had gone off, his eyes stupidly wide, muttering, "Oh—Oh—." When our eyes met, Sergeant Sin clumsily tried to hide his left shoulder with his right hand.

Then I saw. His right arm was gone. Blood poured from the severed stub near the elbow and streamed down to the thighs of the black Vietcong trousers. He tried again to hide his blood-dripping arm as if he were ashamed of the gory stump.

"Medic!" called the platoon leader. "Look after the wounded soldier!"

Two pieces of torn flesh stuck on the rock behind Sergeant Sin, who was bleeding from his forehead. His whole face looked like a mangled mess with the blood streaming down between his eyebrows from the cut. Sergeant Cho Mangil, the medic, crept on his belly to Sergeant Sin, opened his first-aid bag to take out the bandage, and dressed his torn arm in frantic haste. The medic worked very fast to conceal the half stub of the arm, as if he wanted to hide it quickly and see it no more. A while later, the medic dragged Sergeant Sin down and both of them disappeared behind the rock, leaving only the intermittent painful groans.

We waited. The weather was steaming. My eyes tingled with streaming sweat. In the choking silence, I heard Sergeant Sin moan now and then behind the rock. When there was no response from the enemy for five minutes, the platoon leader ordered us to move.

"We have to get out of this place," he said. "I think either there are no enemy in this vicinity, or they still do not know our position. We must move as far away from here as we can before dark so that they cannot get to us."

We fled through the jungle like frenzied animals running for life. I marched breathlessly in a stumbling run, swept forward by the desperate current of fleeing soldiers, occasionally gasping aloud, and I shivered with the frightening delusion that somewhere in the jungle they were complacently watching me and other men on this death run through the entwined branches and vines.

Our advance was hampered by the wounded soldier. Groaning ceaselessly, the bandage on his arm wet with blood, Sergeant Sin was struggling defiantly to hold himself together and follow us at our galloping pace, but he faltered every so often, on the verge of collapsing into unconsciousness. The lieutenant swore at him several times to pull himself together, but deadly pain was not something to be ordered around. It was not right for us to take him with us, I thought. Sergeant Han Taesam carried the knapsack and the rifle for him, but it would still intensify his pain and drive him to a certain death if we forced him to march like this. The lieutenant was infuriated by the delay, yet I could see he was very much worried about the man. He needed some clear-cut solution right away, but he just did not know what to do in this impasse.

We came across a rocky cliff about twenty meters high. We could see a little piece of the sky there. Lieutenant Choe sat down on a turtle-shaped rock and checked our coordinates on his map. He stared at the soldiers crouching around him, thinking, and then called Sergeant Yun Myongchol, the second sergeant of the 4th Squad.

"You stay here with Sergeant Sin," the lieutenant told the second sergeant. "A chopper can land on that rock, so I will have Sergeant Sin evacuated from here. We can't move fast enough with a wounded man. We will never be able to carry out the mission dragging around wounded soldiers, and he could die of too much bleeding, too. We have two hours until sunset, so the rest of us will move away from here as fast as we can and radio the relay station in the evening to have the CP send a rescue helicopter here first thing in the morning. You stay here with Sergeant Sin until daybreak, and then return to the tactical company base with him when the chopper comes in."

Sergeant Yun Myongchol had a queer, dubious expression. His face paled, perhaps because he considered it a death warrant. It was a dreary prospect—a night spent alone with the endless groans of a wounded soldier who had lost one arm in a godforsaken nook of the death-stalking jungle. The Vietcong might be converging on this very spot from all directions, like ants collecting on a dead locust. But the order was given, and a private soldier's life was expendable for the purpose pursued by the whole. He also seemed relieved: he had been given an unexpected reprieve. He was released from the indefinite mission that seemed to be more dangerous than any other. In all the previous combat situations he was an anonymous existence, one in a multitude, who moved the same way for the same purpose with the crowd in an orchestrated mass action. Now, he belonged to a group too small to be comfortable. He, like everybody else, was too visible. An exposed, naked target. But he was getting out now.

"The rest of you, move on," Lieutenant Choe said, picking up his rifle and raising himself.

The platoon leader gave a smoke shell to Sergeant Yun, so that he could show his position to the rescue helicopter coming in tomorrow morning. The enemy might spot the smoke signal, but the lieutenant did not worry about it. They would spot the incoming chopper, anyway. We started.

We camped that night by a dry stream. It began to rain again even before we settled down for supper. Some soldiers had their meal in the rain, but many skipped it because they had not yet recovered from the shock of the three soldiers blown apart by the mine this afternoon. Certain shocks were eternally renewed in battle, and I could never get used to the subhuman deaths by explosives. The platoon leader ordered us to go to sleep with our knapsacks strapped tight in case we might be attacked by the Vietcong at night. We would not delay for a moment our early start in the morning. "We are leaving without eating breakfast," the lieutenant said.

I lay on my side under a tree, squatting like a shrimp, covering my head with the folded poncho, and listened to the raindrops drumming on the ground inches away from my ear, pressed on the stone pillow. Thunder grumbled in the distance. My fatigues, my knapsack, the ground, everything around me was wet, and the rainwater trickled into my jungle boots to wet the socks, too. The radioman was sending out the coded message to the relay station in a hushed, cautious voice to call in the helicopter to evacuate Sergeants Sin Kyusik and Yun Myongchol:

"The bulldozer is all right and cherry bush clover seagulls are on Hong the Magic Boy. One chick is hurt. Report it to Number 6 and send out a dragonfly to the following checker."

I kept thinking and thinking about the three soldiers who had been torn apart. During the night the images I witnessed that afternoon seemed to be mere imaginings. Reality could not be that bad, I thought, and in my mind the three deaths began to lose their reality. I could not know what others felt that night, but I was unable to feel sorrow or even fear. My nerves were benumbed. How could a man just disappear like that in one single moment?

I wished I had some liquor with me. Some very strong drink. I wanted to get drunk until my consciousness relaxed to a normal wakefulness. I might feel grief for the dead soldiers, at least, instead of paralyzed stupor. I wanted to feel fear as a reality. To feel sorrow. I wanted to hear the cry of a baby starting its life. I wanted to lie side by side with Hai on the warm Tuc My beach.

I kept thinking about the soldiers who had died in the afternoon. During the Korean War, when I was a grammar-school child, I marched with my friends along the railroad, imitating the soldiers, singing,

"Marching Over the Piling Bodies of the Comrades." We were so excited whenever we played soldiers, singing the military songs. But it was not exciting at all to become real soldiers and march over the bodies of the comrades.

My comrades were soaking in the rain now, still hanging or sticking to the rocks and trees, for the platoon leader had decided to leave them there untouched. If any Vietcong came to the spot and saw the burnt VC clothing, they might think the dead were their own comrades who had stepped on a mine. Besides, it was impossible for us to remove all those fragments of flesh and bones and the blood spattered all over the place. Min, Song, Corporal Chin—they had been human beings several hours ago. But no more.

Howitzers boomed in the distance; the earth trembled slightly under me. Lying on the wet ground, shrinking myself, I sucked at my wet cigarette, my hand twitching in sudden anger. My hand, holding the wet cigarette butt, quivered, as I lay there, among the shrubs, banished from the reach of anybody's salvation.

I fell asleep for a moment in that uncomfortable posture, but was immediately awakened by a scream of pain. I grabbed my rifle instinctively and rolled over to my stomach, without any definite sense of direction, not knowing what was happening, trying to figure out quickly where to aim my weapon, and muddy water splashed in my face from a puddle. My whole body was drenched and I was shivering from chill. Here and there I saw the soldiers taking cover and preparing for combat.

"I got a VC!" I heard the excited voice of Corporal Chae ten meters away from me. "I stabbed him with my bayonet! I killed him!"

I could not see either of them because it was too dark and the trees so dense, but I heard the platoon leader ask the corporal, "Report the situation. What happened?"

"I was on guard duty when a Cong suddenly appeared just a few inches before me, sir, so I stabbed him," Corporal Chae said breathlessly, trying hard to control his breath. "He's over there, sir."

"Don't raise your head, stupid! How many were they?"

"I don't know, sir. Just one, I guess. I saw just one. Anyway, that VC didn't know we were here and suddenly emerged from behind that fallen tree. He was about to climb over, but I was hiding right behind it. He was so close. I just stabbed him. I drove my bayonet deep into his guts, and then twisted it once, just like in commando training. He must be dead, sir."

"First Squad leader!" the lieutenant called in a loud hiss.

"Yes, sir." Sergeant Chong answered somewhere in the dark.

"Check if other enemy are in the vicinity."

"Yes, sir."

There was a long, nervous silence while the 1st Squad scouted the area. We waited, staring at the dark.

"I feel damn better that we got at least one of them finally," said Corporal Kwon behind me and spat into the rain.

Sergeant Chong Sangchol returned with his squad a while later and reported to the lieutenant. "We couldn't find any sign of the enemy, sir. He must have come alone."

"In this rain?" the platoon leader said, disbelieving. "Keep checking. Something is wrong. Where's the medic?"

"Here, sir."

"You go over there and check the VC Corporal Chae got. Sergeant Chang of the 3rd Squad, you go with the medic and cover him while Sergeant Cho is checking. If the VC is still alive, try to save his life. We can get rid of him any time we want to later, but a prisoner might be a big help to us."

"I understand, sir," Piggie said. "Let's go."

I heard Sergeant Cho and Piggie Chang crawl away toward the fallen Vietcong. The yellow beam of a flashlight searched among the trees. The beam went out.

"Sir," Piggie Chang called.

"What is it?"

"Please come over here, sir."

"What's the matter?"

"It's not a VC."

"What?"

Taking three more men, the lieutenant crept over to the fallen man. The yellow beam flashed again. The silhouettes of the soldiers, frozen among the trees, looked down at the ground.

"My God," the lieutenant said at last. It was Sergeant Yun, in his Vietcong clothes and *non* hat.

"I didn't know," Chae pleaded in a frightened voice. "I really didn't know."

"Shut up," the lieutenant said. "Is he dead?"

"No, sir," the medic said. "He's lost consciousness, but he's not dead. Not yet, anyway, sir."

"Will he live?"

"I don't know, sir. Seems there's not much chance for him to make it, though," the medic said. "The stab is really deep."

"I really didn't know, sir, I really didn't," Corporal Chae pleaded again.

"It was Sergeant Yun Myongchol that Chae mistook for a Vietcong," someone whispered.

"Why the hell did you come after us in this darkness?" the platoon leader asked Sergeant Yun, who had dimly regained consciousness. "Where's Sergeant Sin? What did you do with him?"

Sergeant Yun frowned, his eyes blinded by the flashlight, but he did not seem to recognize anybody's voice. The medic and the lieutenant kept trying to talk to him but he did not seem to hear anything. Nor was he aware where he was. He tried to push his shoulders up to lean against the dead tree. Sergeant Cho quickly helped him.

"What happened to my belly?" he said, looking down at his belly and then touching the bandage tentatively with his index finger. He blankly thought about something, perhaps to figure out what had happened to him. Then, drifting in and out of consciousness, he began to speak incoherently, as if talking in his sleep, sometimes gasping, sometimes his throat gurgling with blood.

"Why did you stab me? I didn't do anything wrong. I really didn't do anything wrong. Sergeant Sin is dead. About forty minutes after you left, I guess, he died. He wept and groaned all the time because his arm pained him so terribly. He wept and groaned until he died. His head rolled down weakly, like a pumpkin falling from the fence. I touched his throat and I knew he was dead. I was scared. So scared. I didn't know what to do about the dead body. I was afraid the Vietcong would come to get me because I was alone. I was sure they were searching for me all over the place. I knew they'd get me and kill me sooner or later, if I just sat there waiting. But I had to do something about the dead body first. I'm telling you the truth. Why did you stab me? Why did you? Sergeant Sin looked so frightful when he died. Dead bodies look so scary. As I sat there with the body, I felt the corpse would suddenly jump up and attack me so that he could take me with him. I was so scared. I couldn't stay with the body. And I was scared the VC would come to get me. I thought the chopper would not come in, because Sergeant Sin was dead. I thought you, everybody, even the guys at the Division HQ knew he was dead. They would not send a chopper. They knew. If the chopper came in, the VC would know right away that something was going on and you didn't want them to know it. You probably radioed the CP not to send the chopper. That's what I thought. What would happen to me, if they don't send the chopper? What could I do, alone in the jungle? By the time it was dark, I was sure the chopper wouldn't come. I'd roam alone, lost, and sooner or later I'd be caught and killed by the Cong. I thought maybe I'd be able to catch up with the platoon if I ran fast enough. It was easy to follow you because I knew which direction you had gone. But it began to rain, and I couldn't find you for hours. I wanted to rest but I couldn't. I had to hurry. You might keep moving all night. I might be lost forever in this jungle. I couldn't go back to the cliff either. I didn't want to go back. If I kept walking all night, I might catch up with you somewhere, I thought. But why do you have to kill me? Why? It was raining so badly. You don't have to worry about Sergeant Sin's body. I got rid of it clean. Nobody would find it. And you don't need to call in the chopper in the morning either. Who stabbed me? Why did he have to do that? You really don't know how hard I tried to find you in the rain. I was so tired, I couldn't see anything. I thought I was going crazy. You'll know how I felt, when you're deserted. A dead body next to you. It was so scary."

The medic lit a cigarette, shading it from the rain with his *non* hat, and put it in Sergeant Yun's lips. The sergeant weakly sucked at the cigarette twice, and then his head rolled down. He regained consciousness twice again before daybreak, and each time he opened filmy unseeing eyes, he raved about the same things.

20

He died just before the sunrise. While we were burying him in the thicket, Chae tried to explain his innocence to the platoon leader, to the squad leaders, to me, to everybody, blubbering, "I didn't know. I really didn't know."

At dawn, the weather turned worse, the gusty wind sweeping the rain like gauzy curtains. The soldiers, the legs of their trousers completely drenched by rain and mud, mutely trudged through the windy downpour that thrashed the trees. Although the overhead foliage provided us with a shield, the march against the head wind was arduous enough, and the wet black pajamas stuck to the skin and also hampered our movements. The soldiers often slipped or stumbled on the stones hidden by the grass; the rocks were slippery and dangerous. The soggy faces did not show any expression, any desire, not even any color. We kept walking in the whirling folds of rain, like banished ghosts, surrounded by misery and loneliness.

I suspected I might be going crazy. Thoughts developed and progressed by themselves without any intervention, judgment or confirmation by me. Various grotesque and eerie thoughts kept flashing through my mind. I tried to drive them away; I thought about Korea, but that was too remote and unreal to dwell on for long. Again and again my mind veered away to the suspicion that Sergeant Yun might have killed Sergeant Sin at the cliff and then hurriedly followed our tracks to join us. No, that was not true, not true, not true.

We were running away from the enemy when we should be searching for them, and we were dying one by one, I thought. The whole platoon would just disappear in the jungle. Had someone sent us into the valley to methodically eliminate us. Who? Was Fate herding us into a slaughterhouse.

No, Sergeant Yun could not have killed his own comrade. I revised my suspicion. But he could have abandoned him at the cliff and come after us alone. If he had, Sergeant Sin might be already captured, tortured now somewhere by the Vietcong. The sergeant might have confessed where we were and what we might be doing. The Vietcong would be chasing us like bloodhounds, examining the wet leaves to track us. I wondered what methods they might have used to torture him.

I asked for two tranquilizer tablets from the medic and swallowed them to calm down, but the sickly, obsessive thoughts would not go away. At times I felt my sight slowly going dim and blurry, and at those moments, I could not even feel the rain streaming down my face. I was falling into a suspended state. I had walked all morning, but when I was having my lunch, I could not remember at all what I had done the past several hours.

The rain began to clear off around noon, and I gradually recovered my sobriety. I slept like a log that night, totally surrendered to the numbing exhaustion. Corporal Kim Chaeo told me the following morning that he had stood my watch, too. "You slept like a stone Buddha, Sergeant Han. I tried to wake you up, shaking and shaking again, but you just went on sleeping like a bear in winter."

I suspected that I had been stricken by dengue fever or some sleepy jungle sickness, but my head was as clear as a crystal ball by the time we started the day's march.

We suffered no casualties for twenty-four hours, and entered another lush forest the next day. Here we could not advance more than 400 meters an hour because the platoon leader decided this dense bush looked suspicious. He pressed us cautiously to check every spider's web and strange foliage shape to check for hidden wires connected to a booby trap. My whole body was steaming. Big sweat drops rolled down my spine to the sacrum, as I had rolled down my sleeves so that spiders and poisonous insects would not land on the bare skin of my arms.

Everything was dark green. I could not see anything except for the soldier wading through the jungle two meters ahead of me. My scalp itched unbearably, my hair was soaked by perspiration and infested with dirt and vegetation crumbs. Constantly I checked my arms for ants, mountain crabs, poisonous flies or string snakes which might have crept into the sleeves to bite me and cause a severe infection that would mean certain death in this isolated place.

Worst of all were "greens," the replacement soldiers who had recently arrived from Korea with the second contingent. The experienced veterans, the toughened grunts, would not die easily because they knew about survival, but they had to share the consequences when a green failed to detect a hidden trap. Also, a tough grunt could last three days with one canteenful of water; a green would run out in six hours and suffer from thirst for a whole day until the next spring or stream. In any combat a greenhorn was a burden. These new chicks were not trained as hard as the first-contingent soldiers and the difference showed.

We found a drain ditch at a cleared site. Several Vietcong had camped here some time in the past two or three weeks. The soldiers came suddenly alert. But we could not find any more tracks. Where was the enemy? The running enemy that refused to be defeated, the elusive and invisible foe who left tracks at one spot, then disappeared into thin air ten paces away? Chasing a shadow that kept fleeing in a circle until we tired ourselves out—that futile race made the war seem ghostly.

Somewhere nearby a Phantom jet was blasting something with napalm, and the whole mountain quivered. We took a break in shade where little grass grew because the sun was blocked by dense trees. I was smoking my last cigarette, my rations were running short like everybody else's. We had not been resupplied for a week. Leaning against a stump burnt by lightning, Sergeant Cho Ichol stared at my face curiously.

"Hey, you're bleeding, on your head."

I had noticed something sticky on my left cheek but not paid much attention to it, thinking it must be dust and sweat. But it was blood that oozed down my cheek. I traced it up to the source with my finger, up into the helmet. In the hair, matted with thick blood, I felt something rubbery. Gooseflesh bristled up all over my body as I touched the foreign existence in my blood-clotted hair. I picked off the soft elastic thing with my two fingers. It was a leech.

"Flying leech!" exclaimed Sergeant Cho, recoiling. Among the jungle creatures, soldiers especially dreaded leeches and string snakes that could sneak into fatigues undetected. "Look out, everybody, we got flying leeches!"

"Jungle leeches," Piggie Chang hissed to his men. "Leeches are falling. Stay away from the trees!"

The leeches fell from trees to land on passing animals or people; the hosts would not know of their presence for quite some time—until the bloodsuckers gorged themselves and the trickling blood showed. The soldiers ran their fingers over the skin concealed beneath their VC uniforms and plucked out the worms, groaning repulsively or spitting in anger, their faces turning pale. Soldiers found the leeches sticking on their necks or in their armpits, tore them off, held them in the air with twig chopsticks and burnt the hideous worms with lighters until they were incinerated. Those who found no leeches on themselves hastily applied insect repellent to their skin and buttoned up shirts to the neck. A few stripped and checked each other's naked bodies.

The bleeding would not stop from the spot in my hair where the clandestine leech had been feeding, and I had to pad the place with a thickly folded bandage. That night we had a very uncomfortable sleep. I heard soldiers slap their necks, fumble with their legs or shoulders, until late into the dark. The leeches were even in boots; the rubbery things could creep in anywhere. I lay on my folded poncho, spread near a decaying tree felled by a howitzer shell. My whole body, I imagined, was crawling with the leeches squirming around inside my clothes. I would doze a while but startle myself awake and fumble all over my body, checking if leeches had infiltrated.

We were scheduled to be resupplied at 0700 hours of the ninth day by a helicopter at a designated spot. We arrived a day early at the drop location, late in the afternoon, because we did not want any enemy who happened to be lurking in the vicinity, to find the supplies before we did and wait in hiding to ambush us when we appeared to pick them up. The drop site was a bare ridge where we could easily locate the supplies thrown from the helicopter.

We spent the night nearby. How the preparations were going for the airdrop was not possible to confirm because our communication with the mobile relay station in between was cut due to the high rocky cliff which blocked the transmissions, but the lieutenant did not seem worried at all. He had made the final check with the CO last night. We thought a skirmish or a serious combat situation was in progress somewhere near Lac Ninh because heavy shelling continued over Hon Heo Mountain and flares kept burning over the dark plain all night. But we could not confirm that either. The fear of leeches had subsided, and even the shrill sound, like navy whistles, of howitzer shells flying by overhead could not keep me awake for an hour after supper.

Around five o'clock I awoke, refreshed. Whatever action that had been going on in the plain was over. As the day broke, the green field began to loom faintly in the grey dawn at the foot of the mountain, and I saw the solitary houses surface like dark islets rising from a sea patterned by squares formed by the rice paddies. Safe-conduct leaflets were scattered all over the bush where we had spent the night, and I noticed for the first time that the rocky cliff had white splotches, gashed by artillery shells. So many had been wasted on worthless targets.

This morning, others seemed to be feeling good, too. They were slowly overcoming their fear. There had been no casualties in the last several days. I even had a vague hope that there was no enemy stronghold anywhere on this mountain. If there was no enemy, we did not need to stay. The battalion commander might decide to pull us out, for we had been uselessly suffering while not seeing even a shadow of the enemy.

As if reading my mind, Corporal Kim asked the platoon leader, "What happens, sir, if we can't find any VC headquarters here because they are not here in the first place? Do we have to search for the enemy stronghold or wait in this jungle until the enemy establishes one? Maybe we'd better settle down somewhere and start farming if we plan to stay here that long."

The lieutenant said, "It may be no problem for you to live here, Private, because you're a mountain boy, but we've got to find them soon if you want to be back to the base in time to start packing for the trip home. I'm sure the enemy is heavily concentrated somewhere. If they are divided into smaller groups, we would have encountered some of them by now."

"I don't mind staying here if we can find the VC," said Piggie Chang, pouring water from his canteen into a freeze-dried food packet. "But I don't like what's going on here, sir. So many booby traps but no VC. How long should we stay here if there's really no VC around?"

The lieutenant looked at the soldiers, thinking, trying to decide if he should tell them what he had known all along. His stiff, military expression relaxed a little, as if saying, What the hell, they have the right to know.

"This mission won't last longer than forty days," he said. "The patrol routes were set up, though roughly, before we left the base because our radio relay has to know where they must move to each day to catch and boost our signals. Our 40-day search route meticulously covers all important areas, and we can believe there's no enemy stronghold in this mountain if we don't find it by then. So, we're returning to the base in a month, even if we find nothing."

I was appalled. The idea of us spending a whole month in this jungle. If we kept losing men at this rate, most of the platoon would be wiped out by the time a chopper flew in to take us home. But the other soldiers seemed much happier to learn that we were moving on any sort of a scheduled plan.

I noticed they had changed. Like children afraid to enter a deserted empty house for fear of its being haunted, then coming to love that same spooky place as a favorite playground, my comrades were gradually becoming friendly with Hon Ba Mountain, where they had spent almost ten days now. They did not fear the mountain too much, and they even exchanged occasional jokes and chattered pleasantly while waiting for the resupply helicopter. The lieutenant tried to make them quiet, but the soldiers did not fear the place any longer.

Chae, however, looked agitated. He had been nervous and fidgety all the time since the stabbing of Sergeant Yun. We avoided his eyes so that he would be less conscious of us and feel less guilty, but it only made him think he was that much more alienated. We knew he was not responsible for the killing, but he himself thought otherwise. He could not sleep well and his face was haggard, his eyes daily sinking deeper into their hollow sockets.

Private Pyon Chinsu frequently cast inquisitive glances at Chae, who was turning into a different personality, as Private Pyon had at Ninh Hoa, and as Kim Mungi had immediately before his death. Was the spiritual terror infecting one soldier after another? Pyon Chinsu was now at peace, detached and aloof, although he was the progenitor of that disease. He was a curious spectator of the fear eating at others, for he himself had gone through the full process and ultimately recovered.

The familiar sputter of a helicopter engine droned in the distance. The sound grew louder, little by little, and then roared beyond the low ridge ahead of us. My heart pounded with the fast sputtering rhythm, as if an old friend was coming. Somebody was coming. Somebody was coming to see me.

The helicopter swooped around the low ridge, into sight. And another, and another. It was not one chopper, but three. I thought it strange because one could carry more than enough supplies for our platoon. The three choppers flew very low, just above the rice paddies, almost touching the ground, until they reached the foot of the ridge where we were hiding, and then suddenly, they began to climb along the slope, almost grazing the treetops. When the triangular formation was about mid-ridge, it sharply broke in three different directions. They were trying to mislead any Vietcong observing them.

The last chopper flew directly to the bare ridge, where we were hiding. Almost skimming the treetops, it quickly hurled down three bulging mail bags. The grass leaned to the ground, blown flat by the rotor's swirling gale, then bristled back upright as the chopper shot off. Like a kite that had just snatched its prey, it flipped itself to change its direction, and sped away over the low ridge. The other two choppers, hovering over the trees on neighboring slopes, unloaded sham mail bags, stuffed with nothing but safe-conduct leaflets and propaganda booklets to convince the enemy that this early-morning mission was merely a psychological warfare maneuver. When they finished the drop, the two helicopters spurted back to join our chopper over the low ridge and the roaring sputter dimmed rapidly.

The 1st Squad, led by the lieutenant himself, lay in ambush for any Vietcong who might approach the pickup area. Pressing down our *non* hats, the rest of us dashed out from our hiding places, plowed through the reeds to where the supplies had been dropped, opened the mail bags and stuffed everything into our emptied knapsacks. We packed all the rations in a flash and scurried away. Like urchins who had just raided a melon patch, we scuttled breathlessly into the bush, chuckling and laughing. Without pausing, we hurried away.

An hour later we arrived at the gorge where the 4th Squad was waiting for us. The soldiers poured to the ground what they had packed into their knapsacks. The platoon leader found several ration cartons containing letters. Piggie Chang did the mail call. Among some two hundred letters, more than sixty were for Sergeant Kim Mungi, the pen pal king.

The lieutenant ordered us to finish breakfast, pack, and fill our canteens in ten minutes to begin today's march, but the soldiers would not do anything until they read all their letters first. I received two—one from my sister, Kihyon, and the other from Kang Inho, a classmate of mine in college.

Choe gave up prompting the soldiers to an early start and began reading his own letters, his bare feet dipped in the cool stream.

"Darn! I've been barking up the wrong tree all the time," Lieutenant Choe said in mock despair, apparently disappointed but grinning.

"Anything wrong, sir?" asked Chi Taesik, squatting beside the lieutenant, his eyes dashing back and forth following the lines in the letter he held outstretched around the radio in his arms.

"You know the school teacher at Haenam, don't you?"

Everybody in the 9th Company knew that school teacher, the army newspaper had carried a boxed story about her and the lieutenant, who had sent her some money so that she could buy an organ for her deprived students. His laudable act of gallantry was publicized both by the local paper and the military tabloid, but neither elaborated the real truth—that the lieutenant had made the donation because the teacher was so beautiful.

"What about the teacher, sir?" the radioman asked, still absorbed in his own letter.

"She's going to marry next month," the platoon leader said, folding the letter and putting it in his breast pocket. "I've been building a fire in the wrong oven duct. And you know what?" He showed the sergeant a photograph. "She sent me a picture of the new music teacher, because she wants to introduce her to me. Look."

"The lost fish certainly looks bigger to me, sir," the radioman said, handing the photograph back to the lieutenant.

Opening my classmate's letter, after finishing my sister's, I noticed Sergeant Han Taesam sitting cross-legged by a tall tree; he was deeply engrossed, reading with a grave expression. "Anything important?" I asked him casually.

"Uh?" Han raised his head to blankly gaze at me for a while, and then he thrust the letter to me. "I was just curious and opened some of Kim Mungi's letters. I came across this one."

I folded Kang's letter and clamped it between my knees to read the letter he had given me. It was in a girl's handwriting.

Dear Sergeant First Class Kim,

You must be safe and alive if you're reading this letter now. Otherwise, you couldn't read this, could you? How do you do, sergeant?

These days my mind is teeming with various thoughts about war. Maybe it's because I have a soldier friend that I've been gradually acquainted with the extreme situation called war. It may sound all too ridiculous to you, who are actually at the war, but these thoughts come and go in my mind all the time lately.

I can imagine profound love between comrades-in-arms blossoming like yellow dandelions on the battleground. I heard some men cherish a comrade's life more preciously than their own in battle. How beautiful it is that a man can sacrifice his own life for somebody else! That indeed is a true love—a true love which cannot be found, in my opinion, between any man and a woman. I hope I can experience such love in my life. To sacrifice one's own life for something noble and sublime—it is a true expression of heroism.

Perhaps it's because I'm a woman that I so often envy a man's world, the brave world in which you can witness and experience bravery, comradeship, heroism, manly sacrifice and idealism. Men are happier than women in the sense that they are endowed with this open and honest context in which they can experience spiritual adventures. I wish I could go to the war and fight side by side with you men, sharing all those experiences. I think I could learn a lot more about life then.

I will go to Pusan and welcome you at the pier when you return home in six weeks. I will bring a big sign bearing your name in big black letters. I want to see you, a brave soldier proudly returning home from the war, the very moment when you put your first step back on Korean soil. I think I will recognize you easily, although I have seen you only through the photographs. (I really like the picture in which you posed with a rifle under a palm tree.)

I want to saunter along the Haeundae Beach for hours with you, listening to your endless story about your life in the war, and listening to the crashing waves of the winter sea. I hope I can do that in six weeks. I will pray for you when I go to the church tomorrow.

From Yun Sora in Taegu

"She writes well," I said, handing the letter back.

Sergeant Han stared at me for a while, dumbfounded, as if I had made a shockingly stupid remark. He sighed deeply, averting his eyes, and then said in a restrained voice, "I'm not discussing her literary style."

"What then?" I said, opening my friend's letter.

After a moment he said, "People just don't know, I guess—about what we are doing here. This girl, for instance. What does she know about us? I think everybody back home is the same. They think we're having a fantastic adventure or something. But what did we actually go through for the past week? Was it a Robin Hood adventure in Sherwood Forest? What's such a big deal that we capture six enemy rifles? What makes it big news? Nobody reports two hundred of us got killed during the Ninh Hoa battle. Why do the government men not want the people back home to know and share with us the pains we go through here? Experiencing them is excruciating enough, why do they try to stop us and the newspapers from talking about them? Why does the press have to keep romanticizing and exaggerating our victories while never mentioning our defeats? Why should we keep those pains as secrets in our hearts, as if they're unforgivable shames? The people back home, the whole nation, is deceived en masse, and they are misled into believing that we're out here picnicking, masquerading as eternally triumphant heroes. I often feel disappointment or disillusionment when I receive letters from my friends back home. What they want to know is how romantic and exotic the palm trees look, how hard it rains during the monsoon, or what kinds of things I can buy at the PX for them when I go home. That's about all. They don't know that each leaf in this jungle emits terror and panic like toxic gas. They just don't know that this war is tearing us into a thousand pieces, destroying our youth, heart, soul and everything else we have. They have buried us alive in this jungle and completely forgotten us."

Although it was still morning, I began to doze.

I could smell the reeking stench from my own body, for I had not taken a shower for nearly two weeks. My body was pickled by rain, sweat, dust, accumulating dirt, and then again by rain and sweat. My scalp was scabby and it itched all the time around the spot where the leech had been feeding. Maybe that creepy worm might have sucked my brain out, too. Both my thighs were sore, because the coarse, sweat-salted underwear kept scraping the skin. The soldiers were losing their appetite; they were fed up and getting sick, literally sick, of the dehydrated food, that looked and tasted like chemical powder. Their faces grew strained, the eyes sinking deeper everyday until they looked like Neanderthal men in black pajamas. The Vietcong clothes, wet with sweat and dirt, constricted my limbs, binding me. My hands and arms were covered with scratches from thorns and briars, and both feet were blistered and swollen to huge dimensions.

Still we had found no sign of any Vietcong or NVA elements.

In the afternoon we had to cross a sunken grassy dell, like a huge bowl. Lieutenant Choe sent out three scouts to check the area. The three-man scout team led by Sergeant Han disappeared into the reeds. Quiet descended from the sky down to the hushed meadow, and I could hear nothing around me except the platoon leader's muffled voice as he occasionally spoke to the scouts on his walkie-talkie, covering his mouth with his cupped left hand, "If you read me, blow twice. Over . . . Good. If you're safe and no enemy is in sight, blow twice more . . ."

The rest of us waited, hidden in the reeds. The sun was hot on the nape of my neck as I was lying on my stomach in the grass, and the heat, held by the grass, made me doze off in an untimely nap.

"Hey, let's go." Somebody slapped my shoulder, and when I opened my eyes, Sergeant Cho Ichol was looking down at me with a disbelieving expression. "Where the hell do you think we are? You really got a nerve, eh, taking a nap on the march. Come on."

Through the stifling, steaming heat we traversed the dell, climbed down a ravine, crossed a gulch, climbed a hill, passed a huge bomb crater, and climbed another ridge. We walked endlessly. When the sun went down, we fell, exhausted, among the rocks and trees into an uncomfortable, reeking sleep but not before cleaning our rifles.

When the platoon leader made the morning roll call to start the march for another day's futile search, Chae was gone.

We temporarily suspended the search for the enemy, and each squad spread out in a different direction. We searched for two hours but Chae was nowhere to be found. Nobody had seen him slip out of the camp last night and we had no idea in which direction he had gone. But we all knew why he had done it. We waited for one more hour with the vague hope that he might come back to us. The waiting was in vain, and we left after an early lunch.

Humping through the bush, I imagined the man roaming somewhere in the jungle, aimlessly, crying. He was a good soldier. He had enough freeze-dried food with him to last for over a week, but what could he do when he consumed all he had? He might wander around until he starved to death. He would never return to us because he no longer could bear the guilt of having killed his own comrade. He would be captured by the Vietcong, if he survived long enough. Then he would be forced by the Cong to broadcast in Korean on NVA radio to persuade the Daihan soldiers to surrender to the noble and glorious National Liberation Front. We often received those broadcasts on the AM band of the military PRC-10 radios during operations in the open field. Why had we become somebody's enemy in this war that actually had nothing to do with Korea?

Among the enemy belongings captured earlier on Hon Heo Mountain, we had found several boxes of leaflets, both in English and Korean. The leaflet, printed in neat handwriting, read, *If a Korean soldier surrenders to the NLF, his life and safety will be guaranteed. His personal belongings will not be confiscated. He can send letters home, and his past war crimes against the Front will not be questioned.* Whoever had written this was either a Communist North Korean or a captured South Korean soldier. During a Bulldozer Operation, the soldiers captured a North Korean rifle that carried the notation *ryon bal,* "automatic firing," in Korean script on the barrel. In this remote region of a foreign nation, North and the South Koreans were confronting each other as enemies in a stranger's war.

21

As the reconnaissance entered its third week more and more soldiers started complaining that whatever we had to go through had better happen quick, or everybody would eventually go crazy in this endless chase of the phantom enemy, who exhausted us simply by not doing anything. The soldiers preferred a hot fight to this maddening, interminable torture, even if they had to suffer casualties.

We did not expect Chae's return any more and the soldiers forgot his existence very quickly. I assumed everybody back at the company base, at the regimental headquarters, in the division war room, and in our fatherland Republic of Korea, had forgotten our existence as fast as we had his. Maybe they had even forgotten that they had ever sent us here.

Our advance was interrupted by a perpendicular rock face that was not indicated on the lieutenant's map. We had to take a detour to reach the ridge above the cliff. The platoon leader decided that we would slip down the gorge to our left, cross the stream, then climb back up the ridge to continue along our planned route. After studying the topography of the gorge and the neighboring jungle through his binoculars, the lieutenant gave his instructions:

"The current of the stream looks rapid, and the slope is steep on both sides. We could be clobbered if we got caught in a natural trap like that. I want the 4th Squad to cross the stream first and take defensive positions so that the rest of us can safely make the crossing. We will give you twenty minutes to go down to the stream, another twenty minutes for the crossing, and thirty more minutes for climbing the opposite slope and taking up cover positions. In the meantime, we will conceal ourselves at the present location and cover you from this higher ground until you safely cross the wild water. We will wait here for fifty minutes and then set out so that we can reach the stream seventy minutes after you've finished securing the area. Now, 4th Squad, move out."

The eight men began to climb down the slope. After the last man vanished through the foliage, we scattered among the trees and took our positions to wait. The lieutenant went fifty meters further down the slope with the 1st Squad to select an easier location from which to cover the 4th Squad in case of an emergency. The 2nd and the 3rd Squads stayed behind. I put down my knapsack and lay on my stomach. The branches and leaves surrounded me so densely that I could not see anything down at the stream. My skin felt sticky with cooling sweat, and the soft soil under my forearms was damp, and the dead leaves squishy, like a wet cushion, under my belly. The wind was dead. I felt drowsy watching the yellow, glossy leaves basking in the little sunshine that trickled in through the canopy of boughs. Yellow color and silence always made me sleepy. I wondered if I had to fight back the drowsiness, but I thought that was not necessary because we had one hour. My vision began to blur slowly. My brain began to fall asleep.

A rifle shot rang out. Just one shot. After a pause—perhaps only two seconds—the whole gorge shook with frantic rifle shots fired in a volley that sounded like thunder rumbling. Then the firing stopped. All at once.

During the eerie lull we hurried down the slope and gathered around the worried platoon leader. Lieutenant Choe Sangjun had been observing the gorge through his binoculars, lying on his stomach on a high rock. He explained to us what was happening: "The 4th Squad is under attack. I can't see the enemy position from here, but they seem to be hiding somewhere on the opposite slope or behind the rocks downstream. The 4th Squad was trapped in the middle of the stream, just as I feared, and I saw someone shot and swept down by the current. Our men are taking cover behind the rocks in the stream, and they seem to be nailed down, because I don't see anybody moving. I wonder why they stopped firing."

Another volley burst crackled somewhere on the opposite slope. Both the enemy and the 4th Squad soldiers opened up and stopped several times.

The lieutenant said, standing up, "We're going down to help the 4th Squad." An agonized despair flashed in his eyes. He knew this skirmish would certainly compromise the whole reconnaissance mission. If we went down the slope and engaged with an unidentified number of the enemy, there would be at least one survivor on the Vietcong side. And that one VC was enough to alert the whole enemy force on this mountain. But the lieutenant could not let his men be wasted, abandoned. He did not need much thinking to make his choice. "It seems the enemy still does not know our main force is here, so, everybody must be extra careful not to expose himself until we spot them first. Even after we make a visual contact, we cannot start firing until I make sure that we can have them all. Remember—we must not lose any of them. We can't afford even a single one slipping out of our grip. Follow me."

"All right, bastards," Piggie Chang said, slinging up his knapsack. "You asked for it, and you will have it."

While we were tumbling and sliding breathlessly down the slope, the on-and-off firefight lasted for another ten minutes. By the time we were halfway, the firing stopped. When we arrived at the stream, everything had quieted except the shattering current violently surging against the rocks. A lone bird squealed somewhere. Concealing ourselves, we observed the opposite slope for ten minutes before going down to the water to see if anything moved. The dead bodies of the 4th Squad soldiers were scattered among the rocks on both sides of the stream. There was no sign of enemy presence anywhere.

It was obvious that the enemy had thought there were no other intruders. The Vietcong had disappeared without a trace, taking all weapons and knapsacks from the dead. We found six bodies. Private Song Namil was hiding in a grove, half-conscious, bleeding profusely somewhere at his waist. Two or three bullets had penetrated through his stomach. Sergeant Cho Mangil, the medic, checked his wound and slowly stood up, shaking his head just slightly, so that Private Song would not notice, to let the lieutenant know that the casualty would not survive.

Squatting before the dying soldier, the platoon leader asked, "What happened?"

Vainly trying to stop the blood streaming from his mashed side with his helpless palm, his one leg twitching spasmodically, Private Song reported to the lieutenant between coughs and groans, that the 4th Squad had started to cross the stream tethered in pairs so that they would not be swept away by the wild current if anybody slipped. Suddenly they confronted, face to face, about 15 Vietcong who were coming down the opposite slope along a hidden path. Both sides saw each other almost at the same time and froze, surprised, the 4th Squad in the slapping choppy water, the Vietcong ten meters up the path. The VC seemed to be on their regular patrol. They faltered for a moment, confused by the soldiers in black clothes. Then someone opened fire from the stream, and everybody started shooting, stumbling, slipping down, hollering, screaming, the water splashing everywhere and the bullets whizzing by.

"We kept firing like crazy, sir, and struggling to get out of the water," said Private Song, looking down at his rent body. The medic pretended to patch it. "I don't know how much damage we did to the enemy, but everybody in the squad is dead, I think, except for me. I don't believe we did much to the Cong, sir. They were on the higher ground and well shielded by the rocks and trees. I doubt if we got even one. When the fight was over, the Cong came down to check if there were any survivors among us. I took off my knapsack and dragged myself into this grove. I didn't know until then that I had been hit and bleeding so heavily. I passed out the moment I saw this blood, and when I came to several minutes later, the enemy was going back the way they had come, carrying all our weapons and knapsacks, the walkie-talkie, everything."

The lieutenant sent the 1st squad across the stream to check the faint trail on the opposite slope, but the enemy was long gone. Somebody must have been killed or wounded on the enemy side, too—so many bullets could not have just evaporated into the air—but we could not find any blood stain or dead body.

The lieutenant wanted to know more about the enemy—"What weapons did they carry? Did they look like NVA regulars? What kind of hat did they wear?"—but Private Song found it more and more difficult as his breath ran short. The private began to choke on his words when he had no more strength left to breathe and talk at the same time. He had to stop talking whenever he needed to gather some strength to inhale, and then, after a sigh or cough, he would go on to tell about the enemy and the fate of the 4th Squad soldiers.

He looked down at his belly because blood continued to seep and soak his groin although the medic had wrapped his waist with several rolls of bandage like a warrior's breast armor. He realized the bleeding would not stop. "Am I dying?" he said.

Private Song Namil did not believe he was actually dying, although everybody else knew he would—in a matter of minutes. He seemed to believe that he would live on, even after he bled all the blood he had in him and stopped breathing. But, ultimately, he had to accept he was going to die when nobody answered his question.

He glanced at the platoon leader and then the medic with pleading eyes, imploring either to stop his bleeding and keep death from taking him away. When neither of them responded to his supplication, Private Song looked around at the other soldiers. He recognized me, his eyes turning bleary, choking, choking again. He said, "You know my sunglasses. I need them when I go home." Then he mumbled something about the chrysanthemums at his home, his eyeballs rolling white, and I heard some cackling sound, like a retch. His mouth gaped as if the tongue were blocking his throat, and then he stopped breathing.

"All right, get ready to move," the lieutenant said, turning away. He seemed to have been waiting for the private to die.

"Sir," Sergeant Han Taesam called.

The lieutenant looked back with a frown. "What?" he said brusquely.

"What about the dead, sir?" Sergeant Han asked. "Shouldn't we bury them somewhere before we leave?"

The lieutenant looked around at the casualties, his eyes burning with fury. "No," he said.

We all looked at him, surprised.

"You will not bury them," the lieutenant said. "Don't anybody touch them. If we bury them, the enemy will know we're here, and they'll start looking for us. We will leave them as they are."

"But, sir—" Piggie Chang was about to protest.

The lieutenant ignored him and went on: "Besides, we've got something to take care of now, and we have to move fast."

The lieutenant was in a hurry. He did not want to lose any time because he knew the enemy was still somewhere near. He wanted to get them. And I knew the lieutenant was infuriated. He was angrily sad for the sudden loss of his men, eight of them, in one single moment, and for having to hastily abandon them without proper burial.

Looking back at the dead scattered by the stream, I was appalled. How could we desert our comrades like that? Leave them like the carcasses of dead dogs? Had we fallen this low? Was the mission really so important that we had to discard our own dead like garbage? What would happen to the bodies. When the sun went down, or even before, animals and birds would gather to feed. Fangs and beaks would tear and chew flesh and feed, eventually leaving only the white skeletons. The corpses would start decaying soon in this jungle heat, and grubs would swarm in the mashed entrails. It was a profanity to desert the dead like this, but a necessity of war. The war made its own rules.

The lieutenant drove us like a mad dog herding a flock of confused sheep, swearing at everybody in sight, growling at us to hurry, hurry, move, catch the fleeing enemy who might still be nearby. If we got them, the lieutenant said, we might find the enemy concentration point, too. But we found no enemy tracks, anywhere. They had just vanished.

We marched until dark, but the lieutenant had to finally admit that the enemy had slipped out of our reach.

The platoon arrived at a green bamboo forest. Its tall bamboo formed a tunnel like the vaulted transept of a grand cathedral. No plants grew in their shade. Overhead the bamboo leaves, that looked like delicate brush strokes in an Oriental painting, were closely knitted into one big green-patterned canopy covering the whole forest.

The soldiers silently marched along the tunnel that was as wide as a truck route, and brimming with a cool green hue. Invisible birds tweeped somewhere in the primordial silence and green mist. The scene was majestic.

Surprisingly, Private Pyon Chinsu had not had any fitful outbursts.

That Pyon was not uneasy at all made *me* uneasy. Normalcy was not normal for him. It was eerie. Our mission seemed cursed. I felt my mental being trying to separate itself from me, from the physical existence that did not function fast enough to be in concert with my mind. I was confusing myself. It was a very strange feeling, but I did not know what my mind was thinking, and I was afraid that my soul would abandon me. But I walked on.

We continued to lose men. Corporal Chon Chonguk, who had mastered the Chinese homiletic classics and composed excellent *sijo* poems because he had grown up in a respected provincial aristocratic family at Hongchon, slipped from a cliff to his death, his spine broken sideways in an L. Sergeants Ryu Chonghyo and Kim Pyong had once fought a "fist duel" on the hill behind the barrack because both of them wanted the same waitress but eventually became such close friends that they always stayed together. When Sergeant Kim accidentally triggered a booby trap rigged to a broken thorn branch, he took Ryu with him. Private Pak Hongtae, in Vietnam for only six weeks, was stricken by dengue fever. Corporal Won lost an eye when he slipped on a lichen-covered boulder and fell face down onto a jagged rock. The lieutenant had to order two corporals to take them down the mountain back to the base.

Only twenty-one remained of the forty-four who had started the patrol.

A cheetah chasing its prey with overwhelming concentration, a galloping horse, a bird skimming over the placid surface of a lake, the majestic submergence of a great big whale—animals at least possessed their own natural beauty. But we displayed only squalor, cunning and insanity in the jungle. The fight was without honor or dignity, without even masculinity—the base acts of a cowardly war. We simply murdered our own species in the most despicable, contemptible, dastardly way. Here even death was insulted.

I had often imagined my own death, wondered what would be the proper attitude with which to face and accept my demise. But I was not sure I would be allowed to die a worthy, man's death here. For I did not have the choice of determining what it should be like. I had witnessed too many beastly and shameful deaths to expect my own to be a respectable one any different from theirs. These dead were denied human dignity.

When Corporal Lee Kwanil had died back at Hill 24, Pyon Chinsu suddenly realized that being killed was an impending, realistic possibility for everybody around us. He wept for hours back at the bunker. The platoon leader was so annoyed that he kicked the private in his side and hollered, "Why don't you drop dead yourself and save us from having to watch a weeping soldier? You're totally worthless as a soldier! A soldier exists for war, and death in battle is the greatest honor for a true soldier. A man at war should not fear death. A soldier should despise defeat and overcome all fear and despair. Look at yourself. What are you? A verminous trash of the human race. That's what you are!"

But the lieutenant had overlooked the basic difference, the distressing fact that he had chosen to be a soldier seeking honor and achievements in war, while we, the drafted private soldiers, had been forced by the system governing the populace to waste thirty months of our precious youth in the army, "to defend the nation from Communist aggressions."

We were not voluntary warriors, but pawns of international politics, an ideological conflict. Not all deaths were the same. If I had to die, I wanted to die like a man. But nobody could choose. Death was not a matter of choice at war.

Well into the bamboo tunnel we found many thick bamboo felled and piled up. The lieutenant checked the machete marks and decided that the enemy had harvested them on several different occasions. We were excited and alert; the Vietcong had been here many times to get bamboo for building shelters and producing crude hand-made traps—the darts, spears, Malaysian gates, spikes.

Taking three scouts with him, the lieutenant himself led the search. We moved slowly, communicating with hand signals in absolute silence. I was tense, my heart pounding away like a mad drum. We would meet the enemy soon. I was sodden with sweat.

The path, much used, was easily traceable, and we found dried feces at one point. The scouts also found a rubber band and some rice grains still sticking to a broad leaf that someone had used as a wrapper for fish-rice. When we came within hearing range of a small waterfall, the scout team moving thirty meters ahead of us suddenly halted. The lieutenant signaled all to stop and disperse. We scattered. Two scouts were dashing back to the platoon leader, stooping low to avoid being observed. They reported something to the lieutenant. Leaving one scout still on the lookout, the two soldiers and the lieutenant hurried back to our position and summoned all the surviving squad leaders and second sergeants behind a young bamboo grove.

"You mean you saw them with your naked eyes?" the lieutenant said in a whisper. He glanced at the direction of the waterfall sound.

"Yes, sir," said Sergeant Chong Sangchol. "We spotted two enemy guards two hundred meters away. The Cong were high in the lookout post of a tall tree."

"Are you sure they haven't spotted us?" the lieutenant said.

"I could not see too clearly from that distance, sir, but they seemed to be loafing away their duty hour, leisurely twining some sort of rope with certain vines. They seemed not to have noticed any of our movements in the vicinity."

"Good," the platoon leader said, his mind made up. "Sergeant Chong, you are going back to the spot where you can observe the enemy without danger of exposing yourself to them. Take Private Yun and Corporal Kim Chaeo with you and continue your surveillance of the lookout post. If they have a change of shift or the lookouts return to their base in the evening, you will shadow them. Remember—you must not expose yourself even if you lose them. If you do lose them, do not rashly wander around until you get caught by the enemy or a booby trap. Hide in a safe place with good cover and wait until they come back. I don't care how many days it may take, you follow them until you find the enemy base. We will wait for you right here for three days. If you don't return before then, we will make our move. Take my binoculars."

The three soldiers vanished along the path through the bamboo groves.

We spent the night in sleepless excitement and anxiety, like young children on the cloudy eve of a school picnic. The next day the three soldiers returned at one o'clock in the afternoon, their bloodshot eyes puffy and their faces gaunt. They had spent the whole night awake in hiding. They looked very tired but happy while they were making their report to the platoon leader.

"We found it, sir," Chong Sangchol said in a gasping, hasty voice. "There is a small brook over two little slopes beyond the waterfall. And along that tiny little brook, meandering through the bush, are about thirty bamboo huts, perfectly hidden from air observation by the trees."

"And the Cong? Did you find them there?"

"There were at least three hundred of them, sir, and they were all congregated along the brook, sitting on the rocks, everybody busy with bottles and tin cans and black stuff that looked like gunpowder. They seemed to be making some sort of weapons, sir. Hand grenades, or explosives for booby traps, I guess. Anyway, they were certainly preparing for big fireworks. With the binoculars, I also spotted the shaded entrances of a big underground tunnel system behind the huts, sir. We observed several women going in and out of that cave, carrying things in baskets."

"That's enough," the lieutenant interrupted Chong's report. "You take me there. Only two of us will go this time, and the rest of you sit tight here. We will be back no later than tomorrow evening."

Sergeant Chong quickly packed his knapsack with the rations and ammunition he and the lieutenant might need for one day, and the two soon disappeared toward the waterfall. We spread out to ambush positions to wait in hiding until the lieutenant's return.

During the night, Private Yun and Corporal Kim Chaeo told us about the enemy headquarters they had observed. The headquarters did not look much different from the one we had destroyed earlier on Hon Heo Mountain, they said. But this one seemed to have separate underground facilities. The scouts had found at least four entrances to the hidden tunnel complex.

The soldiers were very indignant that they had come all the way here, enduring so much sacrifice, but were not even given the chance to see the enemy headquarters with their own eyes. It was infuriating to find the prime culprits who had been decimating us and not even be able to spit at them.

The platoon leader looked fairly satisfied when he returned to our position the next day. "Our mission is completed," he said tersely. "We camp here tonight, and we will start for home tomorrow."

But some complaints were naturally due, and Piggie, who had been fuming all night that we should infiltrate the enemy underground tunnel at night and blow up everything there, protested in a cross voice choking with frustration and resentment: "It's like a murder for us, sir, that we can't even lay a finger on that place after we've gone through so much. Think about all the men who lost their lives so that we could get here. This is crazy, sir. We may lose some more lives to infiltrate the enemy headquarters, but who cares about a few more when we've lost so many already?"

"We have only twenty men left," the lieutenant said. "The biggest damage we can do to the enemy—the best revenge for us is to go back safely to our base and let the whole division go after every single VC in this mountain."

"But this is exasperating, sir." Sergeant Han Taesam sided with Piggie. "So many of us got killed and we can't even take a look at the enemy headquarters, while other guys will have all the action. Let's do it ourselves, sir. Maybe you can get permission from the Division to strike the enemy. We can do the job if we call in artillery or air strikes."

"That's not the idea the Division guys have about this mission," the lieutenant explained, but I knew he wanted to do it more than anybody else did. "You can't kill fleas with baseball bats. We're here now in the first phase of the precision work to pinpoint the enemy and knock them out clean. We've done the pinpointing, and the next team will do their part." Then he said emphatically, his eyes glaring with determination, "But don't worry, I'll give you a chance to avenge the friends we've lost on this mountain."

"How, sir?" asked Sergeant Cho Ichol, his expression suddenly brightening.

"I intend not to report to the relay station that we've found what we've been looking for," the lieutenant said. "At least until we take care of certain things we have to attend to. We're going back to the stream where the 4th Squad was wiped out. First, when we get there, we will bury the dead, if they're still as we left them."

I tried to imagine what they would look like now, left exposed to the elements, scavengers and birds. I forced myself not to think about the condition the bodies must be in. The lieutenant went on.

"After you bury the remains of your buddies, we go into an ambush by that stream. And wait. I'm sure that faint path there must be on a regular VC patrol route, so they should show up sooner or later if we wait long enough. When they show up, we're going to have a real hunt. But there's one thing I want to remind you." He paused. "Our ambush by the stream will have dual purposes—to get ourselves avenged, and to secure a prisoner. We're going to take a prisoner home, although that was not included in our original plan. Just one prisoner. No more. All the other VC we find there we eliminate. We will need a prisoner to secure the information necessary for the future operations over this area. The Division G-2 will need some information, such as how big this enemy headquarters actually is, or if there are any other strongholds on this mountain, or how this region is connected with the Ho Chi Minh supply trails."

The soldiers cheered, but quietly. The lieutenant ordered us to get ready.

22

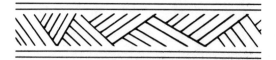

All the bodies were gone. So we searched the area to confirm what had happened to our dead comrades. The 3rd Squad, led by Piggie Chang, went fifty meters downstream until they came across four new graves among the rocks near the path. They dug up one of them to identify the buried body. Piggie Chang reported to the lieutenant that he had found Sergeant Kim Hosik's dog tags in the grave. We could find no other graves or bodies.

"The others might have been swept away by the current," the lieutenant said with a stiffened expression. He tried to conceal his emotions, but I could read guilt and anger in his face. He presumed the Vietcong had buried the dead soldiers, probably to get rid of the stench and clean up their patrol route. "It proves that they do patrol this area regularly. All right, you know what you're supposed to do."

The soldiers carefully prepared for their retaliation, positioning themselves on higher ground so that the enemy would be cornered by the water the way the 4th Squad had been pinned down helplessly. When the enemy was trapped by our crossfire, we could eliminate them all, one by one.

We knew that for all of us, except the two greens who had arrived recently from Korea as replacements, the skirmish by the stream would be our last fight in Vietnam, the last fight in our lives; our Vietnam mission would be over in a month, and we were to be exempted from the operation to be launched over this mountain immediately after our return to the base. Maybe we would go out on ambush missions around the Division Headquarters perimeter two or three more times before our return to Korea, but the survivors from this reconnaissance patrol did not expect to die from those palace guard duties. But I was worried about the last fight *we* were planning to have, the fight we chose as the final one. I hated this mountain, and I thought revenge was not a reason good enough for us to call for our last trial here. I did not want to die in enemy territory in an enemy uniform.

We waited, quietly hiding in the bush, noiselessly "cooking" the freeze-dried meals. The lieutenant cautiously moved around among the trees once in a while, like a slinking leopard, to check if his men were in their assigned positions, secure and safe. The parching sun poured into the gorge. Time stopped in the silence. The only sounds we could hear were the stream tumbling around or over the rocks and some birds warbling somewhere in the trees. We waited.

Eight o'clock in the morning on the thirty-fourth day of our reconnaissance mission, I went down to the stream to refill my canteens. In order to avoid any accidental encounter with the enemy while going to draw drinking water, the lieutenant had instructed us to go to a secluded bend downstream from our ambush spot. When I was about to fill my second canteen, two Vietcong appeared from the bush about twenty meters behind me. I did not see them at first and the Vietcong did not see me either. No one in the ambush had seen the enemy until they suddenly appeared and walked down through the boulders toward the water. The Vietcong walked toward me. The platoon leader could not give an order to open fire, for he did not know yet where the enemy main force was, if there was any, and I was too far away from the ambush point for the waylaying soldiers to get all the Cong who were not visible yet. The lieutenant just hoped I would fill my canteen quickly and turn back, or just look around as a precaution, and see the enemy in time to hide myself somewhere before they spotted me. While I was stooping over the water, the soldiers waited. It seemed nobody could do anything for me.

I finished filling my canteens, picked them up, one in each hand, my rifle uselessly slung over my shoulder, and started back to my position, my back to the enemy. The lieutenant could not wait any longer to trap and strike the enemy. If the VC saw me—as they would soon—they would not walk into the ambush anyway. The lieutenant ordered the men to spread out to aggressively chase and eliminate the enemy, who might be now moving toward the trap but would scatter and flee instantly if somebody opened fire. Sergeant Han Taesam, the leader of my squad, and Private Yun—Boar—were told to take care of the two VC behind me.

At the first rifle shot, I dropped my canteens and threw myself behind a tree stump, pulling my rifle down hastily. I finally looked back to see the two Vietcong and I opened up. Hundreds seemed to have opened fire simultaneously in the gorge. The two Vietcong fell, but I was not sure if I got them, or somebody else. But nobody got them at all. Wriggling like lizards, they slid away through a gap between the rocks and disappeared into the bush. I saw Private Yun roll down the rocky slope, ten meters upstream. His broken bloody leg twisted outward, Boar fell into the water with a big splash. Yun was swept away by the current, crashing against the rocks in the water, spinning, flipping, sinking and surfacing again on the shattered water. He had been hit while coming down to help me out. But I could do nothing except blankly watch his body disappear around the bend. The shooting was going on everywhere and I wondered if the friendly soldiers had been somehow attacked from behind by the enemy.

Hiding myself behind a burnt stump I calmed down a little and tried to figure out what was going on. The rival platoons were exchanging fire all around me; there were at least twenty Vietcong dispersed in the woods less than fifty meters from my hiding spot, and everybody was on his own in his individual man hunt, as both sides mingled with each other in the forest.

"I'm out of ammunition, sir! I'm out of ammunition, sir!" Private No

Hansik, a green, shouted in a terrified voice somewhere in the noisy pandemonium.

"Save your ammo!" Piggie Chang shouted, and another deafening volley engulfed their voices. We had only fifty rounds of cartridges each, and were not supposed to engage in any open combat like this. But nobody could stop it now.

"Where is the medic? Get me the medic! I'm hit!" Sergeant Lee Chin shouted.

"The medic is wounded!" Sergeant Chi Taesik shouted back. Another brrrrrrrup from an AK, and I heard no more shouting from the two soldiers. Messages were shouted aloud, over the rifles, for the enemy could not understand Korean. Shouting to one another was extremely dangerous. The enemy never called out to their comrades, either because they preferred to fight silently to not expose their locations, or because they feared the Koreans understood their language.

"Sir!" Private No Hansik, another green, called. The lieutenant did not answer.

"Sir!" Private No called again, louder this time.

"What is it?"

"I can't distinguish the buddies from the enemy, sir."

"What?"

"I can't distinguish the buddies from the enemy, sir, because they all look alike. I can't distinguish quickly enough . . ."

He did not finish, because another burst of concentrated automatic fire interrupted him. I understood why the green had complained. The enemy was not identifiable at one quick glance because everybody on both sides was dressed alike.

"Take off your hats!" the lieutenant suddenly hollered. "Let your crew-cuts show!"

Another volley. I heard no more shouting. It seemed there were no men in the bush, and only the bullets were fighting each other. The shooting dwindled conspicuously, both in volume and frequency, and there were even brief moments of silence among the burps and volleys and sporadic single shots. When the noise had quieted a little, I looked around and decided that it was dangerous to seek shelter. I felt I was too exposed and crept into a leafy grove only a few meters away from where Private Song Namil had been hiding before his death. I could not know from where the enemy might spring at me.

Soon the shooting became intermittent, the silence lasting longer in the intervals, but a rifle burp went off whenever somebody spotted his target. Sometimes two or three rifles opened up simultaneously at different locations. I was still somewhat dazed, my heart thumping from shock, for nobody had explained to me what really was happening and what outcome I could expect from this situation. Nor did I want to move out to see what was happening and look for the enemy; I was not an aggressive soldier who would go looking for the foe. In fact, I had never considered myself as a soldier, not for a single moment during the thirty months. I had no soldier in my blood. So I stayed in the grove—with only one will, to protect my life.

The raging individual combats in the undergrowth continued savagely, then quieted. But the silence was deceiving. Nothing stirred for a while. Nobody called anybody else lest they should attract enemy fire. Then, all of a sudden, a single rifle shot or a burst would shatter the silence. And then another long silence ensued.

As the intervals grew longer and longer, I thought I had to do something more than merely remain hidden in the grove. At least I should try to find my comrades. Checking every rock and tree around me, I crept out cautiously, slowly, very slowly. I soon found Sergeant Han Taesam near the spot where Boar had fallen into the current. He was sprawled down in the tall grass, breathing heavily, his left ear gone leaving only the bloody root and his chest mangled to pulp.

"What happened?" I asked, lying next to him, practically using him as a cover, glancing around. When I was sure of safety, I leaned over him to check his bleeding chest. "You look seriously wounded. How did you get it?"

He simpered, gasping, and looked up at the sky. "Why don't you carry a pair of spare eyes in the back of your head?" he said.

For the first time I realized Han had been hit while coming down to cover me. "I guess I got five or six slugs in me," he said, faintly beaming. "But I feel all right. Maybe I'm not going to die."

I also thought he would not die. He was bleeding profusely from his ear and chest and belly, but I wanted to believe that Sergeant Han was not going to die.

"What's going to happen to me if I die?" he asked. "I must not die, you know. I have to go home. Somebody is waiting for me. How are things going, anyway?"

Someone opened up, but the burp sounded so distant.

"I don't know what's going on," I said. "Do you want me to call

Sergeant Cho for you?" This was a stupid question. I should have looked for the medic first, but it had not even occurred to me until then. "Your wound needs dressing."

"The medic is wounded himself," he said, coughing with a frog in his throat. "I heard someone say so."

"He may be able to help you, though," I insisted, as if to make up for my earlier negligence.

"Leave him be," said Sergeant Han. "Everybody must be quite busy now." I was not sure if that remark was intended to be a casual joke or an acceptance of the inevitable. "We can wait," he said. "And you keep low. The Cong may spot you. You'll never be safe the second time around."

Sergeant Han was unbelievably calm. When I asked him how painful the wounds were, Han said he did not feel any pain anywhere at all. He just felt numb, as if his whole body was anesthetized, he said. Perhaps something was wrong with his nerve system, I thought, if he really did not feel any pain while his body was so severely damaged. Or perhaps his mind was at ease in resignation, for death was already progressing inside him. When I saw something moving behind a rock and fired in haste, he even joked to me with a faint smile, imitating a drill instructor at boot camp, "Three clicks to the left."

Then his breathing grew uneven. He clutched his bleeding chest once, twice, once again, as he suddenly began to feel the pain tearing at his insides. He jerked his hand this time to grab his torn ear, and a pack of cigarettes that he had been carrying in the fold of his rolled-up sleeve fell to the ground. The cigarettes were Lucky Strike. I wondered why he smoked Lucky Strike which almost all the Korean soldiers just threw away whenever they found any in the C-ration pouch, calling it "Death Strike," because that American cigarette was most often found on dead soldiers. Nobody at war ignored even the silliest superstitions as far as death was concerned. I looked down at the red circle on the cigarette pack, thinking that bloody red was a voodoo sign.

"I guess I'm dying," Sergeant Han said in a choking voice, his mind, as well as his eyes, no longer calm. I had never known before that he had such big eyes; his eyes expanded larger and larger as if the eyeballs would pop out any moment, and those eyes were bursting with fear. His blank eyes looked so transparent that I had the delusion I might be able to look into his brain through those glassy pupils.

I looked around once more and found the lieutenant lying flat on a rock about ten meters up the slope from the grassy patch where we were. I noticed he had been watching us, on and off, for some time, and when our eyes met, I pointed at the dying sergeant and motioned for the platoon leader to hurry down to us. The lieutenant quickly glanced around, then slid backward along the rock.

"How is he?" said the lieutenant, still on the alert, guarding all directions. "Serious?"

I hesitated.

"Sir," Sergeant Han Taesam did the answering himself. "I think I'm dying."

The lieutenant examined the wound in the sergeant's chest. An irritation passed through his expression, because he knew the situation was hopeless, but his voice was calm when he spoke: "The wound is serious, but you'll be all right. We will make a stretcher and take you down to the base as soon as this fight is over. Don't move and stay calm." Then he told me, "Sergeant, you stay here and look after him."

Lieutenant Choe raised his head to look around, and I noticed he was about to move away, leaving the dying soldier with me.

"Lieutenant," Han Taesam called in a new voice that had suddenly changed to a threat. He did not call the lieutenant 'sir,' nor did he use the proper honorific speech that a soldier had to use when addressing any officer. "Lieutenant, you must save my life. You know what I mean?"

The lieutenant's expression darkened when he saw Sergeant Han's eyes flip white. He did not seem to have even noticed the sergeant's impolite speech.

"I know what you mean," Lieutenant Choe said. "Just stay calm, and we will take you down the mountain all in good time."

"Lieutenant, you must save my life."

"I will. I promise I will."

"You will die, too, if you don't save my life."

That was Sergeant Han Taesam's last utterance.

We counted fourteen of the enemy bodies, but found no wounded stragglers. Nor had anyone captured any prisoners. I thought the soldiers had been driven by fury and hatred too intense for them to take any prisoner alive. Vengeance was contagious in battle.

Finally the combat was completely over. I was slowly consumed with an insurmountable grief over the soldiers who had been taken away by death in the past month. I was angry about the panic and fear we had

had to suffer while being stalked, and I grieved over Sergeant Han Taesam's death. Burying the soldiers who had died in this last angry battle, I thought about the endless days we had spent to roam this mountain.

When we finished burying them, the platoon leader gathered us by the stream for a roll call. I did not think the roll call was necessary, for he could see at one glance who were the final survivors. There were only seven of us, including the lieutenant. Besides, we had to leave there as soon as possible because at least five Vietcong had escaped and the reinforced enemy might be on their way to pursue us at this very moment. It had taken almost two hours to bury all the dead, and we were running short of time to safely get out of this gorge before the enemy returned, but the platoon leader wanted to have the roll call anyway. Then I realized why he insisted on it. He wanted to call the names of all the soldiers, one by one, for the last time, to remember everyone who had been in this green hell with him.

The lieutenant began to call the names. And he began to cry. The soldiers cried with him.

The seven survivors came down Hon Ba Mountain forming a short line, like a lone caterpillar worming through the bush.

Two days later we arrived at the barren field thriving with cacti at the foot of the mountain and radioed our map coordinates to the relay station. A Huey helicopter—we did not need a Chinook for only seven of us—came to pick us up in fifteen minutes.

We scrambled up to the chopper, and soon we were in the air. We mutely looked down at the mountain with tearful eyes. The dark green gorges and ridges and summits, and the Valley of Death that looked like a grey patch because of all the dead trees—the panoramic landscape of war was sprawling down there, indomitable, foreboding. I turned my eyes away from the mountain to the Dong Hai sea. Tuc My, Hai's village, loomed far away in the east. We were going home.

Somebody tentatively tugged at my elbow and I looked back. Sitting on the uneven metal floor of the helicopter, Private Pyon Chinsu was staring at me with his bleary eyes. The calm expression on his face had been replaced by a distorted fear: the frightened look, the fear that was his face, his familiar face.

"What is it?" I asked him.

"Where are they?" he said, his neck stiff, his frightened eyes fixed upon me as if he was afraid of looking at anything else.

"Where are who?"

"The other soldiers in our platoon. They all left the company base with us together, didn't they?"

Puzzled, I looked into his eyes. "What's wrong with you?" I said.

"Where are all the others?" he asked. "Are they coming in by other choppers?" He looked for other helicopters with sidelong glances. "I don't see any other choppers."

"What are you talking about?" But I knew why he was talking that way. "The other guys are all dead or missing. You know that."

"No, I don't," he said. "When did that happen? Who are dead? And who are missing?"

"There he goes again," said Piggie Chang from the other side of the helicopter.

The chopper wheeled toward the 9th Company tactical base, flying over the enchanting green patterns of palm trees and rice paddies, carrying the lonely survivors home—including Pyon Chinsu, who abruptly started hiccupping.

23

The greens were shocked to see so few of us return. They turned dumb, disbelieving that such a thing could happen, and actually had happened to the experienced soldiers.

A few days later, the whole division, including the terror-stricken greens of the 9th Company, were thrown onto Hon Ba Mountain to destroy the concentrated enemy position we had located through the costly reconnaissance. While the operation was going on, we remained behind in the trenches to defend the base at night and in the bunkers in daytime. Now "going home" was becoming a more and more tangible and realistic fact for us. But a strange fear began to possess me. I was afraid to go home. I was not sure if I would be really allowed to leave this absurd world, but, at the same time, I was afraid to get out. By what definition was I still "alive," and did "I" really exist when my body was so worn out by physical punishment and the soul so shredded. Would I be able to patch up all the torn pieces of me and restore my old self so that I could recover what I had lost in this war. I worried that it might be impossible, perhaps, for me to return to the peacetime life that had been my own reality only one year ago. I felt like a prisoner who was about to walk out into the strange blinding world into dazzling sunshine after twenty years in solitary confinement. Had I gone back in the evolutionary process to a primitive savage? Who on earth was I?

I had changed so much, and I had learned so many things about the world that other people did not know anything about, that I believed I would never be permitted in their world.

I was afraid to go home.

The Hon Ba Mountain operation lasted for eighteen days, but the 9th Company did not suffer a casualty. They seemed to have given a safer rear guard duty to our company during the operation because our outfit had already suffered such a staggering loss during the reconnaissance patrol. The seven greens returned to the base alive and enormously relieved. Also disappointed. Why did they give such a scary name to that mountain? they wondered. There was not much of a war on that mountain, was there? they said. The torment of a war without combat was as suffocating as a marriage without love. In combat, there was a definite purpose: To survive. That survival urge fed the will to live, they said.

The operation itself was not a blazing success. When the friendly main forces reached the Hon Ba headquarters, the concentrated enemy had vanished without a trace. Nothing remained at the enemy head-quarters except the empty huts and some supplies and weapons abandoned in the underground tunnel complex. Whether a success or a failure, the operation was over anyway.

I went to see Hai twice more—once when we returned from the Death Valley, and once when I went to tell her that I was going home. On those two visits we did not have sex. I did not want to. It seemed she did not want it any more either. I had a strange apprehension that, if we ever had sex again, the bestial lust would besmirch and destroy all the beautiful impressions we kept in our hearts about the one time when we had each other on the moonlit sand. From her calm undemanding expression, I sensed that her mind worked much the same way as mine did in this matter. She did not anticipate or hope for any repeated pleasure. We sauntered up and down the beach, talking, but we did not even mention what had happened that night. Some moments were remembered better when not spoken of.

When I went to see her for the last time, to tell her I would return to Korea, we strolled on the beach, as usual, and exchanged quiet talk for two hours, but we did not utter a single word about my voyage home, as if this was not a parting, as if I would never leave her. Neither of us wanted to talk about my going away, because we did not want it to happen, because we vaguely hoped it would not happen if we did not say it.

Then, as I stood up from the sand to go back to the base, she cautiously caught me by my elbow with her right thumb and index finger. Her eyes glistened with tears when she said:

"Bring me Daihan." She meant, Take me to Korea.

I stared at her, surprised. Hai blushed, hanging her head.

"What?" I asked in a disbelieving whisper.

"Bring me Daihan," she repeated, tersely.

I was at a loss. I realized she had meant it with her whole being. She must have guessed quite a while ago that I would have to leave Vietnam in the spring and probably had been wondering a lot about what would happen to us, to her, when the time came. By now she seemed to have her mind made up.

"But how?" I asked, still puzzled.

"Daihan *linh* go home I look Nha Trang. Daihan bring *beaucoup* things in big box." She gestured how big. "I can go Daihan in big box."

Now I understood. Her suggestion was so preposterous I could not even laugh. At Nha Trang harbor she had seen the Korean soldiers boarding their ships to Korea with huge wooden crates; one crate like that could easily hold ten people. Almost all the soldiers brought home one or two of these wooden containers especially built for them to carry all the PX things they had bought. Watching all those crates going to Korea, she imagined that she could come to Korea with me, if I just let her hide in one of those boxes. She explained to me that she and Trau could squeeze into one box.

"We eat two C-rations one day every day inside box and we all right until Daihan," she said very sincerely.

I was so dumbfounded by her innocent but absurd scheme that I hardly knew what to say, so I asked how she would take care of urination and defecation in the box. That question had been intended to be a joke, but I regretted immediately having said that, because it was an insult to her sincerity. Besides, she did not take it as a joke. With a straight face, she simply said:

"I have big vinyl bags."

I had to get serious too, and with a grave expression, I gave her a long incoherent explanation about the customs regulations, the immigration laws, and many other obstacles she would have to go through in Korea, even if I did let her go with me to Daihan in the wooden crate. Hai could hardly understand all the complicated reasons I was listing to justify myself for abandoning her, but she did not have to. Women could sense what was waiting for them in a situation like this without any wordy explanation.

Leaving Hai's village of Tuc My, I knew I was about to lose a private world that had once belonged to me alone for a limited time. I did not deserve to keep it, because I was a deserter from that world.

I returned my rifle, equipment and helmet to the Headquarters Company and gradually trained myself to the idea of homecoming. Some soldiers took pictures in their bunker or trenches, by the company bulletin board, under a palm tree down at the field, at Ngoc Diem with the Vietnamese farmers. Others rushed to the PX to buy gifts for the families and friends waiting at home, as if they were returning from a vacation tour.

Each homebound contingent consisted of the soldiers who had finished their one-year combat duty with the Blue Dragon Marine Brigade stationed at Chu Lai, the Garrison Intrepid Tiger Division at Qui Nhon, the 9th White Horse Infantry Division at Ninh Hoa, the 100th Logistics (Southern Cross) Unit and the Field Forces Command Headquarters at Nha Trang, the Combined ROK Forces in Vietnam Command Headquarters in Saigon, and the Dove Medical Unit at Vung Tau. For an effective control of this mixed group during the one-week voyage, the soldiers had to be reorganized into new platoons and companies under temporary commanding officers and cabin sergeants. The 9th Division headquarters (hastily building temporary latrines and securing extra rations to prepare for the send-off ceremony) tried to economize their efforts by scheduling the welcoming ceremony for the incoming greens on the same day; it was not an easy task for the division headquarters to assemble all the home-bound soldiers scattered in different locations in the jungle to the division parade ground on the day they were to be transported to the Nha Trang harbor for loading.

The "home-ordered" soldiers had vaccinations, built large wooden crates to contain their belongings to take home, made five copies of the inventory listing the weapons and equipment and other tools of war they were returning, underwent several inspections, and spent the last month's pay to do final shopping at the PX. They sent their personal belongings—the letters they had saved for one year, photographs, plain clothes or shoes, diaries, Vietnamese dolls and other souvenirs—through the U.S. military postal service as parcel post. To the relatives, whom they had not written even once during their year here, the soldiers wrote their first—and last—greeting letters, so that they would not be reproached back home for neglecting their elders. Personal debts among the soldiers had to be settled. Then they received instruction about the voyage home and the recent political, military and economic situations in Korea as well as their duty as soldiers. The worn-out bleached shoulder patches, insignias and name tapes were replaced with brand new ones.

Every night the soldiers held a beer party to celebrate their return. Everybody was willing to contribute a 24-can case of beer for the occasion. Everybody was happy.

In dreams I saw my house, salty sesame leaves pickled in soy sauce, squid sashimi, buckwheat jelly and other delicacies I had missed so long. I also missed the deserted Seoul back alleys during the nightly curfew hours, the pallid street lamps, the moths and mosquitoes and shad-flies gathering around an electric bulb on summer evenings, the dark brown furrows of the snow-covered vegetable patches in the rural winter.

Sergeant Oh Ujin was excited because he could go home early enough to be released from the army in time to register for the spring semester at the Drama and Film Arts Department of Joongang University where he had been enrolled before his enlistment. Everybody had a future and plans, something or someone waiting for them. But what was waiting for me? I was afraid of the ambiguous future. There were no plans or promises, but only dark emptiness in my future.

After returning to the estranged world that had been my home one war ago, how could I secure my own little shelter among the crowd who could not and would not understand or recognize me? How could a soldier join society to work and live among people who would deny all his views and virtues? One was supposed to acquire experience and wisdom as he aged, but in the process of twenty-six years and two wars, I had lost innocence, sense of justice, my humanity, my dignity, without gaining anything. Inside the hollow husk of my being, a persistent anger smouldered.

On the day we were to board the home-bound ship, the 1,820 soldiers of the 7th Contingent left the Division parade ground after the tiring ceremony and headed for Nha Trang. From the truck I looked around for the last time at the familiar and beautifully desolate Vietnamese landscape. Thirteen months and sixteen days ago I had come to Ninh Hoa from Nha Trang along this very road. We were leaving the war.

The soldiers in the truck, sharing the lukewarm beer, joked and laughed and cheered as they left Ninh Hoa. They looked awkward and defenseless because they did not have their flak jackets and helmets on. Their copper-colored tanned faces were shaven and hair trimmed as neatly as if they were going out for their first date. For these soldiers the war, that had been a reality until yesterday, was slowly turning into a past, never to be repeated in their lives.

"Hey, we're really going home. At last."

"Sure we are."

"I can't believe this is actually happening to me. That I am going home alive."

"You remember the day we came to Ninh Hoa along this road? That day I thought, well, I'm never going to see my home again. But here I am, going home alive, thanks to the Cong who so kindly spared my life."

"I remember that day, too. Seems like ancient times."

"Ancient times it was."

The soldiers in the truck ahead of us began to sing a military song we had sung on the night military train coming to Vietnam. Their faces were puffy, for they had been drinking until daybreak at the send-off parties held in every bunker but their bloodshot eyes shone with pulsating life under the field caps that they had been issued in exchange for the heavy helmets. Their eyes shone, for they had triumphed.

Something was missing from my body. I no longer carried with me the two heavy canteens, the harness sagging with cartridges, the bulky knapsack stuffed with rations and the cold rifle that had become an extension of my hand.

I had laundered my fatigues two days ago, but the faint stain of blood still remained on the sleeve. Like that persistent dark red stain, the war would not be erased for years to come. It was Pyon Chinsu's blood that had left the permanent stains on my fatigues; his blood had left that mark on me in the foxhole during the Ninh Hoa battle. Staring at the faint stain on my sleeve, I wondered what kind of a future was in store for Pyon.

Another send-off ceremony was given by the Field Forces Command, ROKF-V, on the Nha Trang beach, on the same spot under the palm trees where the welcoming ceremony had been held for us one year ago. On the plank platform, a fat American colonel and the Korean army officers, from the Field Forces Command and the 9th Division, were seated in four rows on the green folding chairs. The mail truck, equipped with an amplifier and two loudspeakers, played a tape of the White Horse Division Song. The tuba of the brass band flashed in the sun. ARVN Major Don Muoi, the Ninh Hoa Province chief, gave a perfunctory speech that he repeated every other week at the ceremony sending a contingent back to Korea. It was tedious, like all other military ceremonies. The white, red and yellow placards and streamers drooped heavily down from the palm trees. The same cloth decorations hung on the same trees every other week, and the same people sat on the same seats on that platform at every ceremony to welcome the replacement soldiers on their arrival and to send the survivors home. Only the faces of the soldiers who stood before the platform changed.

Somebody kicked me in the calf. I woke up, startled, and reached for my rifle. My hand touched the warm sand. I opened my eyes and saw Piggie Chang standing over me and the blue sky beyond his field cap. I was not on a rice paddy dike, nor in the jungle; I had dozed off.

"We begin boarding now," said Piggie Chang with a grin. "This is the real thing. We are going home."

I raised myself and picked up the duffle bag. The soldiers bustled noisily and hurried everywhere. I stood in line to wait. Two LCUs were waiting near the beach, bobbing with the waves, waiting to carry us to the ship. The sea wind had grown cooler in the afternoon. It was time for us to leave Vietnam.

We crammed onto the LCUs that plowed through the waves to the *USS Geiger,* and then we climbed the tall aslant steel steps to the gangway. We put our belongings on our bunks in the assigned cabins and went out to the deck or the gangway to take a last look at Nha Trang.

After two long toots, the ship began to sail out to the open sea, past the scattered islands, its prow pitching up and down like a huge steel monster butting through the waves with its invisible horns. The palm trees, the white Buddha, and the golden shore slowly vanished into the foggy heat.

I had a hallucination that the distant mountains, slowly vanishing out of sight, were now shaking with howitzer shelling. If the ship's engine was not so noisy, I thought, I could hear the howitzer shells faintly explode in the distance, like soap bubbles popping, *plop-plop-plop-plop.*

PART THREE

24

Tomorrow the deposit was due for the installment savings, my wife had reminded me this morning. Loaded in the bus, with the other urbanites, who seemed eternally beaten and spiritually fatigued, I bumped over the Hongje Pass where subway construction was under way. I plunged into the heart of Seoul. An endless procession of commuter buses charged into the city. Into the chaos and smog and noise and perspiration, the naked fury of the people writhing in their individual struggles for infinitesmal achievements. All these people, all these countless people floundering in frustrated dreams and compromised values. The poisonous metropolis.

The newspapers reported that a mouse will die if it is placed before the exhaust gas pipe of a Seoul bus for an hour. How long could we primates share the toxic gases on our way to the confrontations with one another in the cosmopolitan rat race.

The office girl had put a carnation in a drinking glass and placed it on my desk by the ink stand. The sunlight crystalized in the water drop dangling from the crimson petal.

An editorial meeting was convened by Pak Namjun, the managing director, to hear reports from the managing editor and the three chief editors of Sejin Publishers. I was the chief of the Third Editorial Department.

Lee Wonse, chief of the First Editorial Department, general publications, presented an outdated suggestion: Let's publish a book covering the families who had been separated by the Korean War but had been recently united through the nationwide telethon.

"If we interview the reunited families and compile their stories of separation for three decades, you will have a moving human drama. We can easily sell twenty or thirty thousand copies because there are so many people in this country who have gone through similar experiences due to the war. We're going to offer the merchandise of printed compassion and I'm sure it will sell handsomely."

But the managing director rejected his idea, insisting the emotions and lives of these people, already over exposed by television, were too primitive to do any honor to the company identity if the book were published.

Yet the director half accepted the suggestion by Nam Hosik, the chief of the Second Editorial Department in charge of translated materials. Nam wanted to check the commercial feasibility for a translation of a book by the British woman he had seen on a Merv Griffin show. This young woman, he said, responded to a newspaper ad soliciting a female companion to share a year on a remote uninhabited island somewhere near Australia. She had written a book about this adventure. "You know what she said on the show?" Nam asked. Nobody knew. "She said you could try it if you're bored with your life. Her year was a wonderful and romantic escape."

"That isn't escapism," the managing director said. "That's a response to a challenge."

He was right. That was an act of challenge to hunger, to disease and nature in an isolated and confined situation. And it was actually a challenge to romanticism, too. Her action was not an escape. Like suicide it was an act of will, a great will, demanding the courage to exact it from yourself.

Apropos of nothing, the managing director said to the managing editor, "Should '*tableau vivant*' be included in our primary entries for *the Encyclopedia of Trivia?* I found a two-line exposition for that word in Lee Hisung's *Korean Dictionary* but I couldn't understand what it was and why should it be carried in our trivia dictionary." This remark was actually intended for me because I was in charge of compiling and editing *the Encyclopedia of Trivia,* and I was then expected to do the explaining.

First I told him what the two French words meant separately, and then briefly explained the process of how the choice of individual entries was made. Without much enthusiasm, I tried to convince him that it should be carried in our dictionary. Every week at the meeting the director raised these kinds of casual objections about entries he chose at random while glancing through the galley proofs. This was meant to impress everybody in the office that he was paying close attention to every detail. That gesture on his part occasionally required me to explain to him and other uninterested parties about wolves in India, about ancient Romans enjoying orgies as a spectator sport, and about Mark Twain's *The Adventures of Huckleberry Finn* not being a mere juvenile storybook, as many Koreans believed.

When the managing director had personally proposed the three-volume encyclopedia of trivia, I immediately began to hate that whole idea. Although I always did what I was told, like a good soldier, without any complaint or argument, because they pay me just for that, it never provided me with any consolation, not to say happiness, to devote my life to the tedious work of listing fragmentary knowledge like a contestant in a game show in which human brains decode tidbit facts convertible to monetary values. Peripheral superficialities. The planet Earth governed by a mass of petty spirits after all the giant souls have perished. The change of command between dinosaurs and gekkos.

What significance can a biological existence have in a world without heroes, a world governed by statistics?

Back at my desk after the meeting I found three messages. I called Yo Hyonsu back to be informed that the planned sea fishing to Namyang Bay this coming Sunday was cancelled because the tide would not be favorable. Pyon Chinsu had also left a number. It was for White Violet

Teahouse, but the counter girl could not find any customer named Pyon Chinsu. The third call was from Choe Tokchin, the writer.

After lunch, I dropped by the Seoul Graphic Arts studio at Chungmu Avenue to consult about the cover of the trivia dictionary before going to the Doll's House at the Chosun Hotel to meet Choe Tokchin. Since there was so much time, I decided to walk to the hotel. Trudging among the crowd, watching the people pass, I briefly lost my self-awareness amid the giddy noise and swirl of other human heads and shoulders.

Passing by the Catholic Medical Center my pace slowed despite myself. Feeling a big empty hole in my chest, feeling some sort of absence, feeling something else must be there. Why haven't they invented a shot or pill to cure sterility like other diseases? I had read somewhere that the Abyssinian Emperor Menelik II used to cure his own sickness by eating several pages of the Bible. Would chewing a dose of Chapter 2, Verse 7 of Genesis help anyone have a child? Test tube babies. Cloning. A hatchery where human beings are manufactured in massive quantities. For sale at Sears: perfect Hormel six-year-old female homo sapiens, $700 a dozen.

I passed the old National Theater, dark since its purchase by a banking corporation; the UNESCO Seoul Headquarters that seems to be always in shadow; a hawker dressed like an ancient palace guard, calling passersby to the souvenir shop; a girl with voluptuous young hips packed into tight pants; then the lottery kiosk, the underpass, a roadside vendor selling American sweets—M&Ms, Hersheys, cookies—displayed in her wicker basket, the tangerine booth, the paper boy, the sign saying "Repair Keys." Passing people, passing stories.

The negotiation with Choe Tokchin was brief but satisfactory. Since both of his full-length novels, *The Key* and *The Tale of Twenty-Three*, had been published by Sejin, he took it for granted that we should have the option to publish his third novel, *The Hill-Burners*. Although it was still being serialized in a daily newspaper and would not be concluded for six months yet, several large publishing companies were competing to acquire the publication rights, offering sensational advance payments. Unlike *The Key*, which offended the literary critics with artificial word plays and excessively intricate mechanisms, or the provocative sensualism of *The Tale of Twenty-Three*, *The Hill-Burners* was an historical novel that amply showed the artistic maturity of Choe Tokchin. The managing director cherished an inordinate expectation for its commercial as well as literary success.

Back at the office, there was a message that Pyon Chinsu had called again. He was waiting at the White Violet, the message said, yet the counter girl was irritated by my calling again because she had never heard the name, not that morning, that afternoon, yesterday or ever. Was I making the calls just to annoy her? I apologized and hung up. What could he want after so many years?

I sent the clerk of the editorial bureau to the Korean Publishers Association, and the Ministry of Culture and Information, with copies of our newly published books, then read the latest entries for *The Encyclopedia of Trivia: Max Reinhardt. Tongyang Theater. Pantomime.* Anything to eat away a piece of the interminable afternoon boredom.

Years had passed. I had resumed the ordinary life of traveling back and forth by bus instead of flying *over* by chopper, meeting friends for small talk—about a John Schlesinger movie, flower-patterned neckties, the threat of a fuel shortage—and visiting stuffy little offices (crowded with sick pale people) to get a job, instead of searching for the enemy in the jungle. While I was fighting a war, my friends at home had gone hiking and to the movies. People treated me like a hero from another world. The label attached to me—"the veteran back from the war"—sounded so dramatic. They preferred to see me as this heroic figure rather than realistically scrutinizing my credentials. Some wanted to know how many Vietnamese girls I had slept with, how exciting—*Exciting,* they said—it was to kill a VC face to face, and did the Korean civilian workers really make much money in Vietnam. Nobody wanted to hear what I really wanted to talk about. They could not have understood the nature of the war I had gone through if I told them. I felt like an alien from another planet among these extremely ordinary people.

I got a job on a newspaper. Sometime after the aborted raid by Kim Sinjo's North Korean commando on President Park Chunghee's life, the city editor gave me the assignment to go to Tongduchon and find "this woman," pointing at the underlined name and address in a news article released by the 8th U.S. Army Headquarters in Seoul.

According to the three-paragraph news release, an American soldier, who had been killed in action in Vietnam, was posthumously awarded a Medal of Honor, and the medal would be forwarded to the Korean woman who had been the soldier's "wife" during his service in Korea. The American did not have any other family, apparently. The city editor hoped I might be able to dig out some interesting human interest story behind that terse release, but an hour after arriving at the town, famous for Korean prostitutes exclusively serving American soldiers, I learned that this woman was one of the "GI whores," who had been a "paid wife" of the dead soldier for two years. When I finally found her house after checking several of her past temporary addresses, she was with a Negro soldier in her room.

I was disappointed, having imagined many versions of a romantic story, a beautiful anecdote based on various possible combinations of a Korean woman, an American soldier and the war in Vietnam. I came back to Seoul on the verge of despair. This feeling recurred repeatedly: when a record company PR man tried to buy publicity for a beginning singer by offering me lunch money, or when I had to spend a whole afternoon doing leg work to cover career women at health clubs, or when I had to wait for three hours for an interview to hear everything about the secret love life of a movie starlet whose main and only public value consisted of unsavory episodes exclusively publishable in yellow weeklies. When I realized that a reporter was not necessarily at the vanguard of social justice, I gave up journalism. I quit reporting and joined Sejin Publishing.

It was a mediocre life. Perhaps it was a below-average life led by a below-average person. I did not want the existence of a petty soul physically nourished by fast food and inspired by shallow movies. There must be something worthy, some achievement that would justify the endless succession of empty motions among the sentences and tenses and lead typefaces ranging from Point 7 to Point 9. As if my existence were one of those numerous tiny pieces of type.

As the closing hour was nearing, I found myself waiting for Pyon's telephone call in spite of myself. I had a hunch that he would call again. He had called me after midnight Sunday and twice again today. Why me? Checking the overdue galley proofs and unedited manuscripts as well as the articles and advertisements covering literature and publications in papers, I was vaguely possessed by an uneasy premonition about what Pyon Chinsu was going to tell me.

Filling in the daily report, washing my hands in the bathroom, and cleaning up my desk before leaving the office, my thoughts gradually gathered about the ghost of Pyon Chinsu. Lee Wonse was still grumbling about the managing director's insulting arrogance and wanted to drink off his displeasure with me before going home, but I rejected his invitation because I felt an odd urge, or obligation, to wait for Pyon. I dallied for about half an hour in the office after closing time, reading *Modernization and Agriculture of Korea*. He did not call. On the bus home, I felt some invisible hand was dragging me down by the ankles into a bog of the past, the mire of Vietnam. I could hear the sputtering helicopters everywhere in the enveloping urban noise, and the yellow sunny landscape of the Vietnamese countryside was projected like a monochrome double exposure upon the disorderly shapes of the city. I was plunging into that time past. The decade in between collapsed, perished somewhere.

When a person has gone through a war, that war never ends. The experience saturates. Paralyzes. It is not at all like a nightmare that clears off when one just wakes up. The past covers like sediment and eats away the present.

At school I used to zealously copy down lectures on the poetry of Dryden and Coleridge in those sunny classrooms. A year after graduation, I was hunting human beings. For several years after returning home from the war, I was racked by recollections of what I had gone through. Tens of times I lived again all those incidents engraved in my memory.

Why had I volunteered to go to the war in the first place? Perhaps I had been falsely impressed by the exaggerated concept of heroism in war. The overblown presentation of heroics in literature and movies. The romantic fantasy, even of death as a glorious act. Watching Richard Widmark in a war movie, I used to marvel and cheer in my heart at the tragic gore. I was trained to understand war through stories of someone else, someone else who eloquently persuaded me that war was a sublime moment in which heroic actors, men of action, displayed the most profound and admirable qualities. Or I might have gone to Indochina hoping I could prove, at least to myself, what kind of a man I was. How I would respond to war.

They said the guerrilla warfare in Vietnam was no more than a children's game compared with the war in our country thirty years earlier, and I cherished the dubious idea that there would not be any actual killing around me, us, anywhere. Killing simply did not exist in my imaginary war. In truth, I went to watch the war, not to fight it. And the war, in that strange land in the past, marred the present.

I got off the bus and walked home, up the slanted road, Various scenes had been carved in my memory. My youth. Training for commando attacks in the scorching valley of Yongmun Mountain, the dark night and the military train carrying us south to Pusan, the swaying palm trees at Nha Trang, the night shelling and flares burning up in the black space of darkness, all sorts of tropical plants sweltering in the jungle heat, the soldiers with their bandoliers criss-crossing their chests, the bomb craters, the terrified sunken eyes, the sputtering chopper engines, the wet humid silence, cigarettes glowing red. The scenes flashed without any order or consistency.

And the faces. So many faces. With a frightful feeling that I might be going back to Vietnam to live the death once more, I trudged up the road. My wife was waiting on the porch.

"Did you get the money? For the savings installment?"

I pulled off my socks and threw them into the plastic basket by the bathroom door and said, "I forgot."

"Forgot? How could you forget the money? How could you forget that while carrying all that trashy knowledge in your head?"

My wife slammed the door after her and went out to borrow the money from a neighbor. Sitting alone on the sofa in the living room, I finished reading *Modernization and Agriculture of Korea*. I was hungry but I did not feel like going into the kitchen to see what my wife had prepared for my supper.

I recalled the day when we first met on Hukoan Island. I was on assignment, doing an illustrated series on remote Korean islands. The wind was raging that day because the typhoon had been building up for three days. I went outside to look around the island because I felt too depressed to be cooped up in the stuffy room with the photographer, who spent most of our stranded hours in drunken naps. The wind was so strong I felt I might be blown off the ground and thrown into the sea, but I wandered around, at times reeling against the wind, watching the fishing boats bobbing up and down and clashing with one another at the dock, the closed wine houses for the fishermen who would swarm to this island during the booming corvina season, and the grotesque rock formations behind the village. I decided to climb a rocky hill because I wanted to watch the turbulent sea writhing in the violent weather, and I met her at the foot of that hill. She had come out into the wind for much the same reason as mine, I found out later on our way back to the village; she had been bored "to despair" of reading the same weekly magazine over and over again, for she had nothing else to do in the dusky room where her friend had been sleeping off her hangover all morning.

"We were so depressed and frustrated last night, you know, stranded on this island by the typhoon and doing nothing but playing flower cards in the dismal room and all that, so we, my friend and I, tried a soju drink. It's the first time in my life that I've ever touched liquor, honest, and I did it because I hoped it would help me fall asleep. I couldn't even finish the first shot, but my friend drank almost half of the bottle and passed out."

She had a self-conscious simper on her face when she said that, sitting helplessly on a flat rock at the entrance to the path. She had also planned to go up to the hilltop to see the panoramic view of the island and the sea, but slipped and sprained her ankle when a strong gust made her stagger. She had been waiting there for twenty minutes, she said, waiting for "a knight to pass by and notice the damsel in distress" and rescue her, and added, with a bright smile, that she had been really impressed by the movie *Knights of the Round Table*. She asked me if I could kindly go to the house where she was staying and wake up her friend and tell her what had happened. I offered to take her home myself.

A few days after our first meeting on the rocky path, she and I managed to have three hours all to ourselves at night in the corner room where she was staying with her friend who was having her own secret encounter somewhere else. Somehow it seemed so natural to do so that night, and we were soon in bed together, naked. But I was not ready for sex, for I was apprehensive since I had not bathed for almost a week there being no public bathhouse on the island and the inn having no shower facilities.

When we were in bed one night about six months after our marriage, I remembered that particular incident and told my wife why I had abstained. Telling her I had been very much worried that she might find out how dirty I was at that time, I laughed. I thought it was funny. My bride did not. She mutely gazed at the window through which the bright moonlight poured in onto our bed, sadly thinking about something, and then, after a deep sigh, she confessed.

"That night, I thought you were a very beautiful and romantic human being. I believed you were beautiful, because you were a man capable of restraining yourself even when a naked woman was lying next to you. Like a Buddha or someone. I thought you were a virgin and wanted to save the most precious thing for marriage. I felt something substantial, something real was going on between us. That was why I did not find much difficulty in restraining myself, too, although I had been burning with lust at first, and I experienced a much more ecstatic orgasm from your tender strokes that night than any sex I've had with you since. And now you're saying that it was all because you were apprehensive that dirt might peel off your skin . . ." After a short disbelieving pause, she added as an afterthought, "Maybe you're simply unable to appreciate sex naturally as other people do. You're always thinking about so many things that you can't be faithful to human animality."

Since then, our nights grew uncomfortable. She seemed to feel awkward during the most intimate moments. Her uneasiness made me uncomfortable in turn, and thus we kept accelerating each other's self-consciousness. The secret nightly feast of lust and bliss for others gradually and slowly turned into a ceremonial protocol between us, to something that required careful procedures and stage-setting, a routine that required pretense and sobriety, and at times, when our act was reaching the climax, I noticed my wife controlling her breath, lest any primitive animal sound should escape from her mouth. As the time passed, we grew more and more wary of each other, trying to read the other's feelings when we were supposed to totally abandon ourselves; we simply did not want to reveal our vulnerability to each other.

This physical alienation eventually led us to use separate rooms. Our marriage was going downhill, falling headlong to apparent ruin, and I knew I had to do something, anything, to save us from the destined disaster because I was the man in the family, because the male was supposed to take the leading role in sex, as specified in all therapeutic manuals. But I did absolutely nothing to save our collapsing marriage. I was not a bit willing to fight to save my shattering life.

After throwing the earthworms into the pond of my garden where I breed crucian carps, I went up to the upstairs living room to write a new war poem for the newspaper. When I had called Kim Insuk, the woman reporter covering the literary community for the *Dongnam Daily News* to ask if it was all right to write a poem about the Vietnam War instead of the Korean War, Kim said she would consult with the managing editor. She had called back a few minutes later to notify me it was all right, but she did not seem too happy about my suggestion. Her reluctant consent and her displeased voice gave me the impression that she and the managing editor, like almost everybody around me, considered the Korean War an historical tragedy that we should engrave in our bones and write poems for, but had a bias about the Vietnam War, that it had been a passing event involving total strangers who had nothing to do with our national history. But in my heart, there was the urge to leave a record of an experience that had been more painful and vivid than the war in my childhood. For those who had lived, and died, with me, I wanted to dedicate a small epitaph—my one little poem.

My wife was reading an outdated edition of *Stern* on the sofa so I went to the study and sat before my manuscript sheets. War. War is of original colors. Fragmentary images. Soccer played with a hollow coconut shell on the sand of the Dong Hai beach, on the littered street in front of Ban Cong High School in Ninh Hoa the abandoned body of an American soldier burnt to death by a Molotov cocktail made from a Coca Cola bottle, lethargic vendors in the dirty alleys of Doc Lap market in Nha Trang, soldiers testing which lighter would last longer in the wind by holding out Zippos and Ronsons in the chopper on the way to combat, dark green flak jackets, black blood trickling out of the dead Vietcong's nostril, the canvas camouflage draped over trucks and howitzers, the eerie sense of estrangement when I finally regained consciousness after two days of complete oblivion in a state of malarial coma, used cartridges and empty C-ration cans and human feces and foxholes and black cartridge magazines littering the field where a combat had taken place the day before, a jeep blown up and discarded in the rice paddies, the pleasant heavy feeling of a rifle's weight in my hand and the silent urge to kill during the short moment of loading the gun, the tracer bullets flying away with a long thin red tail during a night engagement. I jotted down the disorderly images that flashed through my mind and then I began to organize them into one single piece of writing.

I heard my wife leafing through *Der Stern* in the living room and I had a queer feeling of missing a step, as if something near me had vanished without my knowing. Something that should be there. What was it that had vanished? No, it was not exactly the sense of absence. Rather, it was an anxiety one feels when he realizes at a particular moment that someone has been watching him for a long while. I put down the fountain pen and looked outside.

Through the window I saw the slanted roadway leading to the bus stop, Pyongchang Nursery where garden trees and saplings were planted closely, the neighborhood fraternity chief sharing a drink with two elderly neighbors under the Coca Cola beach parasol in front of the mom-and-pop store, the ugly skeleton of the sign support erected on the roof of the Citizens Clinic across the street, the acacia trees of Songjong Girls High School, the Kalhyon Apartment buildings on the ridge of the hill on top of which a solitary military billet was perching like a hawk looking out for its prey, and the zigzag alleys among the neighboring houses.

An awkwardly tall man emerged from the alley next to the mom-and-pop store, sidled along the wall a few steps and stopped short by the telephone pole as if hiding himself from something, stretched his neck to peek over at the old drinkers beneath the Coca Cola shade. This man with a crew cut and a blue tee shirt, who somehow looked like a questionable person even at a distance, scuttled along the wall in jerky dashes and disappeared into one of the upper alleys. I decided to go out to the verandah next to the living room to watch this suspicious man although I did not believe any burglar would be dumb enough to prowl around an occupied house.

He appeared again a while later, looked up and down, glanced at the elderly drinkers once more, and then disappeared into the opposite alley this time. He might be one of those daylight robbers who favored suburban residential areas, I thought, returning to the living room and drawing the white gauzy inside curtains so that the prowler could not see me. I felt somewhat ridiculous. At any rate, I could watch what was happening down there, safely concealed from the enemy outside. The prowler, I meant, not enemy.

The man emerged once more, repeated similar motions as before, and then turned into the alley leading up to my house. He kept looking back over his shoulder every so often, hastening up the slanted alley, staying close to the wall. He dashed up about five meters, stopped, looked up and down, and then hurried back the way he had come up. He went down to the entrance of the alley, peeked at the drinkers, hesitated a moment and then dashed up again.

It was then I recognized him. It was Pyon Chinsu.

I went down to the garden and opened the gate, hailing him, "Over here, Private Pyon!"

He recoiled instinctively against the wall of the opposite house, flinching, and cautiously studied my face, after looking up and down the

alley once more. This man stared at me with glassy hollow eyes. The
nerves seemed to have been severed between his cornea and the optic
nerve. He was the Pyon Chinsu I used to know, all right, but he did not
seem to recognize me.

"Are you Sergeant Han?" he asked, doubtfully.

"Sure. Can't you recognize me?"

"It's been such a long time," he mumbled.

"Do you want me to show you my dog tags or something?" I tried to
relax him with a tentative smile. "Come on in, anyway. I've been
waiting for you to call."

Entering the gate, he quickly studied the fence behind my house. I
noticed, with some displeasure, that he was studying the layout of the
house. Even while exchanging mechanical greetings with my wife on
the porch, he constantly cast flashing inquisitive sidelong glances at the
downstairs living room, the master bedroom, the smaller bedroom for
my parents-in-law, the bathroom and even the kitchen. I was somewhat
disconcerted. And offended. For I suspected Pyon Chinsu must have
come to see me for a certain wily purpose. He might betray me for some
reason I didn't know yet, I thought. Upstairs he continued to study my
living room, the bathroom, the study, the two elevated verandahs and
the closet where I kept my fishing tackle. After my wife had gone down
to prepare tomato juice for us, we sat on the sofa facing each other in the
upstairs living room.

"How have you been?" he asked me distractedly, watching the alleys
down below through the sliding glass door opening to the front
verandah.

"So-so. How about you?"

He kept an expressionless silence for a while, as if he had an unques-
tionable right to ignore my words. No, it was not quite that either. He
did not seem to have heard me at all. His haggard face reminded me of
the rusty steel structure of fire exit stairs. We began to ask each other
casual questions concerning personal affairs, like a young boy and a girl
on their first blind date. I felt like I was talking to a zombie; he seemed to
be occasionally catching random words hovering in the air outside his
brain and spitting them out through a mouth that kept mumbling
soundlessly like that of a goldfish. Maybe Pyon Chinsu was dead and it
was his ghost that was sitting before me. In a war some people survive
physically but their soul does not.

I suspected Pyon Chinsu was suffering from some sort of a sickness.

A sickness of war, of Vietnam. He must be ailing, a mental illness. I read somewhere that a group of Vietnam War veterans, who had failed to adapt themselves back into American society, were hibernating in the Alaskan mountains. They must have chosen the way of exile, for they had felt an overwhelming alienation from the ordinary world of the average citizen. For them, psychological coexistence was much harder than a mere physical cohabitation. He would come out in the open, I knew, sooner or later. He would make a confession. I was sure he had one to make.

My wife brought us a tray of tomato juice, pressed dry cuttle-fish, salted crackers and two cans of beer, took the *Vogue* from the table, and went downstairs. As we continued our reminiscence about Vietnam days, Pyon Chinsu gradually relaxed. He even smiled congenially at times as he recounted some weirdly humorous incidents, and we talked about the Operation Buffalo massacre, pen pals, the infuriatingly hot tiny Vietnamese peppers, the flat "dung fish" we caught from the American generating ship at Cam Ranh Bay with the bait of biscuit crumbs kneaded with peanut butter, the Montagnards, exotic gum tree plantations, the Korean construction workers who made a lot of money owing to our military participation in the Vietnam conflict, and going further back. Pyon Chinsu seemed to be more animated as we chuckled about the last training days at Yangpyong. We talked about the night we had had our last drink in Korea at Yangpyong Tavern and our last day in Vietnam.

When we were waiting in lines on the sand of the Nha Trang harbor to board the USS *Geiger* to return home, I saw a young girl in a pale pink *ao dai*, wearing the conical hat, weeping under a roadside palm tree, probably sending off her Daihan lover. When the soldiers began to climb the stairs to the U.S. naval ship, this beautiful young girl, sobbing more and more dolefully, waving her white handkerchief and sobbing some more, finally managed to check herself and cried out towards the ship tearfully, "*Loi chao nhan khi ly biet, Ssibalnom.* Farewell, *Ssibalnom!*" Somebody wicked might have taught this innocent girl that the most beautiful Korean word for one's beloved was *ssibalnom,* mother-fucker.

Recalling that *con gai* tearfully crying out for her *ssibalnom,* I could not help chuckling.

"Why do you laugh?" Pyon Chinsu asked, studying my expression defensively.

I told him.

A little relieved by the humor, Pyon Chinsu tried a bashful smile. "Yes, funny things did happen," he said. "I think the funniest one I ever knew in Vietnam was Sergeant Piggie Chang."

We were still talking when Pyon Chinsu suddenly sprang up. "I must go," he said in an urgent frightened voice.

"Why don't you stay around a little longer and have dinner with me?" I said, rising, but I did not mean it.

"It has been fifty-five minutes already," he said.

I could not understand what he meant by that. I did not ask. He scurried down the stairs to the porch and hastily put on his shoes, not even glancing at my puzzled wife who was awkwardly rising from the sofa, putting down her magazine on the tea table, not sure whether the guest was leaving or not. Pyon did not even say goodbye properly to me at the gate and rushed down the alley like a fleeing burglar.

"What's the matter?" my wife asked me as I was standing blankly by the open gate. "Did you have an argument or something?"

"Nothing," I said, hoping that was true. "Nothing."

From the verandah upstairs, I watched Pyon Chinsu hurry along the alley next to Pyongchang Nursery. Then it occurred to me that he had told me nothing about what had happened to him since his return home. Somehow I got the impression that he did not have any family, and that the present did not hold much for him either.

25

The seagulls scurried
short distances with jerky mincing steps,
pecked at the sand and repeated the same
motions over and over again.

"Have you by any chance been to the
doctor?" I asked my wife.

She glanced at me. "Why do you ask?
Your marvelous sixth sense is at work
again?"

"Did you?"

"Yes I did," she said without a comma in
between.

"What did he say?"

"About what?"

"You know—."

"Having a child?"

"Yes."

"Why don't we just forget about it now? Okay?" she said in a light-hearted voice without any sign of embarrassment or guilt. She looked so confident.

I went out to the beach and strolled alone on the sand and among the pine trees. She remained in the fisherman's cottage where we were vacationing. She was packing, although we were not leaving until tomorrow afternoon. The tide had ebbed so far away that the tall kelp-harvesting poles were exposed naked to the root like dozens of black skeletons in the wet sand. The seascape was clean. The villagers had stacked up more kelp-harvesting poles here and there for later use. They looked like an Indian village of a dozen teepees along the grassy bank lining the sandy beach. The summer vacation season was almost over, even the major resort beaches on the East Coast were closing soon, and this unknown Patjirum Beach on remote Tokjok Island in the West Sea was virtually abandoned now. In fact, my wife and I were the only remaining vacationers at this beach after the camping group of twenty young men and women from a Seoul church had left yesterday along with their noisy hymns and endless prayers which blatantly blared at the villagers through loudspeakers installed in the pine trees.

The nocturnal humans who slept all day long in the summer heat and then lurked around in the dark to hunt for the opposite sex, had all returned to their urban dens, and the distant horizon was calm and quiet under the early autumn sky as transparent as a clean windowpane. I loitered along the edge of the water. It kept sliding up with a gurgling foam and then receding in a hurry, leaving a long, solitary file of footprints in the wet sand. The water would disappear in a new footprint momentarily, and then the impression slowly turned to a little sole-shaped pool. I wondered where all the summer children had gone who had been so noisy and drunk on the scorching beach of littered sand. They might be relishing, or perhaps regretting, the memories of the easy pleasure with which they had cloyed themselves in the indiscreet summer when they used to exist only lustfully. An autumn sea breeze wafted down around the rocky cliff.

Around eleven o'clock, when the tide began to turn and crawl back herding white foam onto the wet flat sand, my wife appeared among the pine trees by the sudden drop at the end of the cliff and leisurely sauntered down the path through the golden rice paddies. She was in her favorite white knickerbockers and white vinyl sandals, and the bottom ends of her bright red blouse were knotted across her stomach.

When I first met her on Huksan Island, she had been dressed much the same as she was now—a bright red blouse, white shoes. Her hair had been trimmed up in a big sweep like that, too. On that island we had loved each other, strolling among the trees swaying in the typhoon. A long, long time ago. Where had that gone? Was it because one's life got contaminated and besmirched as it progressed?

Crossing the dazzling yellow sand, she came down to the water's edge where I was waiting and we mutely walked for a while along the borderline of small empty broken shells swept up by the waves.

"The tide is rising," she said, narrowing her eyes against the sunshine reflected on the waves, gazing at a small motorized fishing boat passing by a rocky islet.

I gazed at a seagull hovering in the air for a moment to land on the waves.

"Tides change," she said, "because of the lunar gravity, don't they?"

I nodded.

"Then, why is the difference in ebb and flow on the west coast so big, while there's almost no difference on the east coast? I don't think that lunar gravity affects the west coast differently. Does it?" She squinted at me and then quickly looked away.

"I don't know."

"Is there anything in this world that *you* don't know?"

Absent-mindedly I gazed at the thirty-eight-year-old face of my wife without any answer, because I had nothing to answer, because I had nothing I wanted to answer, because I had never had anything much to tell her, because all the 14 billion nerve cells in my 1,400-gram brain could not comprehend sometimes even the extremely personal things happening around me, some of them directly happening *to* me. But in my silence, I was thinking—she is thirty-eight years old now. The girl who had been only twenty-three years old when I met her first on the rocky path in Huksan Island one windy day had turned into a thirty-eight-year-old middle-aged woman. And as I was looking up at her face closely to see what changes she had gone through in all those years, I realized that I probably had never watched her face this closely even once in the past ten years.

The clean yogurt-colored skin, the narrow but straight nose, the smooth curve around her chin, the eyes as clear and transparent as the sea breeze, and the sensuous thin lips—it was surprising to see that she had changed so little. I could not find any new lines in her face that had not been there at our first encounter. But where was the love that had glistened then, the love that we had discovered on that windy island? Why, how, had it died without fully consuming itself? Why had we wasted it away?

"Why did you have to hurry the packing?" I said. I squatted down to watch the shrimp ferret about to find the way out, stranded in a small isolated pool in the sunken part of the sand; those little creatures had to wait until the tide came back to let them escape to the open sea before the stagnant water turned too warm and cooked them alive. "We won't be leaving until tomorrow afternoon."

My wife, still standing, looked down at me for a while, studying my expression. "I intend to leave first," she said. "Alone. This afternoon. By the 3:30 boat."

She notified me; she was not asking for my permission or opinion. I raised myself and started to walk again along the edge of the water.

"Why?" I said. "My vacation isn't over until the day after tomorrow, you know." I already knew what her answer would be, but I asked, anyway. "An emergency or something?"

She studied my expression again. She said, "Not exactly."

I looked at her, waiting.

She kept gazing at the horizon with a disconcerted expression; she seemed to find it difficult to explain.

The fisherman on the motor boat saw us, the peaceful vacationing couple on the quiet shore, and waved hello. I did not wave back. Nor did my wife. The fisherman awkwardly lowered his hand, embarrassed, and the sputtering little boat disappeared around the cliff toward Sopo port.

"I decided to leave you," my wife said at last.

Somehow, vaguely, I had been expecting for a long time that she would abruptly say this. "You did?" I said stolidly. I felt like a man on death row on the morning when he was finally called out to the noose. "I guess I don't have to ask you why you made that decision," I said, half to myself.

She gazed at the wedge-shaped track left in the water by the fishing boat.

"I don't think you need any explanations."

She was right.

"Is this temporary or is it going to be a complete termination?" That was all I could ask.

She averted her eyes again to the sea. I also gazed seaward. As if we were looking for an answer out there together.

"I really don't care whichever way you may take it," she said. "Whether we separate temporarily or leave each other for good, I don't see much of a future for us in either case. I am too old now to write love letters or chase a man and get married again. So it makes no difference to me if we get divorced officially through proper legal procedures, or just walk away from each other in different directions. And I don't think it's possible for us to try a second time to recover all the happiness we've lost so far. That's why I believe this is going to be it between us."

A tiny flesh-colored crab scuttled away sideways a short distance on the wet pinkish sand and then halted to warily watch us.

"Maybe we will need some time to think it over," I said, but I did not mean it. "We are not young enough to behave rashly."

She tried a faint unsure smile and frowned to look up at the thin clouds slowly evanescing in the sky. "I've been thinking about this for a very long time," she said. "At first I considered myself a total failure, you know, and I thought it was so primitive and humiliating for me to give up everything only because I could not have a child. However, when I confirmed at the hospital that—"

"Have you had a medical check at the hospital for that?" I interrupted her in a gallant attempt to save her the unnecessary pains of a self-abasing confession. But my chivalry was premature.

"Sure, I did," she said matter-of-factly. "You know I did."

"What did the doctor say?" I asked evasively. I promptly regretted that I had asked it, but it was too late.

"You know what he said, too," she said.

I was confused. "What?" I asked.

"That nothing was wrong with me and I could have as many children as a rabbit, if I wanted to."

I was taken aback. It could not be. She stopped talking, puzzled, when I raised my hand like a traffic policeman.

"You mean . . . you . . . you can have children?"

She halted her pace and looked at me with her clear eyes, mystified. "You thought something was wrong with me?"

"Well, you know . . ."

"But you should know, because you've been to the hospital, too," she said. "What did *your* doctor say?"

She meant that it was I who had to be responsible. If nothing was wrong with her and I was also proven perfectly capable of procreation, then why, why had we not had any children?

"So you knew I'd been to the doctor," I said. But I did not want to tell her about what I had seen through the microscope; if I told her the truth, we would need a lot of explanation between us to verify the unverifiable. "How did you find out?" I asked.

"I just knew," she said. "Did you think I wouldn't know that?" She shook her head, but I was not sure why she did that. "I am your wife," she said. "At least I can read your expression when something important comes up in your life. Isn't that natural?"

I watched the cows chewing their cuds under the pine trees. I was losing something, I thought, and I was losing it very fast. I was losing not only my wife, but I might be losing something *to* her.

Probably taking my silence as a sign of an unspeakable agony, she said a little apologetically, "I understand you've been reflecting on this matter for a long time yourself. You wanted it first. Divorce, I mean."

I was more responsible for that predicament, I believed, than my wife was.

"Why don't we do some serious thinking about this matter?" I said. "There might be some way for us to get out of this. If you insist on leaving this afternoon, I will join you at home tomorrow. We should think it over, sleep on it tonight and—"

"I won't be home tomorrow," she said. Her voice was a little shaky. "In fact, that's why I'm leaving first this afternoon—so that I won't be home when you come back. My parents must have moved my things by now. I found a small apartment for myself. Rented it. My mother gave me the money for that. My father promised to move my things to the apartment while we . . . are vacationing here. I'm taking with me only my dresser, the small desk in the downstairs living room, my clothes and other basic things I might need. I hope you wouldn't mind that. I wouldn't want anything more from you. When you come home tomorrow, a part-time housemaid will keep house for you, so I think it would be better for you to take the morning boat back to Inchon and return home early."

Then, like a real estate broker explaining about a house to a prospective customer, my wife gave me detailed instructions concerning my future housekeeping—how to operate the gas range, where I could find the telephone number of the Chinese restaurant to order my meals if I did not want to cook myself, how to get a part-time housemaid to do my laundering and other chores, and other pathetically trivial things for my domestic life from now on. Her voice, sometimes throbbing, grew faint, and I could not hear any words she spoke except for the droning monotone devoid of any meaning because the valve in my consciousness was shutting down.

I remembered the report about Mars that I had read somewhere last month. The report said there might be some moisture on Mars. Then there must be some life form on the Red Planet that Orientals call "the Fire Star." That life form was not some octopus-like creature with swimming goggles, but certain microbes living in the rocks. Scientists had gathered at Boulder, Colorado, last July to discuss a possible trip to Mars in the next century. The trip would require fifteen years of preparation and six months for the actual voyage. If man could modify the Martian atmosphere and create a body of water, maybe someday the human race might be able to migrate to that planet. Man could create life there through chemical changes by cooling off the atmosphere. If man sent a supermissile carrying all the nuclear weapons on earth to Mars, where Aleksandr Bogdanov, a literary critic and Lenin's friend, once dreamed of building a socialist utopia called "The Red Star," and ignite the radioactive chain . . .

We sat down on the edge of the grassy bank under the pine trees; the rising tide had covered all the vast level sand and was climbing the slope to the bank.

"It's distressing to think how we let ourselves get cornered in this hopeless dead end," she said, slowly drawing a wobbly line in the sand with her index finger. "I feel we are like decrepit people just withering to death. It makes me sad to think that we've done so many things wrong that we can never go back now. There's only an end for us, but no new beginnings."

The whole island felt empty. I wondered how crowded this small island must have been when General Su Din Fan of Tang China arrived here with 330,000 troops on June 22, 660 A.D., for the rendezvous with the 200-ship fleet led by King Taejong of Silla for a joint maneuver to attack Paekche. The war cries and ambitions to unify the three kingdoms had sunk with all the ships and the numerous soldiers into the sea of the oblivious past, and I was on the dusky road to nowhere.

Gazing at the white foam and the waves slapping and crashing on the shore, gazing at the great fountainhead of life, I thought about the Russians trying to create a super race with babies born in water tanks, and I thought about Hai, from whom a sorrowful beauty had emanated at another beach in another time, and I thought that human bodies and souls wear out and disappear into void like any other expendable commodities of life, and I thought I was now waiting for my turn to be exterminated from this world, and I hoped my wife would be waiting for me at home when I returned to Seoul tomorrow.

The sun's rays were collected and refracted in the drop of sweat dangling from her nosetip like a little pearly bead. In that miniature crystal ball, in that tiny little drop of perspiration, the sea was contained as a small replica, like a photograph taken through a fisheye lens.

"Of course we cohabited in the same house, but somehow, all the time, I felt I was living all alone in our house," she said. "I think cold indifference is the cruelest and most vicious hatred one person can show to another."

She talked on and on. I listened. One person talking and the other person listening, but no communication shared. Our conversations were like that, going one way and never coming back. One person talking and one person listening, that was not a dialogue, but a monologue. Alternatively playing the role of the actor and the audience, we never participated together in any sequence of the drama.

Listening to her for almost two hours in a somnambulatory state, I had the dawning thought that she had been feeling the same way as I about so many things in our life. Every single word my wife was saying to me now should have been spoken by one of us a long time ago, but we had not said those things because we had taken them for granted and felt no need to express them. There might have been a salvation if we had not taken so many things for granted. The extended uncommunicative silence we had kept so long, because we did not want to expose our vulnerable parts or unnecessarily hurt the other person by saying a wrong word at a wrong moment, had eventually devastated our marriage.

A lone seagull sat on the sea and watched the horizon, bobbing up and down on the waves.

"Yet I had to go through too much pain and guilt because of that very man who gave me the confidence to make a choice," she said. "That was why I decided to leave you." A short pause, thinking. "To live with one man in love and respect all her life is a true happiness for a woman, but I was denied that. And I do resent that I've failed to achieve such a simple, ordinary happiness. I tried so hard to numb my conscience and justify myself with the popular ready-made excuse that I had all the rights in the world to seek my own happiness away from my lonely and barren life with an indifferent husband. But there was no way to beautify what I had done. Adultery was adultery, and I simply could not forgive my own behavior. There is no beautiful sin in the world."

She was making a confession about something I had never known, but she sounded as though she did not care if the whole world knew it. Besides, the revelation was too sudden for me to accept it as authentic, and I could not understand why she had to abruptly tell me about her "adultery." Was it some metaphor with which she tried to describe her spiritual state?

"It was more painful because you kept quiet, even though you knew it all. You didn't accuse or criticize me. You showed absolutely no sign of violence. If you beat me half to death like an ignorant bully, like a Stanley Kowalski, if you made my nose bleed and my eyes black and blue, if you inflicted some pain on me, I might have been ecstatically happy to see that I *belonged* somewhere—to you. But you just pretended you didn't know anything. I know why you did that. You were too much of an intellectual gentleman to abuse your wife physically. You knew too much to behave like an animal. You decided to ignore me and what I had done. You wanted to believe nothing had ever happened and nothing had ever existed. That made me feel as ashamed as a whore standing naked before strangers in the flesh market. Even though I *was* the culprit who had sinned, it was an unbearable torment to go on living with you, and that's why I confessed it to my parents, to ask for their—"

She stopped, staring at me, her eyes suddenly moistening with surprise and despair, sorrow and resentment, and anger too, for she belatedly realized she had made a mistake. Glistening tears welled in her eyes and trickled down her cheek. Tears, the metabolism of emotions.

"You—didn't know?" she said in a choked voice. The words stuck in her constricted throat. "You didn't know?" she repeated, disbelieving.

"Didn't know what?" I said, my head swimming in confusion—and frustrating grief.

"That there was a man . . ." She could not finish the sentence. I noticed she had used a past tense.

I did not answer.

"You did not know," she said, agonized. "My God . . ."

She looked so lonesome. A sad remorse. A renewed frustration. Her despondent face, sinking into a shocked distress.

"But that man is not the real reason why I am leaving you," she said in a vulnerable but defiant voice. I hoped she would stop the confession before she might hurt herself more deeply. But she did not know how to stop, or when. She went on.

"It's all over, you know, between him and me. I'm leaving you, but I'm not going to him either. Actually I made up my mind to leave you after I had ended that—that illicit relationship with him. I've not seen him—in quite a while."

That night, when she had stayed out, saying that she had to go to the hospital to nurse her aunt, that was the night she had finally broken up with him, I thought.

"I never understood what it was that you sought for in your life. You never told me. I did not ask either, for I might have not understood it even if you told me. We did not talk to each other too much because we did not know how to."

My wife began to cry. She was not weeping or sobbing like a dainty lady; she was crying shamelessly like a mourner. Hugging her knees, dropping her head, she cried like a child. I pitied her. The crisis of love that had been brewing for years was now breaking loose in a few minutes.

She cried about ten minutes, and then cleaned her eyes and nose. She looked at her watch. Then she stared at me with her bloodshot eyes.

"What are you thinking about?" she asked.

"Not much."

"I guess I have to go," she said. "The boat will leave in two hours." I nodded.

She stood up, dusting her hands, and closely studied my face as if I were a stranger she had never seen before. When she failed to find what she had been looking for in my expression, she sighed. She glanced at the rice paddies around the village, at the sea, and then at the rice paddies again. She began to walk through the pine trees toward the village. She did not say goodbye. Neither did I.

26

M y desk was clean.
I excused myself from Nam Hosik's invitation to soju and roast sirloin to "brighten
our spirits from this close weather before
going home," and I dropped by the book-
store in the basement of the Education
Insurance Building and bought a Kundera.
I checked the latest domestic publications,
convincing myself that was also a part of
my work, and then went out to the Kwang-
hwamun underpass, which was sloppy and
filthy with rainwater and wet paper scraps.
The underground path smelled sour in the
stuffy gloom. It was crowded with piles of
evening newspapers, vendors selling book-
holding stands and downtown road maps
and Chinese penmanship books and fold-

ing fans and jumper suits and fishing rods and spools and magnifying glasses and strange medicines and windup toy ducklings, a blind beggar singing to music from his amplifier set, and other human odds and ends. A beggar with an amplifier. The world had changed a lot in the past decade.

Gripping the flapping umbrella with both hands to fight against the crazy rain, I went to the bus stop in front of the Sejong Cultural Center to take a Number 153 bus home. I waited for the bus, the Kundera stuck firmly under my arm, watching three college boys with dirty long hair, tee-shirts drenched to the skin, giggle and chatter before a bakery. The drenched generation. The students had been drenched many times this year by ink-colored black water spurting from fire engine hoses during their anti-government demonstrations.

Somebody held my elbow, as if pinching lightly, and tugged like a prostitute sneaking up on a prospective daytime customer. A woman, forgotten, suddenly coming back to you, her hair all wet in the rain, without an umbrella, her eyes tearful — I was not sure why, but this sentimental, melodramatic image flashed through my mind when the frail fingers touched my elbow. But it was not a melodramatic woman who had returned to me. Holding a big bulky manila envelope carefully under his arms like a precious treasure, his umbrella lowered in front to hide his fidgeting face, Pyon Chinsu was standing by the magazine kiosk.

Pyon awkwardly offered his hand for a shake, an uncertain smile twitching across his sickly pale face. His fingers were thin and tough like steel sinews.

"What's up?" I asked, shaking his hand. "What is it you want?" I asked in a spiritless voice. I did not even feel any anger, like a man too tired from waiting to get mad.

"I've got something to say to you."

Everybody has something to say to me today, I thought. "Maybe we should go somewhere and sit down," I said.

"Where should we go?" he said.

"How about a teahouse? Munhwa Teahouse is just around that corner."

He stiffened, as if suddenly electrocuted. "No. Not a teahouse," he said.

"Why not?"

"Too many people."

Something *was* wrong with him. "Well, where do you suggest then?" I asked. "I don't think we can have much of a talk standing here in this rain."

"Shall I?"

"Shall I what?"

"Shall I choose the place to go?"

"Why not? Go ahead."

I followed him around the cultural center, past the fountain park, past the Municipal Police Headquarters, and by the time we were at the Combined Government Administrations Building, my mind was once again going astray, no longer interested in Pyon Chinsu or what he was going to say or what I had intended to tell him. I was now trying to imagine the natural life of *australopithecines*, my mind wandering, visualizing the anthropologists excavating fossils on a scorching African afternoon, thinking about the early human beings and the very first *Homo erectus*, wondering if they still called Peking Man "Peking Man" or if this designation also had changed to Beijing Man. My brain was again littered with useless trivia and I thought I should not work on the trivia encyclopedia project any more, even though I had no choice. I had little choice about anything in my life. Extremely unproductive and meaningless mental activities. What percentage of my life was wasted while I was wallowing in surplus knowledge that nobody needed? A certain unicellular animal's life span, the diameter of a fully grown sea urchin, *Pelz Nichol*, James Clerk Maxwell's electromagnetic theory of light, conjugation of French verbs, location of Paramaribo, correct pronunciation of Tucson, Emma Goldman's anarchism—why had I accumulated this fragmentary knowledge?

While watching Alfred Hitchcock's *The 39 Steps* a long time ago, I felt a shocking fear that Mr. Memory, who made his living at a bar with his memory power, might be a caricature of my future self. That old man's last stop in life was the crowded noisy bar, where he boastfully told the drunks the distance between Montreal and Winnipeg, or the winning horse of a certain race in a certain year. Was it my final destination? A seedy bar where Mr. Memory might encounter Dan Duryea singing "How Dry I Am" in an episode of Rod Serling's *Twilight Zone*?

We passed the Naija Hotel and headed for the subway station.

"Where are we going, anyway?" I asked.

Pyon Chinsu stared at me suspiciously as if I had asked a wrong question or should have known the answer. Then he looked up and down the street before answering me, "Sajik Park."

"Sajik Park? What on earth are we going to a park in this weather for?"

"There won't be many people at the park because it's raining," he said. I could not understand what he meant by that, but he seemed to have a reason which satisfied him as to why we should go there.

I did not argue with him, but I had to ask. "Where in the park are we going to sit and talk? I may have to buy a newspaper."

"Newspaper? Why?" he said suspiciously.

"Never mind. I'll buy a copy, anyway."

While I was paying the shopkeeper at the park entrance for the newspaper, it suddenly occurred to me that Pyon Chinsu might be a homosexual. That was more than possible. Everything could be explained easily if he was a homosexual. Everything fitted perfectly like the last several pieces of a jigsaw puzzle. His sudden appearance from nowhere, his strange behavior, the situation he was setting up around me, his sickly look, his frivolous and effeminate attitude towards me.

His head leaning as if he found it difficult to carry on his thin frail neck, Pyon Chinsu hastily crossed the children's playground. He was in a conspicuous hurry. I spread several sheets of the paper on the wet bench before Lady Shin Sahimdang's statue, in black bronze standing abandoned in the somber rain, and sat down. Holding my umbrella firmly against the wind, I waited. But Pyon remained silent, as if he had forgotten why we had come to this park in the first place. He kept quiet, restlessly looking around at the paved road winding up to the archery range, the trees dripping in the gathering dusk, and the two young lovers who were busy fondling each other under a red umbrella, enjoying the solitude.

"Are you running away from somebody?" I asked.

Pyon did not answer, his eyes emptily gazing somewhere a little distance short of me; something seemed to be interfering with my blunt question reaching his brain. He looked so dumb and sad in the deserted park, a dreary scene which might have appeared in an old black-and-white De Sica film. If he was really a homosexual waiting for a chance to approach me, he might need some time to muster his courage to make the initial move. Finding an accomplice in shame was never an easy task. But I did not want to wait for him to take the lead in anything. Not today. We were going to have a settlement on my terms, not his.

He just sat there like a zombie, without conscious perception, not knowing who I was, not knowing why we were sitting there in the rain, not knowing what he or I should do next.

Then, putting his manila envelope on his knees, he finally opened his mouth, but his words did not make connections with my questions. "Now I can't go back."

"Go back where?"

The valve closed again in his brain.

I was determined to keep him miles away from me forever. I could not know what it exactly was, but I knew a certain terrifying and gruesome catastrophe was hovering between us like a transparent shadow. By any means I had to exorcize Pyon Chinsu from my life.

"You behaved very strangely the day you came to my house, too. Why did you run away so abruptly when we were not even quite finished talking? You must be running away from something because you've done something wrong."

After a cautious sigh, he said, "You're a poet, aren't you, Sergeant Han?"

It was a digression, but I nodded yes, considering it a remarkable improvement that we had now entered the phase of mutual understanding. And a vague hope flickered in my mind that what Pyon wanted from me was not something ominous or homosexual, but perhaps something motivated by literary inclinations. I occasionally received letters or phone calls from aspiring writers; maybe Pyon wanted some advice or information in the same vein. "How did you find that out?" I asked.

"Didn't you write a poem for a newspaper when Vietnam fell to the Communists? I read it. And I also read the stories you wrote when you were working as a reporter. I mean, the stories about the Vietnamese refugees living at Changjon-dong."

It was a serialized feature I had written about Vietnamy Town, the home for the homeless exiles at the foot of the hill at Changjon-dong, Mapo District, in Seoul. The Vietnamese were barely making their living by baby-sitting or other low-paying manual work ("I tho' Daihans very rich very big country than Vietnamy people because they come Vietnam and fight for us like Americangs. Life very difficult here."). The women, deserted and stranded after their long voyage to Korea to find *Daihan chong,* their Korean husbands, the Korean construction workers who had shacked up with the local girls during their employment in Vietnam ("My Daihan husband tell me come. I come but he no see me."); and all the tragic trite anecdotes of a war.

Hai might have come to Korea with her son Trau, too, suffering from disease and hunger and pirates, squeezed among the boat people on a crowded fishing boat, to find me. They might be living somewhere, Hai and Trau, forgotten, exhausted, wondering where I was.

"Is it to discuss what I've written about Vietnam that we are sitting here in this rain?" I said accusingly. "Why don't you answer some of my questions, too?"

Pyon stared at me like a hypnotized man. Then he said in a distant voice, "I *am* answering your questions, Sergeant Han."

"You are?"

"Yes. Now I am telling you how I found you," he said. "After reading your poem I telephoned the Korean Writers Association to ask for your address. I hoped they'd know, but they didn't. They should know because they must keep the list of writer members or something. But they didn't tell me. Maybe they suspected me because I told them I had been in the same company with you in Vietnam."

"Suspect you? Why do they have to suspect you?"

"I don't know. But people suspect anybody who's been to war, you know."

"Go on," I prompted him.

"Then I read the articles you wrote in the newspaper. They were long by-line stories. One was serialized for several weeks, wasn't it? 'Sorrow Without a Country'—that was the title of that series, I remember. I saw your name printed at the end of each installment. So I called the newspaper, and they told me where I could find you."

"Why didn't you talk to me instead of asking them for my address? I was working for the newspaper at that time."

"No. It was ten years ago that I found out you were a reporter. But I telephoned them only recently. They told me you're working for a publishing company called Sejin. That's where I found out your address. The publishing company. I called the personnel office and they gave me your address and home telephone number as well. This time I didn't mention anything about Vietnam. I lied to them that I went to the same high school with you. That's how I got your phone number. And I called you."

"What was the purpose of going through all this trouble to find me?" I asked, a little intrigued despite myself.

His face turned expressionless again, his eyes losing luster. His eyes are dying, I thought.

"I had to find somebody, anybody, who had been in the 9th Company. In fact I've been looking for the old crew virtually all over the country. I couldn't find many of them. They had gone home to remote countryside villages and I could not get their addresses. I didn't know how to find them. Some, I heard, had gone to Saudi Arabia or Kuwait or other oil-rich Middle East countries to make money as construction workers. The way others went to Vietnam to make money as construction workers a long time ago. I looked everywhere. And you're the only one I could get in touch with in Seoul."

"Why did you try so hard to find them? And me?"

"I thought I might get some help from one of them."

He studied my expression, perhaps to examine my reaction to his statement. As I kept quiet because I could not comprehend where this whole story was leading, he went on:

"I thought nobody could understand or help me if he had not been to Vietnam." A reflecting pause. "You know Sergeant Cha Myongjin, don't you?" he asked me.

"Sergeant Cha Myongjin?"

"Yes. He was decorated twice in Vietnam. I think you remember him because he was in our platoon and we went out together for that long-range reconnaissance mission. I found him. He was one of the few I actually met. But he died before I had any chance to ask him. Maybe I shouldn't have waited so long to let him know why I needed help. You know how he died, don't you? The whole story was reported in the newspapers. He worked at this short-term financing company, and he was knifed to death by a robber one night. In '71. And I also met Lieutenant Choe. Lieutenant Choe Sangjun. The 3rd Platoon leader."

"I think that's enough for the background story. Now, tell me, why have you been chasing me—why did you want to find me?"

Fear began to gather in his face, very slowly at first. The terror intensified to make his facial muscles twitch once, twice, and then several times in a quick succession. He was gasping when he jumped up.

"Have you ever been in the Ten Thousand Mile Cave at Cheju Island? It was so dark in there and I was so scared that I couldn't even breathe when I imagined what would happen if all the electric lights went out."

This sudden incoherent remark brought back to me discomforting memories of Pyon Chinsu. Was Pyon a schizophrenic? And what was in the manila envelope that he was holding so tight in his arms? A bomb? Some sort of booby trap? If I tried to grab him, the envelope would explode and blow us both to pieces.

"Did you call it?" he asked me fretfully.

"Call what?"

"White Violet Teahouse." He nervously cast sidelong glances at me several times, his eyes flashing with suspicion and fear. "How did you know it is at Yaksu-dong?"

He began to rave, talking cheerfully about the wild drinking parties at Yangpyong Tavern in the summer evenings, abruptly switching the subject to the lazy Vietnamese longshoremen at Cam Ranh Bay, and then switching back and forth among random subjects: President Park Chunghee's dictatorship and his political assassination, the Korean students' radical struggle for democracy, American defeat in Vietnam, episodes about transferring the animals from Changgyongwon Zoo to the new suburban park, and the miserable days he had spent at the 102nd Field Hospital in Nha Trang. He just kept on talking frantically, without waiting for my replies or reactions, even panting, because he had to tell everything before he ran out of time, or breath, the confused thoughts swirling in his mind tumbling out of his mouth. Then he asked nervously, his fingers trembling:

"What time is it?"

I told him.

"It has been an hour already," he said, startled. "They will come." He stood up. "Will you hold this for me until I come back?"

He thrust the bulky manila envelope at me and hastily rushed up the cement path leading to the archery range, holding his umbrella very low to hide his face. I thought he needed to relieve himself urgently, perhaps as he had done in his helmet; he was apparently heading for the public latrine next to the swimming pool. I waited for him, wondering what the pigeons were doing on a rainy day like this. I waited in the dismal rain, my mind wandering among the cooing birds. Carneaux pigeons, dragoon pigeons and white maltese pigeons produced large squabs that many people considered a delicacy, but pigeons were carriers of histoplasmosis and psittacosis as well as messages. I watched taxis and buses speed into the dark Sajik Tunnel outside the park, splashing through the water like speedboats. The world was in a hurry.

The envelope Pyon had left with me was rather heavy. I felt it, curious what was inside. He said "they" would come because one hour was up. What did he mean by that? Who was coming? To do what? There was no doubt that Pyon Chinsu was sick.

It suddenly occurred to me that he might not have gone to the bathroom. I hurried to the public latrine to look for him. I was right. He was not there. I looked for him all over the park and even climbed up to the archery grounds, but he was nowhere to be found. Sitting on the lone bench by the ice-cream shop at the park entrance, I wondered why he had run away leaving the envelope with me. I slipped my hand into the envelope to see what was inside. My fingers touched smooth cool metal. I flinched. Then I opened the envelope and looked inside. It was a pistol.

27

When I coughed to clear my throat, the minnows, that had been floating on the shallow surface level of the black water, flipped, splashing and scattering away. Silence returned almost immediately. The bleeding sun had gone down beyond the hills in the west and the herons had returned to their nests after their last fishing expedition. As the day expired a lonely cuckoo began to weep in a gorge behind us. And then another bird, a goatsucker, began to sing *twip-twip-twip-twip* in the woods across the lake. The birds were calling mates with whom to spend the night.

The sultriness quickly dissipated with sunset because the summer was almost gone, and the anglers, who were dispersed sparsely along the water's edge, put on their jump suits or padded jackets to prepare for the chilly night. Quite a few anglers had come to the lake for night fishing, for mild weather over the weekend was rare in this bleak rainy season. Perching in secluded corners, they breathed in the peaceful silence.

A silvery minnow leapt up from the surface near a reedy clump to catch a shad-fly and fell back with a small plop. Insects chirped in the rice paddies over the dike behind me and frogs noisily croaked by the stream below the dam. The moon was so big and bright that I had an urge to yowl at it; this was the sixteenth day by the lunar month. I looked up at the deep black space. Man, a bacterial being in the universe—how pitiful and wretched he is. Love and hate, I thought, how futile and differentially abstract they are. How can the inhuman accuracy in natural phenomena move the human mind so deeply? Where was the end of the universe? What was the ultimate factor of movement in the universe, that St. Thomas Aquinas tried to define as 'God'?

"Chow time! Chow time!"

I was suddenly brought back to the earth by Mrs. Pak's loud supper call as she noisily beat the aluminum lid of the cooking pot with a big spoon to summon us to the meal she had prepared and set on the grass before the tent. I tied the fishing rods to the support poles with a long rubber string , lest a big fish should bite and drag a rod off into deep water. I washed my hands, which were smeared with sesame dregs that I had sprayed into the water to attract the fish, and went over to the tent where Mrs. Pak was waiting, the sleeves of her yellow blouse rolled up. The other members of the Go Anglers gathered at the tent, calling to one another in the dark: *Mr. Kim, are you there? Come on. Supper is ready.* Chattering cheerfully, they sat around on the grass before the steaming hot pepper soup set by Mrs. Pak on the vinyl mat. She had also prepared the side dishes of kimchi, pickled sesame leaves, garlic in soy sauce and boiled bean-curd.

Lee Wonse, the First Editorial Chief, and Kim Hungsu, the copy-reader for the Second Editorial Department, simultaneously offered their first courtesy cup to me. Then they flinched self-consciously and froze, seemingly too embarrassed to say the offering word, their plastic cups still thrust out towards me. I did not know which cup I had to take first; it was awkward and uncomfortable to be given two cups when nobody else was offered a drink. Neither of them could withdraw the cup and offer it to someone else because it was an insult to offer a cup already rejected by anybody. This was a trivial matter of drinking etiquette, but their expressions were visibly apprehensive, as if some sort of conspiratorial guilt was divulged by their act of offering the drink.

Choe Chongju, the former marketing manager who had left Sejin Publishing Company last year to start his own business, producing cassette educational materials, always knew the tricks to help people out of these everyday deadlocks. "Why don't you take both shots?" he said. "You can do Hopalong Cassidy, shooting two guns at the same time."

I promptly took his advice and accepted both cups with both hands. Everybody seemed to be enormously relieved. Choe opened the cap of the soju bottle with his spoon and filled my two cups. Everybody is trying to save me, I thought. I said, "Why not?" Then, I remembered something.

When we were about to leave the company parking lot at two o'clock this afternoon, I noticed nobody would get into the car. They were just looking at me, waiting, even after they had already finished loading their fishing bags and other packages in the Bongo van. They were waiting for me to take a seat first so that they could decide where they would sit. There was no sign of the usual competition for better seats in the front to travel more comfortably during the three-hour drive to Chorwon. I took the front seat next to the driver's, for I was given the choice. Three could sit in front, but nobody took the empty seat next to me, not even Pak Sungok's wife, though her husband was driving.

I remembered, when we stopped at a bait shop at Uijongbu to buy the sesame dregs and fishing rigs and camping necessities, they all tried to avoid my eyes. Then Choe Chongju paid for everything I bought at the bait shop; nobody else's purchases, only mine. And all the way here from Uijongbu, they tried not to talk to me in the car, and when someone did, he sounded unnatural as if conducting a forced conversation. When we arrived at Yonghwa Lake, they all scattered to take their fishing spots, far from mine.

Something was definitely going on around me. The husband is always the last to know, a Western proverb said. Perhaps I was the only one among us that did not know what would happen, because it was happening to me. Or *was* it something about my wife? They might be playing out a charade for me, so that I could take the proper hint.

I excused myself when Choe Chongju proposed to have a flower-card

game or a makkolli rice wine party to wile away the tedious hours before
the fish started to bite around midnight. It was true that I did not like
the card game much but the real reason was my reluctance to be with
them until I found out what secret about me they had been sharing
among themselves. As Mrs. Pak went down to the stream to wash the
dishes and the four men were preparing to play flower cards in the tent,
brightened with all the lanterns and flashlights they had, I went back to
the lakeside, carrying a mug of warm coffee.

I changed the bean powder baits to fresh worms and turned the
carbide lantern backward so that its light would not scare away the fish
in the water. I leaned back on my reclining chair comfortably, my bare
feet dipped in the water, and gazed at the green and crimson chemilight
tips which glinted like distinct fluorescent etchings from the three
noctilucent floats sitting motionless on the surface of the lake. In the
afternoon there had been some wind shifts, but nothing was stirring
now on the water, as glossy and even in the faint starlight as a black
marble floor. Water sleeps, too.

Sporadically along the lakeside, yellow lantern lights glowed in the
dark like unblinking stars. A glowworm glided through the reeds and
vanished like a tiny comet, burning its twinkling white light into non-
existence. An insect disappearing into the lakeside reeds, and a comet
falling across the boundless space. An airplane out on a nocturnal
reconnaissance declaring its existence with the signal flickering at its
wingtips.

A goatsucker warbled again, as if talking in his sleep, in the gorge
beyond the dam. *Twip-twip-twip-twip-twip-twip-twip.* The birdsong
sounded like waterdrops dripping on a thin silver platter.

It was quiet at the tent, where Mrs. Pak Sungok was reading an
Agatha Christie alone with a flashlight. The flower-card game did not
last long, and the fishermen were now scattered again along the dark
lakeside. Once in a while I heard their fishing hooks and lines swish in
the air and the bait lightly land on the water with a cautious plop. The
smell of tobacco burning in Choe Chongju's pipe whiffed to me from
around the corner where an inflated boat was moored.

Gazing at the glowing yellow lanterns dispersed on the other side of
the darkness, I wondered if the keepers of those lights were also
relishing the peaceful loneliness as I did now. The gregarious animals
hiding in their desolate, private darkness. I had come to this dark
shelter to converse with the primitive darkness. *Twip-twip-twip-twip.* I

should find a life worth living, somewhere, somehow, I thought. My life is waning away like the moon.

What persisted were indiscriminative rebellion, ego, anti-heroism, chronic toxication by romanticism, struggles without any purpose or sense of direction, and ultimate denial of my own virtues, if I had any. There are many ways for a man to weave his individual life's pattern. Some historic heroes unscrupulously slaughtered the innocent for personal power and glory, while others amassed wealth at the cost of stifling their souls, and some vainly struggled in the idolatry system established to worship themselves. They dreamed and sought the ways to extend themselves by means of something they did not possess, something they rigged up outside their being in an exaggerated dimension. That was not 'I,' but a fake skin bag bloated by empty air.

I tried to find one working formula to govern my life. But where did I fail? Picking out the wrong types and fonts in the galley proofs, looking for good manuscripts to print and bind as marketable books, searching for new foreign books worthy of translation and sale to domestic readers, writing a few poetic lines once in a while . . . My life lacks—something. Something. What indeed is the proper way to live?

The crimson float tip, that had been sitting still in the formless black space, slowly tilted a little and was dragged some distance to the left, then suddenly plunged into the water. I quickly grabbed the longest of my three fishing rods, and the vibrating pull was delivered from the powerful motions of the carp through the twanging monofilament line and the bending glass rod to the peripheral nerves in my arm. The fish, twisting violently, leapt into the air and, after a brief suspended moment, splashed down to the surface. Lee Wonse rushed to help me, unfolding his net, shouting to everybody who might care, "Mr. Han's got a big one!" Though the carp had made too big a splash for a mere 10-inch one, that was all it was. I managed to pull the fish out on the ground without using the net and slipped it into my icebox. The fish scales glimmered golden reflecting the lantern light. I replaced the bait and cast the hook into the lake. The crimson float streaked across the darkness like a tracer bullet, sat lightly on the surface, sank into the water momentarily, and then the glowing tip budded out of the water about an inch.

Pak Sungok and Kim Hungsu did not even show up and Choe Chongju came only halfway toward me but went back to his chair when he found out Lee had been overly excited. Lee, abashed, could not quickly make up his mind to go back to his spot with the unused net, or stay around for nothing. He decided to stay for a minute and sat on the grass next to me. He offered me a cigarette, smirking self-consciously. "I thought you got a real big one," he said. "The splash made me jump, you know. It sounded like a 15-inch one, at least."

I washed the fish slime off my hands with dirt and water before taking his cigarette. I noticed he was still shunning my eyes. I remembered the two courtesy cups simultaneously offered to me at supper. Then I realized what was going on around me. The reason why they treated me like a horned husband.

"Well, Mr. Lee, when will they post the Candidate List?" I asked him out of the blue.

He was transfixed like an antelope impaled by a pygmy spear. For my question had pierced his heart. "The Candidate List" was a cant expression at the company indicating the guerrilla-style personnel announcement, written in black brush ink on a huge white paper like a funeral banner, posted on the wall in the lobby listing names and new posts whenever they had a major reshuffle that needed a lot of explaining that the executives did not want to do.

"Monday morning, they say."

I did not ask any more. I did not need to. There was no doubt that my name with a new title would be placed somewhere in the Monday morning list on the lobby wall, like an epitaph on my grave. Lee Wonse thought I had known it all the time, because I pretended to. Embarrassed, he picked up the net and hurried back to his spot.

Time stopped. I sat still in the dark, hoping I would blend with and vanish into the hushed night.

Suddenly over the hills on the other side of the lake, a flying engine sputtered loudly like a succession of asthmatic explosions, and a UH-1H helicopter burst out of the dark sky, blinking a red light, its spotlight under the cockpit groping around the empty darkness ahead. This chopper must be out on a night mission, a training exercise of some sort, because the lake was located near "the frontline," the Demilitarized Zone, where North and South Koreas were eternally confronting each other.

Around three-thirty in the morning, a soft drizzle began to spray over the lake like a whispering mist. An auroral circle loomed in the silvery-grey fog around the lantern's glow. I had put on a hooded raincoat and elastic jackboots coming up to my thighs, but the rainwater slowly and steadily kept soaking my underwear. Whenever I changed bait and raised my arm to cast the hook into the lake again, the water drops dangling along the fishing rod trickled down into my sleeve and then to my armpit. The water felt like a cold hand creeping into my chest. The rain had blown out the carbide flame but I did not bother to light the lantern again; I could see the mist rising from the calm surface as the darkness began to peel off from the dawning grey expanse in the sky.

The morning was breaking, the mercurial luster of a new day seeping into the moist atmosphere. While the trees and the water and the wet soil slowly regained their colors, I caught four more carp. Around six o'clock, a cool wind began to blow away the clouds in the sky. Pak Sungok and Lee Wonse crawled out of the tent, yawning and stretching themselves, and came down to the shore.

Yesterday had not ended, tomorrow was already beginning.

28

The ceiling was coming down, invisibly, infinitesimal bit by bit. The movement was so slow that it still remained at the same place, although it had been coming down for a month. Yet, I was sure the ceiling kept coming toward the cement floor by the force of atomically precise physical law. If it kept coming like this for six thousand years, the ceiling would touch the floor, and I would be pressed as thin as aluminum foil.

In three days it would be exactly one month since my name and the new post as Manager for the Sales Promotion Planning Department had been announced on the Candidate List. The designation of my new title had been used so often in the circulars and other official communications in the office that it was usually indicated by its abbreviation but I, who was theoretically in full control and charge of that department, still did not know what I and SPPD were supposed to do for sales promotion planning, or anything else. Even Pak Namjun, the managing director who had invented that official title and assigned me that function, did not seem to know what SPPD should do now or in the future, for he had not yet decided what new—or existing—duties could be given to me and my new office. Therefore, nobody in this company, from the president-publisher down to the delivery boys, knew what work I was undertaking and why I seemed to be doing nothing at all.

In the last reshuffle to "tighten and strengthen the organization," the Third Editorial Department was demolished outright. All the former staff members were transferred either to the other editorial or production departments; and the trivia encyclopedia, as well as other major projects I had been undertaking, were temporarily suspended or cancelled for good. I, the former chief of that slaughtered department, was given a new department, but nobody in the company knew exactly what that department existed for.

That was why I had to spend almost a month like a prisoner in this secluded cell. I was given no one to work for me, nor was I in a position to request anyone. So, I had been "working" all alone in this cell for a month minus three days. A man with a superb brain, who did not know what he was supposed to do—that was me.

The room on the second floor, where I had been in semi-confinement, had been a storeroom for returned books. This morgue for books, that had been urgently converted to accommodate me and my phantoms, was not yet furnished with the new set of office fixtures and equipment usually forthcoming with a newly inaugurated office. Under the excuse that the SPPD functions were not officially defined, the General Affairs Department had issued nothing to my office except one gray steel desk with two big drawers and three smaller drawers—all empty because I had nothing to put in them—and one gray steel chair with a gray vinyl seat (one of its three ball-bearing casters was missing) and one green plastic wastebasket that had required three visits to and one impatient argument with the General Affairs Department clerks for me to get. I did not even have a phone yet; they kept delaying its installation. This cell was not ready to serve as a work place, and the plaster walls were pockmarked with nail scars chipped out like bullet holes where the shelves for returned books had been attached all the way up from the floor to the ceiling and then removed to make space for SPPD. The scarred walls were decorated by nothing, no curtains, no framed pictures or calligraphy scrolls, no blackboard or time table, not even an electric clock. This penal colony was barren and deserted. Nobody had ever even considered the slightest need to furnish an air-conditioner to this stuffy dead storeroom, where only the delivery boys used to drop by in the evenings to check in the damaged copies or unsold old books returned by the bookstores, and I had to fight in this sealed room against the torturing heat that seemed to be avenging the hostile cold weather. The heat packed into the room suffocated me to despair, and that was the reason why I felt the ceiling coming down constantly, imperceptibly, to press me flat.

Buried alive in the cell, I was an outcast in the company. If someone saw me in the hall, he would hastily bow to me halfway and then scuttle off in a frenzy. Nobody came to see me and I felt I met less and less people in the hall or anywhere else in the company as days passed. They seemed to shun my room because they were afraid to accidentally run into me, face to face, if I ever burst open the door and charged out. Or maybe they were disappearing one by one, and some day I might find the whole building empty and deserted.

Maybe they might even forget that I worked for the same company and, one day, they simply would not recognize me if we passed each other in the hall. I would keep on living my life as an intruder, an unauthorized existence, a surplus being.

The six square cement planes—the walls and the ceiling and the floor—were closing in, little by little, interminably, from all directions, halting whenever I looked in their direction, and then continuing their clandestine advance when I looked away. I felt I was constantly watched by an invisible person through an electronic surveillance system. Sitting behind the purposeless desk, I gazed all day long at the door that nobody would ever open, and every single motion and movement I made behind that desk was captured by a stealthy radar device.

I rarely left my office until seven o'clock in the evening. Then slipped out of the company building when I was sure nobody was around. The few trips I made out of my room during office hours were quick visits to the bathroom. On those rare occasions when I ran into anybody in the bathroom, we would exchange uncomfortable, incomplete smiles acknowledging each other's existence, uneasily squinting at the door. And then he would make a quick escape from me.

I did not ask anybody to go to lunch for I might find it impossible to stand their curious sidelong glances and humiliating pity. They pitied me, no doubt, for the banishment and ostracism I had to go through, but they also scorned me for not submitting my resignation and leaving this wretched company rather than taking all the humiliation. I did not want to see or be with anybody, so I brought my lunch from home and ate it alone in my office. I was afraid that somebody would open the door and find me eating lunch all alone, like a monkey in a cage, like an imprisoned criminal feeding himself for a meager survival, so I would consume the whole thing in a breathless gulp and wave my arms to hastily sweep the kimchi stench away from me, out of the window.

I was not sure why, but they did not want me to work for Sejin Publishing Company any longer. That was why they had imprisoned me in this office without giving me any work to do—so that I could take the hint and leave.

Somebody knocked on the door. I stopped my movements. I had not been moving much anyway, but I stopped even that little movement. Who could have come to see me? Why? I waited. I gazed blankly at the door, without answering. Outside the door, silence waited too. When I did not answer for a full minute, a white envelope slipped into the room under the door. I heard the office girl, who delivered the mail to each office twice a day, walk down the hall, away from my office.

When I was sure that she had gone downstairs and the hall was empty, I went to the door and picked up the envelope. The letter did not carry the sender's name. I tore open the envelope. It was from Pyon Chinsu. I went back to my desk and read it:

Dear Sergeant Han,

I hope you're still keeping my iron piece safely. You must not throw it away. It is loaded with three slugs, so it is ready for use at any moment. I am not a spy working for the North Koreans, nor a criminal, nor any suspicious character, so please don't report me to the police or the military authorities. In fact, I want to see you immediately because I have a favor to ask from you. But I was afraid to see you, because you could have reported me to the authorities on account of my possessing a deadly weapon. Anyway,

I have to see you, and I will call you soon. When we meet next time, you must bring that iron piece with you.

I have called you both at the office and at home about twenty times during the past month, but nobody would let me talk to you. They said you've been transferred to the Sales Promotion Planning Department and that department doesn't have a phone. But I don't believe them. So I decided to send you a letter, hoping this will reach you.

I think it's wrong for you to drag this matter on and on like this. I hope everything will be settled when we meet again, next time.

"This is yours."

I thrust the manila envelope at Pyon Chinsu. The envelope, crumpled and stained with rain, was the very one he had given me at this very bench. He had not even sat down yet. With dumbfounded eyes, he gazed at me, awkwardly frozen in a half-squatting posture. He glanced at the bulging envelope and then apprehensively looked around the park, not quite decided about what he should do with the bundle. Along the path to the archery range several old men were sitting on the benches in their old but clean attire—neatly laundered and pressed coats and ramie suits, clean and polished shoes, cheap but well-preserved hats. These old men had nowhere else to go to idle away their hours.

"You wanted this thing back, didn't you?" I said.

With an irritated expression, he warily looked around to make sure that nobody was watching us. Then he took the package and put it carefully down between us on the bench. He looked around the park once more and sat down uneasily.

The sun was still warm for the season, but everything around us had the hue and scent of winter. I could feel it in the cool breeze, and I recognized it in the yearning expressions of the people strolling in the park.

"This is my lunch hour and I have only thirty minutes to spare for you," I said. "So you'd better make it brief if you've got anything to say to me."

I had made up my mind that this was the day—I would see him today—and then tell him to get out of my life. Forever. Although I did not have the faintest idea what he had gone through in the last thirteen

years, I could see something in those unknown years was encroaching
on his soul, but I was obviously not responsible for anything that might
have happened to him since Vietnam. Pyon Chinsu gazed at me with a
frustrated expression.

"It's a long story," he said. "What I want to tell you—I don't think half
an hour is enough to tell it all."

"Then start talking now," I prompted him.

Hesitating, not too sure if he should go on, he gazed at me again. He
took a deep breath to calm himself down.

"You can't even imagine what my life has been like since my return,"
he said, his expression suddenly pacific. His voice was calm. I was
surprised to find such composure in him. "Do you know what happened
to me after I returned home?" he asked.

"I guess you painted billboards for Taehan Cinema," I said matter-of-
factly. "You used to work there before you joined up, didn't you?"

"Yes, I worked there for a couple of months after I mustered out of the
army," he said. "But they fired me."

"Why?"

I watched two college girls leisurely taking pictures on the steps
before the statue of Lady Sahimdang.

After a long pause, Pyon Chinsu said, "I guess I must have been crazy
at that time."

"What do you mean?"

He took out a cigarette and lit it, with the same hand, keeping the
other on the manila envelope all the while, as if he were afraid it might
fly away.

"I hit the PR manager with a folding chair one evening," he said. "I
was drunk."

"Did you fight with him?"

"It wasn't exactly a fight. I just hit him. It was an unexpected
accident, sort of." He frowned; he hated to recall it.

He stared at my eyes, trying to decide if I would believe what he was
about to tell me. Or perhaps he was waiting for me to say something. He
sighed again; he seemed to have reached the conclusion that he had to
speak out.

"I can't understand it myself, but during those first several months,
and even after that, everybody around me looked suspicious to me. They
all looked like Cong in my eyes, you know. I was afraid of everything and
everybody. I feared a booby trap might have been rigged behind doors,

under every desk, or inside the lamp shades, or even in the projector. I was afraid to touch anything at home or in the storehouse at the cinema. You may find it difficult to believe, but I was afraid the paint pail or the brushes or a wood block might blow up, *wham*, if I touched them.

"If I was in a dark alley or ever went to a crowded place like a department store or a soccer stadium, I was restless because I worried someone might sneak up behind me and suddenly stab me in the back. Whenever I noticed a dark object on the road or in the yard, or when I found a human figure around the corner while walking on the street, my hand would stick out instinctively. To shoot, you know. Everything I saw in the dark looked like some target I had to shoot and eliminate.

"Whenever my eyes met somebody else's on a bus or in some other confined place, I could not avert my eyes because I was afraid he might suddenly pull out a gun and shoot me. Even in broad daylight, cold sweat would streak down my spine while I was walking along a street because I would be stricken by a sudden fear that someone could rush up to me from behind and chop at me with a machete. I couldn't even look back. I was afraid there might really be someone standing there with a machete.

"Even now I can't eat in public restaurants because I'm afraid somebody might have poisoned the food. That's why I always carry this with me." He showed me the silver ring on his little finger. Korean soldiers had worn silver rings in Vietnam to test food and water for poison. "For a very long time I suffered from insomnia," he said. "I simply couldn't fall asleep because I was afraid that someone might vault over the fence of my house and sneak in to kill me with a bamboo spear. When I was stricken by such fear at night, I could not even breathe."

"What happened at the cinema?" I said. "You didn't tell me really."

"I got the job back without any difficulty. I guess it was some sort of courtesy for being a war veteran. I don't know. But they did not want me to work there. They didn't tell me so to my face, but I knew they hated me. They never explained but I knew everybody at the PR office was plotting to drive me out with vicious schemes to harass and intimidate me. They would hide my brushes or paint pails, and someone even stole my chisel. They wanted me to get mad enough to quit on my own accord. When I painted Charles Bronson, they laughed at me and said he looked like an opium-smoker. I don't know exactly why they tried so hard to push me out. Maybe they considered me a dangerous person or something because I had been in the war."

"Did anybody tell you to quit your job at the cinema?"

"Nobody had the guts or honesty to say so to my face. Whenever I asked them why they would play innocent, pretending they were annoyed by my unreasonable suspicions. But I knew better."

He glanced down at the envelope between us. A young mother and her daughter were throwing barley to the pigeons on the path by the snack kiosk.

"When it was made clear that I knew, some of them avoided me outright. But I did not want to be driven out by them. I did not want them to have any excuse to fire me. So I went to work earlier than anybody else and worked harder than anybody, too." His eyes flashed to search out his imaginary enemy who might be lurking around us. "Whenever they whispered something about me behind my back, I demanded that they tell me what they had said against me. Then they got impatient, because they knew I was onto them. They accused me of being too touchy. Some thought I was plain crazy. We argued more and more frequently. But I was only being sensible, wasn't I? I had to watch them too, because they might have even worked out a plan to kill me."

Suddenly he started to talk very fast. He was constantly depressed and afraid that everybody in the world hated him and was trying to hurt him by every possible means. Wherever he went, he tried his best jungle tricks to shake an invisible stalker. He took all the detours there were on his way home or anywhere. He always moved in erratic, unpredictable directions, and only when he was sure nobody was around to spy on him. When he arrived home, he never used the regular gate or doors, but vaulted over the fence and sneaked into rooms through the windows. He used to sleep in the basement among the coal briquet piles because he expected an assassin might infiltrate the house and slit his throat open if he slept in his bedroom. He was constantly on the run. He was being chased, by fear, by death. The invisible executioner waited, always nearby.

What he related was typical of a persecution mania. But had I not been possessed by similar images recently while sitting all alone in my cell at the office for hours and hours, day after day? Despite myself, I began to feel a certain sense of conspiratorial comraderie with Pyon as I watched him make this long confession.

After he had been fired by the cinema, he worked briefly as the janitor of an apartment building, then for a small printing shop specializing in business cards, at an electric appliance store, at the locker room of an indoor swimming pool, and at a rice wine wholesalers cooperative office. In the last eight years, he had not had any job lasting longer than a week.

"When I came back from Vietnam, my parents pretended they were glad that I had returned home alive. But I knew they felt differently in their hearts. They didn't want a cowardly son like me to bring shame to the family and the ancestors. My own family turned away from me because I had been such a coward.

"I hated them all. I hated my own family, and I spent nights at inns instead of going home. You will never know how lonely it is to drink alone in a lousy room at a seedy inn, trying to fall asleep. What did I do to be hated so much?"

Gasping, breathless, Pyon Chinsu was talking so loudly that the two girls playing rock-paper-scissors at the next bench glanced back at him. Pyon said he suffered from such terrible insomnia that he hardly slept three hours a night.

Why had he in particular been devastated so irrevocably by the war; it had to be the war that had destroyed him so utterly. I had met many Vietnam War veterans in Seoul who had gone through almost identical experiences. They all had managed to overcome the aftermath and eventually lead normal lives, but Pyon had failed.

"I couldn't sleep unless I took three or four tranquilizers with a shot of soju. You know, Atiban." I nodded; young people used it as a hallucinogen. "Even in that stupefied state, I was always aware of something chasing me."

He had no place to run. What kept chasing him had eaten away his soul and deeply rooted into his brain. The Hell was inside his skull.

I took out a cigarette to ease my upset stomach. A little girl bounced a rubber ball on the ground by the phone booth. The little girl bounced the ball on and on, counting: twenty-six, twenty-seven, twenty-eight . . .

I did not want to listen to his grotesque tales any longer, and I shut out the unwanted sounds from my brain. I tried to remember the first flower-decked hearse I had seen in my childhood. Pyon Chinsu continued to murmur: about grubs sliding down over his skin, about imaginary ghosts haunting him. The man chased himself. Like Guy de Maupassant, who, tormented by syphilitic delusions, believed his body was soused in salt and his brain was spilling out of his nostrils.

His parents in the meantime had decided to send him to a mental institution.

"I had to run away, you know."

On my way to the park to meet Pyon Chinsu, I had expected that I might be able to clean up some cobwebs of my own if I shared a long talk with him, an old comrade. But it had not turned out that way. I was more depressed now, watching a man go to pieces before my own eyes.

"I did not want to go to a madhouse," he said. "That place is full of crazy people, and any of them could attack me at any time of the day. You can never tell what crazy people will do to you. Maybe my family wanted to send me there so that I would be killed by a lunatic. But I didn't want to go. That's why I had to run."

He had packed a Nikon camera, a cassette tape-recorder, some cash, two gold trinkets and several other valuables from the family safe, and then he fled. He left Seoul, went to Uijongbu, an army town to the north, and spent several months there, moving from one cheap lodging house to another.

"I slept at different places every night so that my family would never find me. At the inns, I signed false names in the register. They were not exactly false, not my name, anyway. I used the names of the 9th Company soldiers who died in Vietnam. Nobody would ever find me if I used the names of dead people, would they? But it was scary to spend every night at a strange place. My head kept splitting with unbearable pain and I hated the whole world. I thought I had to stop all that once and for all. I began to think about killing myself.

"But I soon found out that it was even harder than killing someone else."

It occurred to him that he should look for comrades he had known in Vietnam. He presumed these veterans would be willing and experienced. Besides, those who had been to the war with him might be more sympathetic to his agony and need. Up to now, Pyon had located six of his former buddies. They pitied him, bought him a drink, gave him some money or swore at him, but nobody would do it. He even visited our old platoon leader at his home in a military town on the east coast. Pyon Chinsu pretended he happened to be passing and had come to visit as a courtesy. During supper, Pyon told Choe Sangjun, now a lieutenant colonel, the true purpose of his unexpected visit.

Colonel Choe put down his chopsticks without finishing his meal and said, "It is disgusting to have supper with an inferior human being like you. You should be gone when I come back in three minutes to finish my meal."

Nobody showed him to the door, the colonel had ordered his wife and two daughters not to go near "that deplorable imbecile." Going out, crestfallen, he happened to see the objects displayed in the built-in bookshelves in the living room — the artifacts of the prominent military career of Lieutenant Colonel Choe. Name plates, war decorations, plaques and citations from high military commanders. And the pistol. That black small caliber pistol with a bluish glint, captured at the Vietcong 85B Regiment Headquarters on Hon Heo Mountain, and now resting on the bench between us.

Pyon Chinsu looked around once more apprehensively at the people in the park and then pushed the manila envelope about five centimeters toward me. "Please, Sergeant Han," he said in an imploring voice.

I looked down at the envelope, and then at him. "You mean you want me to shoot you, with this?" I asked.

"Yes. Please. The bullets are more than ten years old, I know, but they will work fine. Let's go to a secluded place where nobody will see us, and there you can shoot me safely. We can go somewhere in Samchong Park or to the Pugak Skyway. We can hail a taxi and go there now. Nobody knows I came to see you today, so you don't have to worry about the aftermath. Please. I beg you."

Suddenly I dreaded looking Pyon Chinsu in the eye. I felt the germs of death would immediately swarm to me from him if I did. Watching traffic whizzing by on the street outside the park, I said, "You came to the wrong person. I've seen and experienced enough killing in the war. I don't want any more of it. I can't do what you want me to do. I just can't."

He carefully studied the expression in my eyes, as if trying to read a page from a book full of tiny print. He did not find the answer he had wanted to see in my eyes. He took his hand from the manila envelope. He sighed.

"What should I do now?" he said. His haggard, stubbled face looked sickly, desperate. His bloodshot eyes were viscous with anxiety. Then, he said in a subdued, despairing voice, "I have to go. It's almost an hour . . ." He raised himself awkwardly, whispering down at me. "I will never bother you again, Sergeant Han. And you don't have to be sorry. For not killing me, I mean. I've been refused by too many people to care any more."

I also raised myself, pushing the pistol envelope toward him. "Take this with you," I said. "It's yours."

"No," he said. "I won't take it. I will not need it. I can't think of anybody else to ask. I don't have any more people to see. Maybe I will have to give up the whole idea because nobody in this world will do it for me and I really don't have the courage to put the gun to my . . ." He glanced at the huge garbage can by the swimming pool. "You can throw it away somewhere, or keep it as a souvenir, of the war. Or take it to the police. Dispose of it anyway you want to, Sergeant Han. I don't care." His face was pallid and empty, all signs of life drained out. "I have to go."

Pyon Chinsu turned away and started to walk slowly toward the park gate. I gazed at him, the lonely outcast trudging away to an uncertain future. His whole being reeked of morbid loneliness. And I thought, Where would he go now? What will become of him in the end, after wasting his whole life being chased by phantoms? He may go to an inn at Uijongbu tonight, sign the register in the name of Sergeant Chon Hisik or Sergeant Kim Mungi or Han Taesam, take the tranquilizers with a mug of beer and get some troubled sleep. But what about tomorrow? When will the war end for Pyon Chinsu? Others had long finished with it. Why does it drag on so for him? Pyon Chinsu wanted to be executed because he had been defeated.

"Private Pyon," I called.

He halted at the bottom of the stone steps. When he turned back, his face was shining brilliantly.

Mr. Ahn was born in Seoul in 1941. He studied literature at Sogang Jesuit University, then worked as reporter, columnist, and editor at the English-language *Korea Times* and *Korea Herald*. He has published three novels and has translated nearly a hundred books into his native language. This is the first of his works to be published in English, and the translation is his own.

Ahn Junghyo is a veteran of the Korean army's 9th "White Horse" Division and served in Vietnam.